UNDEAD OATHS

THE UNDEAD GODS TRILOGY

Book Two

Caitlyn Battelle

TWELFTH
HOUSE
PUBLISHING

Undead Oaths

CAITLYN BATTELLE

*To anyone who is still learning
how to love—this one's for you.*

A note to the reader

Please turn to the last page for content guidance.

Chapter 1

Elysia shot through the realms like a fallen star, leaving garnet specks of blood in her wake. She hurtled, steel still stinging against her neck, from certain demise to the sanctuary of death's realm.

Crashing against a cold stone floor, her head bounced helplessly, her body thudding against the long burgundy rug. The wet gurgle of her breath betrayed how close she was to entering the Deathlands traditionally. An oil lamp chandelier swung above her, its light flickering as her vision stuttered in and out.

Hot sticky blood ran from her neck and nose, staining the rug a deeper shade of violence. Beneath the blood, cold swept over her skin, shivers wracking her body. Somewhere in her awareness was the grim reality that she was losing too much blood. She needed to move, or to call out, but her eyes fluttered shut as her hand twitched uselessly in the direction of the imposing double doors. The chill on her skin grew heavier, her bones weighted down to the floor.

Alarmed voices entered the throne room, and dim relief clawed inside her chest despite how the world faded around her. Straining, she managed to loll her head to the side. Worn black leather boots strode closer, pounding against the stone and coming to crouch beside her.

A dark and soothing presence washed over her like a gentle rain. She relaxed into his familiar atmosphere, the endless onslaught of pain growing more distant. Gods, she was tired. She wanted so very much to go to sleep.

"Don't you dare." The words were a harsh order, startling her eyes back open. Though she couldn't see his face, she recognized Aidan's masculine voice, forcing her back from the brink of darkness.

The god of the dead's warm body settled behind her, as strong but sure hands slipped beneath her hair, carefully placing her head onto his lap. He pressed something firmly against her neck, and then his smooth voice took on an undercurrent of anger that heightened as he spoke to someone else.

"Get Maya now." He hesitated. "And bring the dirt."

Elysia stared up at him, mumbling incomprehensibly. "It worked."

One strong, dark brow arched at her.

"Your name," she tried again, still unable to speak clearly.

He didn't respond at first, the lines on his face deepening as his eyes carefully catalogued every injury and spot of blood from the crown of her head down to her toes.

"But what if it hadn't?" The quiet words seemed to be more to himself, but she still caught the here-then-gone whisper of fear.

Her blood stained the whorls of his fingers, but in her half-coherent state all she could think was how much she liked his hands, and how nice it was to have someone touch her so softly. No one ever touched her like this. His hands continued to stroke her hair, and a gentle ease sunk into her body, muting the pain to the point her whole body sighed against him.

Maya, the woman she'd first met in the Deathlands' gothic woods, dropped to the floor beside them, her large, sturdy leather work bag hitting the floor with a smack. Without word or delay, she inspected Elysia. Muttering to herself, she noted her findings. "Concussion. Shattered nose. Chipped teeth. Broken ribs and bruised kidneys. Older half-healed injuries. More blood loss than is sustainable from her neck."

A growl tore through Aidan's chest. "Can you do it or not?"

"Got the dirt," a softer bass cut in, half out of breath.

Aidan spoke again, harsher this time. "*Maya.*"

"I'll fix what I can, but she's too far gone."

Aidan grunted while continuing whatever magic that dripped deeper and deeper into Elysia, turning her to mush. She floated away unaware of the sharp slicing pain on her palm, or how terribly Maya's healing hurt.

The relaxing anesthetic of Aidan's power cut off abruptly. "Elysia, listen to me. Can you hear me?"

She bit back her cry of pain. Bones were knitting, lungs reviving, and none of it was something anyone should ever be awake for, but blue eyes of flame bore down on her, demanding she hear and answer. He squeezed her hand, and blood and dirt wept from the edges of their palms.

"Tell me I can heal you or you're going to die."

Her face scrunched and she mouthed the word. *Yes.*

"Whatever it takes?"

Concern flashed through her, but then her neck became fire as skin sealed, and veins closed. She choked out another yes. Instantly, Aidan's power overtook her, and she sank against him, consciousness fading as he murmured lilting words of promise and petition.

Deep in her own abyss, she never heard his quiet rumble.

"Welcome home, love, I've been waiting for you."

Chapter 2

SHE WASN'T ALONE when she woke. With a bleary gaze on the ceiling, her magic stretched and glanced its fingers against the cold bank of calm with its ripples of worry across the room. *Aidan.* Hastily, she pulled her senses back. She still had no idea what was polite when it came to magic.

Rich hardwood floors abutted sooty charcoal walls. Above her bed was a sprawling dusk painting in tones of cream and purple-gray with hints of stars peeking through. The back of the room boasted an ornate stone fireplace and dark floral rug with two high wingback chairs. Lounging in one of the chairs was a man with black hair, hollowed cheeks, and intelligent bright blue eyes that were locked on her.

All the words she'd prepared back in Relaclave were nowhere to be found. Perhaps almost dying had stolen them. *Thank you* seemed trite, and launching into deal negotiations while in her pajamas poor form. Her anxiety rose as the need for something to say pressed in on her. Moments ticked by as he held her there, ensnared in his cold, burning gaze. The god of the dead finally cleared his throat and broke the moment.

"How are you feeling?"

Elysia ran her hand through her hair, surprised to find it clean and relatively manageable. Aidan tracked her movements as she slipped from the bed and delicately settled into the chair across from him. His brow furrowed, gaze roving over her with worry. Unused to such intense scrutiny, she avoided him, her fingers skimming over the soft pajamas she'd been clothed in. When she spoke, her voice was still thick with sleep.

"Fine. Far too fine."

She left off the unspoken but obvious question. *What happened?* She knew she had been close to death, but now she seemed to be in perfect health. No blood or pain, just a vague lingering fatigue.

His brow smoothed at her response. Relaxing back into his chair, he disregarded her silent question, the hard line of his jaw easing as his lips turned up. "Good."

Her curiosity piqued at this transformation. Where was the rigid man who had refused to bargain with her to save her kingdom? *That* god had been carved from rock, unwilling to bend no matter what she said. Unnerved, she studied him as the last vestiges of sleep left her. She wasn't interested in games or dealing with someone whose personality switched at will, but the god of death was her only choice now. He'd saved her when he could have let her die, and he wasn't looking at her like a nuisance, or some mortal who should have simply said yes to his wretched offer. He looked both relieved and concerned.

"I came to finalize the deal, my, my..." *Grace?* She fumbled over the appropriate title, her eyes dropping to her hands. A thin, smoothed-over red line scored her left palm—it must have been from the king's guards.

Amusement lifted the god of the dead's mouth into a smirk. "Aidan," he offered. "Aidan will do just fine." A certain dark playfulness brought his voice lower. "I'm open to other suggestions if you have them."

She smiled sweetly, her response out before she could stop it. "Like asshole?"

Her hand slapped over her mouth, her dark eyes wide.

Shouldn't have said that. But still. Was he flirting with her? *Couldn't be possible.* No one was arrogant enough to accidentally destroy a kingdom, launch an insane king at the masses, and then offer a damn near useless deal to fix the problem *they created*, only to flirt with a straight face.

Aidan's smirk grew. Holding eye contact, he slowly rolled up the sleeves of his white button-down before leaning in closer to her, elbows on his knees. "Don't doubt your instincts so much. I mean exactly what you think I do."

Elysia blinked, unable to comprehend the utter audacity being lobbed at her. She floundered for a response to shove him back into the corner of her mind labeled *asshole death god*. She forced a sternness into her voice, as if he were an errant child rather than a terrifying god, and sat up straighter. "Then let's be clear, the *only* reason I'm here is to complete this deal and find your talisman. Do you understand?"

The glint in his eyes brightened, and she was momentarily enthralled by the flames, but he acquiesced, resuming a more casual position. "But you will tell me when your wishes change, won't you?"

Her nostrils flared. She was one second away from telling him precisely what she thought of his inappropriate comments when there was a knock on the door. Two women bustled into the bedroom, rolling a breakfast cart over to them. The cart bumped against the edge of the black floral rug, but Elysia's gaze was caught on the skull and dice embroidered on their matching sweaters. Distracted by the familiar design, she couldn't offer so much as a thanks before they left quietly.

Using the breakfast cart as a reprieve from responding to Aidan, Elysia poured cream into a steaming mug of coffee. It was better to ignore him. She knew that. But the desire to tell him exactly what he could do with such statements was almost as diffi-cult to ignore as when Beatriz pissed her off.

She took a few pointed sips, eyes narrowed ever so slightly at him. "I imagine you'll want me hunting for your precious talisman immediately."

The playful arrogance disappeared. "What I want is for you to eat breakfast and to show you our home. You'll find I have no problem making myself clear when I want something—or someone." His fingers drummed on his thigh, his gaze unwavering, making her pulse kick into a higher gear.

Discomfort mixed with dangerous intrigue rolled through her. She didn't understand his angle. *Because there always is one.* But the man *was* beautiful to look at. He could flirt with her if he liked. Didn't mean she had to respond.

Voice unaffected, she redirected him. "Shouldn't we be talking about the deal?"

His blue eyes burned, and her stomach swooped. It would have been wise to take Lily up on that training when she had the chance. Because despite Topp's proclivity for running his dirty mouth, there was something far more unnerving about Aidan's direct, unfiltered attention. Annoyed at herself, she took a long sip of her coffee, trying to work out why such tame flirtation was tying up her insides like she was sixteen and had never seen a man before.

The answer came a little too easily, so she batted it away and looked back up at the god of the dead with an even, unimpressed stare. Topp's insinuations revolved around sex. Aidan was saying he wanted *her.* And she had a rejection wound a prince-wide and a childhood-deep.

Aidan set his tea down and smoothed his hair back into place, suddenly looking more like the serious businessman she had expected. "Yes, you will have an obligation to find the talisman. But if I can give a word of advice?"

She held in her scoff. "I'm not sure you're who I should be taking advice from, given your record."

Aidan dipped his chin. "You make my point. I am all too well-acquainted with how anger can destroy the best of intentions. And while you deserve the space and freedom to heal or not heal after what you've experienced in your short life, the reality is that you're being handed more expectation and responsibility. Are you going to be able to rise to that?"

The enormity of the situation fell like a dead weight, and both of them went quiet. In the past however many hours, she had willingly given up any ties to her family and life in Kava. She had plunged her blade into the guts of the man who had tried his damnedest to ruin her people and landed here in a bloody heap, expecting to make a deal with death. Her kingdom's survival depended on her ability to complete this deal and find Aidan's talisman.

But those were actions. Actions she had known were necessary. Hearing Aidan say she needed to deal with her *internal* shit or else it might fuck everything up? She shifted uncomfortably in her wingback chair. She didn't have any experience with *that*, and there was nothing she hated more than being incompetent.

Thoughts askew, she tried to cover up her helplessness. The idea of baring her soul aloud to a *death god* of all people made her want to get up and leave the room. A grimace twisted her lips. Her near-death experience hadn't brought her to enlightenment nor made her any more prone to wanting to discuss her *feelings*.

"I'll do my job. You can count on it," she said quietly.

Understanding softened his face. "Of that, I have no doubt. We'll get started with business then as it seems more comfortable to you."

Elysia nodded, drinking her coffee and nibbling on a scone.

His face shifted into one she knew oh so well. She'd seen it a thousand times. It was the look of someone who knew a secret and wanted to use it.

Anxiousness turned the coffee in her stomach to acid, and she spoke quickly before he could maneuver their deal even more to his advantage. She set her shoulders primly.

"I'd like to renegotiate. Your terms were terrible."

The terms had been terrible, alright. He was requiring her to find the talisman that would unbind his powers.

Aidan barked out a laugh. One leg kicked out in front of him, he considered her with quiet delight. "Are you always this stiff?"

"You can be direct, but I can't?" *Hypocrite.*

Aidan shook his head laughingly, his smile stretching wide. "You are painfully uptight."

Mouth half-open, disbelief heightened her pitch. "And you are *rude.*" Her posture noticeably stiffened, proving his point—much to her irritation—but nonetheless she pushed back on his observations. "I'm not uptight. I just... Deals are done in a certain manner at court," she finished, both embarrassed and affronted.

His grin widened even further. "That voice you use. What *is* that?"

Her cheeks heated, her gaze catching on the sheen of the scars on his hand. His fingers spread across his jaw and mouth, distracting her. This wasn't going how she wanted it to at all.

"My sister calls it my Crown voice," she admitted begrudgingly. "It just happens, okay?" She crossed her arms uncomfortably and stole a glance at him only to wish she hadn't. The pure amusement hidden behind his hand made her own lips twitch into a smile. Bastard.

The fact of the matter was, the stick up her ass had been installed at birth by her mother, and it was not going to come out without a fight. Not in the presence of a god, anyway. And not that she'd ever admit it.

He held up his palms in placation. "Setting aside the voice, I admire the bold opener. You would have died if it wasn't for me. But please, insult the deal I offered after falling into my throne room nearly dead."

Exasperated, she set down her coffee with a rattle. "I couldn't fight back—I had to let the guards take me. I didn't think it would go that far! And you know what, the voice is called having manners!"

Contrary to his even breaths and calm expression, a dark soot-like fog encased Aidan, his eyes now shining like royal blue coal. Elysia froze. She'd gone too far. She'd pissed him off.

She drew on every ounce of court training she'd ever had, forcing the words through gritted teeth. "I'm sorry, I apologize. The deal is perfectly fine. How do we proceed?" Better to stay alive and work with a shitty deal than to die her first day here.

Ducking her head, she stared at the floral rug, hating herself for rolling over, but she wasn't prepared for immortal fallout. She bit down on the insides of her cheeks. She'd never agreed to such an absolutely gods-awful deal before, and it was going to be inescapably bound by a *god*.

Aidan spoke, his voice smooth and rough at once as his flood of sootlike power tasted her skin. "We both know it's a terrible deal. That's not what I'm angry about."

At his power's touch, an old hunger yawned within her, a hunger she'd been forced to deny her entire life in Kava. She pushed the ravenous sensation down and tucked her feet beneath her on the chair. "It really is terrible. Worst deal I've ever made."

He ignored her, his soot still writhing in the air, tasting her skin and brushing against her hair. "I've kept eyes on you—I was recalling *exactly* how you received your injuries."

Startled, she gripped the arm of the chair. "Like I said, I knew the king was going to make an example of me. At least I got to stab him before he tried to kill me."

"You really knew?" His jaw ticked and her confusion increased.

"Yes."

"You didn't consider escaping? Traveling here before it came to such lethal blows?"

She was quiet. "People needed to know. Everyone thinks Garrison's a hero—that he's golden."

His fingers were drumming again. "I suppose I might owe Garrison one thank you before this is all done."

"What could you possibly want to thank him for?" The soot-like fog had disappeared now, and she mistakenly thought it meant he had relaxed.

"Would anything less than death have made you call my name?"

She flashed back to the king's hands in her hair. Her knees digging into the stage. The crowd of faces and a sword against her neck.

Hand lifting unconsciously to where the sword had cut in, she wondered how that night would form her. If she would rise as Aidan said or if she would fall like the blade that had almost taken her.

Voice sharp, coldness washed over her. "I would have taken the deal, regardless."

He studied her carefully, hunting for any sign of dishonesty. "Is that so?"

"I've lived my entire life on the precipice of death. Bent in half by others' expectations and exploitations. Death doesn't motivate me. The hope of living does."

"What a horrible way to live." Whisper soft, his empathy stole through her practiced guard. "Perhaps, one day when things are not so dire, you will find that here—a life worth hoping for."

She looked away. How could his words be anything but empty? This was the god who had made a deal to wreck the realms. Tucking her hair behind her ear, she refocused their conversation. "My amendments."

"Go on." He listened intently.

Brushing scone crumbs from her hands, she ticked off her demands one by one. "You will give me any information you can to assist me. You will give me free travel between the realms. You will provide coin and resources as needed."

Aidan interrupted her. "As I already told you, you will have whatever you need that is within my power. Travel is outside my grasp, but I will petition the fates on your behalf. They've been known to grant similar boons before."

Elysia considered him carefully, but he shrugged as if it were all simple. "Why wouldn't I help you in every possible way? This realm *exists* out of my power—my power that is immensely limited without the talisman. As things currently stand, the kick-back from my deal with the Kavian king has led to destabilization beyond what you can imagine, not only in Kava, but here as well. At some point, the dead will have nowhere to go. Do you have any idea what will happen if the dead have nowhere to go?"

Her eyes rounded.

He continued. "Your world is also dependent on magic. It may be inhabited by mortals, but it was woven by gods. Without magic, both the land and people will eventually succumb to the inevitable. Kava is a glimpse of what awaits the entire world if Garrison succeeds and we fail."

The stakes were a guillotine above them.

It wasn't just Kava and her people in the balance.

It was the realm of the dead.

The entire mortal world.

Swallowing, she reviewed their terrible deal one last time. "I find the talisman required for you to come into your full godhood, and then you'll help me restore Kava. You can't undo the deal with Garrison, and your powers may still be affected by that deal, but you'll do everything you can to restore our homes, correct?"

Aidan interlaced his fingers and held her gaze. "My offer remains the same as when we originally met."

Overwhelm stole any confidence she'd had. "Please tell me you know where to find the talisman."

But he didn't say the words she wished he would. Instead, he stood up smoothly, his lean muscled frame towering over her and forcing her to look up at his outstretched, waiting hand.

Tentatively, she placed her hand in his, her stomach tightening at the quick brightening of flames in his eyes.

"Are you ready to make a deal, Elysia Parker?"

CHAPTER 3

Elysia walked through the halls with her mask firmly in place. Sweet yet cold and blank, her expression was a hard-won prize from years of navigating the Crown court. Aidan's home was gorgeous, but in her tense state she barely noticed any of its purposeful, elegant design. She put one foot in front of the other with her eyes straight ahead and emotions far from her face.

Sometimes the only choice to be made was a terrible one.

Despite his calm and self-assured appearance, a nervous energy sparked around the god of the dead. His strides grew longer and faster as if he wanted to get to the throne room before she changed her mind. Noticing her struggle to keep up, Aidan slowed his pace, his wool trousers brushing against her hand and making her pulse jump.

Elysia tucked her limbs even closer to her body. She was an imposter. Aidan expected her to be sharp and clever. He expected her to go out into the world and secure his talisman. He didn't know the woman beside him had already been chewed up and spit out, and was without the faintest clue of how to begin finding such a thing.

Wool scratched against the back of her hand again. They were both desperate, she decided. He was desperate to fix his mistakes and she was desperate to save her kingdom. She snuck another quick glance. His nervousness had settled into a determination that made her wary.

He looked like he was marching off to fate or war. Maybe it was both.

There was a dull ache in the back of her skull as his secrets pulled at her. She bit down on the temptation, remembering what happened last time she dove beneath his surface. Her feet slowed as the desire grew sharper. Pausing, she shook off the impulse to sift through his inner life and lingered at a piece of artwork. The dark, earthy oil painting in front of her shone, its shadows dancing unnaturally upon the canvas. *It's magic.* There was so much she had never seen, so much she didn't know about healthy, magically robust societies.

Aidan stood over her shoulder and whispered in her ear. "Stop dawdling."

Elysia swayed toward his voice, accidentally leaning into the firm chest hidden beneath his dress shirt. Aidan froze briefly before stepping to the side, his fingers grazing her lower back. Gentle, relaxing warmth effused into her at every point of contact, a lighter version of whatever he had done to ease her pain when she arrived. Fighting the natural instinct to follow his touch, she arched beyond his reach and continued their walk to the throne room.

"I believe I mentioned the realms are woven by the power of the gods. The Deathlands are an extension of me—the dirt, the flora, the fauna." He gestured and a sootlike haze appeared above his hand. "Raw, unformed magic. You'll see it around me at times. Normally, the entire realm is cloaked in it."

Guilt coated his admission, but she was distracted by the similarity between the raw magic and the soot of her homeland. She ran her fingers through the air, and the magic dissipated. "Reminds me of Kava."

He nodded. "Raw magic is, in essence, decay. The problem being Kava *only* has decomposition. The raw magic accumulates, but the plants, the people, the ether of your kingdom cannot use it, so like any other decay, it rots your home."

"And the people," she finished, her gaze going distant. Clearing her throat, she tipped her face at him. "The sky was hazy when I was first here two weeks ago."

"I've been doing my best to heal what I can. One day you'll see it as it ought to be—the entire realm cloaked in a haze, raw magic at your fingertips."

The hard resolve in his voice almost convinced her that was true. That they would somehow overcome the mountains before them, but no amount of confidence could change the cold hard facts of their situation.

Unthinking, she placed a hand on his arm, fingers touching both skin and the structured cotton of his button-down. The king of the dead halted, the surprise in his eyes making her draw back.

"Finding this talisman is going to be nearly impossible. You're a *god*. If you couldn't find it, then I'm—"

He cut her off. "The only one in any realm above or below that could."

They came upon the massive double doors to the throne room, and she faltered. "There are far better people for this job."

Aidan's hands gripped the swooping door handles as he looked over his shoulder, intensity radiating from his frame. "Did you not hear the song? Did you not fall through dreams and realms only to land at my feet? The fates marked you for death, and *I am death*."

The doors swung open, and Aidan strode ahead, leaving her gaping at his declaration.

A burst of her usual fire had her stalking after him into the chilly throne room with her mouth moving fast. "Excuse me, I think there's been some *very* serious confusion that needs clearing up before we proceed." *There goes that voice again.*

Aidan was back to being infuriatingly calm. "No confusion. Merely facts."

I'll give you some fucking facts. She stomped closer, but Aidan slammed his hands together, and a jarring crack rang throughout the room. Elysia immediately stopped, feet planting and arms bracing out into the air as the floor shuddered. Panic rose as an enormous fissure cracked through the throne room, its jagged crevice growing wider by the second. A wild river rushed violently into its hollow, water splashing and foaming over the spilled black candelabra wax and the burgundy runner.

Feet now permanently glued to where she stood, she gaped at the king of the dead. It was one thing to hear him say the Death-lands were a physical manifestation of his power, it was another to watch the world bend to his command. A soft charcoal haze drifted over the waters of the god-made canal. Soon enough, the fog dampened her feet, leaving the room in a state of eerie, static power.

Hands still clasped together, Aidan swiveled to look at her, satisfaction gleaming in his cobalt eyes. Once more, he held out a hand, beckoning her closer, and a shiver ran up her spine. Steps light, she made her way to him as distrust and misplaced excitement battled within her. Conjuring a chalice from behind his back like a street charlatan, Elysia failed to hide her laugh.

"You'd lose your head for that kind of trick in Kava."

She'd been making a joke, but Aidan was silent, the fleeting compassion on his face saying more than enough. It struck her uncomfortably. In a land where executions happened frequently, humor was a dark, necessary thing.

Crouching down, he scooped up water from the river into the chalice. With drenched knees, he stood and held out the cup to her. Water dripped off his fingers, rivulets streaking down his forearm only to be stopped by the cuff of his rolled-up sleeve.

Why she quivered at the dark splotches on his knees and his river-soaked grip, she would never know. Maybe it was how his steady gaze burned as it turned on her, seemingly seeing past her cracked mask and into the dark uncertainty she hid beneath. Swallowing, she studied the gleaming bronze chalice. Blackened iridescent water swirled in its basin, the water alive and its surface rippling.

Aidan cast his gaze over the crashing waters coursing through his throne room. "This river runs the edge of my realm. If anyone unwelcome were to drink or touch so much as a drop, they would find themselves aflame from the inside out."

Elysia took an involuntary step back, and Aidan's mouth twitched with the shadow of a dark smile. The white cotton of his button-down stretched against his shoulder as he lifted the chalice. Voice low and weighted, it wrapped around her with promise. "As this river separates what is mine from what is not, it will bind this deal between us. Should either of us break it, we will burn like the fire it is. Let no one say the god of the dead does not keep his oaths."

Ice crackled through Elysia's veins and time slowed.

For once, there would be no tricks or turns she could pull.

A vow with the god of the dead was unbreakable. Gods forbid either did not remain true to the end.

Her fingers wrapped around his, the metallic shine of the cup peeking out between them as they held the chalice aloft. "You have a deal." Strong and sure, her voice belied the truth beneath her skin.

Dark fire overtook the blue of his eyes, satisfaction evident in the minute lift of his lips. "To Elysia Parker, the only woman to ever initiate a katabasis with barely a shred of magic to her name. May fate always honor the willfulness within you."

Elysia nodded, silently taken aback. Not difficult, *willful*. Like it was something to be proud of instead of torn down.

Fingers clenching against the cold of the cup, she drank.

She drank deeply of the waters of death, binding herself to both god and deal.

The river raged inside her now, and with terrifying certainty, she knew everything had changed.

Chapter 4

Elysia stared at the inside of her right forearm. She hadn't noticed it yesterday after drinking from the chalice while in her long-sleeved sweater, but today a new mark stared back at her. A permanent reminder of how foolish it was to make deals with gods.

Thanks to her study of banned botany books back in Kava, she knew it was asphodel and narcissus poking out of the strange iron helm on her skin. The skull and dice Aidan had originally placed on her body for travel was now gone, replaced by tiny poplar leaves, which trailed down the shell of her ear.

A deadened anxiety flattened her mood the longer she stared. Elysia flexed her fingers, twisting her arm as she examined the design. It was both brutal and beautiful. She'd chosen this—chosen to help her people, to push back against the decay of her kingdom. But all she saw when she looked at the flora on her skin was deceit, she'd tasted it the second the river water had passed her lips.

She hadn't meant to read him, but his relief had been so palpable it would have been impossible for her not to notice anything. Especially when his guilt had clamped down on her like a vise. Aidan, god of the dead, was telling the truth, but *not* the whole truth.

Fed up with staring at her own skin, she exited her bedroom and silently stormed through the halls. Her sock-clad feet struck down heavily on the deep walnut floorboards. Her mood effused into the air around her—she didn't like being tricked, and the god of the dead was about to find out.

She was moving so fast she almost didn't see him standing there in the kitchen, rummaging through the silverware drawer. Turning around, he held up a bowl of savory porridge and a spoon.

"Hungry?"

She stared at him incredulously. "No, I am not *hungry*."

He pulled out a stool and sat down at the slate counter to eat. He took a mouthful and watched her, seemingly unbothered. Another bite disappeared and she seethed, fixing her gaze on the kitchen behind him as she tried to rein in her temper. Mid-toned wooden cupboards with smoky glass overtook the wall, built around an industrial-sized cooking range. Unsurprisingly, the cupboards did nothing to calm her.

Aidan's spoon rested against his bowl like he was waiting.

Fine. Holding out her wrist like it was evidence of a crime, she spoke her question as an accusation. "Did you know?" She kicked away the fearful part of her brain that reminded her this was a *god*. God or not, she couldn't spend her time cowering.

His expression cleared. "Deals, oaths, magical promises—they always leave a mark. I assumed you knew."

She looked at him like he was dumb. "I grew up in *Kava*. The place with no magic."

"Or you didn't." One scarred hand rubbed the back of his neck before bracing on his thigh. The god of the dead was unperturbed. "If you're ever unsure of something, *ask*. Magic has always been an inherent part of my life."

Dropping his spoon with a clink and pushing back the bowl, Aidan strode over to where she was still haunting the doorway.

He shoved up the sleeve of his black sweater and held his arm out for her inspection. Matching asphodel and narcissus wound up around a small flaming torch.

"I see," she retorted. It was just lovely being completely unaware of what was common knowledge to everyone else.

Tugging his sweater back into place, Aidan deftly plucked her rigid arm away from her body, sliding her sleeve up until he could see all of the flowers and helm decorating her skin.

"Beautiful," he murmured, his voice low. "The flowers are native to the Deathlands. One of my siblings brought them to your realm."

Elysia hastily pulled her wrist out of his grasp. His eyes were doing that damn flame thing again, and she didn't want him to feel her pulse rioting beneath his fingers and get the wrong idea. With her arms wrapped securely around her body, she stared him down.

"I don't care that they're beautiful. I don't like surprises. And I don't like *lies*."

Curiosity emphasized the sharp edges of his face as he tilted his gaze down toward her. "I don't believe I've lied to you, but I do have a solution for fewer surprises." He returned to the counter, eating his porridge and looking far too patient as he waited for her to give in and ask what he meant.

Annoyed, she drew closer, but remained out of reach. "Lies, omissions, same thing. But go on."

"Lessons. With me." Finished eating, he placed his bowl in the sink, and turned to lean back against the dark slate counter. Staring at her, he pushed up both sleeves and folded his arms.

She narrowed her eyes. It was like he was *trying* to put on a show—the forearms, the soft sweater that she'd like to steal, and how it molded perfectly over his wide shoulders. His expression didn't waver. Calm, patient, and ready to schedule all her time locked in a room with him.

"No."

"You're woefully uneducated on all things magic and know

nothing about the Deathlands. Your lack of knowledge is dangerous and needs to be remedied."

All true. Still, she said nothing.

His frustration snagged her attention with a jerk behind her navel. "You do realize you'll be working with me indefinitely as you search for the talisman."

"I can do it myself," she gritted out.

He ignored her. "You wanted all my resources, and *I* am one of those resources. Use me," he taunted, his burning cobalt gaze settling on her. She wanted to punch him. The corner of his mouth lifted like he knew she wouldn't dare.

Fuck. She needed to get a grip. Immediately.

Likely sensing her imminent fold, Aidan slowly walked over. She balked, backing up against the nearest counter. "What? What are you doing?"

Stopping right in front of her, his low voice gained an edge of mirth. "Calm down." Without touching her face, he brought his fingers close to her skin, gesturing for her to turn her chin, but she didn't move.

Inches apart, she could smell traces of bergamot and citrus mixing pleasantly with the warmth of his skin. Trapped and addled by his scent, she held still. His mouth curved all the way up now. "Turn. I want to see."

A rush of blood flooded her face as she complied.

Hands on either side of the counter, their thighs brushed as he studied the leaves trailing down her ear. Elysia barely breathed as his perfectly combed yet somehow perpetually misbehaving hair fell out of place, tickling her skin.

"First lesson. Magic is sentient and impossible to understand. The skull and dice is the mark that usually appears when I make business dealings." His thumb grazed the shell of her ear, and she closed her eyes. "This isn't from me. The fates answered my petition. A little gift, I suppose."

"A gift?" The words barely passed her lips. He was so close. Too close.

"Poplars grow near the water here, much like in the mortal realm. A long time ago, mortals would fall through their waters into mine. It seems they were feeling traditional."

"You mean to say I can travel?" Excitement cut through her nerves—traveling would make her work so much easier.

"You'll need water," he responded, looking down at her.

Slow understanding took root, her excitement fading. "You're saying I'll have to jump into *water* whenever I need to get back here? What about place to place in the mortal realm?"

Frustration added depth to his usually smooth tone. "Traveling between realms is an enormous magical toll. There's a reason it's practically unheard of for mortals. The fates gifted you this because it's outside of my skill set, but being who they are... They never make anything easy. I assume any body of water will do for getting back to the Deathlands from the mortal realm. I'll verify with Maya about traveling from here to there as well as within the mortal realm."

"How symbolic," she muttered. What a pain in the ass it would be to need to find a *body of water* to escape if necessary. Good thing she'd been getting in and out of tight spots for years, no traveling required. She paused, his comment replaying in her head. "What if Maya trained me?"

Aidan's response was flat and fast. "No."

Her eyes grew bigger in exasperation. "You're right—I don't know anything about magic, or talismans, or how to go about any of this, but shouldn't my learning be more important than who teaches me?"

Aidan's jawline came into focus as it tightened, but just as quickly he rolled his shoulders and offered a compromise. "If you're uncomfortable training with me, then you can train with all of us. Myself, Maya, and Grim. But it is necessary for me to be a part of it—you'll have duties for the realm."

She frowned. She wasn't sure she'd have time for *chores* while searching for his talisman.

"Grim?" she questioned. She remembered seeing him during

her first visit but hadn't spoken more than a word to him that day.

He nodded. "Grim and I rule together. He directs the reapers and manages death while I care for the dead and the state of the realm."

Elysia's brain broke. "But you're the only one everyone knows about? The temples, the petitions..."

Aidan appeared pained, which didn't surprise her given that in the short amount of time she'd been awake he'd yelled no less than five times that *he'd be in his office*, which was then followed by a slamming door. He didn't seem like the social sort, much less someone who would be comfortable being worshipped.

"Yes, I drew the short end of that stick. Nobody ever bothers him." He looked wistful before his face settled into practiced acceptance.

"Grim's a god then?"

Aidan resumed his original position on the stool, this time hooking one foot on a rung and drumming his fingers on the counter.

"Correct," he answered distractedly. His bright blue eyes came back into sharp focus. "Bellia first. To the Bone Temple of Ryspur. You should leave as soon as possible."

False cheer lifted her voice. "Oh my gods, what a great idea. You know what I like best about it? The part where you included me in approximately zero of the decision-making process, barked marching orders at me, and still haven't explained what you're lying about."

Aidan brought his hands together and leaned on his forearms. "That was hardly an order."

"Sounded like one to me."

"Then where do *you* think you should go first? Never mind that it's traditional for you to visit the temple and be initiated, and to *not* do so would be a slap to the women and people who helped guide you home." Dry amusement lifted his brows.

Elysia awkwardly paused. *What?* "I—I didn't know that. And

this isn't home," she muttered, hating that she kept running her mouth instead of just asking. She was on edge, still cranky about the marks and questionable guilt he didn't seem keen to give her an answer about.

The hollows of Aidan's face deepened. "Again, please ask if you would like to know something. I would have explained if you'd given me five seconds instead of assuming the worst."

Unsure if he deserved her apology, she shrugged. "Habit." For better or for worse, she was primed to attack at the first sign of being pushed around. It was unsurprising, really, given her history of being lied to and taken advantage of by every single man in her life.

Aidan's gaze heated, his voice dropping lower until it rumbled, drawing her in far too easily with its rich sound. "Trust me, you'll know if I'm giving you an order."

That should be illegal. She unthinkingly clutched the counter as her body betrayed her with a heady slap of desire. Glaring, she dug in her heels. "I need to go to Kava. I have a few things to attend to before I go traipsing about the realms for your trinket."

Dark humor crept into Aidan's tone, and yet it sounded like a warning. "Is that so? You think it's wise to return to the city of your near-execution so soon after?"

"There are things I need to do that are none of your business," she shot back.

A fog of dark soot-stained magic crawled to her, lifting her chin, and forcing her gaze to his. The blue embers of heat in his eyes dashed out to ice as he promised her, "There is *nothing* for you in Kava anymore."

His deathly tone swept through her, emptying her brain of every single decent thought. Looking away, she gathered up the wickedness inside her. She'd had endless practice with a mouthy prince after all. Rolling her words into a purr, she played with a god. "But there is *someone*."

The fog disappeared in an instant. Aidan's brows rose as if he couldn't believe what he was hearing. Marked disbelief filled his words. "What we are doing is more important than some boy who was never capable of loving you."

"Who says I can't do both?" She smiled flippantly, irritated at his response. She'd meant to provoke and instead he'd delivered a hit to both her heart and pride. Gods, couldn't she even piss a man off properly anymore?

Aidan paused, visibly slowing himself down and speaking carefully. His voice was strained. "While I am aware you said that to spite me—I hope you know you are worth infinitely more than what that undeveloped cretin has shown you. Regardless of how disappointing your desires are—I obviously won't force you to go to the temple or stop you from seeing him." His fingers tapped against his opposite arm, but his mouth was shut tight, refraining from saying anything else.

Her stomach dropped, twisting as it went. People in her world didn't talk like this. Pushing off the counter, her voice went rough. "Don't you dare condescend to me about love or self-worth or who I *desire*. You wrecked your realm and my kingdom, remember?"

She stalked over to where he sat like a statue on his stool. Her thumb brushed over his cheek, fingers holding tight onto his jaw in a mimicry of his shadows. "You made a *terrible* deal with a *monster* and now you need *me.*"

Aidan tried to speak, but her voice sharpened, its goal evisceration and distance. "You're a hypocrite. You mock the love I had for Topp, but there's no threat of noose or sword here, and yet I imagine you'll do the same as him. Lie, omit, *betray*."

Aidan calmly shoved off the stool, crowding right back into her space. Body warm against hers, his hands settled on her hips, his words a growl. "I may have learned to communicate, but I spent my mortal life settling things the hard way with men far scarier than a little princess like you. I may talk sweet in your ear and ask all the right questions, but do *not* mistake that for weakness."

Her fingers slid to his, but he clamped down harder on her hips.

"Ask me. Ask me about what you learned as you drank from my waters. Ask me anything and I'll tell you, so long as the fates allow."

Elysia's defiance trickled away, leaving her uncertain. Turning her face from his, she found herself pressed against his neck, the scent of his skin drowning her senses.

"You're guilty," she whispered like a dagger. "And I'm going to find out why."

She made to move, but Aidan held her there, his laugh a low rasp. "I'll warn you now. I've been riddled with guilt for years—a little more won't kill me if it means I get to keep you. But since you can't bring yourself to ask, I'll let you find out what you don't know from the priestesses."

Once again, she strained, trying to leave. His fingers dug in as her breath hitched. "Call me every name in the book, throw my mistakes in my face, but do *not* compare me to that pathetic creature again."

She slipped out of his hold, annoyingly aware of her flushed cheeks, readjusted her clothing and put much needed space between them. "How do you know about me and him, anyway?"

Aidan glanced at her warily but appeared largely unrepentant as he bestowed one more shocking revelation for the day. "I kept an eye on you, of course."

"You *stalked* me?"

Aidan exhaled through his nose as if she were being obtuse. "I think I've already made it clear how much is at stake. So *yes,* I had Grim and his reapers watch over you. They aren't allowed to interfere, and it brought me more anxiety than relief, but I still forced myself to watch over you nonetheless."

Her nose wrinkled, afraid to ask her next question. "How much did Grim and his reapers see?"

Aidan looked disgruntled at the insinuation, rubbing a hand

over his face in exasperation. "Nothing inappropriate if that's what you mean."

Hand still over his mouth, she swore she heard him mutter. *"I'd fucking kill him."*

Begrudgingly, he attempted to explain. "The fates restricted me, as well as every other past god of the dead, from leaving the Deathlands. Between me being unable to leave, and you being unable to access your magic or hold your form here, Grim and his reapers filled the gap."

He shrugged as if the situation made such behavior acceptable.

"You need boundaries." Gods knew what he had seen. She fought the urge to cringe—she didn't owe him an apology for her life.

The skin near his eyes creased as he tried not to laugh and failed. Shaking his head, the dark melody of his voice became forthright and blunt. "Thorn, I would stalk you to the ends of the realms and back again. How's that for honest?"

Her heart stuttered even as she eyed him like he was an insane person. She didn't know why he was calling her *Thorn*, but she doubted it was for polite reasons. Clearing her throat, her Crown voice slipped out inadvertently. "That's unhealthy. And I know unhealthy relationships, so..."

He fully gave in to his chuckle now, the sound leaving goosebumps on her neck. Aidan set his gaze on her, a dangerous gleam entering his eyes as he moved. She held a hand up. "No, you stay right over there. There's been enough of...*this* for one day."

He grinned. "Do I make you nervous?"

She tossed her head. "Hardly. You need house-training."

Gaze locked on hers, his voice was a smooth, slow murmur. "What I'm about to say, I can repeat as many times as you need me to."

Too much, too much. Warmth licked through her, unwieldy and unwelcome. She backed into a cabinet, the door smacking loudly against her head. "We can talk *after* the temple."

Undeterred, his next words almost dropped her to her knees. "Damn the fates except for one thing. They might have never planned for you to reach me, but they made you *mine*."

She started to protest, but scarred fingers covered her mouth.

"And if you hadn't come? I would have stolen you through a crack in the earth and fed you with the truth of your belonging and power until you wanted to stay. Because even though you don't see it, that's what you deserve...love, adoration, *power*."

Stunned, her voice was shaky as she pushed back on his chest. "That isn't a normal thing to say, Aidan. Especially not to a stranger."

Aidan stepped back, allowing her to pass with a smile playing at his lips and his blue eyes victorious. "Wouldn't want you to be confused about where I stand. Besides, we're not strangers—I stalked you, remember?"

Elysia moved stiffly as she left the kitchen, her head rampant with confusion. She stopped two feet out of the doorway, looking over her shoulder. "You don't have to do that—convince me of something that isn't there to motivate me. I meant it when I said I'd do my job."

CHAPTER 5

WHAT THE FUCK is a dead man's remedy? Nothing on this cocktail menu made any sense.

Despite Aidan's *you should leave as soon as possible* orders, he'd been nowhere to be found all day. His office had been unusually empty and anytime she ran into a stray reaper, they hurried away before she could ask them where he was. Like any good snoop, she'd used this time to poke around the house, and even pilfered a few fountain pens from his office. His desk was lined with color-coded jars of them—and now he was a few pens short. She smiled. She might have only known him for a short time, but she had him pegged, and it pleased her no small amount to mess with his fastidious order of things.

Knowing he'd be pissed if she traveled off to the mortal realm without speaking to him, she decided to venture into the village. In her initial travels to the death realm, she'd only seen a bit of the woods and the estate—there was an entire realm to explore though, and the local village seemed like a good place to start. Nestled in a valley, the estate was snugly surrounded by rolling hills and patches of the scraggly woods she had seen on her first visit. A well-worn dirt path directed her up over a hill all the way to the cobblestone streets of the village.

The houses she passed looked like smaller versions of Aidan's home. Dark red-brown brick with black trim and iron accents. Moving further into the village, she found not only red-brick offices and storefronts but also smooth, creamy plaster buildings with the same dark trim and dark roofs. Windows were decorated with planter boxes, and she imagined they would be filled with bright red flowers come spring. Sooty fog reminiscent of Kava caressed the open air, but unlike her home, the buildings remained clean and presentable. When she inhaled, the tinted and speckled air didn't stick to her mouth or lungs. People leisurely unlocked their shops, waving and chatting to each other like it was routine.

Now, her ass was on a barstool as she scanned the cocktail board looking for a single drink she recognized. Giving up, she perused the liquor shelves instead. Elaborately cut bottles glowed and swirled. One bottle in particular caught her eye as flecks of light sparked in the dark blue-green liquid.

"Want a taste?"

Elysia turned her attention to the blonde bartender. He pointed at the bottle. "The starshine? Do you want a glass?"

The lights within the bottle grew brighter and Elysia smiled, enjoying the simple show of magic. She started to say yes before remembering she couldn't pay. "I mean I do, but I don't have any money."

The bartender grabbed a beveled cocktail glass with one hand and the starshine with the other. "Just get here?"

She nodded as he poured the shimmering liquid out.

Pushing the glass at her hand, he settled back against the bar. "Did housing already set you up? You'll find a job soon enough."

Elysia combed her hair into a ponytail, grumbling. "Something like that."

The bartender's eyes latched onto the floral helm peeking out as she tied her hair back. He whistled. "I thought I recognized you. Elysia Parker, the mortal we've all been waiting for."

He grinned cheekily, and Elysia pulled her cocktail closer,

suspicion rankling her. "Why in the realms would you recognize me?"

Corking the starshine, he threw her a look. "I live here permanently. I care about what happens to my home."

She frowned at him and sniffed her drink. *Floral, but sweet.* "That's not an answer."

He shrugged, evading her question, but still stuck out his hand, introducing himself. "Herman."

Placing her hand in his, he flipped her wrist and jerked her half over the bar to examine the design more carefully. Elysia wrenched back, but what the man lacked in height he made up for in muscle. He released her, and she smacked onto her ass, the stool wobbling beneath her.

"Aidan's driving you to drink already?"

"Don't. Touch," she bit out.

She didn't know who she was allowed to stab around here. Could you even harm someone who was dead? Ignoring him, she took a cautious sip of her drink, liking how it slid down her throat like warm honey. Lightness hollowed her bones and her scowl fell away, replaced by an unfamiliar easy smile. Downing the glass, she held it out, silently asking for another. The quiet glug of the starshine stopped as the spout tapped against the rim.

She swirled the drink, her chest feeling looser than it had possibly ever been in her life. Every last tension and anxiety were gone in an instant. She couldn't even remember why she'd been in such a mood walking in here.

Toying with the bevels of the glass, her gaze roamed around the small establishment. Five barstools and a couple of small round tables made it an intimate setting. Candles wavered in the low light, and the heat was positively toasty compared to outside.

"I shouldn't be here," she acknowledged, thinking about Kava and the temples.

"In my bar? How barbaric. Tell him you're your own person."

She shook her head, lips splitting into a grin. Herman was a lot more tolerable after a drink or two. "In the death realm. Or in charge of finding Aidan's talisman at all."

Herman poured himself a thimblefull of something red and fiery. "You think you're the wrong person for the job."

She snapped her fingers and pointed at him. "Exactly. You get it."

He considered her, his blue-gray eyes more serious than she'd been expecting. "On the contrary, I think you've been through a lot, and it's easier for you to think you'll fail. Easier to expect that both you and others will let you down. That everyone else lies and manipulates as much as you've had to."

The airiness of the starshine rippled as her natural emotions tried and failed to affect her. Her brow wrinkled as she grasped for wariness or even confusion, but it was futile. They all drifted away like little clouds of nothing.

"What do you know about what I've been through?" Perfectly at ease, her question had no bite, only curiosity.

Polishing off his drink, he topped hers off again. "What can I say, I'm a fan."

A frown started, but then left as her smile widened. "Find the talisman. Go home to Relaclave." She nodded to herself, the room shifting with prisms of beautiful light. It was simple, she just needed to start. How hard could it be? She was born to find secrets, and the talisman was simply an object of power—hidden like a secret.

It was time to go to Bellia.

DROPPING her jacket on the floor, Elysia stood in the foyer of the estate. She was humming tunelessly, staring at an oil painting of Aidan's dogs, when the hairs on the back of her neck stood up. Twisting on stockinged feet, she found him striding closer, holding an open leather-bound ledger with his sights set on her. His mood wasn't difficult to decipher, if his tightened jaw and harsh gait were anything to go by. *Serves him right*, she thought, giggling. She hoped she'd stolen his favorite pen.

Elysia gave the worst curtsy of her life as he approached, almost falling over. "Your Deadliness." Tiny spheres of light floated around his head, drawing her attention as she watched them shift colors with delight.

His expression flattened and the ledger snapped shut. "I didn't realize day drinking was how one showed their commitment to the job."

Elysia kicked her jacket out of the way, enjoying how Aidan's gaze slid over to the motion in annoyance. "I couldn't find you. And it's a well-documented part of the Parker process. You should just be glad it didn't involve drugs."

Aidan placed a hand on the credenza, leaning his weight onto it as his irritation melted into tired patience. "Potions *do* have drugs, Elysia."

She paused. "Oh." That explained a lot.

She'd promised herself she would never do drugs. Alcohol on occasion, but never drugs, not after watching her sister fall in and out of sobriety for years. The guilt she expected to overtake her escaped her reach though, and she grinned to herself. No wonder people were into this.

Aidan's shoulders dropped, his head tilting as he watched her. "Yes, *oh.*"

Tossing the ledger onto the credenza, he grabbed her hand, pulling her along through the house until they were in what looked like an infirmary. The small amber potion bottles here looked decidedly less fun than the ones at the bar. Instead of beautiful shimmering colors, they were filled with dark, murky liquids and floating herbs. Raised lettering on their labels said things like *anti-diarrheal* and *Aidan's migraines.*

Her mind flashed back to the meela's tincture, and she grimaced, waving her hands. "No, no. No, thank you. I'm good. Drugs wear off."

Aidan grabbed a particularly sludgy bottle off the shelf and uncorked it. "That they do. But you were expected at the Bone Temple hours ago, only you disappeared, and no one knew where you went."

Elysia poked him in the belly, making him jerk back in disbelief. "Nooo, I looked for *you*, and I couldn't find *you*, so I found... other activities."

Aidan fought a grin. "I had to go to the prison. I'm half-tempted to leave you like this for a while. Alas, responsibility wins out like it always does."

She nodded sagely, some distant sober part of her relating to what she heard in his voice. "Truth."

Aidan handed her the bottle, but she pushed it away, wrinkling her nose as the smell wafted from it. "You know, some people would argue that I deserve a little respite after *almost dying*. Unsurprising behavior for someone who rules over the dead, though. How lively could you be?"

Aidan looked at a loss as she cackled and snorted at her own terrible joke. Still laughing, she didn't see him change tactics. Faster than she could track, he was tipping her head back and pouring the tonic down her throat as she gagged and spluttered.

Wiping her mouth, she scowled at his satisfied expression. "*Hey*. That's my move." All at once, reality slammed into her, the beautiful, honeyed warmth and kaleidoscopic lights fleeing to another dimension. She stood still for a moment, jarred by the abrupt return to reality.

Aidan glanced at the bottle before tossing it into a bin. "I *did* learn that move from you, but we can talk about that another time. You need to get to Ryspur, *now*."

She barely held back the retort that she was going to Kava. Per the usual, life was easier when you simply told people what they wanted to hear but did what you needed to do. It was better that he didn't know. He'd just worry and waste more precious time trying to sway her. If he did realize what she'd done thanks to his stalking ways, it would be too late, and wouldn't that just suck for him.

He handed her a small coin purse, which she shoved into her trouser pocket. "Tell me you're going to the Bone Temple."

Elysia fixed her face like a good little indentured woman. Gods knew she'd had enough practice doing it for everyone else. "I'm going to the Bone Temple," she parroted back.

"*Only* the Bone Temple."

A dark tendril of soot tilted her chin, and she sighed, answering him. "I am to go to the priestesses. Only to the priestesses. And then return to you, my deep, dark deadliness."

Grimacing, he dropped her chin. "Again, if you want to give me a nickname, I can think of a few others I'd rather hear."

"Dream on, dead boy."

"You don't even understand how ridiculous that statement is."

"I thought we were bonding." Elysia smiled with her lips closed, blinking up at him with her big brown eyes.

He shook his head. They were back at the front door now, where she put on the shoes and coat she had just taken off. Aidan looked down at her, becoming serious. "Twenty-four hours. Twenty-four hours max, and you're to report back here."

She saluted sarcastically before holding out her hand and curling her fingers. "I need a dagger."

"I would have to be decidedly insane to arm you at this point."

Eyes narrowed, she kept her hand out. "You would have me defenseless?"

He just looked at her.

"Soot and storms, I'm not going to stab you with it. Probably wouldn't even kill you anyway," she grumbled.

Aidan's blue eyes lightened. "You're right, it wouldn't, but somehow I don't think that would stop you."

She smiled sweetly. "Maiming is fine when killing won't do."

Defeated, he released a slow, suffering exhale and pulled a sheathed dagger out of his back pocket. "Thought you might want one."

Red gems encrusted the bronze handle. Weighty and just right in her hand, she grinned until Aidan plucked it back out of her palm. She started to protest, but then the man knelt on one knee, his hands sliding up her thigh, carefully buckling on a leather holster and securing the dagger against her. Hands still pressing into her thigh, he looked up and Elysia almost combusted on the spot.

His fingers squeezed gently. "See something you like, Thorn?"

Her eyes pinged around the god below her, from his hands to his face and back again. "Absolutely not," she mumbled with bright red cheeks.

Aidan grinned. "And where are you *not* going?"

She pursed her lips in silence.

"It feels like I shouldn't have to say this, but stay away from the king. Stay away from his spawn. If you set *one* little foot in that godsforsaken land—"

"You'll wait for the next fated mortal girl to tumble through her dreams into your Deathlands? You need me every bit as much as I need you, so I'd be careful with those threats." She kept her voice pleasant.

An inhuman growl sounded in the back of his throat as his hands tightened on her thigh. "Try me, just try me."

Elysia blinked, her tenacity running from the room like she should have.

Smiling at her stunned silence, Aidan took advantage of her mouth not flapping. "You go to Bellia. You learn what you need to learn from those who have kept the god of the dead's stories alive. And you come *home*. No detours." His final words were both a threat and a warning.

She twitched, growing damp with perspiration beneath her heavy sweater. He needed her. And couldn't stop her. It would be fine.

She managed a nod.

"Good. I spoke with Maya and while you will need a natural source of water to travel from the mortal realm to here, you should be fine without water for all other travels. The fates' mark on your ear allowing you to travel is a boon, and I am *asking* you for the last time to not abuse it or endanger yourself. Can you respect that?"

Not waiting for an answer, he spun her around and gave her a little push as if she were about to go through the front door instead of disappearing from one realm to the next. She forced herself not to look back. She really hadn't planned to do this two inches away from him. It kind of ruined everything, but she was nothing if not determined and possibly obstinate. Leaning away from him, she whispered as quietly as she could.

Gage, Gage, Gage.

But not quiet enough. She could still hear Aidan's curses ringing in her ears as she landed.

CHAPTER 6

ELYSIA DUCKED a fist flying at her face. Classic sounds of a bar brawl—glasses breaking, noses crunching, obscene hollering—crashed around her. Elysia dropped to the ground, grinning as she crawled as fast as she could on her hands and knees to the edge of the room.

Popping back up, her blood sang as she took in the ransacked tavern. Throats were slit and boots were stomping unmentionables. She winced as someone got thrown into the fireplace.

By the gods.

This was why you never snuck up on Gage.

A man spotted her and came at her with a roar. Grabbing the wooden chair beside her, she clobbered him as hard as she could. Wood splintered with a sickening sound as the chair broke against his face. The man slumped to his knees before falling sideways. *The chair won that round.*

Elysia scanned the room, trying to stay out of the fray. It was terrible, she supposed, but she'd secretly been dying to do that ever since she'd first seen Jessa attack without mercy and with only a chair during Topp's traitorous raid below the sea.

Not subtle, very effective.

A familiar hand grabbed her by the collar and yanked her

close, throwing her behind him. Elysia huffed at the manhandling. "For fuck's sake, I'm fine. Did you see that chair move?"

Gage let a throwing star rip across the room. "You shouldn't be here."

The fighting simmered to a low boil as Gage's men cut down the last few people standing.

Elysia peered around Gage's shoulder at the final scene.

Blood. Guts. Excrement.

Gage did not have a glamorous job, she decided. The smell started to waft in the heat of the small room, and she involuntarily gagged.

Smirking, he glanced back at her. "Yeah, you're just an old pro now, aren't you?"

Elysia cut him an unimpressed look. Not everyone could be known as Kava's Shadow. The title had clearly gone to his head. "I need to talk to you."

"Yeah, I kind of got that when you showed up in the middle of a job."

Gage snapped out orders to his men, who were already dragging bodies and gathering previously unpaid coin that was now paid in more than full. He pointed to a set of wooden stairs. "Let's go. I don't want anybody to see you."

"I don't think there's anyone left to see me," she muttered as she stepped delicately over the human remains littering the old porous wood floors. Some stains never really did come out.

Wooden beams vaulted the ceiling and soft lanterns lit the upper room. Blazing in the back was a woodfire stove with a kettle hanging off to the side. A small bed covered with handmade quilts was tucked against the wall.

Gage sank into a chair near the fire. He stared at her, his face an emotionless brick.

"Why are you looking at me like that?"

He pressed two fingers against his lips, incidentally smearing blood and grime on his skin.

Eyes downcast, he wouldn't look at her. He stared at the fire, the floor, anywhere but her. "I failed you. I never should have let you near that ball. *You could have died.* And I couldn't do a damn thing. I knew, I knew I should have sent you away."

Elysia was silent, her own eyes wide and soft. An unfamiliar ache took up residence in her chest. Gage carried no blame, she had made her own decision, but the fact that he *cared.* Her own parents had stood by like statues as her head almost rolled. While Gage, like every other decent parental figure before him, struggled not to bear the burden for her.

She put her hand onto his, wrapping her fingers around his palm. Finally picking up his head, Gage met her gaze, and it was enough for a dark wave of guilt to crash over her. Another unfamiliar first, she realized her choices had caused *him* pain.

Voice breaking, his pain seeped out. "You disappeared. Into thin air, and I had no idea if you were okay. There was blood on Garrison's sword. I just kept praying that you made it back to the death realm in one piece."

She squeezed his hand. "I'm okay, look at me—all healed."

"You look like nothing ever happened."

Releasing his hand, she sat back in her seat and lifted her chin, so the faint pink line on her neck showed. "There's still a few scars."

Nodding, he pointed at the floral helm on her forearm. "You took the deal."

"What other choice did I have?"

His dark eyes flashed at her response. "Fates know that you would have ended up there somehow."

"What's that supposed to mean?"

Gage's thick, dark eyebrows drew together, but he didn't answer.

She tapped the arm of her chair impatiently. "I get it. You're mad, but I don't have time for brooding or coddling. I'm not supposed to be here, so if there's something you need to say, then say it."

The sound of a tinkling collar broke the tension, both of their heads turning to the source of the sound. A small black, copper, and white long-haired dog bounded up the stairs, racing over to Elysia, where it sat down staunchly. With its lips peeled back in a fierce growl, all five pounds of the animal were menacing...and adorable.

Gage's eyes grew wide, and he inhaled sharply. "What exactly is your proclivity for unnatural creatures?"

Elysia looked between him and the tiny dog in confusion. "You mean the raccoon? I've told you. She was Topp's rehab project. The dog is unfortunately Aidan's."

Gage's eyes hadn't left the dog. "Not a terrible choice even if I don't like it."

"Yeah, because taking care of a dog is exactly what I need to be focusing on right now." Aidan was going to be getting an earful when she returned.

Sighing, she grabbed the ball of fluff, pulling it onto her lap. The dog gave her a solid lick before showing Gage its teeth again in warning.

"Can't wait to see what you bring home next. Did I mention the raccoon showed up again? I can't get it to leave."

Preoccupied, Elysia didn't hear him. She ran her fingers through the dog's fur, checking its collar for a tag.

She squinted.

CRUSHER

How fitting. She looked down at the pint-sized dog. "You should have been called Daisy or Sweetpea." The dog grunted disagreeably.

Drawing her attention back, Gage questioned her. "Where are you headed?"

"About that, I need a favor."

He folded his perpetually tanned light brown arms, already looking like was going to say no. "Why do I feel like I'm not going to like what you're about to say?"

She offered him a rare, genuine smile as she scratched the pup's ears. "Because you actually know me."

He snorted. "That I do."

Looking at him seriously, she held his gaze. "I want in."

The words weren't even fully out before he was shaking his head and frowning.

"Will you at least hear me out? Aidan's going to be sending me all over the godsdamned world in search of this talisman."

"And how is the Reyez family going to help you with that?"

"Don't be dense." She spoke crossly now. "You don't have to like it, but you know it's practical. Your family's business sprawls all over this side of the world. Either I have their protection, or I will inevitably come up against them. You call me family, now make it true." Her words ended in a growl.

Gage stared at her before finally speaking. "You don't know what you're asking."

"I know exactly what I'm asking."

He pulled out a small knife and toyed with it as he settled in to clean the battle out from beneath his nails. "Really don't think you do."

"Then tell me," she demanded fiercely.

Gage gave a dry laugh and looked up at the ceiling. "You want in the family? Do you know the cost of being in this *family?*" He gestured grandly at the tavern below them. "This is a casual Monday, Elysia. Do you think I can just brand you and then you'll get a free pass? You're already indebted to a death god. Isn't that enough?"

She snarled right back at him. "You're the heir to the entire organization, so yes, I *do* think that you can do that, and I need you to, so that I don't end up dead as I hunt down treasure for said death god."

A bitter silence fell between them.

"What good is he if he can't protect you?"

"You taught me to protect *myself.*"

His voice softened. "You know you can't escape him, right, Lys? Not even my family's that good."

"Godsdammit Gage, I'm just trying to cover my ass. Will you help me or not?"

Despite what he showed her, Elysia could tell he was angrier with her than he had possibly ever been before. He never spoke much about his family or the Reyez empire, and she'd never forced it, but things had changed, and he knew it as well as she did. The Reyez family brand would mean she could find a safe haven in almost any city she entered. Maybe she would get lucky and not be in need of their protection, but she'd be stupid not to have it.

Frustration all over his face, Gage wrested the bloodied signet ring off his finger and used an iron poker to start heating it up in the woodfire stove.

Trepidation snuck into her tone. "I thought you just tattooed people."

She'd seen the men lined up in his house while the tattooer inked a dark, thick band around their ring fingers.

Married to the family and only the family was what they said.

He crouched in front of the stove, holding the ring over the open flame. "My men do wear the band. You are not my men."

Gage walked over to her and placed one hand on her shoulder. He held the ring with a tea towel, and there was gravel in his voice when he spoke. "This is going to hurt, but you can't move, or else we'll have to do it again, and the blurred burn will shame you. Understand?"

Elysia grimaced, bracing herself. Eyes shut, she grunted her permission. "Just do it already."

The next thing she knew, she was biting back a scream and the smell of burnt skin was singeing her nose.

He pressed harder, the signet ring shoved into the sensitive hollow of her throat. "Don't. Move."

Tears streamed down her face, but she didn't move. Slow breaths puffed out of her nose, her shoulders gently rising and falling while Gage's fingers dug in.

"You're almost there." The ring seemed to be one with her

skin, burning through the layers of flesh, ensuring it would brand and not heal. An eternity later, he pulled the ring out of her flesh. Gage's gaze shuddered, locked onto the small, angry mark until he turned away with his mouth tight. He hadn't wanted this for her.

She grabbed his wrist. "I'm sorry, but thank you."

Turning back to where she sat, he pressed his palms down on her thighs, bent over so they were face to face. "Pray you don't need it. Because no one becomes family without a cost. Not even you. And if by some miracle this all ends? You'll still be family—no matter how long you live."

"Whatever it takes." Steel girded her words because it was true. She had no choice but to go wherever this journey took her.

He grabbed her palm and pressed a kiss over the faint scar. "Send word if you can."

She nodded, standing up and preparing to leave. Her chest burned with pain, but a mischievous spark still entered her eyes.

Gage took a wary step back. "What, what are you looking like that for?"

She grinned and tossed the snarling ball of fur at him.

Gage's blanching face was the last thing she saw, and then she was gone. Elysia laughed. She could've sworn she heard Kava's big bad Shadow hiss in surprise.

CHAPTER 7

ELYSIA STUMBLED, her knees hitting crumbling white stone steps. She brushed the dust off her smarting kneecaps and stared at the ancient temple before her as the wind whipped furiously. Tucking her hands into her sides, she lowered her face against the stinging winter cold and began her ascent.

Up on a thick platform, the bone-white walls of the temple jutted against the dusky bloodred sky. Domed and octagonal with dark windows, it was eerie how the temple loomed over the rest of the world. Instinctively, she kept her steps silent and cautious. Off-white dust drifted into the wind like smoke, but she refused to look out below as the steps grew steeper.

Though her chest and thighs were burning, she heaved herself over the hanging edge of the temple's platform and stood. The wind was even worse this high, her hair cutting against her skin. She held it back with one hand and swept her gaze over the desolate sea of tombs that rolled out in waves as far as her eye could reach.

A fraught silence prickled against her skin. She studied the temple at her back. It was *too* quiet. The kind of quiet that made her fingers itch for her dagger. Aidan had said they were expecting her, but he wasn't even allowed in this realm. Maybe he was wrong.

In the distance, a strange howl pierced the silence, and Elysia fought to temper her unease. The beasts of Bellia were nothing like those of Kava. Bitter winters and beautiful temperate summers gave way not only to bears and wolves, but to shifters and magical creatures she'd only glimpsed in Topp's books. The kind of creatures that a mere dagger would not even be worth raising against.

With the sounds of Bellian beasts at her back, the temple invited her closer. She approached, snatching her hand back from the temple wall before it could touch what she now realized were actual bones pulverized into compacted form. Little shards stuck out in odd places, ready to slice the unsuspecting person who was unfortunate enough to trail a hand over the walls.

Elysia pushed against the heavy black door until it slid silently on a well-oiled track. The door clanged as it closed behind her, the sound echoing throughout the empty temple. All at once, candles burst to life. Flames danced inside hanging lamps, and fat half-melted candles were strewn about the bone-dust-covered floors.

At the center-back of the temple was a throne. Enormous and intimidating, it was a massive puzzle work of perfectly fitted skeletal remains. She drank in the silent and still room. It was death made into art. There were spiraling columns of spines, interlocking femurs from which lanterns hung, and more pulver-ized dust pounded into symbols on the black floor. Every sculpture, every detail was death given form.

While most of the old Kavian beliefs had been lost, there were many who still held the old superstition that the spirit of a person lingered in the bones. If the old Kavian beliefs about bones were true, then the amount of power in the very structure and material of this temple was inconceivable.

Footsteps echoing, she walked closer to the skeletal throne, her gaze snagging on the golden coins clamped between teeth and pinched between creeping tarsals. Snug within the eye sockets were dark, glinting bloodstones that she imagined their master could peer through to see his earthen temple.

Unlikely, but in the flickering candlelight, the gemstone eyes seemed to follow her, pressing on the strange guilt she carried for ignoring Aidan's wishes. Given Crusher's unexpected appearance, she wouldn't be surprised to find out the hypervigilant pervert was still stalking her. Glancing around, she scanned for a reaper or priestess lurking in the shadows but saw nothing except what one would expect inside a temple.

Burnt-out and still-flickering tealights, food offerings, and curios were scattered about the base of the throne. Despite her non-religious upbringing, she knew each little candle signified a petition or prayer. It was a foreign curiosity to her—praying to someone or anything with expectation for response.

Kavians still used the term undead gods, but to Bellians it remained true.

Kavians said it scoffingly. Bellians said it reverently.

It was difficult to extricate the jaded ideas she carried about the gods. In Bellia, the gods were the ones who placed each and every magical gift like a benevolent seed into mortal souls. In Kava, that connection was long gone, and they were left with not only soot-ridden skies, but bodies.

Bitterness twisted her mouth as she stared at the hopeful petitions around her feet. Undead or not, she wanted nothing to do with them. Aidan with his broken powers and useless deal. Not to mention every other god who must have watched as her people fell from their curse.

It was obvious that mortals and their small magics and lives did not matter to such beings.

Her attention turned to a bronze bell hanging from a rope of spines near the throne. Dangling from the clapper was a skeletal arm with its hand reaching out, waiting, and beckoning her to ring the bell.

The bastard could've warned her that she'd have to shake hands with death.

She supposed she already had.

Disgust curling her lips, she placed ice-cold fingers into the skeletal ones above her and pulled. The bell tolled and tolled until the temple hummed. Vibrations rose from beneath her feet. Movement stirred down below as if the temple had only been in slumber.

Gods, what had she done?

She backed away from the bell, her boot crunching on a teacup filled with frozen coffee. She staggered backward, unsteady, as she hastily made it to the door only to find it sealed and locked. Pulling to no avail on the handle, she swiveled, pulling out her dagger. Then the lights went out.

Without the flood of candles, it was utter blackness.

A womb of death, and her within it.

Elysia blinked wildly, bidding her eyes to adjust, and as they did, the shadowy outlines of people took shape. People who had formed a circle around her and the throne.

As one, they began to sing.

The haunting melody had never failed to draw a tear to her eye all those nights she had fallen from her bed to the Deathlands. Now, encircled by priestesses within death's temple, the familiar voices enraptured her just the same as they had the very first time all those months ago.

She could see now that the priestesses' robes were simple, dark, yet elegant. One part of their faces were painted like carved bones and the other half sensual and lush. They were beautiful, but haunting.

One of the priestesses floated forward, stopping within a breath's reach of Elysia, and smeared white paste along her cheekbone, jaw, and lips. A second priestess took her place, painting her left side with wine-stained lips and smoldering eyes. Shocked, a natural sense of alarm grew within her as strangers invaded her space. Still, she fought to hold still as they finished their work.

Together with efficient, nimble hands, they removed Elysia's clothes. She shivered, her skin peppering with goosebumps as they placed a heavy robe over her and clipped bones into her hair.

The priestesses returned to their places and spoke in unison.

Not one, but two.
A mortal, a god.
One to revere and one to dread.
Fate's true challenge.
And life's last quest.

The sudden silence that followed was jarring. The priestesses broke apart and with their movement, the door and windows slid open, allowing in the yellow light of the moon and sharp evening wind. A murmur of excitement zipped through the women and people around her, but Elysia was still reeling over the realization she had been hearing *them* every time she fell asleep, only to wake in the Deathlands.

Their chant played back in her mind, her stomach plummeting with a sickening swoop.

She tried to slam down her walls, to push the words away. But the chant persisted in banging around inside her skull. The god of the dead never worked alone. She gripped her dagger tighter, refusing to consider the final line.

The sick feeling lurched from her stomach to her throat.

She shouldn't be here. She was just a gossip-ridden, cursed woman who hid in libraries and pantries to steal people's secrets. Anything involving a *life's last quest* was not for her.

A bone-painted face popped up in front of Elysia, eyes and face aglow with excitement like this was all good news and they were at a party. Words flying fast, the woman tried and failed to hook a chummy arm through Elysia's.

Undeterred, she chirped away. "You've finally come! We've been waiting *so* long for you to arrive. We even sang every night to guide you home."

Elysia's distress leapt to new levels. Mouth seemingly stuck shut, her gaze darted around to all the people paying rapt attention to their exchange and then to the door.

Another priestess, who walked like a warrior of death rather than death's handmaiden, hushed the bubbly acolyte before speaking. "Let's take our guest below. I think a little food and warmth might go a long way."

Elysia's shoulders dropped just a fraction. Food, warmth. Those did sound agreeable. Far more agreeable than whatever prophetic nonsense had seemingly already been set in motion without her consent or knowledge.

All the stories she'd studied before seeking out Aidan crept through her mind. How sometimes the mortals ended up wishing the gods had never noticed them at all.

Too late now.

There hadn't been a single story about the god of the dead always taking a mortal within the *Travels of the Undead* text, but then again she hadn't been able to find any other books to study given Kava's shitty picked-over libraries.

The warrior priestess made a parting motion with her hands, and the floor slid open, revealing stairs down into the heart of the temple. She guided Elysia down the bone-white steps until they exited into a torch-lit hallway. Eventually, they entered a large dining hall filled with long wooden tables and benches. Many of the people who had participated in the ceremony were already seated, still in their face paint and digging into food.

"Sit." The warrior directed Elysia before walking off, only to return a minute later with steaming mugs of broth and a basket of rolls.

Tall and sturdy with obvious muscle lining her arms and tight, twisting braids adorning her head, the priestess looked like she spent more time sparring than praying. She held out a warm deep brown hand, offering Elysia a mug before sliding onto the bench across from her.

"So, you're her." She appraised Elysia with intelligent, watchful eyes.

Elysia didn't respond at first. Based on what had just happened above, the priestesses likely had certain expectations that she had no desire to be held to.

Gripping the hot cup of broth, she answered bluntly. "If you want to think so, be my guest. What *I* know is that I made a deal with a god in hopes of saving my kingdom from his mistakes."

"You scorn fate so easily."

Elysia barely refrained from rolling her eyes. *The fates this, the fates that.* "My people don't have gods. We don't have fates. Only their consequences."

At that the woman smiled. "I'm Nia."

"Head meela?"

Nia nodded, still looking Elysia over like she was going to discover a secret, or maybe a more suitable option for their god. "I'm responsible for the temple and the people who inhabit it. How strange that the fates-chosen mortal would be from a kingdom where you've been taught nothing of the gods. Your stories lost and magic dried up like wasted grapes."

Ignoring her comment, Elysia let her gaze run over the walls of the dining hall, carved and painted with figures and glyphs. Her natural curiosity came out, and she tipped her head at the art. "Are those the stories of the past gods of the dead?"

The careful etchings and rich paint ignited an unexpected wisp of longing in her chest. She didn't necessarily wish she had grown up with gods or religion, but maybe she did wish Kavians had *something* that connected them beyond their own flesh and blood to the world and divinity that ran through all things. Beyond that, a people who didn't know who they were or where they came from were a weak, unstable thing. The loss of ancestral knowledge and practices cut them off in a strange, inhuman way from both the natural and spiritual world.

Nia smiled fondly at the walls. "They are love stories. Stories of life and death. Stories that stick to your bones and revive your spirit."

Walking over to the wall, Nia took a moment to run her

fingers over the textured art before speaking. She pointed to a faded drawing in the center. All the other stories crowded out from this piece as if they were its offspring.

"The first god of the dead. He saw the mortals with their hopes and their passions and desires. He saw how they hoped yet lost course again and again. His heart was struck by this plight. How the dead would come through his land with their regrets and soul-deep aches."

Her fingers traced down to a sealed scroll. "He began offering deals to mortals. Assistance for their paths. But as can happen with gods, he often lost sight of what truly mattered to these mortals, what had drawn him to their plight in the first place, and he began to offer deals to whoever could offer payment. The god of the dead, no matter who it is, always has a certain affinity for wealth..."

She returned to the table to finish the story. "Wealth to a certain degree may be neutral, but the methods, the godly hubris —that's where the problems came in. But temples were being built and payments were flowing."

"What went wrong?" Elysia sipped her broth, listening intently.

Nia smiled wryly. "As you know, all it takes is one bad deal for consequences of catastrophic proportions to occur."

Elysia's face must have given her away because Nia laughed, a short hoarse sound from her chest. "Yes, all the gods of the dead seem to have a few things in common. But I'm telling you this story because it's why you are here now."

Elysia raised her eyebrows, waiting.

"The first god of the dead made a deal with a mortal man that led to the mortal's death. A terrible deal—the kind young mortals ask for when their desperation for change outweighs their sense. His sister was far more cunning. She came to strike her own deal and brought with her an offering of tea. The god of the dead drank the tea only to realize she'd tried to poison him. She'd been bold enough to believe she could kill the one who rules over the dead with mortal herbs."

Nia grinned, clearly loving this part of the story. "That's the kind of gumption that wins gods and starts wars."

"But *did* she kill him?" She glanced at the wall, thinking the recipe might be useful.

"Of course not! Gods are not so easily killed. Something you ought to remember. *But* the poison did weaken him enough that he made a deal for its antidote."

Elysia recounted the story in her head, trying to keep up. "And that deal impacts me now?"

"Correct. The deal was that the god of the dead would never rule alone again. He would be tempered by a mortal with limits to his power."

"And he agreed to that because...?" Elysia was starting to question if any of these men had ever cut a winning deal before.

Nia made a soft noise of agreement. "There are theories. The most common being that the fates became intrigued and intervened."

Elysia paused, remembering what Aidan had said about the fates and the damper on his power. "Right, that's where the talisman comes in then. More meddling of the fates."

She stared into her mug, soaking in this new information. So, Aidan was after the mortal counterpart required of him as god of the dead along with the talisman. Lifting her gaze, she spoke from her gut. "I'm not her, I won't be her. I'm a mortal who wants the god who fucked up her kingdom to fix it. If he believes I'm the mortal to his god, then he should've made a better deal, but he didn't. All I've agreed to is finding a talisman."

Nia responded with infuriating calm. "Then you have nothing to worry about. Find the talisman and be on your way."

Elysia eyed her. "You wouldn't have a map, would you?"

Grinning, Nia started eating from a small board of cured meats and cheese. Between bites, she asked a pointed question. "If you could overlook the deal that wrecked your home, what's your take on him?"

Elysia flushed, covering her mouth as she spoke around her food. "Overconfident and annoying."

Nia's chiseled cheeks curved in amusement. "That all?"

Frowning, she chewed her food. It hadn't been long, but so far, he'd spent most of his time in his office, working and scribbling in his ledgers. When he wasn't busy looking worried, his attention was heavy on her, his communication blunt with a heated edge.

"Unexpected," she grunted begrudgingly.

"Aidan is unique amongst the gods. He tends to those who have passed. Makes deals with the living to align broken fates, or at least he used to. He's far more aware of mortal realities than most of the gods who dip in and out of their lives."

Elysia waved a chunk of bread. "You don't need to do this. The whole talking up your boss bit—it's just like I told him. I'm committed to my job, my kingdom, and that's it."

Nia continued evenly. "He is also stubborn and terrifyingly powerful even when limited. He can dry the life from the most succulent of beings. He may be god of the dead, but he carries the weight of death within him. It's not a weight meant to be borne alone."

Elysia dusted her hands off. "Well, I guess he better start dating then. Is this all I'm here for? I have things to do." Irritation had her eyes flicking to the exit. She'd been initiated, so if this was just going to be *ten reasons to date the god of the dead*, then she was ready to leave.

"You've never been in a temple before in your life and you don't have any questions?"

She'd gotten drunk and smashed a bottle against Aidan's skull temple in Relaclave—didn't that count? She pushed her empty mug away. *Fine.* "Aren't you bored here? You don't seem like the priestess type."

Nia's gaze homed in on the new, angry branding nestled in the hollow of Elysia's throat with recognition in her eyes. "I've retired into this position and was specifically brought on for my skill set." She looked back up, speaking wryly. "You're sorely mistaken if you think there is anything *boring* about managing an underground temple full of women and folks who are obsessed with death of all things."

Elysia grinned in spite of herself. "Do you mean to say temples have assassins? Wouldn't that fall under Grim's work?"

"Grim and Aidan work closely together. This is as much Grim's temple as it is Aidan's." Nia's focus slipped, her knowing gaze heavy on the fresh burn still tingling Elysia's skin. "Wish I could be a fly on the wall when our god sees *that*."

Elysia sniffed, her shoulders drawing tight and her back straightening at the implication. As if she gave a rat's furry ass what that man thought about her ensuring her own protection. "He's the reason I needed it, so whatever his grievances may be, he can shove them wherever he'd like."

Nia's eyebrows rose.

"And if this is his grand plan—sending me to chitchat with his priestesses about his many wonderful attributes, then I think we're all going to be waiting a very, very long time for me to find the talisman."

"I'd send you away too if I had to deal with your shit attitude all day."

Elysia glared. "My attitude is not shit."

Nia shoved the bench back with a scrape and stood. "You want to know more?"

Elysia trailed behind her into the dormitory portion of the temple, stopping in front of a rounded, bright pink door. The shocking color of the paint stood in severe contrast to the bone dust and dirt surrounding them. The door opened before Nia could so much as lift her hand to knock.

The overly excited woman who had spoken to Elysia earlier stood in the doorway smiling with the enthusiasm of a child. "*Finally*, I've been waiting."

Reaching out, she dragged them both into her room, her smile growing bigger by the second. "Your hunt has begun!" She waved her arms out wide theatrically, and Nia sighed in exasperation.

"For fuck's sake, Sera."

The woman briefly narrowed her eyes at the Head Meela and then promptly ignored her, continuing her speech with vigor and fast-moving hands. "Your hunt has begun, and you seek to thwart our god's plans as none of the mortals have ever sought to do."

Elysia glanced at Nia. Was this woman for real?

Face bright, she whispered conspiratorially. "We have a bit of a bet going on if you'll be able to pull off securing the talisman but still evade Aidan's clutches. The odds aren't good, we've asked, but I'm rooting for you!" She elbowed Elysia as if this would be cheerful news.

Nia twirled the tasseled rope around her waist. "You do realize what happens if Aidan doesn't find his mortal?"

Elysia jolted back to attention, her gaze shooting between the two women. "My job is the talisman. I find the talisman and he fixes things." Her voice grew weak as she realized exactly why he'd sent her here. All his comments about her being his—the bastard had meant it in a literal, fated sort of way, not just an overbearing *I'm a god who gets what he wants* kind of way. He'd thought she'd take the hit of *immortality* better if it came from a third party. Don't stab the priestess and all that.

Her voice went lethally quiet. "That wasn't part of the deal, and I have no interest." He had another thing coming if he thought she was going to roll over and accept this minor addendum to their deal. She was going to burn him alive, and she was going to enjoy it.

Sera whispered again, sounding awestruck. "Look how furious she is. Do you think she'll try to fight him? Oh, I hope she does."

Nia looked at Elysia without a shred of pity. "Remember that commitment you mouthed off about only minutes ago? To your job and your kingdom?"

A heated tension radiated throughout her body so hard she could've sworn she was vibrating in place, but she had no words. Silent, overwhelmed, and furious didn't even begin to cover it. She wanted to scream in all their faces that *this wasn't the deal* until they got it through their thick skulls. She'd agreed to find a talisman. She had *not* agreed to co-rule the realm of the dead and lose her mortality. Her duty was to Kava. The Deathlands were his.

Given that punching a priestess wasn't an option, the desire to bolt jittered through her now, demanding she get away from this place. She needed to be alone. She needed to be above ground and anywhere but here.

Noticing her distraction, Sera grabbed both of Elysia's wrists firmly. "Look at me, right here."

Elysia's eyes snapped to hers.

"Good. You will travel to many lands and many places. You will come across faces new and old as you search. Friends will be foes and foes will be friends. Each lesson harder than the last until you hold the talisman in your hands."

Elysia's face contorted in disgust as her panic ebbed. "*Enough.*"

Sera sighed and broke character. "You can't just *find* the talisman. You have to earn it. The fates will reveal the talisman if they deem you worthy."

Hope bloomed in Elysia's chest, and she gripped Sera's wrists tighter. "And if I fail? A new mortal will be chosen?"

Nia cut in now. "If you fail on purpose, you'll wish for death over what the fates will do."

Elysia flinched, but Sera's grin was wide and buoyant. She turned to Nia with a squeal. "She honestly wants to bail. Bail on *fate.* Ugh, I love a reluctant hero. Best. Death voyage. Ever."

Elysia spoke through gritted teeth. "It's a job. Not a voyage."

Sera looked at her in amazement. "Incredible. But no, it really is a death voyage. You'll see!" She winked, and Elysia thought about stabbing her in the eye.

"None of this was included in our original deal." She was practically begging the head priestess to hear reason.

"Perhaps you're not remembering everything then."

Elysia's brow scrunched in disbelief. "I'm fairly certain I would remember the part about being forced to co-rule over the death realm and go on a death voyage."

"He told you to look, didn't he? Gave you a chance to see what he couldn't say because of the fates and their restrictions—a chance to examine the fine print."

Elysia stopped, her body automatically recoiling at the memory of diving behind Aidan's barriers for even moments. She released the echo of the remembrance with some effort. "We both know that's not how deals work. Whatever way you want to spin it, it was shitty to not say it outright."

"Maybe he's better at deals than you thought."

Nia chuckled at Elysia's pissed-off expression. "On that note, you have now been formally inducted into the mystery of the death voyage, so our work here is done. Time to send you back. And in case our god doesn't bother to tell you—you're welcome here anytime. The Maidens of Death are now yours as well as his to call on."

CHAPTER 8

The cobbled streets of old Relaclave felt good beneath her feet. Solid, dirty, and familiar—she couldn't help but grin. The grin was also due to thinking about how a certain chthonic deity was probably pulling out his dark, perfect hair and begging the fates for a new mortal while blue fire burned in his eyes. *Bastard fucking deserves it.*

If she couldn't drop out of this *death voyage*, then perhaps annoying him into submission would do the trick. She eyed her mark's sleek silver hair as it shone in the dim, overcast light of Relaclave. Looking sharp in a man's oversized wool coat and a burgundy scarf, Beatriz Parker swaggered through a door the color of a blackened berry.

Elysia let out a jaded snort and shook her head.

Of course, her sister was sweeping through that particular doorway in the middle of the godsdamn night when any normal person would be sleeping. Swanky drug dens and bars had always been her stomping grounds, but Elysia had naively wished to believe that she might be keeping her proclivities within the walls of the House now that she was so in *love*. That perhaps love had become her drug.

I am...an idiot. That wasn't how these things worked, no

matter how much anyone wanted to believe so, and Elysia knew it damn well. If anything, she was grateful Beatriz had decreased her use. Apart from a few occasions, most of the times she'd seen Beatriz the past few months, her sister had been coherent and seemingly herself.

Eyes still on the door, she chewed her lip. She wasn't sure if it was worth trying to speak to Beatriz now. If she wasn't already high, then she likely would be within the next few minutes. Elysia braced herself to travel through nothingness back to the death realm, before remembering she needed a godsdamn body of water. *Why can't anything be easy?* She was still bemoaning the fact she'd have to get wet when her ears pricked, and she heard a silent tune no one else could.

She looked up at the gray sky and pursed her lips. This was just the kind of thing that would get her caught. It was specifically the sort of thing she shouldn't do right now with a bounty on her head. But the music pulled on her strings, and her sister really was just through that door. A magic-addled smile swept her face as she went trailing after that silver mane, swinging her hips to the tantalizing song in her ear.

Hand on the iron door handle, she stumbled to a stop. There within the transom window above the door was a purple flower with sprays of greenery. *Her* purple flower. Someone had pried apart one of her pieces and slotted the flowers into the glass of the window. But why?

She opened the door with some caution. The melody that had drawn her to the door dipped sweet and low, soothing her anxieties. It buzzed and hummed in her ear as her eyes adjusted to the darkness of the club. Her magic beckoned, drawing her eyes to the fading form of her sister slinking down a brocade-papered hallway.

Elysia rolled her neck, fighting with herself internally. Yes, the magic pulled her, tugging incessantly, but her logic and experience cut in, reminding her that she didn't want to see her sister like this. Eyes void and soul seemingly outside her body.

With a tired sigh, she shoved her discomfort away and kept her feet quiet, staying a few paces behind Beatriz. Her sister greeted a severe-looking man and folded her tall frame into a leather booth. Elysia waited until Triz stared at a menu and then ducked into the booth behind the man she was meeting. Invisible to Beatriz and perfect for listening, she settled into eavesdrop.

Her cursory glance at the man, blonde hair slicked so tight it must have pulled at his scalp, confirmed this was business not pleasure, but then again, no one was ever more Beatriz's type than when they had drugs in their pocket. The purr in Beatriz's voice rolled out and Elysia barely refrained from making a retching noise. If she had a Crown voice, then her sister had a man-eating voice. It was shocking that anyone fell for this shit.

"Ramsey, what do you have for me?"

Elysia listened for the sounds of him digging in his pockets, but instead a server hurried over, delivering two glass tumblers with haste. Phosphorescent liquid swirled, glowing a distasteful neon green, immediately reminding Elysia of the potions in the death realm.

Beatriz held the tumbler up, inspecting it as one would a fine gem.

She gave it a loud sniff. "Luminous with notes of green apple. How is that possible?"

Elysia wondered the same thing. Fresh fruit. Candy. All delicacies and flavors that were difficult to come by in Kava thanks to the lack of sun, magic, and insane importing costs.

Ramsey's grin was evident in his tone. "A perfect addition to our lineup. Don't you think?"

Parker through and through, her sister held her secrets close, it seemed.

Elysia chanced a peek through the crack between the wall and booth. A lazy but pleased smile curled Beatriz's lips. "Possibly. What does it do? And whose magic is this?"

"Hallucinogenic trip. Maker doesn't want to be known."

Her sister sighed. "No name, no purchase. The Nightshade Market can't afford anymore fuckups."

The man gave an understanding nod but shrugged all the same. "You know how it's been. That rebel group getting busted has everyone scared shitless and pulling their stock."

Beatriz pinned him with her hard gray eyes. "You're willing to vouch for the supplier?"

"Absolutely."

She smiled. "Your head if you're wrong. But I'll take it. We'll be in contact."

Ramsey made to pull on his coat, but Beatriz leaned across the table.

"Any word?"

Pity lowered his voice. "No, ma'am. We've got everyone we can spare keeping their eyes and ears out all over the kingdom. There was a tip a couple hours away in Valka, so maybe that's something. There are rumors too... About people crossing the borders and getting their magic back. Probably bullshit, but you never know."

Beatriz's jaw tightened, worry and stress sharpening her features. She leaned back, sliding down to the seat. "Right. Thanks, Ramsey."

A quick handshake and both parties departed. The man headed to the front door and Beatriz cut over to a back exit. Elysia trailed behind her, no longer bothering to hide her steps.

Her sister leaned against the soot-covered plaster wall outside with her arms crossed, singing to the shadows. "Come out, come out, whoever you are."

Elysia shook her head and bit back a grin. Her sister was the dumbest person alive. Pulling out her dagger, she twirled it as she stepped into the warm glow of the streetlamps. With a flick of her wrist, the dagger flew, slicing through the edge of her sister's long wool coat.

Beatriz yelped and dove in the opposite direction, tumbling along the nasty cobblestones.

Elysia cocked her head innocently. "Beatriz! What are you doing on the ground?"

Scowling, Beatriz appeared murderous. "This was expensive!"

Elysia backtracked. "Oh, I'm sorry, is it Madam *Nightshade* now? Or is that just your drug market? I'm a little confused on the details."

"You're a fucking little shit, Elysia. Almost dying then disappearing." Beatriz kicked a cloud of rocky soot in Elysia's general direction. "I should kick your ass."

Elysia held out a hand to her sister. "Missed you too, and I'd love to see you try."

As if on cue, Crusher waltzed into the alley. All five pounds and some fur of her.

Elysia closed her eyes. "Fuck *me,* today is the worst. I thought I got rid of you."

Crusher curled up by her feet, eyes moving between the sisters with interest.

She held up a palm before Triz could squawk her mouth. "Don't. Just don't."

"It was a raccoon before, right? Was I high that day? I swear it was a fucking raccoon." The skin between Beatriz's brows creased as she evaluated her memories.

Elysia frowned. "Beatriz, you met the damn raccoon. Its name was Lina, remember? This is a *dog.* Have you completely melted your brain?"

Triz stared at the dog, still unconvinced. Brushing off her hands, she gestured at the street. "Come on, let's get you out of sight before we're both beheaded in front of dear old Mother. It'd make Father far too happy to get rid of us both at once."

Elysia grimaced and rubbed her neck.

"Too soon?"

"Way too soon."

"You're very precious about near-death experiences for someone who makes such stupid decisions all the time."

Elysia looked at Beatriz incredulously. "As if you're any better."

"What are you even wearing right now?" Beatriz plucked at the heavy black robe draped around Elysia and tapped at the bones in her hair. "Are you *naked* under there?"

"I am," Elysia admitted, her mouth twitching. She really did look ridiculous.

They both smiled a little.

"I saw you try to get to the stage."

Beatriz pulled up the collar of her coat, hunching her shoulders. "Don't be gross."

"Gods forbid I try to thank you for giving a shit that I was about to die."

Beatriz pulled a hat out of her coat pocket and slammed it over Elysia's head, pulling it down so far she could barely see. "Shut up, Elysia. We've got business."

And with that, she stuck her arm through Elysia's elbow and glared at anyone who came within five feet as she marched them through the late-night fog-ridden streets. Soon enough, they were clomping onto Spirit Street, both flinching at the smell.

"At least no one will care if they do see me over here."

Beatriz grunted in agreement, but still slapped at Elysia's hat, forcing her face down. "No one likes a narc, but keep your head down, will you? Stop being so stupid all the time."

Elysia's gaze flicked dangerously to her sister's. Taking a breath, she reminded herself that wrestling Beatriz in the middle of the street wouldn't help with not being noticed. Silently, she stuck out a foot, smiling as Beatriz almost ate shit on the vomit- and piss-scented street.

"Oops."

Beatriz righted herself with a glare. "Be nice to me or I'll slip something in your drink, and you'll wish you had stayed in the death realm."

Elysia drew back, sniffing. "You wouldn't."

Beatriz threw open the door to the Salty Rim, sauntering in

like it was a palace instead of the shittiest dive bar you could find this side of Relaclave. Slamming the door shut with a backward kick of her booted foot, Triz turned to Elysia. "The woman does realize that the name of her bar is disgusting, right?"

Elysia's brow quirked as she looked around the empty bar. Must have been near closing time. Beatriz just cocked her head and waited for it to click.

"Oh my gods. You are *disgusting*. Don't you dare say that to Jessa."

"Say what to Jessa, dead girl?"

Elysia's gaze shot over to the owner of the Salty Rim, who stood staunchly behind the bar. A rugged beauty with a bite like a snake, Jessa wasn't someone Elysia enjoyed pissing off.

"Do *not* call me that. I called Aidan 'dead boy,'" she grumbled.

Beatriz plonked onto a bar stool and grabbed the drink that was clearly Jessa's. Swallowing a mouthful of gin, she considered the nickname. "Dead girl. Death's bitch. There's potential there."

Elysia took a seat while staring daggers at them both. Why in all the realms did she come to see these two? She was likely to be fed to whatever demons Aidan kept for defying his orders, and what did she get out of it? These two idiots.

Jessa stared at the dog pawing at Elysia's leg. "I've told the prince and I'll tell you—there are no *animals* allowed in this gods-damned bar."

Elysia threw up her hands. "She's Aidan's. If you can get rid of her, then be my guest. Also, how is Larky?" Guilt rose in her. She wished she could take her cat to the death realm, but that wasn't fair. It was better for Larkspur to live with Jessa now.

"Good. He's gotten fatter. Sits in the window all day and cops an attitude like you wouldn't believe about his breakfast."

Beatriz grabbed the bottle of Sap and poured out three healthy glasses. "You really are this death god's bitch. Babysitting his dog and everything."

Elysia rubbed her temples, but Beatriz pressed an icy cold finger to her lips to shush her. "You almost got your head chopped off, cracked out into thin air, and now you're here, right as rain and on dog duty. Explain."

She choked down a little gin, knowing it was going to hurt to say aloud. Telling these two would be the grimmest form of reality check. Gripping her drink, she forced it out. "I met with the priestesses of the Bone Temple in Ryspur tonight. There were some unmentioned details to the deal."

Her mouth thinned as she paused, and Beatriz motioned for her to elaborate.

"Historically, the god of the dead is required to have a mortal co-ruler...who becomes immortal. There's this *death voyage* where you earn the talisman. I guess the fates are involved."

She took a much larger swallow of gin, carefully watching their faces to see if they thought she was insane yet.

Jessa surprised her, laughing so hard she snorted and choked. "Oh, that's amazing. At least you thought he was hot, right?"

Glaring, Elysia bit down on the inside of her cheek. "It's not funny."

Beatriz whipped out a handkerchief, rolled it up, and tied it off in a circle. Dropping it onto Elysia's head with a flourish, she dipped her chin mockingly. "Once a throne hunter, always a throne hunter."

Throwing the handkerchief aside, Elysia shoved a hand into her hair, frustration hardening her words. "I'm in over my head. I have no idea how to *earn* or find the talisman, and I don't want to be a *god*."

Neither woman said anything to that, which only made her feel worse.

Elysia smiled bleakly at her sister. "Maybe you were right. Kava's a shithole and will die a shithole because I don't think I can do this." She stared into her disgusting glass of Sap, wishing it could be literally anyone else responsible for this.

Beatriz started coughing, swiping at her tossed-aside handker-chief, but the force of her cough had her bent over and grasping, unable to find the cloth. Tiny black specks dampened her fingers and flew through the air.

Time froze and Elysia's brain went completely silent.

Delicately, she picked up her sister's hand. Dark soot-riddled droplets stood out in contrast to her light skin. Elysia dropped her hand, nodding silently with her eyes open, but unseeing. She made to stand, but Beatriz clamped a hand onto her shoulder and shoved her back down.

Her sister was Fallen now. Nothing escaped the soot in Kava, not even its people, and once it was inside you, there was no future outside death.

Voice rough, she towered over Elysia. "Don't you dare look at me like that. You never once pitied me as I drank and smoked and wrecked my life every way I possibly could, and you sure as the realms aren't going to now. Do you understand me?"

"Because that was your *choice*!" Elysia shouted back into her sister's face, tears blurring her vision.

Beatriz lifted her chin, mouth tight. "It's going to be fine. So just calm down and forget about it."

"How long?"

"Can we not do this? There are more important things for us to discuss."

"I said, *how long?*"

"She's already held on for over six months. Stubborn shit." Jessa crossed her arms, ignoring Beatriz's irritation.

Elysia swallowed this information, but her fast words and high pitch gave her away. "Okay, okay, so we just need to work harder. Find the talisman. Aidan gets his magic. He fixes Kava, and you'll be fine. Yeah, it'll be fine."

Hot tears threatened to break free now, and Beatriz swore. Slapping her hands firmly to the sides of Elysia's face, she gave no room for argument. "Look at me, dollface, it's okay. I was never supposed to live this long, anyway. And trust me, I'm doing everything I can, but you're not responsible for this."

The tears rolled, but Elysia nodded, clutching onto Beatriz's wrists. "You can't die, Triz. I won't let you."

"Want me to piss you off?"

"You can try," Elysia hiccuped.

"You're how the Nightshade Market started."

Jessa took a gulp of gin. "Here we go."

"How could I have possibly started the Nightshade Market?"

Beatriz removed herself from Elysia's death grip and grinned tauntingly. "Father wasn't the only one who realized you were a magnet for finding magic."

Elysia's already heightened emotions turned volatile, storming through her, ready to attack if her sister answered wrong. "You knew." It wasn't even a question. Her hands clenched.

Beatriz held up a finger. "I didn't know about the realm traveling. Which is what you told me about that first night! So, before you even say it, I wasn't lying when I was surprised. I thought you had things under control."

"As if that's the point! Did you know about Father then, too? Just couldn't be bothered to care that I was being exploited when you were doing the same thing?"

Red crept up Beatriz's neck onto her face. "Do *not* compare me to him. I knew he was a pain in your ass, but I didn't know the extent of it until you told me. Maybe I should have asked, but you're not exactly the most forthcoming person. You wouldn't have told me shit even if I'd tried to suddenly swoop in and play the part of big sister. So yes, I saw an opportunity and I took it, okay? The Nightshade Market allows people to make money from their magic and for people to get things they need that don't exist here anymore unless they're imported at astronomical costs, and I'm not going to apologize for that. Even if I die, the Nightshade Market is a good thing, and I did that!"

Tears brimmed once more in Elysia's eyes. "Fuck you, Beatriz. Fuck you for being a shit sister and fuck you for trying to die."

Sharp as glass, Beatriz pulled her sister into her arms where all her edges couldn't cut her. "I know."

Elysia breathed in her familiar mixture of smoke and something crisp yet earthy. "I'll find the talisman, okay?"

Jessa pushed their glasses at them. "I didn't realize this was going to be a Parker family sob fest."

Both Parkers glared now, but Elysia wiped her eyes. "Anything else anyone needs to share?"

A guilty look flashed across Beatriz's face, and Elysia gaped. "Are you serious? There's more?"

Jessa leaned back against the bar and crossed her ankles. "Ask her to tell you more about the Market."

"Beatriz," Elysia said warningly. Her magic was already stretching, though. Cloaking itself around Beatriz, attempting in vain to suss out all her secrets without a tenth of the power she needed to do so. Even so, a few telling images flashed through her mind. Disbelief colored her voice. "Drugs, alcohol, gambling—those are one thing. You're dealing in magical weapons? Who would you even sell them to? And what for?"

As soon as the words were out of her mouth, she tensed in knowing, leveling her sister with a parental stare. She'd literally introduced Beatriz to Gage. The heir to a sprawling criminal empire who was the only one of his family forced to maintain his reign without magic.

"Figured it out, didn't you? It's all for the cause though. Almost. Some of it's just for money." Beatriz shrugged as if they couldn't all be saints.

Elysia took a deep breath, mumbling at the floor. "I regret coming here. I thought it would help and it didn't. It really didn't."

Beatriz polished off the rest of her drink. "Personally, I feel *great*. So fresh, so open."

Jessa made a disgruntled noise and pointed a dish towel at her. "We need to up our weapons supply."

"Need more money for that."

Elysia cast her gaze between them. "You're supplying rebels with weapons."

Jessa narrowed her eyes at Beatriz. "She's stingy enough about it."

"I've *told* you—I can't just be giving everything away for free. I have a business to maintain!"

"People don't need downers and make-believe trips! They need healing tinctures and a way to defend themselves!"

"Those drugs are what's funding your bullshit ragtag crew of misfits, so maybe we don't bite the hand that feeds us, huh?"

Sarcasm fell heavily from Elysia's mouth. "There's nothing like your friends running an entire illegal operation behind your back for the gods know how long."

Jessa didn't bother to look chastised. "You had enough to deal with. The partnership is still new—we just used to buy from her."

"What she means to say is they'd be lost without me." Beatriz looked down at Jessa pompously.

An easy smile touched Jessa's full lips. "Have I ever mentioned what my gift is?"

"No." Beatriz made a face like she didn't give a fuck and rattled her glass.

Jessa leaned across the bar, her fingers tiptoeing up Triz's chest. "I can control pressure. Have you ever seen a human explode?"

Beatriz turned an unpleasant shade of white and leaned away, her voice faint. "Understood."

Elysia was both impressed and aghast. "Even here in Kava?"

"Magic here is so touchy. I never know if I'm going to give someone a nice, threatening squeeze or blow their lungs apart."

Both sisters went silent, taking this in. No wonder people were so scared of Jessa. Forget her studded plank, she'd likely blown someone up and everyone was too terrified to ever mention it again.

Suddenly, the door flew open, and a man staggered in, leering at all three of them. "How much?"

Jessa immediately grabbed her plank. "Bar's closed."

His leer only grew. "I wasn't asking for a drink."

Beatriz made a face of disgust. "As if one of us would even look at your shriveled, smelly—"

"Please don't finish that sentence." Elysia watched the man stumble closer, his hand reaching for what was likely a dagger.

Jessa clambered over the bar, plank ready, as Elysia whipped out her own knife, but before either of them could do a damn thing, Crusher vibrated as she leapt to her feet. The snarling animal guarding their front was no longer a pint-sized lap dog, but a creature large enough to swallow a man whole. Her glorious black and copper fur gleamed as her lips peeled back, revealing sharp, terrifying teeth.

Drunk and without any sense of self-preservation, the man took another step. Crusher lunged and tore off a sizable chunk from the man's ass.

Jessa spoke in a restrained hush. "Elysia, you need to call it off."

Eyes on the enormous beast, her voice trembled. "Crusher, come here."

She turned her head and looked at Elysia with baleful dark brown eyes.

"You can't eat him." Thanks to the shake in her voice, her statement sounded far too much like a question, but nonetheless, the dog lowered its head and forcefully nudged the now profusely bleeding man toward the door. With one final ram of her head, the interloper was flung outside. There were a few mutters about *crazy bitches,* and then he staggered away into the night, bleeding and moaning.

"If you shrink down, I'll go back." She didn't need anyone else seeing a dog bigger than a horse in Jessa's bar. One person rambling about it was just drunk nonsense. More than that meant executions.

Crusher heaved a great sigh as she returned to her previous form. Totting back over to Elysia, she looked up expectantly as if she should get a treat.

Jessa's voice quivered as she roared. "Get *out* of my bar. *All of you!*"

Chapter 9

Elysia landed heavily on her ass, sopping wet and pissed off. She'd had to jump into the Valvere Sea to travel back, and there was nothing she hated more than wet clothes sticking to her skin.

Gathering her bearings, she tried to figure out where she had ended up. She still didn't fully understand how traveling worked, and she wasn't ready to swallow her pride and ask Aidan for tips.

Intense music vibrated up from the floor, beating inside her chest like a second heartbeat. It must have been almost dawn, and she was tired and bewildered. Brass horns—much like the ones attached to record players in Kava—were fixed up high in the corners of the room, music booming out of them. She stared in confusion, unsure if it was a different technology or magic making the speaker work.

A masculine grunt drew her attention, and Elysia gulped.

The two gods on the mats kept breaking apart and then clashing together again like angry, thundering cymbals, and she was more than a little awestruck.

She hadn't expected this. Not with his lean but solid swimmer's body, rumpled button-downs, and constant mugs of tea. But she had been mistaken not to look past the polite scraps he offered to put her at ease. And maybe if she was honest, she'd been a little bit afraid to see the god rather than the man.

Because stripped to the waist and gleaming with sweat was the scarred and shredded body of someone who was more than familiar with a fight. Grappling against him, with his brown skin equally sweaty, was Grim. The god of the dead dealt a blow to Grim's jaw that would've knocked a lesser being out, but Grim grinned as if it was nothing and dropped his shoulder to go for Aidan's gut.

Elysia came to her knees, sopping robes hanging off her, completely entranced with the show and wanting nothing more than to continue peering beneath his high-strung, overworked façade. Seeing him fight should have made her nervous. It should have made her want to tuck her tail and hide in her rooms until his frustration blew over, but instead she drank it in. She wasn't a stranger to rage or violence, and this was an orchestra of it with their bodies playing both conductor and instrument.

Grim's eyes darted to her as he dodged another hit. "Aidan."

Aidan undoubtedly knew she was there, but he ignored Grim. Shooting forward, he took him down to the mat. On his knees, he loomed over his sparring partner, his pale face a chiseled mask of concentration as he fought to keep him down.

Gods above and below. Her mouth went dry, and heat sank in beneath her skin. This was *entirely* different from watching Gage and his men spar. When she watched them, she was focused on their footwork, their style, and how she could translate it into her own body.

All she was learning right now was what incredibly deep shit she was in if her libido had anything to say about matters. With her eyes still glued to them, Grim reversed their positions, and she willed herself to get up, to leave, to do anything other than continue to ogle the man of her nightmares.

He tricked you, she reminded herself.

That has nothing to do with sex, the demon in her mind countered, looking at the hard lines that disappeared into his shorts.

Her inner logic waved its last flag, screaming it was a trap.

Allowing herself one more creepy, lingering stare, she abruptly ripped her gaze away and stood up in a flurry of seawater and heavy robes. She needed a bath and to go to bed so she could wake up with her sanity restored. Without a clue where she was within the sprawling estate, Elysia trudged off to find her room.

The music cut.

"Going somewhere, Thorn?"

Elysia shuddered. *Illegal. His voice should be illegal.* She turned to look over her shoulder, ignoring how his muscled chest heaved with exertion and his cold blue eyes seemed to heat as they stared at her.

"To bed."

He took slow steps in her direction. "Yes, I imagine you are quite exhausted."

"I am," she answered as primly as anyone with seaweed stuck in their hair could, turning her back to him.

A large hand slammed the door shut just as she was opening it. He was close enough she could smell the warm heat rolling off him, taunting her. Bergamot and amber enveloped her as he lowered his face to her ear. "Going against my advice twice in one day. I can't say many would be so bold."

Her pulse increased, beating against her throat as his low, smooth voice curled around her. Still, she pried his fingers off the door, letting go of them like they would contaminate her.

"You said you wouldn't stop me."

Aidan allowed her removal of his hand, spinning her around, so they were face to face. "Was seeing your friends and parading through the city where your head is wanted worth breaking my trust?"

She scoffed, an almost hysterical laugh coming out of her mouth. "Oh my *gods*. The amount of delusion required for *you* to talk to *me* about breaking trust. When were you going to mention the unspoken immortality clause? Never? Just hoped I wouldn't notice?"

Blue fiery eyes held hers, and as much as Elysia wanted to eviscerate him, to dig her heels in and scream at him for what he'd done—she didn't.

She spoke again, but this time with an assured coolness she didn't remotely feel. "And yes, it was worth it. Because taking steps that will aid me in finding the talisman and to work with the people of my kingdom is more important than accommodating whatever personal deficit drives you to be so overbearing." She looked up into his hard face, refusing to back down or away from him. Seawater dripped from her onto his bare feet, but he didn't move, both of them holding the other at an impasse.

"Grim, get out."

Grim silently shot her a *shit luck* kind of expression as he took a wide berth around the two of them and used a different exit. The door latched quietly, but the sound still made Elysia's heart jump like a rabbit given how intently Aidan continued to stare at her, his jaw working like he also was fighting the urge to let her have it. All feelings of victory evaporated as the seconds extended and she waited for him to strike back, her anxiety ramping higher the longer he said nothing.

As he was wont to do, Aidan did the opposite of what she expected, abruptly moving away from her, and giving her room to breathe as he paced along the edge of the sparring mat. Stopping, he stuck one hand behind his head, tugging at his hair and gesturing at her with the other.

"Fine. Tell me then. Tell me what was so important that it demanded your presence not once, but twice in that festering city where anyone would turn you in without thinking twice."

Given he was still covered in sweat and shirtless, it was practically obscene the way his muscles rippled. She narrowed her eyes. As if a man that old didn't know what he was doing.

Her shoulders tensed as her natural defensiveness grew, but still she held her tongue as her brain struggled to find a way to explain she didn't know how to give up checking in on her sister, and it mattered to her what was going on in Relaclave.

When she didn't speak, Aidan shook his head, misunderstanding her silence. Resigned disappointment dulled the usual fire in his eyes now. He made a dismissive motion with his hand. "Go to bed then. We'll talk once you've slept."

Confused, she grappled behind her for the door handle. "That's it? You're dropping it?"

Aidan gave her a tight, close-lipped smile, his dark eyelashes lowering as he cast his gaze over her from head to toe. "To be clear, I am gloriously angry with you."

Her stomach dropped out as Aidan took small, measured steps back to her. His hand gentled on the curve of her throat, thumb brushing over her erratic pulse like he could hear it. Voice dropping to a murmur, his blue eyes held her hostage.

"There are a million ways I could pry the answers I want from your lips." His fingers drifted to almost touch her mouth, but then dropped as he took a step back. "But pushing you will not get me where I want to be."

Face scalding, she blinked, trying to force herself to remember that he was a manipulative twat. Her mind and body fought as she turned to flee but paused, speaking haltingly in a tired voice. "I hate that you didn't tell me. You said you didn't want to start this relationship with lies but giving me a chance during negotiations to examine you with unpracticed magic isn't the same as being honest."

Aidan ducked his head, shame darting through his face as his hands went behind his back. "You're right, and I'm sorry. I wish there hadn't been restrictions on what I could say, but it doesn't change what happened, and I understand why you're angry."

Elysia took in the slight hunch to his shoulders and found herself confused by the raw emotion in his voice. The ache and fear in his words. He was showing her his stomach, knowing she could plunge the knife. Exhausted, her scorn was long gone. It would no doubt return, but right now she was left with only one quiet, doubtful question. "Are you? Sorry?"

He met her gaze now, his words strong and straight from the

chest. "Yes, while there were restrictions, the truth is that I was afraid. Afraid you would run screaming back to Kava, and I would never see you again while the future of Kava and the Deathlands hung in the balance. But I shouldn't have taken that choice from you, and I am as sorry as I am able to be for securing the most important deal I will ever make in my long, immortal life."

She nodded. "I hate what you did, but I would have done the same."

Aidan's brows flew up.

Elysia lifted a shoulder, lips gently pursing. "It's not a compliment. You did what you needed to do to guarantee I'd make a deal. It was manipulative and shitty, and if you do it again, I'll figure out how that one bitch poisoned a god to start all of this and try it on you."

A hint of a real smile played at his lips, but he graciously accepted the gift she had given him in laying down her defenses with a dip of his head.

Elysia walked slowly back to her room, replaying every moment of their conversation in her head. Aidan was *not* what she was used to, and she had no idea what to do with that.

Chapter 10

Elysia sat on a footstool in the living room, anxiously tapping her foot while Aidan scratched away in one of his seemingly endless ledgers. He always had them. Leather-bound ledgers of different colors. Brown, burgundy, navy blue. She had no idea what the god of the dead could possibly be tracking so meticulously, but he didn't seem to feel the need to share despite constantly working on them.

Aidan lifted his eyes from his work to stare pointedly at her foot. She halted the motion and sat on her hands to keep them from taking over the movement. "I thought we were going to be working."

Aidan tossed the heavy leather book on the cushion beside him. "I don't see how we can if you don't want to talk about yesterday. You're free to do as you like in the meantime."

Her mouth dropped open. "So much for not pushing me into talking," she muttered.

He twisted a fountain pen between his fingers, addressing her complaint drolly. "I'm not going to waste my time making plans with you if you're just going to go do whatever you want the second my back is turned."

Elysia scowled. "You're being unreasonable. It was easier to do what I needed to do than to try to convince you there was any merit in going back to Kava, which there *was* even if you won't admit it."

Aidan dropped the pen. "Forgive me for valuing your life even if you don't. But please tell me what required your presence in a city where you tried to assassinate the king and were almost executed."

Irritated, she planted her feet and leaned toward the couch. "Don't act as if you care about me beyond your own machinations. It's transparent and beneath you."

"If that's what you need to believe, then fine by me. Carry on thinking so lowly of yourself. Either way, no one could blame me for wanting to protect my most valuable asset."

Oblivious, Maya and Grim strolled in, her chattering away and Grim's face serious as he listened to her. They both stopped, eyes going between Aidan and Elysia, likely feeling the strained tension. Maya shot Grim a look, shoving an elbow into his side.

"You said you weren't going to tell him!"

Aidan's head tilted dangerously as his eyes narrowed on Elysia. He was clutching the pen again. If he squeezed any tighter, he would likely end up with ink all over his palm. "Tell me what, precisely?"

Maya's face cleared. "Nothing."

Grim rubbed at the stubble on his chin and nodded at Elysia. "You said you wanted to hear about it all from her."

Aidan's simmering gaze swept the room. "Maybe I've changed my mind."

Maya looked contemplative for all of two seconds before airing Elysia's secrets. "*Personally,* I think the Reyez branding was a good move. Strategic given the situation. And it's not like Aidan's a stranger to such empires with his...history." She smiled like she'd poked a bear but was excited for it to attack.

Grim, on the other hand, groaned quietly in the back of his throat and edged for the hallway. "They need to figure this out on their own."

Maya peeled off her jacket, unbothered by the mess she'd made. "What's the point of friends who don't meddle? Besides, we don't have time for glaciers to melt."

Elysia frowned at that. She was pretty sure she'd just been called an ice-bitch, but she was too busy watching the god of the dead move through a multitude of restrained emotions to tell Maya to fuck off.

Dark soot-like shadows crawled out over the floor, creeping closer to where she sat. The shadows gently swathed her ankles. "Show me."

She refused to give in to such bullying. "You said you wouldn't push." She threw a hand at the soot-shadows caressing her. "*That* is pushing."

Aidan eyed her like he knew she wasn't really that bothered, but nonetheless, the shadows disappeared along with the searing intensity he'd been damn near choking the room with.

Taking a deep breath, she watched as Aidan ran his fingers through the thick wave of dark hair close to his face. Tiny, smooth slivers of skin that looked like knife scars decorated his hand. Noticing her gaze on his hand, Aidan's lips curled halfway, but his words were dry.

"You were gone for less than a day and you joined a *gang*?"

Elysia's mouth flattened. There really wasn't much to say to that. Instead, she begrudgingly tugged her dark green sweater down to reveal the still red and angry branding Gage had left behind.

There was an inhale of disbelief followed by a flurry of movement. Head down and eyes intent on the mark, his fingers ghosted over it. Concern and anger warred on his face. "This was completely unnecessary."

Elysia stiffened. "It was *completely* necessary. I'll have protection and somewhere to stay no matter where the death voyage takes me. If anything, you should be thanking me for being willing to take such measures," she hissed.

"Thanking you?" Aidan looked up at the ceiling as if pained.

"Throw me into the pits the day that I say thank you for wearing the brand of another man and his *gang* upon your neck."

Elysia flushed. "Don't be so judgy. He practically raised me."

Aidan became deadpan. "Because that makes it *so* much better. You're aware that you have to be alive to complete the death voyage? And that there will be a cost for their help?"

"Then I'll pay it," she gritted out, her nose practically bumping his.

Aidan laughed, rubbing a hand over his face. "If I were a lesser man, I would banish it from your skin, and cover you head to toe in the symbols of our realm, so no one would mistake where you belong."

Elysia's eyes grew large.

Preying on the subtle shift in her reaction, his hands wrapped around her calves, and the sensual velvet of his voice returned. "But you don't want to talk about yesterday, and I would hate to be manipulative or disrespectful."

His hands left her body, and then Aidan was once again on the other side of the room, faster than she could track, lounging on the couch, one ankle crossed over his opposite thigh, looking unrepentant about the little push and pull show he had just put on.

Deliver me from this man. Elysia collected herself, forcing her Crown voice to make an appearance. "That was inappropriate."

Aidan's grin took up his whole face, white teeth flashing and his fingers thrumming against the couch arm. "My sincerest apologies."

Elysia straightened her back and looked down her nose. "Your bad behavior scared away your friends."

"Good, they're more annoying than gnats." Aidan stood. "If you're not ready to work together, then I have a realm to run." And with that he walked briskly out of the room, ledger tucked into his side.

Elysia stared after him, unsure if she'd really done anything wrong other than follow her own plan instead of his. Turning her attention to the crackling fireplace, an invisible cloak of heaviness settled over her. She didn't like empty spaces in her day. Her life had been a series of crises, one extending into the next, leaving her wound tight and uncomfortable with something so simple as sitting on a footstool in front of a fire.

The brief quiet brought up all the thoughts she'd been avoiding, causing the pressure in her chest to build and build until she couldn't breathe. In losing Topp, she had lost both love and her oldest friend as well as the life she had expected. She'd gone on to stab a monarch only to find out she was now possibly eternally bound to the god of the dead. Her fingernails dug into the heavily embroidered footstool as her vision tunneled into the flames.

Aidan wanted to talk.

But there were words she didn't want to think about, much less say aloud.

Her sister was dying, already living on borrowed time. And instead of being there with her, she was supposed to go treasure hunting. Dark thoughts overwhelmed the corners of her mind. Even if she knew exactly how to find the talisman, her gut sank with the terrible certainty that Beatriz would likely be dead before anything could be fixed. Her infuriating, unstoppable big sister, taken out by the ravaging decay that was a consequence of the poor choices of the man down the hall.

Elysia's heart became heavy as a rock. She knew what it was to be lonely, but a world without Beatriz was one she didn't care to know at all.

CHAPTER 11

A HEAVY, singular knock pounded against her bedroom door. Elysia glanced up from the book she was trying and failing to read. Begrudgingly, she pulled herself out of her warm, soft bed, and wound her damp hair into a bun as she walked over. She paused, cautiously let her magic slither out, tasting the energy of the person outside the door. After years of her magic being inaccessible, it was still strange to have it just be there, ready and waiting for her to call upon it.

Unsurprisingly, it was Aidan disturbing her at this hour.

His head thudded against the wood with exaggerated impatience, voice rumbling through the door. "Are you enjoying feeling me up?"

Embarrassed, she flung open the door. "That is *not* what I was doing!"

"Could have fooled me." He tossed a heavy coat at her and set off down the hall.

Elysia scrambled to grab it, running after him. "Excuse you! Are we going somewhere? I'm in my pajamas for the gods' sake."

Aidan stopped abruptly. "Sweet of you to think of me, but we're just taking a short walk. I want to show you something."

Realizing what she'd said, Elysia grumbled after him. "Maybe I was talking about the other gods."

"Sweetheart, I'm the only god you'll ever be talking about."

One arm into the coat, Elysia blinked before hastily pulling on the other arm along with her boots. How did someone who looked like a fucking accountant keep spitting lines like that? It was both confusing and arousing, and she needed it to stop already.

Outside, they walked side by side, cutting through the dead winter lawn with Crusher tagging along at their feet. Elysia glanced surreptitiously at the man beside her. Hands shoved into his long wool coat with his black hair mussed and a tiny ink stain on his cheek, she hated to admit that maybe the look was less accountant and more bookie.

His gaze twitched toward her. "Yes?"

"I can't decide if you're an accountant who sometimes fights or a bookie who drinks too much tea."

A blinding ear-to-ear grin split across Aidan's face. "Do you have a preference between the two?"

She considered the question. "Both have their merits if you're into that sort of thing."

"Good answer," he murmured.

She snuck another quick look at his angular profile, wondering if it would kill the attraction between them if she got to know him. In her experience, it was a foolproof method with ninety-nine percent of men.

Aidan glanced back at her as he stepped onto the narrow dirt path that led into the Bonewoods. "Do I even want to know what you're thinking?"

Elysia scooped up Crusher, snuggling her soft little body against her chest. "That maybe instead of avoiding you I should do the opposite and see if that handles whatever this is." She looked up at him, completely serious. "Could be worth a shot."

He held a branch out of her way. "Not following."

She ducked under the tree limb. "You know how it is when

people first get together. Sparks, butterflies, ripping each other's clothes off. But then eventually, they see the cracks and realize they can't stand the way the other person breathes. Maybe if I'm lucky, that'll happen with you."

Aidan's jaw was practically in the dirt. He finally looked away, disgruntled. "Right."

Elysia's cheeks pinked. "I just mean you broke my kingdom and already omitted the immortality thing, and I don't want to forget that just because you flirt and look like *that*. And you're a little intense—we just met, you know?" *Ohmygods, why couldn't she shut up?*

Aidan blew out a slow breath, the air crisp and white. Hands back in his pockets, he looked resigned. "I deserve that. And this probably isn't going to help with the intensity front." He stared off into the Bonewoods, suddenly seeming indecisive.

Crusher whined, and Elysia soothed her without thinking, rubbing her ears, and giving her scratches.

Aidan pointed at a small structure in the distance. His voice was dry. "We're almost there, so if you could please refrain from ruining my most lethal guard. She's taken centuries to train."

Elysia's gaze drifted to his. "Centuries," she repeated. There may have been a slight crack in her voice.

He smiled easily enough, not bothering to respond.

"You said you made the deal with Blatz when you were young. That you were young and angry."

"Young for a god," he corrected. "I still am."

Visions of women she'd known being married off to crusty, repulsive men filled her mind, and she shuddered. So, he *was* a dirty old pervert.

Aidan looked like he already knew he was going to regret asking. "What?"

Elysia smoothed the disgust from her face. "You might be young for a god, but by my standards you're past senile."

"Does that mean you've been trying to take advantage of the elderly? We have laws about that here."

Elysia glared at him. "Fine. Age and time are...complicated for gods."

He smiled again.

Silence fell between them as they continued to trudge through the Bonewoods, the same ones that had frightened her during her first visit. The trees' gothic fingers all pointing in judgment looked different to her now. Less terrifying, but still poignant in their beauty. Curiosity overcame her, bringing her to break the comfortable silence.

"This isn't what the Deathlands always look like?"

Aidan's eyes hardened, his cheekbones becoming pronounced in dissatisfaction. "My realm is not in as much immediate danger as yours anymore. It's unstable and will eventually collapse if I never come into my full power, but I've worked to mitigate the damage. I worry that could rapidly change."

A gust of wind blew the loose, damp tendrils of Elysia's hair against her face. The structure was clearer now. It looked like some type of shed. "Because of Garrison?"

Aidan nodded.

Elysia started to muse aloud, hesitant to voice her suspicion. "Topp mentioned Garrison can divest people of their magic, or even life itself if it's someone who didn't retain any magic. Is he... accessing death magic?" She knew she was right when his jaw tightened.

"A drop in the ocean of my power and look what he's doing with it." He glanced at her. "Magic and life force are intertwined. He can just as easily kill someone with magic, he just has to strip the magic first. I'm sure he's realized this by now."

Elysia absorbed this. "Can't we just kill him? Deal broken and problem solved? How did he end up with any of your power, anyway?"

Frustration laced Aidan's tone. "Possible but difficult. He is no longer entirely mortal."

She balked. "But all mortals' magic comes from the gods, and we still live and die."

Aidan shook his head. "Diluted magic that comes from a well-spring we created specifically to imbue mortals with a trace of our abilities. Blatz has my direct, unfiltered power in his veins."

"He's a demigod. *But how?*" Dismay colored her voice.

"The fates don't care for their plans being upended. I allowed the deal, but Garrison sought it. From their perspective, he was spitting on their mortal design, their *gift*. He wanted nothing more than magic to be completely gone, and he got his wish, but they punished him for it as they punish anyone who goes against them. Gave him a drop of the darkest magic one can hold to see if he would hold true to his dogma or spiral."

"He didn't last very long," she whispered, not even noticing the glass building in front of her.

"Yes, and he is going to be a problem, but for now, tonight, let's forget that. I dragged you out here to give you a present, not to depress you further."

Wrapped up in their conversation, it wasn't until Aidan prompted her that she finally noticed the gorgeous small glass building only steps away. Dark iron framed the gleaming panes, and wrought iron flowers crawled over the glass door.

Elysia lowered Crusher to the ground, pausing only the shortest of seconds with her fingers on the door handle. "Is this what I think it is?" Excitement flew through her. The door was already springing open before Aidan even had a chance to answer.

She ran inside, stopping in the middle of the glass house to spin and look around. There were sturdy worktables and shelves filled with pots, dirt, and trays for organizing seeds. Heart in her throat, she looked at him. "You made me a life-size flower house?"

Aidan leaned against the wall next to the door, watching her. "I believe they're called greenhouses."

"But it's for me? And plants will actually grow?"

Walking over to a mound of rich, dark brown soil, he ran his fingers through it. "While it is winter here, and it's not as good as it will be one day when the Deathlands are healed, it's something —a start."

She examined the seeds, already itching to see what could grow in this strange realm. "You knew about my flowers? Because you're a stalker?"

Aidan nodded shamelessly, not bothering to correct her as he allowed the dirt he was holding to run through his hand back onto the pile. "I wish I could tell you that my intensity will lessen, but that would be a lie. I am obsessive, focused to a fault, and riddled with self-doubt and anxiety that you can't imagine. But I don't want to put that pressure on you—I know you don't want to be here. And I understand more than you know what it's like to be thrust into a role you didn't ask for or want. But I can't dictate the fates any more than you, and I, personally, am glad that it's you here." He cut off abruptly, once more covering his mouth as if stopping himself from saying anything more on the matter.

She looked at him with her guard a hair lower than usual. He was still the bane of her existence, but it might have been the best gift she'd ever been given. "I like the greenhouse, Aidan."

He smiled, the anxiety in his stance easing at her words. "Thought you might."

Elysia set the seed organizer back where she had found it. "I still plan to find a way out of the latest *addendum* to our deal. A thoughtful bribe doesn't change that."

"Expected and understood even if I feel I must note how futile that will be." A mischievous glint burned in Aidan's eyes as he prowled over to her. "But what if we made a little wager?"

"I am not *betting* with you. What is it with everyone and betting around here? Even your priestesses are gambling on us. And look at where the last deal with you got me." Elysia crossed her arms, scowling up at him.

"Locked into an exciting voyage to save not only your kingdom, but realms beyond, with the promise of immortality beside the most handsome of the gods?"

Elysia stabbed a trowel into the workbench. "You are genuinely insane."

The light humor disappeared from Aidan's face. "No, I

simply have had longer to know you than you have me, and as you seem to be caught on—I've been around a *very* long time. I would hope that I would know what I want when I see it after all these years."

Elysia's brows drew closer in suspicion. "How didn't I ever notice a constant reaper tail?"

Aidan breezed past her question. "Because you couldn't see them. Now, we need to finalize this wager you keep asking for. If you're certain you'll want to leave at the end of your voyage, then there's nothing for you to lose. I'm prepared to set the odds entirely in your favor." His voice had switched from the hard, but thoughtful god who gifted greenhouses to the man who clearly enjoyed cutting deals and taking bets.

Squaring her shoulders, she looked him dead in the eye. "It's not even a question—I'll want to leave."

"You want to go back to the family who exploited you. To rekindle the love that never existed between you and Garrison's spawn. Makes perfect sense."

"What I *want* is to remain a mortal who lives in the mortal realm and to live a normal life free from insufferable gods."

"Okay, a bit of wager, a bit of a deal. If at the end of your voyage, talisman in hand, you want to return to the mortal realm and live a perfectly boring life, then we will find a way."

Elysia grabbed the trowel back out of the table and stuck it at him. "According to you, that isn't possible."

Crossing his arms, Aidan's fingers pressed into the wool of his coat. "I can't promise mortality, or escaping ruling entirely, but I can promise the freedom to live in the mortal realms for much of the year. You would still need to fulfill certain obligations here."

Hesitation held her in check. "Why would you offer me this?"

Fire bloomed in the heart of his cold blue eyes. "It's as much freedom and choice as I can offer you."

"And?" She narrowed her eyes.

His lips turned up with utter confidence. "Because I'm certain you'll want to stay."

She stared at him in exasperation, dropping her arm and the trowel down by her side.

"Mark my words, by the end of the voyage, you'll want to stand beside me with a crown on your head, making our enemies shake when you walk into the room."

"Hardly." Again, he had to be insane.

His grin was vicious as he strode closer, his earlier uncertainty long gone as he took hold of the lapels of her coat. "It won't even be a question. But don't worry, I won't gloat. Won't even bring up this conversation."

His proximity and wild presumptions sent a blazing mix of furious heat and electricity down her spine, and yet her dark eyes gave none of it away.

"*Hands*," she said coldly.

Aidan released her, conjuring the same goblet he'd used that day in the throne room when she'd unknowingly drunk her mortality away. He held it out daringly. "Do we have a deal?"

Voice even, she pointed out the obvious. "You didn't state the rest of the conditions."

He lifted the cup. "You wanting to stay *is* all I could want. No further conditions."

She shook her head in utter amazement. "I cannot fathom the level of self-assurance required for you to believe I'd want to stay."

A small dimple she'd never noticed before appeared near one side of his mouth. "The odds are in my favor. You'll see."

She pushed the cup back to him. "Because *death voyages* and forced immortality are the foundation of all great relationships."

"No, but trust and friendship—learning about one another as we navigate the obstacles of fate—might be more romantic than you'd think."

A laugh burst out of her. "This is going to be easier than I thought if that's how you think of romance."

Aidan set the goblet down, his gaze sharp and altogether too perceptive. "Possibly," he acknowledged. "Or perhaps you're unfamiliar with what it looks like for two people to know and care for one another beyond sex and separate ambitions."

Elysia blanched, drawing back like he'd struck her, but Aidan caught her waist. "It wasn't an insult. You survived a land that wanted you dead for existing. I could never fault you for any of it. You could go on a murderous revenge spree, and it would be understandable. You deserve *more,* is all...so much more."

She didn't know what to say to that—she had wished for someone, anyone to see her without judgment for so long. For them to know all the horrid details and actions that haunted her with shame, and to still look at her like she was whole and wonderful and something more than what had happened. He couldn't possibly know everything, or he wouldn't dare to make such statements.

She took hold of the goblet, speaking in a low voice. "You don't know what you're talking about."

"I've made choices I hated too." He held her gaze easily. "Yours don't scare me."

Elysia drank without hesitation, handing the goblet off to Aidan and wiping her mouth with a smirk to cover her discomfort. "To being the first platonic co-rulers of the death realm."

Aidan choked, water spraying out of his lips, and Elysia smiled as she swept out of the greenhouse with a new pep in her step. Her wrist burned as the floral background of her tattoo expanded around the helm, marking her skin with Aidan's promise to give her as much choice as the fates allowed him.

Chapter 12

Elysia was both unsurprised and unimpressed that her death voyage was beginning where the disaster that was her life had begun. She'd returned to her bedroom from the greenhouse to find a sealed envelope on her pillow. The fates had finally spoken, and she'd leave the next day.

Afraid to travel directly to Lynd, she'd taken a risk and traveled to Rollie, landing somewhere in the tunnels, and scampering away before he could see her. Elysia crept through familiar tunnels and hidden stairs until she finally dropped into the castle kitchens, startling the daylights out of the closest kitchen worker. The girl shrieked as if Elysia were a ghost, dropping the large copper pot she'd been transferring to the iron stove.

Broth splattered everywhere, and the girl groped for words. "You're, you're *her*." Speaking in a hushed tone, she looked around frantically to see if any of the other workers had noticed that the prince's almost betrothed, now fugitive of the kingdom, had just landed right in the midst of their roast beef preparations.

"You will stop that at once," Elysia chastised in a mimicry of her mother. She could practically see the nonsensical words building up against the girl's sealed lips, but not a single one was uttered, her eyes round with fear. Pleased the girl had stopped yammering, Elysia pulled her into a corner. "Where's Lynd?"

The worker nervously played with her apron, still looking around as if someone might do something about the rogue wanted woman holding her captive in the corner, but the kitchen was a tired, well-oiled machine and no one even bothered to glance up from their work.

"She's not here anymore. They questioned her about you, and no one's seen her since."

Elysia closed her eyes. That was not what she wanted to hear. Bracing herself for the answer, she asked the next logical question. "She's dead then?"

"No..."

Elysia didn't need her magic to know this girl knew more than what she was saying.

"Tell me *now.*" She growled. If the threat wasn't clear in her voice, then it was in the defined point of her dagger now tipping up the girl's chin.

She pressed back against the wall, whispering, "I think she's at the House."

"You tell anyone I was here, and I'll slip into your room when you're sleeping and end this conversation. Do you understand?" She dug the dagger into soft skin, knowing her visit would be gossip fodder within minutes. Elysia smiled as she disappeared. She hoped it made Garrison scream when he heard she'd been in his kitchens.

***

Elysia traveled to the Doorman, and by the gods, did she immediately regret it.

She truly would never be able to unsee such a thing.

Her sister's bare ass and tits. Stalking closer to the Doorman, who was sprawled like an artful goddess across her silk bedding and practically purring as she enticed Beatriz closer.

Elysia's voice came out in a hurried squeak as she slapped her hand over her eyes. "Oh my gods, *stop, stop, stop.* Please, for the love of all that is good in this wretched world, stop."

Her sister's annoyed voice scratched at her ears. "You have the worst timing of anyone I've ever met, Elysia. I've half a mind to throw you outside and call the king's guards."

Elysia peeked through her fingers, only to see her sister still as naked as the day she was born, glaring forcefully. The Doorman had rolled over onto her stomach and was watching as if this were an entertaining bit of theater rather than her sex life being interrupted.

"How was I supposed to know you were here and doing *this?*" Elysia hissed right back. Grabbing a pillow off the floor, she shoved it at her sister's tits. Gods, it was like they were staring at her. How did someone built like a knife manage to have tits like that? The gods were unfair. Very, very unfair.

Uninterested in modesty, Beatriz chucked the pillow straight back at her head. Elysia ducked. The pillow soared past and crashed into a fake potted plant, knocking dirt everywhere.

The Doorman emitted an aggrieved sound. "Perhaps we can jump to the part where you tell us *why* you're interrupting our evening? I only have so much time before guests begin arriving, you know."

Elysia stared at the ceiling since no one seemed to feel the need to put clothes on. "Yes, because I *wanted* to have to bathe my own eyeballs later. Can you just tell me where to find Lynd? Some girl in the castle kitchens said she was here."

Both Beatriz and the Doorman's eyes narrowed simultaneously.

"You went into the *castle?*"

Elysia flinched, hurrying to defend herself. "I had to! The fates sent me to find Lynd. Take it up with them!"

Beatriz took a stomping and naked step closer. "You are the most idiotic, frustrating person I've ever met in my life. You can't keep coming back to Relaclave! We've got things handled here, okay? The market, the rebels, just leave that business to us."

Elysia deflated. "I know, I know. I won't come back unless it's necessary, but what if you need something? How are you supposed to contact me?"

Triz spoke slowly. "Elysia, you need to do *your* job. The talisman is your only concern."

Her heart dropped even further, and she mumbled, embarrassed. "The fates really did tell me to find Lynd, but you know I worry about you. You've made it impossible not to over the years. And now, what if you die and I don't even know?" Her fingers intertwined fretfully, and she avoided her sister's gaze.

Beatriz's face softened, but the Doorman interceded, and she spoke far more gently than her other half. "Lynd is in the kitchens, of course. We'll be shipping her out as soon as we can. Not even I can hide her for long without consequence."

Elysia nodded mutely and slipped out the door to find the kitchens. She'd known it was a risk coming here. But the instructions had told her to visit the safest place in the castle, and as far she was concerned the safest place in the castle was a person, and her name was Lynd.

Elysia reached the kitchens and poked her head inside, stilling at what she saw.

Lynd.

Working dough like any other day.

But with half her face bruised and a bandage wrap poked out of her shirt collar.

Elysia swallowed and walked in tentatively, her steps weighed down with a sense of responsibility and guilt. Choking on the rising panic, she flung it away. *Beatriz is dying, and Garrison went after Lynd.* She blinked away tears. It wasn't Lynd's job to make her feel better.

Clearing her throat, she spoke nervously. "Any maple cakes today?"

Lynd dropped the dough, her head jerking up as she gasped.

Hurrying over with flour covered hands, she immediately admonished Elysia. "You shouldn't be here. There's a warrant out for you—you need to leave."

"I know, but I think you know why I'm here."

Lynd's mouth tightened, stubbornness setting into the lines of her face. "I know no such thing."

"I can't leave until you tell me whatever it is."

Lynd's voice became fierce. "It's not your job to deal with gods or fates. Let someone else handle this mess. Look at how they string you along even now, making you beg others for what to do."

Unshed tears pricked Elysia's eyes once more, but she swallowed the burn. It was a funny thing to hear her own justifications validated by someone she loved. Somehow, it almost made them easier to let go. Because none of this was her fault, but that didn't change the fact that she was tied up in it all now.

Elysia could see her battling over the right thing to do, so she pressed a little harder. "I need to know whatever it is, Lynd. Can't leave until I do. Then I promise I won't come back."

"Not like you to make promises you can't keep."

"I'll do my best not to come back," she amended with a half smile.

Lynd watched her through hard eyes, not looking like she believed her. She continued to work the dough as if she could knead and punch through whatever it was that kept her from speaking plainly as she normally tended to do.

"Never was much a believer in the undead gods even before the Fall. Maybe they exist elsewhere. But not here. Not for us." Dropping the dough, Lynd finally relented, knowing she had no choice. "Three people visited me."

"And?"

Lynd stared past Elysia, clearly swimming in the memory of the visit. "They told me to tell you that your voyage begins where you last left your heart. That you must take it back to begin."

The name she hadn't allowed herself to dwell on since waking up in the death realm whispered through her mind. Everything in her body screamed *no.*

She didn't want to see him.

If she didn't see him, she could pretend it had all ended with a dance. When the truth was, he had plunged the dagger into her heart the night he had left her on a beach to die. He'd twisted it even deeper in the woods as he screamed in her face and asked for answers. And then shattered her to nothing when she finally accepted that he would sell her out in a heartbeat if it meant achieving his goals.

Drained, Elysia leaned back against a counter. Gods help her, but she wanted to go back to the death realm and lick her wounds in peace. But she couldn't, not until Lynd told her the last bit of information she was still refusing to hand over.

Elysia's magic wanted to dive in, peeling back Lynd's armor, but it banged to no avail against its own weakness in this land. "Whatever it is you're hiding, it could get me killed. Now isn't the time to protect me."

Lynd glared. "You're barely grown."

"To you." Elysia smiled, looking at her hands.

"Yes, to me, and I'm the only one who matters, got it?"

Laughing tiredly, her wan smile held. "Yes, ma'am."

"They said that you need to remember your voyage, or you'll fail before you even begin. That the talisman is yours to find and the king is his to destroy."

CHAPTER 13

DRIPPING WET, Elysia held unnaturally still. Water rolled down her neck and off her body onto the hardwood floor, making an ungodly amount of noise in the midnight silence.

She rested her hand on a wooden beam next to her, squinting into the pitch black. Stacks of old ledgers. Half-finished cups of tea on every surface. An enormous fireplace with one of the dogs sleeping in front of the still-smoldering embers. *Was she in his office?* Her heart picked up as realization dawned.

No, no, no. This wasn't happening. This was *not* the message she wanted to send. It was okay, she assured herself. She just needed to be stealthy. In and out like she had so many times before. He never even had to know.

She twisted away from the bed where the god of the dead slumbered. Her sea-drenched boots squeaked loudly, and she closed her eyes with a silent groan. Maybe she could just transport herself—

A sleep-heavy voice interrupted her.

"You're in my room."

Even riddled with sleep, the satisfaction was evident in his low voice.

Elysia resigned herself to her doom.

She attempted to run her fingers through her clumpy hair, and the exasperation shone in her voice. "Trust me, I didn't mean to be."

Aidan sat up, the blankets spilling down to pool in his lap. His light skin stood out in the dark, the curves of his well-formed chest and the shadowy lines of his arms drawing her eye as he stretched the sleep away. She hastily tipped her chin up to the ceiling before he caught her staring. What was wrong with her life that this was the second time in one evening she was looking up at a ceiling in order to avoid seeing naked bodies?

"Is it that hard to keep some clothes on?" she grumbled, refusing to look down.

A moment later, a quiet, raspy chuckle had her chancing another peek. Aidan's stomach flexed as he laughed, and hers clenched in response. *Immediate regret, back to the ceiling.* She flicked her eyes up.

"You're the one who chose to travel into my room in the middle of the night." Likely remembering where she had just been, concern deepened his voice as his feet swung to the floor. "What happened? Are you alright? Grim didn't alert me, but they can't always track you."

Elysia waved him off, grateful to see he at least had shorts on. "Everything's fine." Goosebumps rose on her arms, and she rubbed them uncomfortably. Gods, wet clothes were terrible.

Aidan sank back onto the bed in obvious relief, his brow creasing in confusion now that he knew she was safe. "Then why are you here?"

She edged a few steps back. "Because I'm bad at traveling?"

Standing, Aidan waved a hand as he walked over to her, lighting the fire and several candles. He stood close enough that he could likely smell the fish on her and she grimaced, discreetly trying to sniff herself. Yep, fish.

"Traveling is *very* sensitive. You weren't thinking about me, were you? Because if you recall, this happened last time as well."

She frowned as if his insinuations were ridiculous. "Hardly. I was thinking about how the fates must be complete assholes to make me go see Topp." The truth was, she still hadn't asked how traveling worked, which meant she was thinking of both locations and people's names while hoping for the best. "Do you mean to say I can just think of...wherever and it would work?" She tried to keep her words casual, but Aidan didn't seem to hear her question.

His blue eyes became harsh, but his faint smirk was telling. "You don't want to see him."

"Of course, that's all you heard," she grumbled. "But no, I don't want to see him, *obviously*."

"Because?"

Elysia yanked on her wet shirt, frustrated by his question, and simultaneously overwhelmed with the urge to rip off every stitch of wet, disgusting clothing. "Because I *loved* him and he left me to die. Because I feel like the stupidest person to ever grace the realms every time I think of him. Because all I want to do is make him feel every bit as broken and worthless as I did when I finally realized he never cared about me like I did him. But that would be impossible. Because he would have to actually give a shit about me to feel anything."

Her chest heaved, and she could only imagine how wild she looked standing there in her sopping, horrible clothes with wet hair plastered to her skull as she yelled about her ex-boyfriend. "Now will you please explain to me how traveling works? I don't want to end up in your room again." This was the second time he'd seen her soaked like a drowned rat and that was enough for her.

Aidan's forehead scrunched, compassion and amusement contorting his face. "May I?" He gestured at her clothes.

She looked back at him in question.

"Fix your clothes. It seems like it's bothering you."

She flushed. "Oh, sure..."

In a flash, she and her clothes were completely dry and devoid of any sea stench. Her body instantly relaxed, the high-strung tension fading, and making room for a sweeping wave of tiredness. Wavering on her feet, she grabbed hold of what she had thought was a wooden beam but was actually his bedpost.

"Better?" Aidan perched on the end of his bed, looking her over as if he expected to find further ailments. "And yes, you can simply think of wherever you would like to go, but you need to be familiar with at least some detail. Traveling to people is still an option if it's easier."

Elysia nodded sheepishly, embarrassed she'd said so much. "Sorry."

Aidan leaned back on one hand, completely at ease. As if he was fine with being woken up in the middle of the night even if it was just so she could rant about her ex. His low melodic voice held a note of confusion as if *he* couldn't understand why *she* would be apologizing.

"There's nothing to be sorry for—I *want* you to come to me like this. The fates are going to ask more from you than you could ever expect. None of this is meant to be done alone."

She paused. Now they were *both* confused. He kept shifting between what she had deemed his hard, no-nonsense bookie self and his reasonable, even slightly soft, accountant self. The gentle reasonableness left her vaguely stuck, unsure if she could really believe the words coming out of his mouth.

"No," she decided. "I shouldn't be talking to you about this."

"I'm exactly who you should talk to about this," he countered easily.

She kept walking backward, bumping into ledgers and stray decorative pillows as she tried to reach the door. "I'll talk to Maya if I need to, it's too weird for me to talk to you about him."

"Elysia." Aidan's firm tone had her freezing.

"Yes?"

"You are not stupid because your ambition blinded you to his. You are not worthless because someone, who was never meant for you, didn't choose you. That man will regret leaving you on that beach till the day he dies, but you don't have to carry the weight or shame of his mistakes. That is *his* burden to bear, not yours."

It was a terrible thing not to be worth loving, but she'd already known that thanks to her parents. Topp Blatz hadn't stopped at reinforcing how difficult to love she must be—he'd proven that she wasn't even worth keeping alive. And yet, she had gone back to him. In the Lovestone Woods. At the Raven Ball. Hoping to erase and drown out the voice that constantly reminded her of how horrible and pathetic she really was.

Aidan's words found the barest sliver of a crack in her armor. The quiet certainty in his words stole in through the crack and pierced the dark hollow of her chest. A single silent sob choked her. Fending it off, she shuddered. The last thing she wanted to do was cry in front of Aidan.

He didn't say anything else. He didn't say it was okay, or offer any of the other sweet but empty platitudes that people say. But he returned to her side, offering his steady presence, and the rhythmic stroke of his hand over her back as he pulled her into him.

With her forehead tipped against his bare chest, she allowed herself the moment, knowing it wouldn't last.

CHAPTER 14

ELYSIA STOOD in front of a mirror, strapping blades to her body. Her usual dagger just wasn't going to be enough if she had to see Topp Blatz's stupid face. No, she was going to need more than that. Tossing a small throwing blade into the air, she caught it easily, feeling the weight before sliding it into the chest harness she'd found in her closet. Blade after blade slid into tiny slots until the raw emptiness she'd woken with quieted, and the hardened shell of Elysia Parker, daughter of the Crown, reemerged.

She had no practice with breakups. Topp Blatz had been her first everything. Crush, kiss, *almost demise*. The usual events in every young woman's life.

The closest thing she had to a relational example was her sister, and Beatriz had either slept with or swindled half the city. Rolling out of beds without so much as a *thanks for the orgasms*, her sister used to leave people behind as if they could have been anyone or no one. Elysia wasn't sure this was the best model to work from, but it was all she had, and treating Blatz like he was no one was better than letting him see her break. If he could leave her to die, then she could steal back the heart that he'd never deserved in the first place and be on her way.

Easy, she told herself. It was a lie she desperately needed or else her feet weren't going to move.

Elysia glanced at the weaponry room door, knowing Aidan was waiting for her to emerge and go over the plan before she catapulted herself to wherever Topp resided. She grimaced. She'd rather get her teeth pulled out than have to discuss the patheticness of her heartbreak with Aidan. Almost crying in front of him had been a failure of her fortitude that wouldn't happen again. No, like most things in life, she was better off doing this alone.

Scrawling out a short note, she slapped it on the knives table and traveled to see the one man she had hoped never to lay eyes on again.

"OOF." All the air in her body expelled itself in a forceful whoosh. The familiar scent of a woodland storm and ozone cloyed her senses, while the deep voice only inches from her ear sent wary prickles up her spine.

"The dagger on your hip is about one inch from guaranteeing Kava has no heirs, so if you don't mind..." Broad hands took hold of her waist, lifting and adjusting her slightly.

Elysia scowled, digging her elbows into his lower ribs as she attempted to lift her head only to smack it on wooden boards. Dust showered down on them both, damn near sending her into a coughing fit.

Great. She'd found him, alright. And was immediately on top of him. This was going swell.

Heartbeat a heavy thud against her ribs, its rhythm was as uneven as the rickety motion beneath them as she grasped for something, anything to say to hide how unsteady she was. She'd strapped on blades and set her court mask firmly in place, but nothing ever prepares anyone for coming face to face with the person they once loved who had broken their heart.

She hadn't seen Topp Blatz since they'd glided past their

intended engagement and straight to treason on the Raven Ball dance floor. She'd then disappeared to the death realm with blood dripping down her neck. Elysia gritted against the twinge of hurt still lingering inside her. Betrayal was as familiar to her as breathing, and yet, she feared the prince's may have broken the last piece of her that secretly wanted to believe in even the possibility of goodness in another human.

Brown hair askew and mirthful green eyes locked on her, the prince wasn't bothered in the slightest by their compromised position. His lightly freckled face stared up at her, his initial surprise at her unexpected entrance fading as he waited for her to respond.

"Are we beneath a *carriage* right now?" As soon as she said it, all the sounds around her clicked into place. The wheels cracking against the road. Hooves clopping smoothly.

"Better question. *How* in the many realms did you get here? And keep your fucking voice down." Ear to his chest, the rumble of Topp's voice vibrated through her.

"That's none of your business." She dug her knee into his groin as she squirmed, grinning when he grunted. "Now where are you going?"

"I'm getting out of Kava for a while."

Elysia paused. The Crown Prince of Kava was leaving his own kingdom beneath the floorboards of an old carriage. Well-founded trepidation had her whispering. "Is he after you?"

Topp's fingers dug into her waist reflexively. "I've never seen him like this before. It's bad, Lys, really bad."

She nodded, chin against his chest, his coat rubbing against her skin while his masculine scent tried to confuse her senses. For the first time though, it wasn't sweeping through her like a relaxing or enticing drug. Instead, a quiet hesitation labored over her internal brakes. Maybe her body had finally come to the realization that Topp Blatz wasn't a poison to the masses, but he was hers, and she didn't have time to play in toxic waters.

"Where exactly are you wanting to go?" she asked as if this was a perfectly normal position to be having a conversation.

"Bellia, to start."

Another bump in the road had her cursing as her skull cracked against the floorboards above. Still wincing, she made a fast decision. "Tell me exactly where you want to go."

"Saarspur."

He didn't deserve her helping him. She would be well within her rights to leave him beneath the floorboards of the carriage, escaping his own kingdom, and the pettiest part of her soul wanted to do exactly that. But the newly emerging, awkward part of her that was *trying* to be a better person who cared about what happened to her kingdom knew that Topp's chances of getting out of Kava were slim to none. He didn't deserve her help, but Kava deserved a chance at a different future, and for better or for worse, Topp Blatz was going to play a role in that.

Aidan had never clarified if she could travel with more than one person, but she was about to find out. Elysia gripped Topp around the middle and whispered their destination, Saarspur, Bellia's largest city, aloud three times for good measure.

Elysia landed in a crouch, snow crunching beneath her boots and skyward pines all around her. The crisp forest air was a relief even as her ears burned from the cold. Head snapping to the right, a loud thud reverberated into the woods. Encased in snow, Topp let loose an impressive string of curses. Stunned, he remained flat on his back, staring up at the trees until his broad face finally broke into a wide, genuine grin. Elysia tilted her head back as well, taking it in. The branches and needles of the trees above inhaled in unison, appearing to sway and pulse as if they were all one system instead of endless separate trees.

Still sprawled in the snow, Topp threw her a look. "So, that's how you found me. You can travel now."

She nodded, but he was distracted. He was still staring at the sky, grinning. "Gods, I love this forest."

Brushing snow off herself, she stood. "Been here before?"

Topp pulled himself out of the snow and nodded. "Many times."

He carefully examined their surroundings, likely trying to determine where in Saarspur they'd landed, and while he studied the land, she studied him. Cool bright light bounced off his skin, highlighting tired smudges and green eyes that were not nearly as electric as she knew they could be. Tension pulled at his shoulders, creeping up into his neck and thinning his lips. Faint lines had started to settle into his skin, marking the price of these last few months and years.

Unaware of her observations, Topp lifted his broad chest, pulling in a giant lungful of forest air with a grin. "Forest smells proper here. Unlike Kava."

Elysia shoved her cold fingers into her pockets, nodding in agreement. "Who knew a forest could smell like anything other than decay?"

Grabbing her hand, he locked his eyes on some distant edge of the forest she couldn't see or sense. "Come on, civilization is that way."

Elysia gently dislodged her hand, and Topp's eyes flicked to the movement, his brow creasing before resignation came over his face.

His mouth tightened. "Right, habit."

Habit. A single, loaded word that set off the loneliness she could never quite kill. It emanated from the cavity in which her heart was supposed to reside but, per the fates, was in the pocket of the man beside her.

Now that she was here, stomping through the snow with Topp Blatz only a hand's reach away, she wondered how in the realms she could ever steal it back, when giving it had never been voluntary.

Snow swirled gently through the air. A single snowflake landed on Topp's pink nose, chasing away her thoughts and bringing a smile to her lips.

Wiping it away, he opened the conversation with an air-stealing statement. "You stuck a dagger into my father's guts and disappeared."

She froze, her hand shooting out to grab the nearest tree. *Fuck*. She'd been so caught up in seeing Topp, she'd forgotten that she'd tried to *murder his father* the last time they'd seen each other.

He looked at her out of the corner of his eye, his breath huffing out in tiny white clouds. "You went to the death realm, I presume, and *now* you almost ruined my escape—which took a lot of work for me to organize, by the way."

Elysia tugged the collar of her jacket up higher, ensuring the Reyez branding was hidden, and let her hair fall over her ear, feeling extremely conscious of all the new marks on her body. Feet moving again, she fixed her gaze ahead.

"That covers it."

He grabbed her shoulder, bringing her to a jarring halt again. They were never going to get out of the forest at this rate.

"No, it doesn't."

Frustration crinkled the skin near his eyes, but Topp didn't press, choosing to drop her shoulder and stalk away. She eyed him curiously now. Topp Blatz showing restraint? She didn't trust it for a second.

As they trudged on, the wind began to whir. It grew louder, an overwhelming static buzz filling the air as the wind frenzied. But it wasn't just the sound—the wind was picking up snow and ice, spiraling the frozen precipitation faster and faster in a moving cone-like spiral. One arm thrown up against her face to protect her eyes, Elysia dropped to the ground in a panic as she tried to understand what was happening.

In the eye of the windstorm was the one and only Crown Prince. Lost to his own frustration, he appeared immune to the destruction he wrought. Ice and wind cut into Elysia's skin. Screaming as loud as she could, she tried to get his attention. "Topp, you're hurting me!"

She wasn't sure how he even heard her considering how the wind was swallowing all other sounds, but his influence cut off abruptly. Elysia collapsed to the snow in relief, bringing her hands to her face. Her fingertips came away with tiny pinpricks of blood.

Looking both startled and guilty, Topp crouched beside her. "Shit, I—" He brushed a hand through his hair, completely befuddled. "I have no idea how I did that, Lys, I'm so sorry." He frowned and wiped at the blood speckling her face with his sleeve.

She stared back at him equally perplexed. "I know we're not in Kava, but your magic still shouldn't work. Try it again," she urged, no longer giving a shit that her face was a bloody mess.

The crown prince closed his eyes, faded freckles dusted with snow, and the air danced again, picking up in intensity as it went. He opened his eyes and it stopped, returning to its lazy stirring through the trees.

Her brown eyes met his green, both gaping.

Voice rough, Topp spoke. "Something is changing, Elysia."

She swallowed. *Everything* was changing.

CHAPTER 15

ELYSIA SAT AT A STICKY, beer-covered table, waiting for Topp to return with their drinks. She looked out the window back in the direction from which they had come. The Endless Forest remained in a constant state of gloom with only tiny swaths of bright, shooting light breaking through before disappearing again. Deep within its reaches, the trees and snow muffled sound, blanketing the world in a beautiful silence. Just like at the Bone Temple, the unfamiliar cries of creatures she didn't know escaped into the air. It was unnerving how they were the singular sound to escape the forest's persistent quiet.

No mortal could possibly step foot into that forest and think they would be the one to conquer it. Elysia wasn't especially familiar with the magical creatures that lived in its darkness, but she was positive she didn't want to meet them.

Bringing her attention back to the tavern, her magic crawled out, slinking over floorboards and half-spilled beers in search of the juiciest secrets this Saarspur bar could offer. Excitement surged right as Topp plunked down two sloshing mugs of brown ale.

He shoved one at her before heaving himself into the chair across from her with a grin. The rowdy tavern fit him. If you threw on his usual battle axes and added a bit of facial hair, he would have looked like every other burly Bellian man currently tipping one back in the fire-warmed room. Elysia listened to the rapid Bellian. Side by side on the same continent, Kavian and Bellian were closer to dialects than separate tongues. Still, even though she could follow along, it wasn't without concentration and some confusion.

Tucked away, their knees bumped under the table, his warm thigh now touching hers. Elysia grabbed her mug of beer, wishing the tavern wasn't so fucking packed, and took a sip, mulling over the flavors. She wasn't used to beer, and couldn't decide what to make of the bitter, roasted taste.

"My magic is working here too," she commented with a raised brow.

Topp chewed on this, drinking most of his beer in one gulp before shrugging. "What isn't strange in the world right now? None of the rules are real anymore."

Elysia laughed roughly, putting her chin in her hand. "Isn't that the truth."

Topp continued to drink his beer while fidgeting with his coat. He stopped abruptly, switching to bouncing his leg before setting his mug down. "Things've changed fast in Kava."

"The kind of changes that lead to a prince smuggling himself out of his own kingdom?"

Splotches of red appeared on his high, wide cheekbones as he messed with his already unkempt hair. "It was too risky to stay. My father has lost his fucking mind, and it was getting harder to believe that I wouldn't be a casualty sooner rather than later. And I'm no good to anyone if I'm dead." The words sounded like he was convincing himself as much as her.

Skeptical surprise shone across Elysia's face. "He'd really leave himself without an heir?"

Topp leaned in closer across the small table. "I'm telling you. He's *changed*. Ever since the Raven Ball, it's like he's just completely gone off the deep end. Lysia, he's been threatening other kingdoms with that disgusting magic and traveling to small cities, testing his ability on our own people. Can't be long before he tries his hand at other kingdoms."

This information rattled around within her.

"Since the Raven Ball," she repeated flatly.

Topp gave a tight nod, his eyes scanning the tavern. Seemingly satisfied, he leaned back even though there was nothing relaxed about the posture or his face. "He had this woman half-starved and locked in a guest suite. He went to her immediately after you disappeared. Stomach still bleeding, medics trailing after him, raging about the god of the dead and demanding she tell him what was going to happen."

She gripped her beer tighter. "Did you catch her name?"

"No, but she was one of the rebels in that group you met with. I recognized her."

Her stomach sank, hating that she'd called it. Victoria's premonitions were always right according to Mari and Jessa. "What did she tell him?"

He gave a slight disbelieving shake of his head. "She laughed. Tried to attack him even though she looked like she was about to join the dead herself."

"And? Did she say anything?" Now her knee bounced beneath the table. *Please let her have lied.*

"She spoke of a mortal who would release the death god from his chains, and an heir who would claim justice."

Shit. Victoria couldn't have made it plainer than that. "He knows."

"Your warrant went out immediately, and I bet mine isn't far off."

She scratched at the sticky table. "He's not going to stop until he finds me, is he?"

He shrugged. They both knew the answer to that question. Standing, he excused himself to the bathroom. When he came back, he wore an all too familiar look upon his face.

Topp Blatz wanted answers after all.

Before he could start in, Elysia opened her mouth. "You want to know why I'm here? I'll tell you."

Suspicion narrowed his eyes. "Just like that?"

She waved her hand. "Like you said. Everything's changed." *And I have no idea how to succeed at this mission, but the one thing we never did was tell the truth.* She hoped she didn't regret this.

The prince wore an expression of wary determination as he nodded for her to go ahead.

Taking a big breath, she spoke fast, anxious the prince would make a scene. "I tried to make a deal with the god of the dead before the ball. He offered a terrible bargain though, so I turned it down. Except then, when I found out what your father was going to do to me... Plans changed."

Darkness flooded the prince's face. "You knew? You should have told—how bad of a deal, Lys?"

She looked off at all the cheerful Bellians instead of at him. "I agreed to find his personal talisman so he can regain his power and help fix Kava."

Relief relaxed Topp's body, and he stretched one arm back with a grin. "That's not so bad. Your magic could help you with that, couldn't it? Finding things?"

Elysia smiled wanly. "Oh, but there's more... I, unknowingly, agreed to partner with him. Permanently."

The prince looked ill now. "What do you mean, *partner*?"

She looked away. "It means the fates have sent me on what they call a death voyage where I have to prove myself as worthy of earning the talisman and standing beside the god of the dead, and you're my first stop."

Topp's brow pinched before he spoke decisively. "No, impossible. You are *mortal*. Mortals can't partner with gods."

Elysia took a long drink of her beer, waiting for him to get it all out.

"You can't possibly mean—" He grasped for words, not wanting to come to the logical conclusion.

She slammed her drink down. "Oh, but I can. When I say partner, I mean it in every sense of the word. *Immortality.*"

For once, the prince didn't get angry. A heavy sigh rasped through his thick chest. "So, you're fucking a god then?"

Her mouth fell open. "Everything I just said, and that's what you heard?"

The prince had the decency to look at least semi-abashed. "Seemed relevant."

"How in the realms is *that* relevant?" she hissed.

He looked at her like she was stupid. "Because why are you here then?"

Elysia reared back. "The fates sent me to talk with you."

"Sounds made up. Like you just wanted a reason to see me."

"You think I'd risk my neck coming to see you because what? Because I wanted to have sex with you?"

His gaze drilled into hers. "No, but I thought you might because you still love me. That you wanted to help me finally, even though I told you to stay away." He chewed his bottom lip. "But you're right. That's impossible after what I did."

Her anger bottomed out, scraping over the well of hurt and heartbreak she hadn't wanted to acknowledge. *Fuck.* This was exactly why she was here. To have *this* conversation. She was going to punch the fates in the face if she ever met them. Bunch of drama-seeking assholes.

"Whether it's possible or not, I have to let you go, Topp." Her voice was so soft she was afraid he wouldn't hear her, but he nodded, his throat bobbing as he did.

"We were two kids with no idea how to love, and I think, I think we really hurt each other. Probably as much as we loved. You left me on that beach, and we went about everything the wrong way, but I have a job to do and so do you, and I think we need to be able to help each other without this"—she gestured between them—"getting in the way."

The prince nodded at the table. He looked pained but calm. "Are you with him then?"

Elysia flushed, shaking her head. He laughed bitterly.

"It's not like that."

"Sure, it isn't." His fingers tapped against his glass, his face hardening into one he used with sycophants and men who followed his father. "Finish telling me everything, Parker. Every last detail of these deals and how they affect Kava."

She studied him. It was the best response she could have hoped for, but instead of being relieved, she was weary. She had known nothing she could say would break his heart. But she was only now realizing that maybe you weren't supposed to have to trick or force people into paying attention and caring. Maybe they were supposed to be obsessed with you beyond the taste of your skin or the value that you brought. *Dream big, girl.*

Elysia motioned to a server and requested another round. The drinks arrived shortly, and Topp whistled at everything she unloaded onto him. He eyed her with renewed intensity that made her hackles come right back up.

Frowning, she snapped at him. "What? Why are you looking at me like that?"

"Because you're more important than I am."

She blinked.

"I should help *you*." He nodded, clearly warming to the idea even as she wanted to shriek and run away.

"No."

Topp kicked out his long legs, knocking hers. "Why not? If you're how Kava gets fixed, then my priority should be you. It's only what's best for Kava." He smiled roguishly.

"Topp, *no*, you can't help me with this. You just can't."

"Why not? Sounds like your voyage is happening topside, and we both know you could damn well use a guard."

"Excuse you, I can take care of myself."

His brow creased, eyes darting to the knife harness and dagger on her waist. "You weigh a hundred pounds soaking wet. You're not going to win every fight no matter how *skilled* you are."

She wasn't short and had more than enough muscle packed

onto her that every bit of his comment was ridiculous. A hundred pounds, her round, muscled butt.

"Kava's Shadow trained me, himself, you arrogant piece of ass."

His grin stretched wide. "Did you just call me a piece of ass, Parker? I'm flattered."

She threw her head back. "Oh my gods. You can't come with."

"You're being unreasonable. Who says two people who used to love and fuck each other can't work together amicably?"

She stared at him, her mouth half-open in absolute horror. "Me, I say so."

Topp put a hand over his heart. "I have to do what's best for Kava, and if following your fine ass around is it, then I'm willing to make that sacrifice."

"I hate you."

Laughing, he polished off his second beer. "No, you don't. You only wish you could."

Ouch. That had been a little too on the mark, but Lynd's message from the fates crashed in between her ears, and she paused, trying to remember exactly what Lynd had said.

"Topp... One of the things the fates said was that we have different missions."

He looked at her askance. "You're just saying that to get rid of me."

"No, I'm serious. Gods, I wish I could remember what Lynd said, but *oh*—the king is yours." She nodded feverishly, one hand pressing down on the table.

"As in..." *Kill my father?* He let the unsaid words hang in the air between them.

Elysia deflated, smiling weakly. "I'll let you decide what that means," she offered delicately.

The prince grabbed her unfinished beer. "We could swap if you want? I'm sure your death god would love me."

Snorting, Elysia gave him an actual grin. "If only."

Topp looked into her now empty mug. "You want some food? I'm starving."

She nodded, waiting until he stalked off to the bar to slip off her stool and back outside. *Some guard he would make.* Elysia leaned against the wooden slats of the tavern, letting the cool air clear her thoughts. She just needed a moment. Her insides itched, and there was something screaming in her brain for her to put as much distance between herself and everyone else that was getting difficult to ignore. She had zero practice with emotional vulnerability and—surprise, surprise—it was *awful.* Rip your skin off and jump into the lake so you can travel back to the death realm awful.

Elysia exhaled, watching the white air puff away as she walked around the side of the tavern. Was this what other people dealt with *all the time*? Shit was for the birds. Maybe she *should* go find the nearest body of water before Topp found her and reinstated himself as her personal guard.

Her gaze on the forest, she didn't pay any mind to the crunch of boots behind her. But then the noise stopped, and with the sudden silence a prickle of unease ran up the back of Elysia's neck. Right as she began to turn, the cold metallic cut of a blade pressed lengthwise into her throat. The arm wrapped around her chest from behind held the blade easily, their grip and posture confident.

Elysia's nostrils flared in irritation. All she'd wanted was a *moment*. One single moment to clear her mind. *Wrong day, bitch.* Both hands gripped her attacker's small wrist, her body turning and twisting beneath the woman's arm. One hand still squeezing her attacker's wrist, she shoved her opposite hand between the woman's shoulder blades, forcing her to bend in half.

The knife clattered down with a dull thud against the snow, but the woman wrenched out of Elysia's hold, kicking the knife away and turning toward her.

Elysia ripped two blades out of her chest harness and stared at the narrow dark blue eyes glittering back at her. Lanky and lean, the stranger looked far too at ease for someone who was now without their weapon. Breath rapid, Elysia's hard gaze never faltered as she took a step closer, her magic creeping out and verifying what she'd already gathered. Her attacker knew how to get in, out, and wipe her blade clean before anyone else even knew she was there.

In other words, Elysia found herself facing a fair match.

She darted in, her offense practiced and without error, but the woman moved fluidly, avoiding her with a laugh. Annoyed, Elysia tried again, mentally trying to place the woman's familiarity. There was something about her eyes—the small size, the shape. Maybe it was the point of her chin.

Focused on the blonde, Elysia failed to realize there was a second, far more concerning threat lumbering up behind her. A massive hand grabbed her shoulder, whirling her around and latching onto her throat. Feet dangling, Elysia scrambled to dislodge the giant's hold, swiping with her daggers.

Unamused, he lifted her higher, where she couldn't reach him.

Fuck. She was losing air. Black danced on the edges of her vision.

The blonde ambled closer. The winter sun bounced off her face.

"You stole my kill, Elysia Parker."

Stunned, Elysia blinked, but the man squeezed harder, until black dots became an endless, airless sky.

CHAPTER 16

Elysia woke to angry, incessant snarling.

Gods, she felt like shit.

She'd only been choked out once before. She hadn't minded. She was always trying to get Gage's men to practice harder with her, but Gage, on the other hand, had made sure the man joined her on the dirt, out cold and with a bruised windpipe.

Last time she'd woken up to careful ministrations from Gage's practiced hands. Today, her wrists and ankles were chafing against ropes that tied her to a chair, and she had no idea where she was. Another sharp snarl echoed out, and her lips turned up at the sight of Crusher, world's best Deathlands hound, standing on her feet and warning everyone off.

The lanky blonde sat on a stack of crates, twirling and tossing a blade to a silent rhythm, likely blissfully unaware Crusher could swallow her whole. *Fucking Aidan.* Such a stalker.

"Quite the undead pet you've got there, Parker."

Or maybe the woman did know there was something odd about Crusher. Elysia shifted, trying to determine just how tightly her hands were bound. If Crusher hadn't grown ten sizes and eaten her kidnappers, then she figured she wasn't at death's door yet.

"Can't say she's mine, but she *does* have an unexpectedly large bite." Elysia smiled pleasantly enough to unnerve her new friend, who just squinted at her and continued twirling her blade.

Abruptly stabbing the blade into its sheath, she leaned back and kicked her long legs out with curiosity on her face.

"So, it's true then. The gods are rumbling once more in Kava."

Elysia lifted a shoulder. "Hardly." She waited for the woman to make her move, but she was staring at Elysia like she was an enigma.

"Rumor has it you were trained by Kava's Shadow."

Elysia kept her face straight. *Where is this going?*

"Rumor also has it that you made a kill in a room filled with royals and walked away."

Ah. This wasn't going anywhere good then.

Elysia sent out her magic silently only to recoil at what she found. Notes of sharp abandonment buried beneath a blazing fury. This woman had turned her pain molten and forged it into the weapon that was herself.

"Scarzan," Elysia breathed. "He really did sell you."

The woman's smile was tight, but her voice was even and matter of fact. "He always did have a terrible gambling problem. But I'd say it all worked out in the end."

The man who had squeezed the consciousness out of Elysia lumbered back into the room. All six and a half feet of him made her nerves twinge. This was why you weren't supposed to get caught. Because instead of fighting one person, now she was tied up and going against gods knew how many.

Topp's warning that she wouldn't be able to win every fight played back in her head. The size of the man's neck alone made her all too aware of her shortcomings. Anxiety unspooled in her stomach as she scanned the room. They were in a work shed. Tools, carriage parts, and sled equipment took up most of the space. Gods, maybe Crusher really would have to eat them. She nudged the tiny dog with her foot, but she did nothing. *Figures.*

The man brushed his hands down the woman's shoulders. "So?"

She kept her eyes on Elysia. "Haven't decided yet."

Crusher growled again and Elysia smiled, nudging her once more. *Yes, eat them, do it.* Who needed the fifteen blades no longer strapped to their body when Crusher was hungry?

"Look. You stole my kill, and in my world, that means I get to kill you. But here I am with such a *tricky* little situation given the friends you keep." She spoke casually as if this was a perfectly normal conversation to have.

"Friends like the god of the dead?" Elysia drawled right back, meeting her eyes with unwarranted confidence. "I've been to the temple here, you know. The Bone Temple in Ryspur with the priestesses who sang me such a pretty lullaby? You're familiar?" She leaned forward as much as the ropes allowed. "I used to hear the lullaby in my dreams. It was so nice to finally hear it in person."

The woman stilled, her breath catching. She had grown up in Bellia. A land where the gods were active, loved, and feared. Elysia had no idea if she was religious, but if she was as comfortable doling out death as she made it seem, then it was likely she was familiar with the god of the dead's customs. She might even believe she would be meeting him one day when her own light went out. Elysia had no problem capitalizing on that religious fear if it meant keeping herself alive.

The woman's hand tightened on her blade's handle and then was towering over Elysia in two smart bounds. Crusher just huffed as if the woman holding a blade to Elysia's throat were no more than an annoyance before promptly disappearing into the ether.

So much for the help. She couldn't wait for the earful she'd likely receive back in the Deathlands. Something about managing to get kidnapped in less than five hours flat of being gone.

"It's true then? You're the mortal to his god." The blade nicked against the sensitive line of her scar.

Elysia's insides squelched. She didn't even know if that was a good thing to these people, but she'd already dove headfirst into mouthing off about the death priestesses. Elysia hid her uncertainty beneath a blank face, but then the heavy silver ring on the resident muscle's hand caught her eye as it gleamed in the light. She gave a slow, knowing grin.

"Pull down my shirt."

The woman laughed. "Not my type, pretty girl."

"Pull down the damn collar of my shirt. You think I know Kava's Shadow, well, I do. And I'm marked." Elysia all but growled the order.

"Bullshit. Gage doesn't even—" But the man gently moved the woman aside, as she continued spitting about Gage. With one enormous finger, he pulled down the collar of her shirt.

"Fuck." He let her shirt snap back up, his lips twitching. Elysia was fairly certain that was akin to a full-bodied laugh for this man. "She's serious."

Disbelief crashed across the blonde's pointy face. With Crusher gone, she marched back up to Elysia fearlessly, ripping at the fabric of Elysia's shirt with her whole fist. "By the gods..." She brushed a finger over the brand, her face stretching into a wide grin. Throwing her head back with a laugh, she smacked Elysia on the back as if they were old pals.

Slicing through Elysia's bindings, she stuck her knife away and held out her hand. "Emmellin Reyez, formerly Scarzan."

Elysia rubbed her wrist and slapped her hand into Emmellin's. "Elysia."

Emmellin looked at her seriously while still holding her hand. "You're family now. And as family, I can let this one go, even if it was my lifelong goal to take revenge on my father. Consider it a welcome to the family gift, but don't take my kill again, understand, sweetheart?" She made it sound as though she were being generous.

"Is there a list?" Elysia asked dryly. "You know, of people I ought not to kill?"

Emmellin's grin came back. "Oh, I like you." And then she punched her.

A clean, practiced punch that knocked her right back out.

ELYSIA DECIDED that she wasn't sure about this new friendship. Given that she had been knocked unconscious and woken in strange surroundings twice since it first commenced only hours ago. At least this time she was in a comfortable bed with the smells of stew and spices warming the air.

She damn near yelped when Emmellin spoke from the corner of the room where she was sprawled on the floor with a book. "Bet you're hungry. We napped ya before you could get your dinner at that tavern. That was the prince, wasn't it? Think we could make him pay for you?"

Elysia rubbed her temples. Being knocked out twice in one day couldn't be good for anyone's health. "He's not really in a position to call on the Blatz wealth at the moment. Has a wicked temper too... I'd be careful there. You should know he's a damn good tracker."

Emmellin popped to standing and made an unconcerned face. "Prince or not. Magic or not. He'd have to be dumb as shit to come *here* wanting to fight. You've been running with Gage too long. Things are different here in Bellia. We don't care if he's a prince or some asshole who owes us money. And we've all got magic."

Elysia recalled what Topp had told her about the king and grimaced. They had magic for now, anyway.

Emmellin pulled her off the bed. "Come on then. Let's get you fed, and you can meet the family. Gage has been very naughty keeping secrets, and *you* are going to share them. How are we supposed to maintain a successful and unchallenged crime empire when our heir doesn't even tell us he's been training and harboring the mortal to the god of the dead? His job was to keep an eye on you, not adopt you. He is in *so* much trouble. Just wait till you meet his mom."

What? Gage was supposed to keep an eye on her? But she wasn't given any time to dwell on that new information. Emmellin took hold of Elysia's wrist and didn't let go until she'd yanked her down several flights of timber stairs into a large open kitchen and dining room. The smells alone made Elysia's stomach rumble. There were large iron pots that she had no doubt had been simmering for hours. Platters of cheese and cured meats. Vegetables roasting to perfection.

And about ten Reyezes of all different ages staring at her like she was a disease.

Emmellin shoved Elysia in front of her. "Elysia Parker, everybody. Poisoned a whole court, killed my father in the process, and was chosen for the death voyage." Emmellin glanced wickedly between Elysia and her family before uncere-moniously pulling Elysia's shirt down once more. "And she's *ours.*"

There was a moment of silent surprise before cheering and banging broke out. Elysia wasn't sure she'd ever been more off-kilter. She would've thought that years of following Gage around would have prepared her on some level for the people who had raised him, but then again, she was wrong a lot lately. Emmellin shoved her around, introducing her left and right to the warm but rough crew surrounding her. Food and drink were in her hands before she even knew what had happened.

Later, once everyone had piled in around the long wooden table, a young boy with dark hair and matching eyes threw down his fork in a fit of frustration. "Uncle Gage can't just *mark* some random lady. She hasn't earned it."

Elysia couldn't help her smile at his indignation, but she wiped her face clean when she realized several faces around the oval table were considering his words.

She set her drink down and met the young boy's eyes. "Lyon, right?"

He nodded and shoved his hair out of his eyes so he could properly stare daggers her way.

Elysia spoke slowly, caring for her words. "Gage, your uncle, took me in when I was smaller than you. He is not my father or my brother or lover. But he *is* family."

While not every person in the room was a Reyez like she had first thought, the man who came to stand behind the small boy looked so much like Gage that it made her heart hurt. Elysia blinked at the familiar dark brown eyes and lithe body movements.

The man spoke. "You say he is family, then we would like to see just how much like family you are."

A thick woman wrapped in a gauzy cream dress glided down the stairs. Her black hair was spiced with gray and coiled into a strong knot atop her head. Elysia automatically sat up straighter, her heart rate increasing. *Gage's mother, Sylvia Reyez.* The queen of this family, this empire then.

She paused above them all, but she stared directly into Elysia's own brown eyes. "Emmellin has brought us a gift in allowing us to know the one my son has given his life to guide and protect as was his sacred duty. But my family is right to test you. Our family's protection and resources do not come free."

Elysia swallowed.

The woman laughed, but the sound only made Elysia's nerves jump higher. She came closer, swiping a piece of fruit from the table. "Your king grows paranoid. You disappear beneath his sword, and now his son slips out like a thief in the night? Both of your warrants have been sent far and wide."

Topp had a warrant now too? She knew Topp was expecting it —that was why he had left—but she still struggled to keep the surprise off her face. Garrison being willing to take the chance of harm coming to his only heir was a shock, but then dreadful realization sank within her. If Garrison was a demigod, his lifespan had just expanded. He could make a new heir without hesitation now.

Sylvia's gaze glittered. "You need us. But you will be tested like any other Reyez initiate, no matter your status. Consider your test to be one of Gage as well. You are his first protégé after all. He has no partner, no children. Just *you.*"

As much as she wanted to travel out of there lickety-split and not look back, she knew she would need their protection and assistance, and more than that, she didn't want to let Gage down.

Elysia straightened in her seat and kept her voice level as she met the queenpin's gaze. "Name your test."

Sylvia Reyez evaluated her and smiled coldly. "A court-raised woman trained by the heir of a criminal empire. Yes, I can find a useful test for you."

Chapter 17

Out of all the places Elysia Parker had gone snooping, this might've topped the list.

The Lights was the newest and most popular club in Saar-spur. Located in the Endless Forest, it was slung up in the farthest reaches of the branches. Just looking at the club had made Elysia uneasy. The roofless club stretched through the weakest and smallest branches of the pines, gently swaying in the evening winter wind. Architecturally, it was, in a word, precarious.

Elysia wasn't used to magically designed buildings. She now realized she had a strong preference for concrete, structural beams, and buildings that were connected to the ground. The Lights gave her the distinct impression that one body too many within its doors would send the whole place crashing down, leaving them all impaled on the excrement of what was once a very stupidly constructed club.

Despite its stupidity, The Lights, she had to begrudgingly admit, was beautiful.

Dazzling, colorful lights shimmered and waved through the night sky, and because The Lights didn't bother with a roof, its inhabitants were able to be as close to the gorgeous expanse of starlight as humanly possible. The pines of the Endless Forest were only a fingertip's reach away, rustling in the wind and scenting the air perfectly.

But Elysia wasn't here to luxuriate in the beauty of the night sky.

She was here to steal the plans for some new magic-fueled gambling machine. The Lights was one of the few clubs not owned or under the protection of the Reyez empire within Saarspur, which normally they would have been willing to overlook so long as The Lights didn't cause any *problems*. But The Lights had procured a new distributor. This distributor was bringing in all sorts of fresh products—drinks, drugs, games, beauty potions. It looked like the beginnings of someone edging in on their market. And the products were good too. Creative, underground types of ideas that Bellia, one of the richest and most stable kingdoms, hadn't seen in a long time.

The Reyez family had no desire to stamp out such ingenuity. They wanted to poach it. And that started with an introduction —one Elysia was guaranteeing when she stole the foreign distributor's newest design. Everyone knew theft and blackmail were how all great working relationships began.

Elysia sat at the bar, sliding her hand up and down her thigh. The rhythmic, smooth sensation beneath her palm was a poor attempt to quiet the steadily growing alarm within her, but unsurprisingly did next to nothing to rid her of the distracting tension in her neck or silence the inner voice demanding her to get the fuck out and forget this club. Elysia forced her hand to still. She couldn't be giving herself away like that.

At least her dress was pretty if it was what she ended up dying in. The deep, sensual green of the fabric was woven with a warming magic, so that even with the blustery chill, her muscles were as warm and relaxed as her nerves would allow. Long sleeved with a wide boat neck and slim-fitting body, the dress moved with her rather than constricting her motions. Resting on the seat of her stool was a cropped black jacket with a high collar and golden brass buttons.

Unable to help herself, she ran her thumb over the soft fabric again. It was unsettling to realize just how crippled Kava must have been in the years that followed the Fall. Buildings that had once relied on magic needing to be reinforced and reconstructed. Clothing, crafts, and every product you could think of suddenly needing to be produced in a mundane manner. She wondered how long it took people to learn how to make something as basic as food without magic. It must have been a disaster. And yet now, Kava boasted electricity and steam-powered engines. The rest of the world found them strange and unnatural, but she knew they were survivors. It took a rugged, immeasurable sort of strength not only to keep your creativity but to find the will to create something new in the face of your entire world breaking. And her people had done so, over and over.

Elysia played with her drink as her magic crawled through every corner of the club.

Money, sex, impulsivity, and longing.

People who were here to escape. People who were here to amplify. People who had felt nothing for a very, very long time. The rare few who were just genuinely enjoying themselves.

Elysia bit back a sigh of frustration. She'd been hoping this would be good practice for searching for the talisman given that she'd never used her magic to search for anything specific before. It just dragged her around and she hoped for the best. Elysia rattled the ice in her glass. It looked like she was going to need some magic lessons after all—from Maya. Aidan could bite her ass if he thought she was going to fall for his bullshit just because he'd been nice to her when she was about to cry. Her throat thickened with discomfort just thinking about that interaction. She was letting him get too close. They didn't have to cry on each other's shoulders to work cordially together.

Her glass hit the wooden bar with a thud, her eyes latching onto a newcomer. Stuffed into a three-piece charcoal gray suit, the man strode through the club with a quiet but powerful energy. She tracked him as he cut a sharp, direct line to where she sat. Her interest thrummed higher as she freely perused her mark. Light skin, dark brown hair tinged with red, and a neatly groomed beard paired with muscles that were ready to bust out of his finely made suit. Elysia's magic slithered out, and she inhaled a nibble of his secrets. Flashes of violence ripped through her mind along with numbers and a sense of astuteness. As a former unbranded Reyez enforcer turned businessman, it all made sense. *Interesting, indeed.*

She smiled lazily, tipping her gaze up from the well-oiled leather boots now standing an inch from her stool all the way up to hard blue eyes.

"Welcome to my club, Ms. Parker. Given our mutual friends, I assure you that the sizable bounty on your head is all but forgotten." Her mark stressed the word *sizable* while his gaze drifted from her face to roam all over her body as if the gleaming pinkish-red skin of the Reyez brand would suddenly make itself known from beneath her dress.

Resting a hand on the bar, he leaned against it. Intelligence shone in his eyes, giving away how he'd moved from mere muscle to owning a club like this in the heart of Reyez territory. He leaned in as if they were having a private moment, waiting a few seconds to speak. Elysia sensed eyes on them from around the club as he held his position near her ear, but she maintained her indifferent posture. As if people hadn't stared and panted after the Crown Prince. She was immune to such rabble. Heat rolled off the club owner's body, and his voice this close to her neck made her skin crawl.

"The games here really are unique. You'll have to let me know how they compare to Kava's."

Elysia maintained her half-lidded stare, giving him a barely perceptible nod. "As you're well aware, our games rely strictly on cunning given that we cannot use magic to," she paused, opening her gaze to better meet his, "*enthrall* the masses."

He smiled mirthlessly, dropping a handful of gaming chips onto the bar in front of her. "Perhaps you should let your cunning rest and allow us to enthrall you then." With that, her mark stalked off, the crowd giving him an easy berth.

Elysia's nostrils flared the second he was gone. He knew. He didn't know exactly why they'd sent her, but he'd taken a solid stab in the dark with that little quip about the games at The Lights. *Fuck me.* She might as well have strolled in here with a banner that said, *Hi, I'm a Reyez initiate and I'm here to steal from you! Would you like the bounty on my head before or after you kill me?*

But Simon Maspan was her mark, and there were *rules* she had to follow.

Rule number one. No fated magic or underrealm creatures. In other words, no magical traveling, or man-eating pint-sized dogs.

Rule number two, as spoken by Sylvia Reyez. "There are no rules. Steal the damn plans, or we'll kill you and send you back to Gage as a present because both he and our death god deserve better than some girl who can't even steal or kill properly."

And then she'd been given an address, the whisper of a name in her ear, and instructed to be home by dawn before being booted out the door with a hearty chorus of *may death guide you,* which was quite possibly the creepiest farewell she had ever received.

Maspan kept proving himself to be unfortunately capable. His security and employees communicated like a practiced team. There were magical eyes on the walls that she didn't understand, but intuited were watching as the paintings blinked and swiveled. Elysia slid off her stool, slipping into her jacket. Letting her magic out to play was her best bet at this point—one way or another she had to find those plans.

Elysia quietly followed her mark onto the terrace, awed at how cozy it was without the frigid wind or snow pelting her in the face. Past the perimeter of The Light's terrace, winter raged on, but inside its bounds, guests enjoyed the magic of a perfectly pleasant winter night with stars twinkling above.

Staying in the background, she mulled over the few tidbits and images she'd managed to extract from his psyche. Maspan kept looking at his head of security with the type of suspicion that would have made most men run. He was nervous then—about the incoming game plans and possibly even her. She'd also learned that Simon hated casinos but loved money, and he was very, very excited about *something*.

Which made sense.

Given that the new game plans were being delivered tonight.

Elysia dropped her head back against the wall to better see the sparkling swaths of night sky. Thanks to the magic, she didn't even feel a breeze. Gods, she could get used to this.

Eyes snapping back to Maspan, she observed how he moved from person to person, room to room, dropping a hand on a shoulder or a quick word with a grin, but he was monitoring. Expectant and cautious.

Well, he should be. She took another sip of her drink and wondered who would be delivering the new plans to the club and if the head of security was going to be a problem. It was getting late, and she wanted to get this over with. Dropping her drink onto a table, Elysia decided to move things along.

Strolling through the club, she grazed her hand over walls, windows, and doors. A new building like this didn't hold nearly as many secrets as the beauties in her home city, but nonetheless, she let herself revel in the sly, deceptive nature of The Lights. All at once, she knew she'd found what she was looking for as the feeling of it hooked behind her navel, and pulled, pulled, pulled.

Unlike in Kava, where she had no control, Elysia now grabbed hold of her magic, wrestling it until her mind cleared a little, and she managed to slow her feet, only hesitating when her magic tugged her right back out the front door. Halting on the threshold, she almost lost the thread as her logic fought back against where the magic demanded she go. The twinge of fear in her chest reminded her of every time her magic had almost been the death of her, but still she followed it out the door and away from the bouncer to the side of the club.

Her heels echoed against the smooth black deck. Stopping, she searched for where her magic could possibly be pulling her as she rested her hands against the railing. The hook behind her naval yanked, demanding she go up over the barrier and out into nothing. Fingers gripping the railing, she pursed her lips as she looked out into the pines. Her stomach clenched and she took an instinctive step away from the ledge.

She'd scaled rooftops and spires and run along soot and rain-slicked tiles. But no one would recover from a drop like that. She rubbed the still tender Reyez branding as she tried to talk herself up.

You can do this. You're a mediocre thief, who's terrible at poisons, and you're not about to let down the only man who's ever taken care of you.

With that, Elysia hiked up her dress, revealing several small blades strapped to the insides of her thighs. Twisting her thigh harnesses, she settled them properly, no longer caring if she had suspicious bulges beneath her dress. Climbing up and over the railing, her now bare feet rested dangerously on the deck's edge as she clung to the railing behind her. Bracing herself, she let go of the railing, and took one terrible step out into nothing.

A soundless scream tore from her throat as she dropped.

CHAPTER 18

ELYSIA PLUMMETED. Needles and branches scratched and broke against her body, slowing but not stopping her descent.

Until all at once, she crashed against an invisible barrier. Bouncing lightly, her body finally settled against the mesh. She allowed herself a few breaths to reorient herself and ensure nothing had been broken before heaving herself into a sitting position. The mesh net swayed with her movement, causing her stomach to lurch once again.

Elysia exhaled harshly. *Maspan is a masochist if this is how he always enters his home.* Coming onto her hands and knees, she crawled in the direction of a concrete terrace. No longer at the highest level of the forest, she guessed they were halfway down to the forest floor. She chanced a glance below, and panic surged through her, leaving her stuck and panting. Despite being able to feel the mesh netting below her, all she could see was air and the straight drop to the ground. The discrepancy between the visual and tactile information left her panicked with black spots dancing in the corners of her eyes.

Gripping the netting until it cut against her fingers, she forced her eyes shut. *Feel the net, just feel the net.* Eyes still closed, she inched along even as her body begged her to remain glued to one spot until Maspan inevitably found her and killed her.

Thank the gods she hadn't screamed. If she was lucky, security wouldn't come running, and she was far enough down that she doubted they could see her through the pines.

Cool, damp concrete let her know she'd reached the landing, and she damn near whimpered as she pulled herself onto its solid surface. Crawling ahead, she planted herself against a curved wooden door set into the arch of a stone cottage. Breathing rapidly, she pressed her cold fingers to her face trying to regain some semblance of control.

Spine adhered to the door, she kept her hands on the surrounding concrete arch as she slid back up to standing. The world swayed, but Elysia pivoted on her bare feet to look at the door instead of the giant free fall in front of her before her panic could resume. A quick test of the door handle confirmed what she had assumed. *Locked.* Pulling up her dress, she grabbed a thin instrument tucked beside one of her knives and set to work. The familiar work of picking a lock soothed the last remnants of the terrible shaking, buzz still present in her limbs after falling like a brick from The Lights. Soon enough the door swung open, and with her mind clear and satisfaction warming her chest, Elysia entered the stone cottage.

It was a funny thing—but she had missed this part of herself. Maybe it wasn't a skill to boast about, but she'd been trained by the best, and getting in and out of buildings, hunting for informa-tion—it truly was what she felt most at home, most like herself, doing. Quiet confidence hummed inside her. The last few weeks had been a nightmare of incessant, tumultuous, life-changing revelations. She had no idea how to complete a death voyage or emotionally process the expectation of becoming the partner to a death god. But picking a lock? Breaking and entering? She could do that just fine.

She scanned the room, thinking of the man who had raised her and trained her to be fierce instead of helpless. Who had given her the skills and grit to back up her mischievous gifts. She owed him more than she knew how to say, and tonight she honored that.

Elysia glided to the office, careful not to disturb anything as she slipped through the small home. Her magic was silent now. Not a sound or tug to be had as she rifled through his desk, cabinets, and papers. Elysia slammed a packet of papers down onto the desk, trying to force her magic into guiding her again. But silent it remained as the clock on his wall ticked, reminding her that her time could run out at any moment.

Her heart picked up as she crept through the dark, refusing to admit what she already knew.

The plans were not here yet.

Her magic had delivered her to where she needed to be, but she couldn't just manifest the plans out of thin air. She was going to have to hide and wait. Unsurprisingly, Maspan's home was sparse with not so much as a closet in the office for her to hide in.

Gods above and below. She was going to hate this.

Elysia shoved open the office window and stuck her head out. No impossibly slippery and soot-covered Kavian roof could have ever prepared her for this. Pulling her head back inside, she danced in place, shaking her hands out. *I can do this. I have to do this.* She was still standing there, putting off the inevitable, when a key caught in the front door.

Shit.

Elysia threw herself out the window, hanging off the roof as she weaseled the window back shut. The last dangling bit of her was just disappearing out of sight onto the roof when voices grew louder. The cold metal was frozen with ice and snow, leaving her with damn near nothing to hang onto.

Hands and feet steadily turning numb, Elysia considered the tree branches around her. If her hands grew so frozen they couldn't grip, her safest bet was to launch herself at a tree and hope for the best.

Voices carried out through the bare crack she had left in the window, recognition startling her to the point her body jerked. Elysia scrambled to gain purchase as she slid toward the edge. Bare feet catching against the sharp metal edge of the roof, she scooted her ass back up. Her feet were already painfully numb, and she knew they were going to be a bloody mess before the night was over. As if her feet weren't already scarred enough.

Elysia gripped the roof tighter this time as she listened and waited to hear the voices again. Because if her ears didn't deceive her, then she was about to unleash her holy wrath.

Familiar, addictive anger coiled tighter and tighter in her chest. Hot and heady, she wanted to fly in through the window and kick her beloved sister in the cunt. The woman had expanded to *Bellia?*

Elysia growled silently, her frozen fingers flexing against the roof. At least she wouldn't feel it when she punched her sister in the fucking face. And if Gage knew about this, she'd chop his balls off. It was one thing to supply weapons, it was another to send her overly confident and underprepared sister into danger. And after she was done with Gage, she'd kill Beatriz for getting her friends involved in this shit. Leashing her anger, she listened, taking in the details of Beatriz's new game plans.

She called it twenty-one. A game of magical roulette where every spin was a gamble. Spot seventeen promised a beauty elixir that erased every line and blemish, but slot nineteen would fix the contestant with a body-wide green rash that smelled like fish. Each spin completed offered the contestant more money, but they had to reach certain spins to keep their cash. Make it to spin five and keep ten thousand. Make it to spin eleven and get twenty thousand, but only spin nine? Back to ten thousand. The grand prize for completing all twenty-one spins was a hundred thousand in Bellian currency. The closer you got to winning, the more dangerous the game became, and considering the contestants had to sign a waiver allowing for death and injury, the stakes were certainly high. Beatriz finished her spiel by reminding Maspan that the game would be updated monthly, keeping the prizes fresh and the game new.

Elysia wanted to bang her head against the roof. How in the realms was her sister producing this kind of design in *Kava?* The kingdom where even if you had magic it didn't work correctly.

Beatriz wrapped up her presentation, and Elysia could practically feel her sister's smug certainty all the way up on the roof. Everything about her closing remarks screamed she knew this was a done deal.

But there was that second voice again.

Yes, she was going to kill her sister for getting Remy involved.

If her sister wanted to run her harebrained magical black market in a city where it could get her executed, that was her choice. But Remy Peraldine was better than Beatriz's bullshit, and it boiled Elysia's blood to think Beatriz had somehow bullied her into helping with this mess.

Yet it was Remy's voice that rang out smooth as silk, finessing the finer details of the deal. Soothing Maspan's jagged complaints as if she could just run her manicured fingers over their edges and dissipate them into the evening air.

Elysia began to struggle to hold on to the roof, blood dripping from her frozen bare feet. She cringed as she watched the dark red droplets bead and fall, hoping against hope that they didn't splatter against the window. Straining to listen over the wind to the now quiet murmurs, Remy reviewed numbers while Maspan gave grunts of affirmation.

What her sister didn't realize was that dealing with Maspan was less roulette and more certain death. If they had bothered to study their mark, then they would have known this was a man who had dealt far longer in blood and broken bones than he had sky-high clubs, and he hadn't gotten to where he was now without relying on old skills.

The wind shrieked through the trees now, and the eerie sense of foreboding pulling on her navel grew stronger than Elysia could bear. That man didn't have any intention of paying for something he could simply take, and she wasn't about to let her sister and oldest friend die in the middle of the godsforsaken Endless Forest over the dumbest game she'd ever heard of in her life.

Elysia relaxed her frigid muscles, lamenting the enormous tear that occurred as her dress caught on the ice as she slid back down to the roof's edge. Hunkered down in a dangerous squat, she gripped the roof's edge and waited.

The clinking of glasses. Liquid splashing over rims. And finally the toast.

"To my club's newest centerpiece." Maspan's deep tones carried easily out into the night.

Elysia dropped silently into a dead hang, ramming the window upward with her bleeding feet and sailing inside. She was almost standing when Maspan's giant fist slammed straight into Beatriz's face. Her sister crumpled, flying back into a cabinet before sliding down to the ground, dazed but still conscious.

Her gaze flicked away. Elysia knew she couldn't help her now. Vision narrowing to the beast of a man in front of her, the sweet clarity of a fight flowed through her. This arrogant piece of shit had planned to kill people she loved. Any lingering remorse over the Reyezes' requests disappeared as she ripped two blades free, ready to face the man in front of her.

Maspan straightened, and Elysia dropped into a slide that delivered her perfectly to the back of his knees. Blades in an X, she sliced efficiently, bringing him down to the floor.

Elysia staggered to her feet, memories of practicing with Gage flitting through her mind. How he'd forced her to learn how to butcher animals—to practice the unique force and angle required for a throat versus knee. She'd had to learn the feel of slicing through tendons and cartilage rather than the softness of flesh.

Because of those lessons, her mark crashed onto his palms, bleeding out from the backs of his legs. She could hear Remy and someone else beyond the rush in her ears, but she wasn't done. Elysia stomped on his wrist, forcing him to drop the knife he had pulled out, and crouched down to where he made guttural noises as he shuddered. Elysia watched curiously as his teeth shortened and lengthened.

"You're a shifter," she said quietly without emotion. "I've never seen someone shift."

Rage filled his eyes, but she didn't care. Her blade caressed his face as she whispered. "I've met the face of death, and now you'll meet him too."

One more quick draw of her knife, and her mark had been dispatched. Elysia pulled a coin out of her pocket, slipping it in between his teeth. Religious she was not, but she knew it was tradition, and she wanted to be sure this asshole got to meet Grim and Aidan.

The girls were squawking, but Elysia's skin still vibrated and the violence inside her was turning hollow. Slowly, she wiped her blade on her no-longer-beautiful dress. She looked at her feet, not yet feeling the true extent of pain she knew she would once she came down.

The room had finally gone quiet, and she could hear that now. She needed to turn around, but she didn't know how to—she'd just killed a man, and they'd all watched her do it.

A voice she hadn't been expecting broke the silence. "Not bad for a Crown bitch."

Elysia whipped around to find another familiar face. Green catlike eyes and black hair in two tight braids that wound around her head, Jessa met Elysia's bloodied appearance without flinching. Gratefulness flickered in her chest. She couldn't have stood it to see the fear or disgust that she knew her sister or at the very least Remy were likely feeling.

Jessa slapped a hand onto her shoulder. "Your way was neater anyway."

Elysia looked away from Remy, who was administering unwanted first aid to a swearing Beatriz. "Neater?"

"Haven't you heard? Everyone's got their magic back outside of Kava."

Elysia swore faintly. "Oh my gods. You were going to blow him up."

Jessa nodded matter-of-factly. "Except I haven't ever managed to narrow it down to a single human before. Probably for the best you swung in."

Elysia ran a bloodied and likely frostbitten hand over her face. "Amazing."

Beatriz appeared to be a little light on her feet but was nonetheless trying to push off Remy's support. "You really are the worst busybody I've ever met. I'm in a different *kingdom* for the gods' sake."

An old, slow-burning rage licked at Elysia's wounds. Words like ungrateful and undeserving flashed through her mind. "The response you're looking for is *thank you, Elysia, I'd be dead without you, Elysia. I'm a fucking idiot, Elysia.*"

Remy's dark brown eyes were enormous as they swung between the two Parker sisters. Jessa just grinned and stepped back to lean against the office wall.

Beatriz shoved Remy off and staggered closer, her voice scathing. "I knew what I was doing! I brought the nerd, and I brought the muscle! This isn't my first time, you over-controlling pain in my ass."

A muscle in Elysia's jaw jumped. "I wasn't even here for you."

Beatriz blinked, her face clearing. "What?"

Elysia stalked out of the office, her tone turning cold. "We don't have time for this. Maspan has security crawling all over the place, and his men know you weren't supposed to walk out of here. Escaping the forest is going to be a nightmare."

Jessa came up behind her, peering out one of the windows. "Thought you could travel now."

"I don't know if I can manage an entire group, but I can try." She'd gotten Topp here easy enough, but doubt sprang up as she considered the three women next to her.

Jessa quickly shook her head. "No. I've seen what happens when traveling goes wrong."

Oh. Maybe traveling with the prince hadn't been so wise after all.

Remy spoke quietly, hanging onto whatever scraps of calm she had left. "I have an idea. But you're not going to like it."

Minutes later, Elysia was shivering in the rapidly dropping temperatures of the Endless Forest. Her dress may have been made for warmth, but it didn't replace layers or a coat, and her cut-up bare feet and hands were killing her. Worse than that, she was back to clutching the invisible net outside the stone cottage, but this time with three more bodies weighing it down until it sank dangerously in the middle, making her swear as it creaked.

"Ready?" Elysia's question barely carried over the wind.

Petrified, Remy said nothing. Beatriz nodded grimly, looking disassociated and slightly green as she stared through the invisible netting to the ground. Naturally, it was Jessa with her eyes squeezed shut who spoke through gritted teeth. "Stop talking and just do it already."

Knife arm up, Elysia paused, giving them each a hard look. "If a single one of you makes so much as a peep, I will leave you in this godsdamn forest." She brought her blade arm down, cutting through where the net attached to the concrete landing.

Remy's scream was loud enough it was probably heard all the way in godsdamned Kava.

"Shut up, shut up." Elysia hissed, but there was nothing to be done about it.

If Maspan's men hadn't already realized something had gone wrong with their boss's meeting, then they definitely knew now, and Elysia was sure they'd be taking an alternative route than the nightmare bridge to get them down to the forest floor.

Trees and branches flew past as they clung desperately to the netting, which had now twisted into an invisible rope. A branch cracked against Elysia's ribs, forcing all the air out of her body, but she clung on, knowing that letting go would likely mean death. Using her feet, Elysia propelled them away from the trees the best she could after watching Remy smash her nose. Pine needles cut and scratched against skin, and then one by one they all thudded against the base of a pine. Slowly, she pried her cold fingers free of the netting, crashing down into the snow and dirt.

Looking around at her ragtag, busted-up crew, Elysia could hear Gage in her head.

We are not saviors. We are not rescuers. We get in. We get out. And we do not take deadweight.

All three pieces of deadweight groaned and swore.

Elysia stared at the shoveled path that led out of the forest. Lit with golden light, it was the fastest and clearest route out. She was barefoot, and she was afraid the girls wouldn't make it through the knee-deep snow.

The sound of heavy footsteps and low voices rumbled closer, hastening her decision. Into the forest where hypothermia was likely, or onto the golden path where they'd be spotted and over-taken with swiftness.

Gage flitted through her mind one more time, but she pushed back the rush of shame threatening to slow her down. She was going to fail her mission and her mentor, but she saw no other path.

Elysia slipped back into a cool, detached headspace even as in her gut she knew they were neck-deep in shit. Security was already in sight, the dark shadows of weapon-clad men peppering the trees. And then the sky crackled, lighting up the darkness as the wind screamed and rain fell down in icy sheets.

Low growls carried to her ears past the wind and rain, and the hairs on her neck stood on end. *Maspan was a shifter.* She shoved at her friends, who were behaving like disoriented cats. "Onto the path, go, go, go! If they're shifters, they'll be able to see us anyway in the woods."

A pair of feet landed solidly behind her, the crunch of snow reflexively making her whirl, blades out. Knife to artery, Elysia's shoulders collapsed as a hysterical laugh won out.

"Going to kill me, Parker?"

"You're a fucking asshole." A wild surge of hope flooded

through her, never happier to see the man who had not so long ago left her for dead.

"Would you have me any other way?" The prince had found battle axes and was already pulling them out, his wet hair plastered to his skin and green eyes blazing unnaturally.

A half circle of wolves slowly crept in, forming around their group, but Elysia grinned, pressing her back against his.

She lifted her knives back up.

CHAPTER 19

THE WIND SHRIEKED as the air around them began to vibrate, even the ground shaking as heavy snow and ice loosened. The whirling vibrations increased until the rumbles deafened everyone, the women clapping hands over their ears and wolves whining at the sound. Picking up snow and ice, the cyclone grew and grew until, with a tree-shaking boom of thunder, it released, tunneling for the wolves and incoming men.

Shocked, Elysia's gaze slid to Topp. Fingers gripping his axes so tight they were white, he furrowed his brow in concentration as he swept the cyclone along, tearing up snow, dirt, and trees. One by one the men who hadn't shifted burst out of human skin, turning into wolves and bears, darting out of the cyclone's path. Seconds after the first thunder, blinding lightning cracked through the trees, and a shifter yelped, diving and rolling out of its path.

Elysia stared at the burnt scorch of earth, overwhelmed with the terrible and unfamiliar feeling of being helpless in a fight. *My magic is no good in combat, and I can't fight a fucking bear.* Topp's chest heaved with exertion, and the remaining shifters were shaking out their fur, beginning to advance again. Slowly, they encroached, eyes yellow and snouts curled in permanent snarls.

Topp was raising his axes now, determined exhaustion lining his face. Elysia's eyes darted between Topp and Jessa. They needed to act now, or they were going to be torn to shreds. Stomach sour, she barked out her order. *"Rip them apart."*

Two pairs of green eyes locked on her, but she didn't flinch. "I said, *rip them apart.*"

Jessa hardened in understanding, and then animals and trees exploded, both gore and wood splinters flying through the air. The shifters who didn't explode dropped to the earth, rolling and crying out as their oxygen cut off until all at once they stopped, bodies still and eyes lifeless.

Topp's bright eyes grew dim as he gazed down at the destruction they had wrought, and Elysia dropped to her knees, the snow soaking through her green dress. Something in her wanted to keel —to collapse and wordlessly scream into the now mundane winds. Topp's large, calloused hand appeared in front of her face. Tiny drops of blood were splattered against his freckles. Placing her hand in his like she'd done a hundred times before, Elysia stood, allowing the brutal wind to whip her long dress around her.

The cold settled against her heart. *Every step is one closer to the talisman.* Elysia clung to this hope. And with that, she silently began to trudge along the golden-lit path out of the Endless Forest to claim her place in the Reyez Empire.

BLOODY AND MUD-SPLATTERED, they arrived.

Remy was likely traumatized. Topp hadn't stopped asking Elysia questions about her *kidnapping* since they started walking, and Beatriz and Jessa were plotting something that she pretended she couldn't hear.

The front door swung open. Emmellin grinned, letting out a loud whoop as she turned and jumped onto her husband, legs wrapped around his middle. One arm thrust in the air, she yelled into the house. "Parker returns! Pay up, assholes!"

And with that, she directed her enormous husband to carry her to each and every person who had seemingly bet against Elysia's success.

Elysia watched from beneath a lifted eyebrow. Nothing like knowing almost the entire room thought you were going to fail and die.

Her sister and Topp loomed over her shoulders, curiosity getting the better of them. With a ready sneer, Beatriz took in the handful of crew members eyeing her little sister with unveiled disdain. "No wonder Gage was willing to cut himself off from magic to get away from you all." Cold and angry, Beatriz was past snippy and well into bitchy territory.

Topp gripped Elysia's shoulder protectively, his eyes focused on the mixed reactions of their hosts. He murmured into her ear, "Let's go before—"

Emmellin hooted and slid off her husband in front of them. "Well, I'll be—a *prince*." Her gaze snagged on Elysia's feet. "Fuck. Those are the ugliest feet I've ever seen. You should take care of that. Looks like frostbite over all those...scars."

Elysia's still-frozen ears turned hot with embarrassment. She had managed to hide her feet from everyone, including Topp, until now.

"They're fine," she muttered, barging into the house with her motley crew trailing nervously behind her like a bunch of weird ducklings.

Elysia snatched the tube with the roulette plans from her sister. Beatriz tried to dive for them, only for Jessa to grab hold of the neck of her shirt and yank her to a full stop. Marching over to where Syliva Reyez watched imperiously, Elysia held out the tube with a glare and spat at her feet.

The room took a collective inhale, silence falling heavier than the snow.

Sylvia grasped the tube, but Elysia ripped it backward, pulling her in close. There was shifter matter in her hair, and she was careening dangerously close to not giving a shit if she walked out of this house alive. She held the Reyez queen's eyes. "You're going to pay her."

She released the tube, and it was likely only years of training that kept Sylvia from stumbling back. "You're going to pay my sister for the plans. You want me to steal? You want me to remove a mark? Fine. But what you don't do is send me in unprepared to keep people I love alive." Heart thundering, the fear she'd kept a grip on was slipping. She gestured sharply at Topp and Jessa. "The only reason we walked out of that forest is because of *their magic*. Your son trained me to be a thief. To sneak in, sneak out, and fight *mundanely* if needed. You want to test me? Fine. But do *not* bring my people into this without warning. Do you understand?"

Nose to nose, Elysia didn't dare blink or back away. An eternity slipped past as she waited to be cut down, but neither Sylvia nor any other member of the family moved.

A slow smile crept across Sylvia's face, but her eyes remained two chips of hazel ice. The effect was terrifying. "Your test was not of strength or skill."

A buzzing noise filled Elysia's ears. *This fucking b—*

"You grew up alone. From my son's messages, you are guarded, difficult, and trust no one."

Her hackles rose.

"He also was willing to stake his life on the fact that in spite of how everyone failed you, you would die fighting for your family." She nodded at the extremely tense group of Kavians behind them and then gestured at her own people. "To be in *this* family, you must be capable of being *loyal* to something beyond yourself. And your strange collection of friends...is a start."

Elysia's anger pitched low, still a dark hum in her veins. "You wanted to see if I would take the plans and leave them to die."

Sylvia gave a perfunctory nod. "Consider that I also gave you a chance to save them. If you hadn't been there to steal the plans, Maspan would have handled them quite easily."

Her fingers flexed and released by her side as Jessa grunted her dissent.

Beatriz slapped away Jessa's hand that still clung to her collar, strolling over with far too much confidence. She looked down at her sister. "You're trying to tell me you joined *the family*?"

Exhausted, Elysia was well past explaining her actions, but Sylvia intercepted the question.

"Many think of us as criminals, and we are—but we are also the foot soldiers of death's many faces. Who do you think pays for all the temples? Who do you think pays for all the impoverished and orphaned women who find shelter and now walk in their halls? People are taxed heavily enough. We can't expect them to drop their coins at the feet of their gods. We fill in what is needed and take care of our own."

Elysia glanced at the enormous home she stood in and made a face. They *more* than took care of their own. Beatriz slid Slyvia an oily grin in response to the woman's rather polite description of the family business. "You misunderstand. I have no qualms with your *business*." Her eyes narrowed as they went back to Elysia. "My issue is with this one."

Sylvia's lips turned up at the sibling dispute. Facing the entire room of Reyez family members and scraggly Kavians, she raised her voice. "Clean up. Take the night to rest. Because when you wake—we celebrate our new initiate and explore fascinating foreign business opportunities."

Beatriz muttered a quiet, *"Fuck yeah,"* garnering a few chuckles from around the room.

The crowd dispersed, and Emmellin corralled the tired and quickly fading crew up the stairs and down a hall filled with guest rooms.

Taking the first available room, Elysia shut the door before anyone could say a word, threw the damnable roulette plans to the side and sank onto the bed, staring off at nothing. Limbs heavy and brain numb, it was several minutes before she finally glanced at the bathing room. She had to bathe. She *needed* to bathe. But her body wasn't moving, and her feet hurt so badly she wanted to throw up.

She dug the heels of her palms into her eyes. She could've lost her sister tonight. She was likely going to in the next few months anyway. Elysia pressed harder as if that would shut up the thoughts inside her head.

The door banged open, and Elysia's head shot up. Beatriz led the unwanted invasion with everyone else trailing in behind her. Door shut, Topp leaned heavily against it with his arms folded.

Plopping down beside her, Beatriz slung an arm around her shoulders. Suspicious, Elysia stiffened before finally relaxing into her sister's side. She couldn't remember the last time they'd hugged. Head dropping against her shoulder, the tension in her chest loosened.

Beatriz allowed the awkward side hug to go on for a record-breaking ten seconds before turning to Elysia with her sharp gray eyes entirely too focused for three in the morning.

"Elysia Penelope Parker, you have some serious fucking explaining to do."

Was nice while it lasted. Elysia grunted, wriggling out of Beatriz's hold as Jessa hopped up onto the small writing desk and crossed her legs. "Your sister's right."

Elysia was too tired to draw up the required scorn or disbelief. "What about your *international* black market? You forgot to mention that the other day, didn't you?"

The apples of Jessa's chiseled cheekbones turned pink. But Beatriz turned solemn, her voice uncharacteristically soft. "You killed a man for us, little sister. You would've stayed and bled out with the rest of us if it had come down to it."

"And you went toe to toe with *Sylvia Reyez.*" Jessa's voice shook slightly, reminding Elysia of just how reckless that choice had been.

Uncomfortable, her gaze darted to Topp, but if she was looking for judgment, she wasn't going to find it in him. Not when it came to doing what needed to be done.

Elysia scraped at the dried blood on her hands, unable to keep her voice from being harsh. "I told you two to be careful. You can't just walk into deals without any research or protection when you're moving the type of product that you are. You're both smarter than that."

Her voice heated as she continued flaking dried blood onto the cream rug beneath her feet. "And why did you have to drag Remy into your underground bullshit? Couldn't you have just left her alone? She was *safe*. Why do you think I've ignored her and Daphne since this started? It was to keep them *safe*."

Remy's voice was an even thing amidst the rising tension. "I will remind you that you do not get to make those decisions for people, Elysia. You tied your life to a god's, protected us when it would have been smarter to run, and you won't even let us stand beside you? If we are yours, then you are ours as well."

A lump lodged itself in Elysia's throat. She was making up for years of blood on her hands, but somehow, for her it was *expected*. She had no such expectations of other people. Years of being alone in both her fears and successes had taught her not to rely on the fickle caring of other people.

Remy moved like water, gliding closer to Elysia with her usual fearlessness returning to her eyes. "*I* went to Beatriz. It's my job to pay attention to the businesses within our city, and while it may surprise you, I support what she is doing. Call it what you wish, but she's creating a market for our people to build something of their own. And I think the time is coming when we are going to need as much ingenuity as possible."

Tension spiked up Elysia's neck into her skull. "How bad is it in court?"

Remy's manicured hand flexed. "Garrison is in a frenzy. He won't stop until he's exterminated magic as far and wide as he can. We all know what almost happened to Kava after the Fall."

Topp spoke up for the first time. "He's whipped the people into chaos as well. He'd already built a base of fear around magic, and now he's capitalizing on it. Staging events that make it look like people with magic are violent and depraved. He's going to have a ready and willing army."

A throbbing ache banded around her head now. "It was all to be expected."

"It's still a nightmare," Topp replied, looking worn. "I received word that he intends to allow Kavians to keep their magic when they cross the borders. It will be a reverse of the Fall. Kavians slaughtering and pillaging the kingdoms that did the same to us when we lost magic. No doubt he'll take it away once he's used them to achieve his ends."

Elysia turned back to her oldest friend, hoping she would hear her earnestness through the tired rasp of her voice. "I liked knowing that at least you and Daphne were safe. I never had such hopes for me, or Beatriz, or anyone else in this room, but I thought maybe you two could be."

Remy grabbed her hand. "I do not wish for immediate safety, but a lasting one. I'm *good* with numbers and business. You know that. Let me do what I do best for something worthwhile."

Elysia looked down at their interconnected hands, her pale, mottled, and bloodied fingers wrapped tight with Remy's smooth warm brown ones. She squeezed Remy's hand. "You already were. You were the only one who was. That's why you deserved to keep your peace. But if you want to turn my sister's ill-thought-out bullshit into something lethal enough to wreck a kingdom, then *okay*."

Remy smiled. "*Okay.*"

The women filed out shortly, leaving Elysia alone with a pair of bright green eyes that belonged to a man who used to make her heart race. She traced the outline of his broad shoulders and strong jaw with her eyes, too tired to feel anything but oddly comforted by his presence.

Pacing over to the window on aching feet, she looked out at the fat flakes of snow lazily drifting down from the sky. "They're going to create a network of magical deviants. Probably blow up the castle or something equally insane."

Topp's low chuckle sounded closer than she expected, and she turned her head to find the warmth of him right behind her. Sweat and the scent of a crisp summer storm filled her nose. It was three in the morning, she was exhausted, and it would be so easy to simply keep turning, until she fell into him. She doubted he would stop her. But behind the tired impulse, she knew she didn't want that at all. She wanted comfort, but she didn't want him.

Topp wrapped a single arm around the front of her shoulders and rested his chin on her head. "I don't know how to do this."

Elysia remained silent, flicking her face up at his. He looked down softly at her. "Part of me thinks I should chain your wrist to mine and guard you like I said."

Her mouth flattened. "Because I'm what's most important for Kava."

"You *are* what's most important to Kava."

Elysia deflated, giving a clipped nod to the harsh but expected answer. The Doorman's words came back to her. *That man has a destiny to fulfill, and love will not stop him.*

Quietly, he spoke against her hair. "And you'll always be important to me."

But never important enough, and never for the right reasons.

She stared out the window, knowing what came next. "You're leaving, aren't you?"

He nodded and pulled her tighter against him. "I thought about what you said, and you're right."

Elysia looked up at him, feigning shock. "I don't think I've ever heard you say that to me before. Can you say it again?"

Leaning down, he whispered in her ear. "Elysia Parker, you were right, and I was *wrong*."

Exhausted delirium must have taken her because uncontained giggles had her bending in half until her eyes watered and she hacked for air. "See, that's what it sounds like when you're actually funny."

A small smile warmed Topp's face. "I know I don't have the right to ask this, but—" Uncertainty flashed across the prince's face as his cheeks turned red. "Never mind," he mumbled, running his fingers through already messy hair.

Curiosity piqued, Elysia stepped out of his grasp so she could face him and pushed gently on his chest. "Say it."

The court- and forest-raised man in front of her ducked his head, refusing to meet her gaze. "I would like to be your friend."

A sharp pang cut through her chest. Out of all the things, she hadn't been expecting that. She spoke cautiously. "Friendship, like any relationship, demands trust."

He nodded, fully flushed now and still staring at his feet. "Which is why I don't deserve it." He heaved a breath. "I'll never be able to apologize or make up for what I did—for this *version* of me that I've become. I know I have no right to ask you for friendship I likely can't uphold."

"You're right," she said, but reached for his hand, thinking about how grief and pain had warped the best person she knew into this angry, confused man. With thoughts of the boy she'd once known and how much she sometimes hated who she'd become, she offered Topp Blatz a reprieve from his guilt. "Did you know Jessa was in love with Syren Herrin?"

He frowned. "The healer? That—"

"That I picked out of a lineup for your father."

His face cleared as he took in the extent of what she was saying.

"Jessa chose to help me anyway because of how important this is. I wouldn't say we're friends, but we're...something like it?"

Topp nodded, studying her intensely like it mattered what she said next. "Where does that leave us?"

"Maybe try to not leave me for dead or double-cross me, and we can revisit this conversation?"

Topp shoved his hands into his pockets with a grin she knew stole hearts all too easily. "Only because it's you, Parker."

She rolled her eyes with a smile, knowing better now than to fully believe him.

He stopped outside the room, the lines around his eyes deepening. "You take your path, Lys, and I'll take mine. If they intersect... Well, then I would be the luckiest, but somehow, I doubt two curses make a right."

She huffed. "Just don't die, okay?"

The prince's warm hand latched onto her waist as he swept down to press his lips to her cheek. "Take care of yourself, Parker. I'm sure I'll see you."

CHAPTER 20

Topp Blatz would never argue that he was the smartest man. But he wouldn't have said he was the dumbest either.

His head cracked above him, causing a loose clod of the gods knew what to crumble down his face and into his eyes. *Fuck me.* He'd sworn he'd never come back down here again after the last time. Topp rubbed his eyes, straining to see in the dark. Having had a taste of his powers, and then being forced back into stunted scraps was like ripping away a drug he hadn't known he needed.

He stalked further into the dark, continuing to question his own mental faculties.

Slinking around underfoot the man who had raised him and now had a warrant out for him admittedly wasn't his wisest decision. Worse than that was being back in these godsforsaken, shit-infested tunnels like he was a rat instead of a fully grown man.

Another clod of dirt disintegrated over him, and familiar tension cramped his lower back as he tried to make himself shorter. He was always stressed. His muscles wouldn't have known what to do if they weren't tight enough to pop his head right off his body. Swiping dirt off his face for the second time in less than five minutes, Topp eyed the tunnels with disdain. He doubted they were going to last much longer.

One cursory sweep with his meager power confirmed it. The wildlife was starting to clear out. And when the animals left... humans would be wise to follow.

He had walked into the tunnels in a foul mood, though. The dirt and shit, along with who he was about to see, were only making it worse. He scratched at his face and ended up with dirt under his nails. Elysia had gotten into his head alright. Spitting out words about their relationship in that tavern he hadn't wanted to hear, trying to taint the only good memories he had over the last few years.

He'd known their relationship hadn't been perfect, but for him it had been his only reprieve. She wanted to write them off as surface and sex, but it had sprung from friendship, and that part of them had never died. It'd just been suffocated and neglected by the weight of their secrets and duties. Now, she couldn't even stomach the idea of him in her life. He'd seen the hesitation on her face when he'd said they could work together.

He swatted at an insect. He wouldn't want to be his friend either. But in some ways, as long as Elysia loved him, then it was like the better, younger part of him was still alive. Like there was still hope he could get back to himself.

But she didn't love him anymore, and he should know better than to think he could ever go back.

Topp turned a corner. *In another life...*in another life, it would have been them. Him working with animals. Her slung over his shoulder, screaming like a lunatic as he carried her off to their favorite spot in the Lovestone Woods. She could have been a journalist. Put her godsdamned nosiness to good use.

She was a pain in his ass. The best friend he'd ever had. And she was proving to be a nightmare to get over.

Dim lights wavered in the air, drawing his eye.

"I might be an asshole, but at least I'm trying," he muttered to himself.

A dry voice responded from much closer than he had expected. "And all these years I thought you had no idea."

For fuck's sake. Topp shook off the temptation to pick Rollie up by his shirt and throw him into the nearest wall. Might take the damn place down if he did.

"Rollickus." The name came out more growl than greeting.

"Crown squinch." Turning away, Rollie strode off into the soft flickering candlelight. He didn't bother to look back as he spoke. "Why are you here, and how do I get you to leave?"

Topp prowled close behind. "You know this place isn't long from collapsing, right? All the animals are gone."

"Of course, I know." Haughty as ever, Rollie's nose might as well have been in the air.

Topp's teeth ground together. He was trying to be *nice*. Fixing his voice, he tried again. "I've got a proposition for you."

"No."

Sighing, he ran a hand through his hair, grimacing as dirt clouded into the air. "You haven't even heard what I've got to say."

"Once a squinch, always a squinch."

Topp's nostrils flared as he lost the battle with his temper. "Rollie, do you want to die down here in the fucking tunnels like some kind of vermin, or do you want to help me warn as many rulers as I can about my father?"

With white hair and pale skin, Rollie looked ghostlike in the dim light. "I know this might be too complicated for your tiny royal brain, but how is *warning* people that a deranged ruler is going to tear out their magic and ravage their lands going to do any good? Doesn't really stop it from happening."

Topp decided right then that Rollickus Timmons was the human equivalent of a sliver in your asshole. And considering that Elysia was no longer his girlfriend, he wasn't sure he had any reason not to throttle the infuriating and precocious man.

His tone was chilling. "Do you have a *better* suggestion? Should I let them be completely blindsided then?"

Rollie marched into his lair. "Yes."

"Yes, what?" There were stacks of books everywhere, like he had pillaged a library.

"Yes, I have a better plan than that." His tone made it sound obvious.

Topp shoved his hands into his pockets lest they got any ideas. Like squeezing Rollie until his eyes and tongue popped out.

"And that would be..." he drawled, pushing his irritation down.

Rollie gave him a hard look and spoke slowly as if to a child. "Tell the rulers if it makes you feel better, but they're not the ones you need to speak with."

"And who would you speak with?" he pressed, curiosity overriding his annoyance. Rollie was the smartest bastard he knew, and he'd known it'd be easy enough to provoke him into laying out a better plan. The key was not killing Rollie before the wisdom was imparted upon him.

"The ones who follow the paths of the undead gods."

Topp's heart skipped a beat, and his voice went low. *This* was why he had come here. "What makes you say that?"

Rollie slammed a thick worn-out book down onto the table between them. "Because if you want to get shit done, then you're going to need to make them notice."

Topp ran a finger beneath its title, *The Histories of the Undead Gods.* "Make the gods notice?" Skepticism rang through his words.

"How do you not know any of this? Did you not learn anything living in other kingdoms?"

Topp's cheeks heated. "I learned plenty."

Scoffing, Rollie muttered to himself about *royal educations.* "I'll keep it simple, so you can understand."

The prince gestured for him to get on with it. It was like Rollie *wanted* to be punched.

"A long time ago, all the gods died because they got *bored*, and a lot of humans died because of the chaos. And before you ask, yes, gods can die... It's difficult and messy, but if they try hard enough, they can kill each other. Thus, the fates made new gods and introduced a drop of magic into our mortal lives and assigned each other roles."

"And how does this help us?" Topp kept his voice gruff while fighting to keep a grin down. He knew if he walked in here with a shit plan that Rollie wouldn't be able to help himself. Insufferable know-it-all.

Rollie shoved the book aside and flung down a map. Unfurling it, he stuck candles on its edges to hold the paper flat. He pointed at a handful of red circles. "Do you know what those are?"

Peering closer, Topp nodded. "Temples."

"Temple locations are not random. They're built over ancient founts of power. Liminal spaces where even mortals can knock on the ground and hold the ear of their god."

Topp folded his muscular arms. "Let me get this straight, you think the gods will devolve into petty drama and chaos if mortals lose magic."

"Correct—it might take a century or two for them to get bored enough, but it's inevitable."

"And you think if we somehow manage to inform the gods of what my father is doing, then they will..." Topp trailed off, his brows raised in question.

Rollie shoved the candles aside, allowing the map to curl back up with a snap. "How can someone who traveled half his life be so uncultured? It's not a question of *managing* to get the gods to hear us. It's possible and happens every day. The more pressing concern is how long it will take them to get off their asses and do something about it."

Exasperation overtook him. "You want to petition the gods like a religious fool. That's the entire plan?" Doubt was starting to creep in now.

Rollie scowled as shadowed light bounced off his glasses. "I've done the research, and I'm telling you it's possible to prey on their insecurities. Even gods are afraid of death. They won't want a repeat of history." A gleam entered Rollie's blue eyes. "Speaking of death... Do you have any way to contact Elysia? A direct connection to the god of death would be invaluable."

His jaw clamped shut. "No."

Rollie cast him a knowing stare. "But you've seen her?"

Topp gave him nothing more than a clipped nod.

"And you didn't think it would be helpful to secure continued communication with her? She's working with a *god*."

She's probably doing more than that. Topp stepped away from the table, leaning against a wall and immediately regretting it. "There are other gods. We don't need hers."

Rollie's lips flattened. "I'm not even going to respond to that."

"Oh, fuck off, Rollickus. Do you want to storm some temples with me or not?"

Excitement flashed across Rollie's face. "You're in?"

Gods save us all. "I'm in."

Rollie raced into a different room, yelling at the top of his lungs. "I'll get my maps and books. We leave in an hour."

Topp's face dropped into his hands. This was a mistake. He just knew it.

TOPP WASN'T PARTICULARLY high-class for a prince. He dreamt about a cabin in the woods. A sanctuary where he could take in more animals. Small creature comforts like his favorite imported coffee and a good fire.

But he had found a line, and that line was made of wretched, rotting bodies.

Piled all around and above him were bodies in various states of decomposition. The stench alone was quite possibly going to be what finally took him out of this world. Unlike him, shoved in amongst the corpses, Rollie sat up on the driving bench, chortling and yapping away with his friend, Mortie, the local dead dealer.

Mortie was a strange fellow. He took in the dead and cared for them.

Buried them. Burned them. Studied them.

Topp hadn't known that Rollie even knew how to chortle, but there was that sound, driving him toward his own premature death due to insanity. He closed his eyes, trying to block it all out, but with every bump that tossed him up and then back down onto the bodies, his eyes reflexively flew open, forcing him to endure this endless ride wide awake.

Eventually, the wheels stopped squeaking and feet hit the ground near the wagon with a thud. The stained linen cloth over all the bodies was thrown off, and the moon shone down on the prince. He blinked up at its fog-covered yellow light. It had been hours then, *hours* of riding with the dead.

Rollie grinned down at him, and Topp's blood pressure threatened to burst. "Let's get a move on, *Your Highness.* We've got a traveler to catch."

"Get. Them. Off. Me." If only he could murder someone with his eyes.

"Now, now. That's just disrespectful. That's someone's grandma losing her bowels over the top of you."

This isn't happening. But it was. Mortie strolled over, oblivious to their bickering, humming to himself as he gently moved the bodies off the prince, leaving him with suspiciously wet clothes and a strong desire to strip naked despite the damp cold.

Rollie hadn't bothered to wait for him, already weaving through the cemetery plots with obvious familiarity. Squelching after him with a grimace and a grumbled thanks to Mortie, Topp found Rollie waiting next to the cemetery's rear gate. Dead grass covered the land as far as the eye could see. He sometimes forgot that they were lucky to have the decaying Lovestone Woods in Relaclave. Much of Kava looked like this now—withered grasses and cracking trees.

"Do you really expect me to travel with you smelling like that?"

Topp bit down, refusing to give in to Rollie's obvious baiting. He would never understand how Elysia could stand this little prick of a man.

Rollie buttoned up his coat, still grinning as if he knew it was only a matter of time before Topp exploded. A dark human-shaped shadow expanded, growing taller as it came around the side of a chalky mausoleum. Unlike the shadow, the human attached to it was incredibly small.

Wool cap shoved over thick corkscrew curls, and scarf wrapped halfway up her face, the woman was all eyes. Even with the scarf muffling her voice, no one could have missed her revulsion. "What in the realms is that smell?"

Rollie looked up at the moon and smiled. "I had no idea when I woke up this morning that today was going to be so utterly amazing. You know, I don't really like surprises. Or leaving my tunnels and studies, but somehow this does make it worth it." He motioned between them. "Topp, this is Lucy. She's one of the rebels who managed to escape with her life the night you fucked us all over. She'll be traveling us out of Kava."

Topp pretended that ignoring Rollie was getting easier. Ignoring him was just a muscle. It was going to burn before it got better. Or he would snap and kill him like a bug. One of the two. He turned to the new arrival, shoving his guilt down where they couldn't see it. "The smell would be me. Rollie thought our best means of escaping Relaclave without me being seen was...with Mortie." He hooked his thumb back at the older gentleman, who was now hard at work excavating new graves.

Appalled, her mouth turned down as she looked at Topp and the wet marks on his trousers. "Rollie, I told you I could meet you in the city."

"Ah, I wanted to chat with Mortie. It's good to get some air, you know?"

Topp glared at Rollie. "Is that right?" Glancing down at the small woman, he faltered. "Are you sure you're going to be able to travel us both?" He gestured at about the level of her height and looked at her apprehensively.

Both of her extremely small, mittened hands went to her hips. "Are you implying that I can't do my job because of my *stature*?"

Gods, he was tired. And apparently, he couldn't say anything right. "I only meant the pair of us might be heavy—I don't know how traveling works."

She softened slightly, but her voice retained a prickle. Turning to Rollie, she lifted her chin. "You were right. *Squinchy*."

He was giving up. He was going to take a vow of silence for the rest of this fucking trip.

She held out a mitten to each man and took hold with a surprisingly firm grasp. Narrowing her eyes, she stared them both down. "If either of you let go, it's not my fault where you end up."

Topp glanced between them. "Where *are* we going?"

Ignoring him, Lucy looked at Rollie with a pout. "You're sure I can't come along? I could help."

Rollie shook his head, not even noticing how the woman's gaze trailed over him. "You know you're needed here."

Her playfulness disappeared, but she still gave him one last reminder. "Can be back in an instant. Just send a signal."

And with that she winked, and they were dropped onto the warm sun-beaten steps of a temple in Sherod, a small seaside village in Aruza. Topp blinked at Lucy in shock—there weren't many travelers who could handle that great of a distance. She'd traveled with three people over not only the entire landmass of Kava, the mess of small kingdoms below it, but also the Flustran Sea to reach Aruza. Lucy disappeared with a little wave and a confident grin.

Topp stretched, enjoying the satisfying crack in his sternum as the sun sank into his skin for the first time in the gods knew how long. He'd never minded the lack of heat in Kava, but a little sunshine could fix a multitude of ailments. It was amazing more people didn't die of some wet, fungal disease with the ceaseless rain and perpetual damp.

He looked at Rollie's translucent skin and grinned. "Hope you like sunburn. And that girl was into you."

Rollie blinked and answered seriously. "How would I know? I've never been in the sun." He stopped, brow creasing. "Into me?"

Thrown for a moment, Topp paused. "That's not what I... You know what, fair enough. But you probably should find a hat at the very least and keep your long sleeves. And yes, she's interested in you."

Rollie nodded, staring at his hand like it might become red before his eyes before turning abruptly back to Topp. "How do you know that? She didn't say anything."

He stared out at the blue sky with one hand shading his eyes, smiling at the sight. "The way she looked at you. Was obvious."

Rollie reared back, his voice vaguely uncertain. "You couldn't possibly know that."

Topp sighed, dropping his hand and looking at him. "You're gonna have to trust me on this one."

Based on the intense expression on Rollie's face, the prince had finally found one thing he was smarter at than the genius beside him. He pointed up at the temple. "So, we're starting with the original temple of pleasure then? That's one way to ease a heartbreak," he muttered with his focus drifting over to the temple's entrance.

Rollie's gaze snapped to him. "She finally dumped you? Took her long enough."

Topp let out a long, slow breath, refusing to look at his new travel companion. "Nice, Rollickus, thanks for the tender care. And no—actually I don't know." Now that he thought about it, he wasn't really sure when they had officially ended things. The night on the beach? In Bellia? It didn't matter either way.

"That doesn't make sense."

Topp stripped out of his heavy coat, folding it over his arm. "No shit."

"You couldn't possibly have been the one to end it."

He began to walk up the sand-covered steps. "Unlike you, she did actually like me, you know. Lys and I had a lot of fun before it all went to shit."

Rollie looked at him as they heaved themselves up the large steps. Sun beating down, he squinted at the prince, shaking his head. "She fell for the carefree, responsibility-avoiding prince who was never going to come near her secrets and escaped with her to the woods. You fell for the compliant girl who was happy to keep her distance and never asked for more." He wiped sweat off his pink forehead. "But Elysia isn't compliant, she'll lie to your face and do what she needs to do behind your back without even blinking. And you're not carefree, you're bitter and angry and blinded by ambition. Relaclave carved you down to your truths."

Topp let out a rough laugh in the back of his throat, giving Rollie a considering glance. "But you couldn't tell that girl liked you?"

Rollie shot him a look. "Not the same."

His thighs strained as he took another step. Oddly enough, something about the honesty of Rollie's comments comforted him. If only because it made him realize it would always be more complex than that. He might have liked her sweet, compliant court mask, but he had loved seeing the devious wheels of her mind spin. It was only when their ambitions and secrets had clashed that everything came apart.

The ultimate truth, the one his mind wanted to avoid, was that it didn't matter. He'd wrecked their lives without blinking and left the woman he'd loved to die. He knew exactly what kind of man that made him, and it wasn't good.

Hot air burned his lungs. It was a game of kings, gods, and fate now. The only kind of person he needed to be was one who stayed alive long enough to save his kingdom and avenge his family.

Grunting, he yanked Rollie up another step before the man teetered backward and broke his neck. "Enough feelings. Pick up your fucking feet before you fall to your death."

Red-faced Rollie nodded, sweat dripping down his temples as he stood, pinching his side. Topp's expression flattened. He should have known Rollie was going to hold him up. He never even came above ground, for the gods' sake.

A sweet jasmine breeze floated past, and Rollie swung his head, sniffing the air. "I normally hate perfume, but that smells amazing."

Topp's instincts kicked in, his head swiveling as well. The scent smelled *unnaturally* good. Lesson number one of nature—the most beautiful things were often the deadliest.

The thought had barely passed through his mind when his muscles locked, and his knees hit the hard steps. Collapsing, his head cracked against the sandstone steps. His green eyes attempted to search for Rollie, but neither of them were able to move.

CHAPTER 21

TOPP STIRRED, coming to slowly with his face smooshed against cold white tiles.

"Now, now, Prince, couldn't have you causing a scene on our Lady's steps."

The woman's voice swirled around him, sensual and familiar. Gods, he knew that voice. If his brain could just stop swimming, he could place it. Topp attempted to twist, hoping to confirm his suspicions, but his muscles ignored him, still largely paralyzed.

A small throaty laugh taunted him. "My Lady and I simply have a few questions for you, Your Highness, and then you'll be on your way. I assure you, you're as safe as ever."

Topp had been stripped down to his undershirt and shorts and tied up like a pig that wasn't going to make it through the day. *Safe as ever, my ass.* Whoever had tied him up like this surely fucking wasn't.

The prince mirrored his captress, his low voice rumbling right back at her. "And whom do I have the pleasure of speaking with?" He strained his neck, still trying to see her, but he couldn't so much as lift his skull. From what he could see on the floor, he was in a spa dressing room. A row of single benches sat between tall, stacked cubbies where people had shoved shoes and clothes.

Clean robes were neatly folded and waiting to be used while woven straw bins housed dirtied towels. Refreshing eucalyptus and lemon permeated the thick moisture-laden air, making him believe there was a hot spring or sauna nearby.

A soft clicking of heels brought the woman to his side. Silky fabric swished near his nose as she crouched down, her full heart-shaped face and curves swallowing his vision.

Topp flopped back, giving up on moving with an unimpressed sigh. First, he got shoved in a wagon full of dead people, and now he had to deal with this conniving, altruistic bitch. His green eyes stared at hers, his tone derisive. "Saved your girlfriend's life a few days ago, which means you owe me, *again*. Funny how that keeps happening."

A small hand snapped out, hoisting Topp up with surprising strength. He was looking straight into the face of Relaclave's very own Doorman.

He smiled amicably now. "To be fair, Elysia saved her life first because we all know Beatriz is an impulsive, money-hungry idiot, but *then* I helped save both of their lives. Still counts, right?"

The Doorman's eyes narrowed, her delicate but wide nostrils flaring, clearly torn between kicking him while he couldn't move and demanding to know what he was talking about. Face smoothing, her painted mouth set into a determined line. "Tell me why you're here. My Lady does not cavort with the sons of other gods."

Annoyance crept into Topp's voice. "Because I have *any* idea what you're talking about." An uncomfortable pins and needles sensation flooded his limbs as the paralysis slowly dissipated. Glancing around, he questioned her roughly. "Where's Rollickus? I know he says things, but he doesn't mean to—you can't hurt him. Elysia would murder us both."

The Doorman released her grip on the prince's shirt, striding away and settling onto the smooth light-toned wooden bench like it was a throne. "Rollickus is perfectly fine. And you know exactly what I mean, Topp Blatz. You don't belong to this house."

Understanding dawned. "I'm the heir of *Kava*, which means regardless of where my shred of magic came from—I don't belong to any house or religion."

The Doorman's gaze held a hint of laughter as if his objections were cute like a child's. "You know that's not how it works."

Able to sit up, the prince awkwardly pulled at the ropes cutting into his ankles until they unraveled, coiling in a heap on the floor. Biting at the bindings on his wrists, he spoke around a mouthful of rope. "I don't care how it works. I've taken no vows, completed no rites. Until then, I belong to no god or house."

The Doorman stood, sweeping her silk magenta skirt out like a fan, golden wrist bangles chiming. "Not all of us can afford such naivete. You'll see."

A short man with black hair and a white linen uniform walked in and shot Topp a dirty look before speaking furtively into the Doorman's ear. She nodded and held out a hand to the now standing prince. "Come. Rollickus is ready, and my Lady shall have her answers."

Topp complied, knowing it was the fastest route to achieving his own ends. He'd wondered if she was religious. It seemed like every time he went to the House he'd noticed a new painting or icon that had reminded him of the goddess of pleasure. Hadn't ever considered she was a *priestess* in the original temple of Aruza though. *What a busy, busy woman.* Incredible she'd never been caught.

Rubbing his wrists, he took his time following the Doorman, his feet striking against the cool tiles. She strolled ahead, leading them out into a room so humid his skin immediately perspired, tiny droplets bursting along his forehead. Lush greenery and bright tropical flowers surrounded the in-ground hot spring as steam rolled off it into the air.

Sun drenched the room, shining in through the glass roof that peaked above them, and sitting at the water's edge was a shirtless Rollie. Clean and fresh in a pair of loose linen trousers rolled up above his ankles, his feet dangled into the water. He popped a grape into his mouth, almost choking when he noticed Topp. Unlike Rollie, who had apparently been given the guest of honor treatment, Topp was still in his underclothes, smelling like the dead with rope burns around his extremities.

Hacking as he swallowed, Rollie continued methodically pulling grapes off the vine and tossing them into his mouth. "How'd you piss her off already?"

The Doorman smiled, relaxing onto one of the beige cushioned lounge chairs. She gestured elegantly to Rollickus. "See? Perfectly fine. Now tell me why you're here and we'll see if it meets my Lady's price."

Rollie paused with a grape halfway to his mouth. Indignation increased his volume. "You know exactly why we're here, *Lily*. And you want a price?" He jerked to standing, knocking half his grapes into the water. "I knew we should've started with the temple of ration and reason."

The Doorman looked scandalized. Topp hadn't even known her name till now. Tilting his head at her with an easy grin, he pretended to dust off his hands. "You heard the man. Looks like we're off."

Rollie was already shoving his blonde head through his new lightweight long-sleeve shirt, grumbling about where his books and maps were. "They better not be *wet*," he groused, hair erratic and glasses askew.

The Doorman recomposed herself and swung her high-heeled sandals to the slippery floor. Crossing her legs, she exposed a slit of freshly sun-kissed skin. "It's true then? Your father intends to eradicate magic as far as he can?"

Topp leaned against the wall near the archway they had entered through and studied her, positive she already knew what Garrison was doing. "Have you not been in Kava?"

"In and out. I oversee Kava's temple—the House as you know it—but lately, I have been needed here at home."

He snorted, shaking his head. "I knew there was magic involved in the House."

The Doorman smiled lazily, accepting a beverage from a server. "Kava and its residents lost their magic. My god did not. She simply...gave us a little boost. Not much given the restraints and how wicked the fates can be when spurned, but even a little goes a long way somewhere like Kava."

He nodded, thinking of how Elysia had responded to the House. While he didn't fully understand her magic, it made sense that she'd been unable to resist the thrall of a house soaked in a god's power.

Rollie marched back in with his books shoved into a lumpy drawstring bag slung onto his back, rolled-up maps poking out the top. He nearly slipped on the wet floor, but the Doorman barely spared him a glance. "Sit down, Rollie, this conversation is finished when I say it is."

Amused, Topp walked over to the hot spring, stripping off his shirt and slowly submerging himself into its waters. Like he was going to turn down the chance to bathe in a heated indoor spring after the day he'd had. *Not fucking likely.*

The Doorman watched him indifferently. "So, you plan to visit the temples and what? Petition the gods you don't believe in?"

Rollie, who had resumed his position by the water, twitched in irritation. "No, we want *you* to petition your Lady. Who knows how long it will take Elysia to find the talisman for the god of the dead. We need to involve the other gods—make them realize how easily history could repeat itself, make them *want* to get involved."

Her thumb rubbed over flawless skin. "Yes... The death voyage could take years, and Garrison could wreck the world by then."

Topp flung his head back, shaking water and wet hair out of his face. "Did you just say *years*?"

The Doorman tucked her smooth black hair behind her ear. "Oh, yes. Based on our records, it all depends on the initiate. The fates can be so fickle about these things..."

Rollie's shoulders dropped, his face going bleak. "We're

doomed. Elysia is going to *hate* not being in control. She'll get so pissed that she'll go after the fates instead of working with them."

Neither the prince nor the Doorman disagreed. Elysia had spent her whole life under someone else's thumb. She wasn't going to be amenable to someone new holding power over her even if they were the ones who crafted fate itself. Topp scrubbed at his body with the hot water, ridding himself of the stench of death. Whatever the death voyage entailed, she'd likely try to circumvent it to get the job done faster.

The Doorman opened her mouth to speak when the hot spring roiled to life, churning its waters slowly at first but then picking up speed. Alarmed, Topp dove for the water's edge, hauling himself out before he could be dragged into the current. Water boiling now, the Doorman lowered herself onto one knee, hissing at them. "Make no promises and whatever you do, do *not* look her in the eye."

Head ducked, he fought the insane urge to look. A goddess was about to emerge out of the water's depths, and he was going to miss it. His neck ached with how hard he drilled his gaze to the floor.

Wet feet slapped closer, and Topp's pulse grew wild.

Water droplets hit against his bare back with a sizzle. Muscles bunching, he remained bowed even as rose and jasmine stirred him to move. Long fingers with well-kept short nails trailed over his cheek. A luxurious wave of sensual power drowned him, turning his skin sensitive and blood hot. It was all he could do to bite back a groan. The fingers gripped his hair, forcing his head to turn.

Gaze on the soft stomach of a goddess, he exhaled into her grasp. The goddess of pleasure gleamed in the natural light. Waist length rippling black-brown hair and dark eyes, her naked golden skin shone as if there were specks of literal gold beneath its surface.

"You are not mine." Her gaze shifted to Rollie. "And neither is he."

The Doorman kept her eyes low and her voice a soothing caress. "They say they have news of the death voyage. That the king of Kava may eradicate magic before it can be completed."

A myriad of colors flashed within the goddess's eyes, and what Topp saw in her temper chilled him. Beyond the shining allure of her beauty was a core of ice that no touch could possibly thaw.

"He wishes to play games with my youngest brother, the baby of our family? To steal the magic we have generously bestowed upon the mortal children?" Her stunning face hardened protectively, but Topp could scent the fear beneath her bluster.

Keeping his head down, he stole a glance at the Doorman, hoping she would capitalize on the goddess's evident concern. His gut soured when Rollie spoke around a mouthful of grape, his voice flat.

"Your *little brother* is the one who made a deal that gave the king the power to destroy magic." Rollie popped another grape and the Doorman paled. The prince had grown up with Rollickus. He knew that Rollie despised hierarchy. It was one of the few things Topp had always liked about Rollie, but something told him the dripping wet, naked goddess might not understand or appreciate Rollie's disregard for title and stature.

"His only plan for cleaning up the mess he made is through Elysia. What happens when she finds the talisman? Doesn't sound like he even knows."

Blatantly ignoring every one of the Doorman's stipulations, Rollie made hard eye contact with her now. "The fates seem to care more about her jumping through their hoops than the situation up here. And has anyone considered she might purposely fail? Like, have you met her? She doesn't enjoy being told what to do. We need another plan. A fail-safe."

Topp's fingertips brushed the floor as he readied himself to launch between a man who wasn't even his friend and a goddess. This kingdom-saving excursion was going to be over before it began because Rollie couldn't keep his fucking mouth shut.

But to his surprise, the goddess merely appraised Rollie with new interest. She flipped her long, thick hair behind her shoulder. "You will work for me when order is restored," she purred, one finger tipping beneath Rollie's chin.

Rollie set down the grapes, finally looking alarmed. "Pleasure isn't—no, no thank you." His already sunburnt skin turned red.

The goddess smiled like sunlight hitting ice—sharp and blinding. "It is invaluable to have devotees who are immune to the many charms of my House. *And* it will anger my dear sibling."

Squeamish, but curious, Rollie looked her over as if she really were an employer for him to evaluate. Topp had to shake his head. Who knew if Rollickus had ever even been with anyone, and here he was judging the *goddess of pleasure* like he had any right.

Still blushing, he questioned her. "And what do you propose for our current problem?"

The goddess offered Rollie her arm. "Let's walk, my pale little dove. I'm sure we can find an answer."

Brows in his hairline, Topp finally unfurled his large frame as they exited the hot spring room arm in arm.

"Did that just happen?" His voice sounded unnaturally high to his own ears.

The Doorman collapsed to the floor, moaning. "I think I just aged twenty years—all the plants in here used to be mortals."

CHAPTER 22

"TELL ME, what good does it do to hate the role you have been given?"

Sylvia Reyez spoke like a philosopher rather than the head of a sprawling criminal empire. Elysia slowed upon hearing the poignant question, coming to stand beside Sylvia. Feet covered in ointment and wrapped in bandages, it had been no small feat to shove them into the leather boots she now wore. Every step made her want to break down and ask if they had a healer, but she hadn't decided if she could trust her new *family* with something like that. Better to wait until she was back in the Deathlands and Aidan could force Maya to be of assistance.

Clasping the railing, both she and Sylvia looked out at the celebration that was well underway in the forest-protected back-yard. Glowing orbs decorated the looming line of pines, and flags with the family crest were hoisted into the air, snapping in the wind. Family members milled about, happy for the excuse to eat and drink.

She'd been relieved that no one seemed too fussed about whether she participated or not even if the all-day affair was theo-retically in her honor. At least until Emmellin had pounded on her door, shoved her into the bath, and threatened to drag her out naked if she wasn't ready in fifteen minutes.

So, now she was here. With Sylvia Reyez philosophizing next to her like a damn monk. Elysia's gaze slid to her before slowly returning to the ecstatic children racing around in the freezing cold, up to their knees in snow with sticks that flung sparks out into the air. She almost smiled at their shrieks.

"And what role would that be?" she asked lightly, going back to Sylvia's initial question. She could play along. *Maybe.*

Unamused and uninterested in feigned confusion, Sylvia's tone was iron. "Answer me—what good does it do to hate the role you have been given?"

Like mother, like son.

"No one likes having their choices taken away," Elysia answered tonelessly, wishing she could escape to where the food was.

"Then make a different choice." Shrewd hazel eyes turned on her, expecting her to bend, to comply.

Annoyance stoked somewhere deep inside her that had nothing to do with Sylvia Reyez and everything to do with her past. She gripped the wooden banister tighter. "There *isn't* a different choice. I either complete the death voyage and become even further bound to your god or destroy any chance at a future for our kingdoms, and as you can see, I am *here* and doing my job." Why was she being lectured again right now? She shifted on her aching feet, the smell of something sweet and spicy calling to her.

Sylvia scoffed, blocking Elysia from passing her on the stairs. "It is the height of hubris to not see what is in front of you simply because you did not choose it."

Elysia bit down on the inside of her cheeks, willing herself not to insult the matriarch of the Reyez family. "I'm here, aren't I? Completed my first instructions from the fates."

The reprimand on her face was eerily familiar to the one Gage often wore. Apparently, it was a family skill to be able to make someone feel two inches tall without saying a word. "Yes, you cut the princeling loose. Good riddance. That's not the same as claiming your divine role."

She poked Elysia in the chest, her fingers tapping against Elysia's sternum hard enough that she swatted at the offending hand. "There's a force right here. And you're wasting it. Lamenting, pretending you don't know, all the things people do instead of seeing and acting on the truth. Forget what you thought you knew and embrace what you know *now*."

Frustration loosened Elysia's tongue. "And what is it I'm supposed to know? That this is all a load of shit, and I'm stuck in the middle of it? If you have any real advice, I'll take it, but until then—" Her voice cut off as her eyes landed on a muscular, lithe body she'd recognize anywhere.

Flying past Sylvia, a heady rush of relief swept Elysia down the stairs. Her painful feet were forgotten as she threw herself off the last step into the open arms of the only Reyez who was truly family to her. "*Gage!*"

Arms wrapped around his neck, she clung on hard. She tried to release her tight hold when embarrassment hit, but he held her there, perfectly comfortable and at ease. His woodsy scent covered her as she relaxed, his strong hands squeezing her. Gently, he lowered her to the ground, holding her away from him so he could look at her. "Well done, kid."

Elysia failed to hide the smile breaking through. The warmth of his pride was a drug, and she couldn't get enough. She wavered, her hands sliding to hold his wrists. "I thought I failed you. There were all these shifters, and I—I'm useless here, Gage. My magic isn't made for fighting."

The skin near his eyes crinkled, and he slung an arm around her shoulders, steering her out the sliding glass door and away from his mother to the deck. Leading her over to a split log bench, he grabbed a blanket out of an ottoman and tossed it on her lap. Coming back over with two steaming mugs of mulled wine, he lowered himself onto the bench, staring at the yard and forest that had once been his home.

"That's the point of our initiations. To see how someone responds when their back is against the wall, and all their normal moves don't work. Testing whatever might be a weakness or danger to the family."

Elysia's head turned slowly, her eyes flashing. "Did you *know* she was going to put them in danger?"

Gage's full lips stretched, showing off his beautiful smile as he shook his head. "I wasn't allowed to participate. Something about being biased."

Elysia relaxed slightly, but kept her eyes narrowed on him. "It was fucked up. Your family is crazy, and coming from me, that's saying something."

He took a sip of the steaming wine. "Tell me about it."

She huffed. "Your mother was just spewing nonsense at me about embracing my *divine* role. What does that even *mean*? She basically told me to quit whining and throw myself at the death voyage. Or maybe Aidan. I'm not sure." Elysia took a gulp of her wine and hissed as her tongue burned.

"Ah, the 'if you're a warrior be a warrior, if you're a scholar be a scholar' talk."

Brow lifting, she looked back at him in question.

Gage stretched his legs out and threw a bare arm around the back of the bench, seemingly unbothered by the cold. "She gave me that talk a million times. It might come as a surprise to you, but I wasn't exactly excited to be shipped off to a magicless kingdom to watch over a little kid when I was the heir to all this."

Elysia choked, red wine spraying out into the frosty air. Wiping her face, she looked at him in shock. "No."

His mouth quirked, and he leaned in closer, squeezing her thigh. "Yes."

"But I thought you were there to establish a foothold in Kava." She set her mug aside, ready to demand answers.

He lifted a shoulder, his short-sleeved undershirt puckering against his upper arm. "I mean, that kept me busy and was good experience, learning to build from the ground up rather than relying on what my mother built here, but no. I was sent to watch over you."

Astonishment rocked her. Emmellin had made a vague comment about Gage being supposed to keep an eye on her, but with everything going on it hadn't truly registered. Before she could make any further assumptions, Gage stood and leaned against the railing of the deck so he could face her. "One of our girls is a seer. She had visions of you for a year straight. Eventually, she had one of you and me. All we knew was that you would be important to our House. After conferring with the priestesses at the Bone Temple, it was decided the family needed to keep you safe. That *I* needed to keep you safe."

Elysia was reeling. "You were family to me," she whispered.

Gage clasped a rough hand on her chilled cheek, already knowing where she was heading. "Don't."

"But—" Wet flakes of snow caught in her eyelashes and children screamed in the background.

"No, you know how I care for you. I left my family, my world, the magic that was a part of me—and I poured all of that into you as much as you let me."

Elysia swallowed hard, her own hand reaching up to touch his. "Thank you."

Gage turned their hands, kissing her palm. "It only took most of your life to get you to warm up to me."

Snorting, she pulled his toasty hand out in front of her to inspect it. "What kind of magic *do* you have?"

"Ah, little of this, a little of that. My parents come from different backgrounds."

She stared at him expectantly, but when he didn't answer her magic slid out playfully.

He danced back as if that could stop her. "Hey, I didn't teach you to be a cheater!"

Laughing, she pulled it back in. "Actually, you did."

Ripping his shirt overhead and throwing it aside, Elysia blinked. "It's freezing, what in the realms are you—" The rest of his clothes hit the deck. "Oh my gods, why does this keep happening?"

Gage paused, unabashedly naked. "Who else took off their clothes?"

Hand over her eyes, she hissed at him. "Does it matter! What are you doing!"

There was a strange groan, and when she dared peek out again, a large cat was butting its head against her.

"You're a *kitty*!" Elysia's delight stretched across her face as she smoothed her hands over the lush fur of the beautiful creature in front of her. As tall as her chest, his fur was a blend of creams and grays with darker spots throughout, perfect for blending into winter foliage. Reaching up to his ears, she marveled at the tufts of fur sprouting off the tips. "No wonder Sir Larkspur hated you. He was probably ready to pee himself every time you walked by."

The big cat made a chuffing sound, then stepped back and within seconds was once again a naked, muscular man. Reaching for his clothing, Gage spoke in a pained voice. "I am *begging* you to never call me a kitty again."

"Ah, but you're such a pretty kitty."

Gage glared at her. "I could kill you faster than you could blink. You'd never hear me coming."

She gave him a look right back. "That's just rude."

"No, your fucking cat is rude. All eight pounds of him trying to mark all over my house because he could smell me but knew I couldn't do anything."

Elysia's lips pressed together as she tried not to laugh, but it was useless, her entire chest shaking as the laughter broke free. "Larky made you his bitch."

Sighing, Gage sank back onto the bench. "My mom was right, you know."

"About what?" Still chuckling, she didn't catch his tone shift.

"You really do need to consider what it would take for you to embrace this." He held up a hand before she could respond. "If only for your own sake, Lys. I'm not a stranger to sacrifice, and the first few years I was in Kava I was a miserable, pissed off son of a bitch, and I made it damn near everyone's problem. I caused fights, ended fights, took jobs I shouldn't have just to see what would happen."

Elysia picked her mug back up, afraid to ask her next question. "What changed?"

He looked at her softly. "I finally let myself care about the little kid who hadn't asked for shitty parents or to be stuck with illegal magic in Kava. I knew I wouldn't have been much without my family, and that keeping you safe meant more than just making sure you didn't end up dead."

A dull swath of emotion blanketed her, weighing her down and seeping into her eyes.

"Sometimes we find ourselves along the way, Lys. You just throw yourself in with everything you've got and when you finally look up, you might be surprised at the person you find."

"That makes more sense to me than whatever the fuck your mother said before," she sighed and scooted closer to him, knocking into his side. "Triz is sick."

He tensed against her. "Sick?"

She could feel his gaze, but she looked straight ahead, not wanting to see his reaction. "The soot."

A rumbly lamentation rolled in his chest. "I'm sorry, kid."

She stared out past the lazy snowfall to the trees. The small orb lights flickered as the snow hit them before brightening again. The effect was mesmerizing as they dimmed, then glowed against the dark. "I thought you might have known since you've been working with her."

He leaned back, guilt turning his mouth down. "About that."

She waved him off, still watching the snow drift and fall against the forest. "I don't have it in me to care. I had been hoping that being over the border—with magic working—that it might heal her, but she said she hasn't noticed any change. Her magic didn't change at all here in Bellia like everyone else's did. Guess the damage is done."

Gage made a noise of empathetic consideration, and she finally looked at him. "In the Deathlands, raw magic looks like soot. Do you think that's what it is? People's own magic unable to take form and killing them?"

Gage looked troubled as he pulled her in close. "I don't know, Lys, I don't know."

Together they watched the snow fall, neither saying a word.

THE PARTY WAS OVER.

The Reyezes drank, ate, and danced until the majority of them had passed out in varying states of disarray. Elysia tiptoed past, smirking at the sheer number of weapons strapped to the bodies sprawled out on the floor, furniture, and even the stairs.

Beatriz was face down on a couch, her silver hair fanning out. She had fearlessly danced and bantered with the Reyezes all evening, riding the high of the deal she'd struck with Sylvia.

Triz had never really met a stranger. It was only a matter of if she felt like being charming or biting that day. She'd been charming enough tonight that she was walking out a much wealthier and better-connected woman. Between Gage's recommendation and her throwing free party potions and elixirs at anyone who would try them, it'd been an easy sell.

The Kava black market was officially in Bellia and backed by the Reyez empire, for a cut, of course.

Her sister turning flush with excitement as she shook hands with Sylvia Reyez had stirred a million memories in Elysia. Sitting next to her father, watching him work—how uncanny his instinct for a deal or worthwhile product was. He'd never needed her for finessing a deal as much as for detecting bullshit.

She dodged another passed-out Reyez on the stairs, heading to her guest room. She didn't even know the obvious, common types of magic, much less the softer, more hidden kind, but she knew that somehow what Triz and her father did was more than mundane skill. And now she'd never know what her sister's magic could be—because of the fucking curse. *The curse that's all Aidan's fault.* She ignored the thought even though it whispered to her at the most inopportune times. That she was supposed to become immortal and stand beside the god who had ruined everything.

Elysia checked all her weapons at least three times. She was stalling. It was time to return to the death realm, and she couldn't stop fixating on what it meant to embrace her *divine role*. Her chest tightened as she re-examined all her actions since she'd landed broken and bleeding out in the death realm. She had gone to the Bone Temple, been civil to Aidan, and commenced with the death voyage. Whatever was so apparent to everyone else was clear as mud to her.

Sinking onto the vanity stool, she stared at her reflection only to look away. It wasn't that she was apathetic. Her kingdom was on the line. People were sick and dying. Beatriz could fall down dead any day. Magic was in danger of being lost.

She wanted to be *that* woman. The one who magnificently and heroically rose to the occasion. The one who easily let go and moved on, smiling as she went.

But she wasn't.

She was the angry woman. The woman who was tired of being exploited, unseen, and told what to do. The woman who wanted to take every order and shove it down the throat of the person giving it to her. She'd stabbed a king in the gut and yet she still wanted to burn. *What would be enough?*

She had no idea, but she knew the Reyezes were right. Somehow, someway she needed to find a spark within her empty chest. Because until this became *her journey* instead of a *death voyage* thrust upon her, she was going to be banging her head against a wall.

Remy's smooth voice slipped in through the crack in the door. "Can I come in?"

Seeing Elysia nod, she came in, shutting the door and easing herself onto the edge of the bed. Face drawn, she clasped her hands. "There's one more thing you should know before you go."

Elysia waited.

"On the chance you end up back in Kava, you ought to know that Daphne is with the Crown."

Remy cut Elysia off before she could reply. Disgust wrinkled her nose. "No, she's *with* the Crown. She knows everything, and she's with the king. It looks like Garrison is taking precautions for a new heir."

Revulsion smeared her face. "*That...* That is not possible." Daphne wanted money and an easy life, but that didn't mean she wanted a crazed king.

Remy quietly observed Elysia's internal struggle. "I couldn't believe it either... And I'm there witnessing it more days than not." She looked tired as she rested her chin in her hand. "You know she loved Topp."

Elysia's answer was whip-fast. "She did *not* love Topp. She loved the Crown that came with him. She hated his dirty hands and his animals and everything that actually made him good."

Remy met her eyes and let Elysia's own words hit their mark.

Shoulders sinking, she braced against the sting of betrayal even though it was closer to grief.

Message delivered, Remy stood to leave, but Elysia caught her hand. "You're the most brilliant person I know, use it to stay alive, won't you?"

Dark shadows smudged beneath Remy's eyes, but she let a little of her practiced saunter out as she made for the door. "You're looking at the woman running the money for Kava's underground. Does she look afraid to you?"

Both women laughed as the door shut, but the echo of it sounded an awful lot like *goodbye, I love you, I hope I see you.*

But as old friends often do, they kept the words inside. Both turning their faces in the directions of their own paths while holding the other somewhere safe where no one could touch.

Giving her weapons a final pat, Elysia departed from Bellia, using a small stream just beyond the forest line behind the Reyez house to travel back to the death realm with her mind heavy and unease curdling in her gut. It was one thing to have a heart to heart with Gage, the man who had raised her, it was another to bare her shortcomings to the god whose help she needed to save her kingdom. She landed in her room at the estate, and cleaned up for bed. She could only imagine how smug he would be about her crawling to him and needing help.

Snuggling in beneath the covers, she put it out of her mind. Talking to Aidan could wait until tomorrow. She needed rest and fortitude for that type of torture. Sleep claimed her with swiftness, her dreams blissfully blank throughout the night.

CHAPTER 23

Morning came entirely too soon, and with it the unappealing task of discussing her *divine role* with the god of the dead himself.

Elysia stood outside Aidan's closed office door. Hands gesticulating in the air, mouth moving silently, she froze when the door swung open. Dropping her hands to her sides, she cleared her throat awkwardly. "Hi."

Aidan dropped one shoulder, leaning against the doorframe with his arms crossed. Black shirt unbuttoned at the neck and vest completely undone, he looked overworked and perfectly rumpled.

"You've been standing outside my door for at least five minutes."

A hot flush spread from the apples of her cheeks to her hairline. "I wanted to talk to you."

"The floor is yours."

His face remained impassive, and Elysia's hand went to her neck, her mouth opening and closing like it was her first day speaking.

Aidan simply waited.

"I wanted to talk to you about something that has been brought to my attention." Internally, she winced. Per the usual, in her discomfort she ended up sounding stiff and formal, when really, she wanted to climb out of her skin.

His brow lifted like that wasn't what he had expected to hear. Stepping aside, he gestured for her to enter his office. She hurried past him, pacing on the rug in front of his desk. Hands in front of her stomach, she stopped and looked at him where he rested against the edge of his desk.

"I promise I've been trying. I took the Reyez mark. I had a terribly honest conversation with Topp in hopes of passing the fates' first instructions. I completed the initiation for the Reyezes. I *killed* a man for them! And all I keep hearing is how *obvious* it is to everyone else that I'm going through the motions." Her fingers gripped the chair in front of her until her knuckles turned white. "I will do whatever it is I need to do, but the fates haven't delivered any further instructions. It's like they're torturing me."

Slipping his hands into his pockets, Aidan's mouth turned up as he listened, nodding almost imperceptibly at her frustration. When she was quiet, he looked at her intently. "Are you wanting empathy or ideas? I can do either."

Elysia stopped, thrown off by his question and open face. She hunted for a microexpression, a tensing, *anything* that would indicate judgement, but she found none. Deflating ever so slightly, she leaned forward, elbows resting on top of the chair. "Both?"

"You're doing your best with an impossible task. Matters of the heart or spirit rarely cooperate with timelines no matter how much we try to force or cajole ourselves into feeling a certain way. But you did what you could with the prince—you laid it all out there, so it has a chance of healing rather than festering. And sometimes it appears we're *going through the motions* when really, we're too overwhelmed to feel anything at all. Numb is never just numb."

She'd been studiously staring at the pattern on the armchair when her head shot up at his final words. A sense of resonance spread like light within her as she nodded emphatically. She hadn't expected Aidan of all people to be the one to reflect exactly what was happening inside her.

The words for *thank you* were stuck and unwilling to come out, so instead she asked another question with a scratchy voice. "The fates are being quiet. What do we do?"

Pushing off the desk, with a smile that made her battered heart go weak, Aidan strode past her, snagging her by the wrist as he went. "We train."

DRESSED in loose pants and a soft long-sleeve shirt, Elysia bounced on her feet in the sparring room. Today it was quiet. There wasn't the swell of music or of two gods crashing against each other. There was only the nervous racing of her pulse and the soft patter of her feet against the black cushioned mat.

Aidan watched her bounce for a moment, appraising her with a short nod, and then began to unbutton his shirt. Her eyes went to how his fingers slowly and methodically undid each button, before darting to his face.

"What are you doing?" she asked sharply. She might be new to magical training, but she was positive it didn't require a striptease.

He shrugged out of the button-up shirt and tossed it to the side, pulling his undershirt free from his black fitted trousers and stretching his chest. A partial grin curled up his face as he released the stretch and rolled his shoulders out.

"You look wired, so I'm going to wear you out."

Her mouth dried. *Wear her out.* She was slow to answer, studying the smirk on his face and trying to decide if he knew what he was saying. No, this was a desert, and he was a cactus that looked like water.

"You want to spar?"

He nodded, taking a weighted step that had her moving back two. His grin widened as he paused. "What do you normally do when you feel like this?"

"Make Gage spar with me until I can't think, or run until my legs and brain give up." *Have sex with Topp until I pass out.* She heated—she probably didn't need to mention that one.

He tipped his head at her in reply and removed his belt. The metal buckle made a clank against the hardwood floor outside the mats.

Oh. He was giving her an outlet before they practiced using her magic. She reassessed him silently. "I told you before that I'll do my job—you don't need to baby me or whatever it is you're doing."

Aidan gave a short laugh. He didn't move an inch as his intense blue eyes scanned her from her long brown ponytail to her feet and back up again.

"Noticing your discomfort and addressing it is babying you?"

She folded her arms. "Feels like it." She itched to do exactly what he was offering—to spar and train until she couldn't breathe —but the way this man *noticed* everything was too unsettling. Her entire life had revolved around and counted on people not noticing.

Aidan nodded and walked loosely to the center of the mat. "Me paying attention feels unsafe." He looked up, his face clear of any mocking or condescension. "That I try to understand you." His low, rich tones cascaded over her, both alleviating and exacerbating the high pitch of anxiety strumming through her.

"It's unnecessary." Her gaze went to the door. She could just go for a run outside. She'd barely seen a quarter of the estate grounds.

"Elysia, I don't need you to trust me with your life right now. I just need you to spar with me and let a little steam off before you have a panic attack."

His matter-of-fact tone had her almost smiling. She *was* a little worked up. Taking a step closer to the center of the mat, she tightened her ponytail.

"Okay, let's go," she muttered.

Aidan didn't wait for more permission than that. He kicked

her feet into a better stance, and Elysia responded just like she would have if Gage had done so, moving into her fighting posture. Adjusting her arms, he looked her over and nodded at what he saw.

"Good," he murmured, stepping back, but catching her chin so she looked up at him. "How about this? You don't have to trust me. It's not a requirement or expectation. Just keep talking to me. Keep coming to me when things are good, when they're bad, all of it. Use me to win your freedom."

Something in her loosened at his words. The idea that she didn't *have* to trust him. She didn't *have* to suddenly be a healthy, well-functioning sort of person, when the truth was, she might never be. Going to his office and explaining what was going on had been difficult, but Gage's words were in her mind—maybe if she just kept taking steps, she'd wake up one day and be surprised at where she was and who she'd become.

Elysia nodded, and instead of making a big deal about it, Aidan simply settled back into his own stance before looking at her evenly. "For the record, I like your thorns. All the most beautiful flowers have them."

Stunned, warmth bloomed in her stomach, but she deflected. "Ready?"

He nodded and they began. His easy movements and ability to dodge every punch and kick reminded her once again of training with Gage. And even more so how he seemed to be studying her, taking notes on what she was doing all the while, never so much as catching the edge of a blow.

Muscles finally warm, she pretended to grow frustrated, making her movements appear tired, choppy, and ill-formed. It was juvenile, but as expected, Aidan relaxed, slowing his responses to hers. *His mistake.* Darting in, she landed a kick behind his knees, grinning as his legs buckled while her foot was already slamming into his back. He crashed face first down to the mat, and she dropped as fast as she could, ripping one arm behind his back and squishing his face to the floor.

Hot, sweet victory flooded through her as she dominated him. Breath heavy, she laughed openly only for Aidan to twist his head so he could look at her.

"Oh, you think that's funny, do you?"

Faster than she could blink, Aidan rolled, pinning his knees around her hips and gripping her wrists above her head. Leaning forward, the heat of him settled against her, and she damn near moaned at the sensations that shot through her.

Blue fiery eyes set on hers, and Aidan rolled his hips once more as he brought his face closer to hers. "Are you feeling better, Thorn, or do we need to go again?"

Flushed and sweaty, she squirmed, but his grip and knees only tightened, keeping her firmly pressed against both him and the mat. Eyes narrowed, she spat her reply.

"Again."

Releasing her, he smoothly pulled her to her feet and gave one sharp tug on her ponytail. "Good. Now, set your feet."

And then they went again and again and again. Hands grappling and bodies tumbling as they became acquainted with the touch and feel of one another. She wasn't sure how long it had been when she finally collapsed with her face falling against his chest and his body lax beneath her, both of them panting on the sticky mat. Breathing in his warm citrus and bergamot scent, she jerked back realizing she'd been collapsed on top of him a little too long, and awkwardly rolled away into a sitting position.

Leaning back on one arm with her legs out wide, she caught her breath with her brain blissfully quiet. It wouldn't last. Just like the expansive feeling in her chest would soon give way to tension, but for a little while the sweet exhaustion and satisfaction of running herself into the ground offered relief.

Glancing over at Aidan, she almost choked when he reached back and pulled his undershirt over his head. Skin dotted with sweat, he wiped at his face with the cotton shirt before noticing her frozen expression. Laughing, he chucked the shirt at her and grabbed her ankle, yanking her closer and pulling her foot into his lap.

Except then it was his expression freezing as all his laughter disappeared and a single finger tracked lightly over what she knew was a slew of hideous scars. Some raised, some flat. Purple and mottled pinkish red. The soles of her feet were not dainty or something that she wanted anyone to see.

Gaze even, she refused to let her voice waver. "They're old. Nothing to worry about."

All the warmth leached from his eyes, leaving them a cold glacier blue. The ice in his eyes flowed downward, turning him into a chiseled and frigid thing. His words were slow and purposefully drawn out. "Tell me what happened."

She shook her head, watching as a soot-like fog silently lazed out from the outline of his being, blending in with the black mats. "You're overreacting."

Embers melted the ice caps that were his eyes as blue fires roared back to life, and his thumb pushed into the arch of her foot, smoothly sliding against her strained muscles.

Eyes shuddering, she swallowed a sound of surprise. *Gods, that's amazing.* "I'm serious. They're old. Maya couldn't do anything about them." She had already asked when she showed up with frostbitten toes after Bellia, but given how long ago the original scars had happened, Maya couldn't help.

His thumb stroked again, finding the perfect rhythm and pressure. "Tell me. Just give me a name."

She relaxed even further, sinking back onto her elbows. "Or we could not talk, and you could just do that."

"Please tell me." A dangerous politeness infused his tone. His fingers wrapped around her ankle and gently lifted her foot to his mouth as he pressed his lips against the scars. Mouth still against her skin, he spoke again. "Elysia, tell me what happened, or I'll have to stop." His lips brushed over her ankle, barely touching as he lowered her leg, and resumed rubbing her foot.

Elysia could hear the smile in his voice but knew better than to think she'd won. Smooth light touches stroked up beneath her training pants against her calves until the touches turned to gentle kneading.

Groaning, she gave in. It wasn't like he could do anything from down here, anyway. "My father. He didn't like when I used my magic for my own purposes."

Aidan switched feet, silently allowing her to continue.

"He much preferred when I was gathering blackmail and gossip for *him* to use." She scoffed and adjusted her position so she could rest her leg more easily against the warmth of Aidan's lap.

"Why the feet?"

She opened her eyes now, looking at him as she answered. "Because in Kava I don't have any control. I fall into a trance sometimes when my magic takes over. The magic doesn't care—it just wants me to spin to its tune."

"He tortured you."

"He wanted the pain to remind me, to stop me from getting lost in it. But it doesn't work like that." Her voice went distant. "I could be bleeding out and I might still follow my magic. It's a fickle master."

Aidan stretched his hands up over her calves again, running his fingers up and down before sinking back into the overworked muscles. "Your magic is not your master. Kava is in a state of decay, and it's not your fault you couldn't stay coherent. Not everyone's magic functions like yours—I imagine it was akin to flooding your system, then shutting it off. Flood, dry, flood, dry. You were high and your body was desperate for its natural state, which is to always seek power."

Elysia considered this, her brow puckering when his fingers stopped. She wriggled her foot impatiently, and Aidan laughed, gently slapping his hand against her foot. "Greedy."

Fully blissed-out with her hands behind her head, she smiled up at the ceiling. "I've never had a foot rub before."

His hands paused before resuming their luxurious, almost

sedating strokes. His voice was rough when he broke their silence. "Are you feeling up to working with your magic?"

She propped herself back up, tugging her hair free from its ponytail. "What are we going to do?"

Aidan rested his hands on her bare feet, his mouth curving slightly. "You're going to practice one of your co-ruling duties."

Her eyebrows went up as she finally and begrudgingly pulled her feet back. "Which would be?"

Aidan stood and offered her a hand. "A skill I could never master."

CHAPTER 24

Rollie and Topp stood on the same steps they had days ago. This time Topp didn't smell like dead bodies, and they were both freshly washed and clothed courtesy of the Doorman's sharply tender care.

Rollie was fidgeting next to him, his fingers vibrating. Topp ignored him, resonating with his urge to move. Rollie was just like an easily stressed-out cat. He wanted to be inside, working on his projects, and now one of his projects had taken him out into the world, and it was all a bit much for the senses.

Running into the Doorman had thrown him. Conniving, law-breaking icon of Relaclave—she was a dangerous nuisance. The steady stream of favors between them over the years had grown out of control. Numerous times they'd refused to see each other, knowing it was never social nor an easy request. He'd consider calling her a friend if it wasn't for the fact that he was certain she'd beat him to death with his own crown if it ever came down to it. Never mind that he'd helped her smuggle her brother back to family in Aruza when his magic had grown uncontainable. And now she had Beatriz whispering in her ear. Beatriz, who had always hated him for the freedom he'd been granted as a man that she'd had to steal through scandal after scandal.

Maybe saving Beatriz's life would finally put him on the Doorman's good side for more than five minutes. She owed him for that, and he wouldn't forget.

Rollickus sat down on the sandstone steps, face scrunched in concentration. He tapped the step, skin already turning pink from the midday sun. "Porous. Just like I thought."

Topp held in his sigh. "Great, next time we'll bring masks. Is the traveler going to be here soon?" He wanted to get away from this temple before the Doorman or her goddess changed their minds and turned them into matching palm fronds.

The fact that the goddess had been willing to hear them out had been a feat. She hadn't agreed to do anything, but he considered it a success that they'd gotten her to pay attention at all.

Rollie stood up, brushing at the wrinkles on his lightweight trousers. "She'll be here, stop fussing."

"I'm not *fussing*."

"You sound fussy."

Rollie pointed at Lucinda, who was climbing up the steps now. "See." Much like last time, she only had eyes for Rollie and didn't seem to even notice the prince.

"Good morning, Lucy." Topp greeted her, attempting to be cordial, but she ignored him, her fingers skating over Rollie's wrist as she asked how things had gone.

"Holding grudges then," he muttered to himself since no one was going to answer him.

Rollie conferred with Lucy before nodding with vigor and telling Topp to *hold on to his pants* point two seconds before they were all yanked through space and spat out at the mouth of a new temple.

The temple of pleasure had been warm and dusty. Almost unassuming in its sandy earthiness until you realized your inhibitions had fled and your desires had begun to slink in time with the temple's tempestuous heart.

This temple *gleamed*.

It gleamed like fresh golden coins and the tears of the poor it didn't care about. White shiny walls with malachite spikes jutting out from the border of the temple ensured no one rested or took shelter in its shadow. Matching green tiles created a footpath to its entrance, and on either side of the path were golden statues planted into white sand that glinted in the sun.

Topp took one look at the statues and groaned. He fucking hated this place.

"Really? Did we have to go here next?" There was no point coming here at all, and if Rollie had thought to actually take anyone's opinion other than his own into account for once, then he would have told him that.

"Seemed most logical." Rollie waved to Lucy, who blew him a kiss, but his attention was already fixed on the intensely immaculate temple.

Lucinda disappeared and Topp had half a mind to ask her to take him with her.

"What's your issue with the god of the undead gods?"

Topp grimaced as some of the acolytes came into view. Their silk robes shimmered, gathered and tied off strategically with precious stones. "Have you ever met someone who worships this god?"

Rollie threw serious side-eye his way. "No. I never left Kava until this." The *obviously* was implied.

Topp scowled at the acolytes, ensuring they kept their distance.

"They're *insufferable.* They worship wealth and spend their days blustering on about how useless the other gods and temples are when the only reason they have so much money is because they demand it in exchange for petitions."

"So, what you're saying is that we can buy our way into an audience." With that, Rollie set off down the sparkling green-tiled path, heading straight for the acolytes. Topp grabbed Rollie's arm, stopping him in his tracks.

"I'm telling you it's a bad idea. Call Lucy back," he growled.

Rollie shrugged him off, annoyed and already decided. "You're a prince. This will be easy."

Topp fought the urge to shake him. He was the one who had traveled and been to these temples before. This was supposed to be a partnership, but it was seeming more and more like a one-man show. He grasped for patience he didn't have and tried to explain his point of view.

"Rollie, there is no god here. There's no one to petition or call upon. You have to trust me," he hissed after him, but it was too late. The acolytes had recognized him, their money-sniffing snoots twitching as they now watched him like sharks who had scented blood in the water.

"Prince Blatz, our god welcomes you. Were we aware of your visit?" The one speaking smelled like salty olives and alcohol twice baked in the sun. Fucking vile.

Topp's favorite and most familiar mask clinked right back into place as if it had never left. Bored. Rash. Expectant.

The Crown Prince.

"I didn't realize I had to send word to be received properly." Pleasantries didn't belong on a man like him. He gestured to his side. "This is my advisor, Rollickus."

Rollie pushed up his glasses, looking down his nose at the acolytes, and Topp smirked as they shrunk back unconsciously. The man had absolutely no idea what a natural he was, but Rollie's aloof countenance was perfection beside his rugged but quiet aggression.

Striding past them, he ignored their startled exclamations and cries for him to wait. His boots cracked against the ceramic tiles as he entered the temple, spraying bits of sand and dirt all over the pristine floors. He stood inside the foyer, not bothering to hide his irritation and distaste. Nose wrinkled and lips curled, he realized they'd managed to make it even more repulsive since the last time he was here. Golden fountains, golden statues, paintings of their god showered in wealth.

Idiots. Everyone knew the god of the dead and the goddess of pleasure were who to petition for wealth. The god of all gods didn't even exist. Not that'd he been convinced any of the gods existed until recently. But it was a testament to the temple's fear-mongering that they managed to swindle the people of the White Sands for so much money when no other region even acknowledged the existence of the god of the undead gods. Likely because it was a farce and this temple belonged to an old nature god no one paid attention to anymore.

The acolytes rushed in, the heavy gold-coated doors banging behind them. Topp barked out orders, demanding rooms and food for two. Breathless and red-faced, they stammered after him, assuring him they would find him suitable accommodations. Topp reached over casually, his knife plucking off the pearl holding together the nearest acolyte's robe. Bending over, he picked up the pearl and examined it. He smiled unpleasantly as he dropped it to the floor with a ping.

"We came for an audience with your god."

The acolyte clutched his robes to keep them from falling as his eyes blinked in stacks of coins. "Yes, yes, I will pass that on to our high priest."

Topp patted the man on the head, his voice rumbling. "Good. You do that."

They'd only been in their shining, marbled rooms for minutes when a knock came. Topp remained lounging in a white wicker chair near the balcony and nodded for Rollie to open the door. In strode a man with blue eyes and light sandy brown hair cut tight. A foreigner most likely then, given most of the people in the White Sands boasted perfect rich tans of medium to deep depths year-round along with dark hair and eyes. The man scanned him boldly before offering a practiced smile.

"Our humble temple is honored to host you, Prince Blatz. The god of the undead gods welcomes you to his home."

"I'm sure he does." His words hung in the air awkwardly as the priest quickly ascertained how this meeting was going to go.

Readjusting, the priest got to the point. "You wish to gain an audience with our god? Does this mean you follow the true path? We would be glad for you to become a member."

Topp's mouth almost lifted. *The true path. Membership.* Maybe he should be more cultured, more open. He'd spent time in so many kingdoms. Visited all the temples. Watched a goddess stalk naked and dripping wet past him only days ago. But in his heart, he was a Kavian—the gods were dead, and if they weren't then they must be real fucking assholes. All he heard when this little man spoke was the ting of coins and the ramblings of delusion.

He casually rested one elbow on the arm of the wicker chair. "You can guarantee an audience?" Skepticism flattened his tone.

The priest folded his hands at his jeweled waist. "I imagine that idea might be difficult for someone from a godsforsaken land like yours. You never learned how to hear the call of divinity in your ear." False, condescending empathy oozed from the priest's words.

Sonofabitch.

Topp smiled and glanced out the window before responding. "I don't need to hear a voice to know when someone's full of shit. I can do that all on my own."

The high priest pretended to be confused. "Why would I work to petition an audience for you when you hold such disregard for our practices? I couldn't in good conscience call in my god to be greeted by such sacrilegious sentiment."

Gods, this was why his father didn't force him to do the endless meetings. Inevitably, there always came a point where the bullshit was so thick that he cracked—and apparently, he wasn't supposed to call the bullshit, bullshit. That was offensive. People didn't like that. Too bad he didn't care. "You'll do it because I'll pay you."

The priest nodded and considered this. "There is a high price, indeed, to feel the presence of the god of gods."

Topp's voice became dry. "How else would you pay for your tasteless art?"

He kept his composure as he waited for the priest to reveal his price. The price didn't matter. Because whatever price they demanded was one he couldn't pay. It wasn't like he had access to the royal coffers—he'd left his own capital city in a wagon of corpses.

The priest adjusted his stance, his warm turquoise robes rustling with the movement. "Our house, as you can see, is not in need of funds."

Topp grew impatient. "So, name your price."

The priest finally dropped the polite veneer. "We want to know where the girl is. Your ex-girlfriend, betrothed? Wanted by the king of Kava and rumored to be courting death. So much mystery surrounds her, don't you think?"

Topp fought his beast, overcome with the desire to grab his axes or divest this toad of the air in his lungs. Externally, his mask never slipped. "If it's not her bounty or mine you're after, then what could you possibly want?"

"Your father is readying to move into Sagondia. When the time comes and he marches into the White Sands, we want a bargaining tool to keep him out of our temple. We decided she'd be easier to hold than someone like yourself." The priest sniffed as if Topp was a wild animal better left outside than in their unholy temple.

Sagondia. *Gods.* They really were running out of time. He expected his father to go after easier kingdoms, ones he could have ransacked without his foul powers, but Sagondia? Garrison would have to sail the Valvere Sea and navigate the dense, jungle-ridden mountains that swept most of the land. The roads weren't straight or even connected, and the majority of villages and cities weren't on maps because of their kingdom's intense paranoia around outsiders. Kava might have been a larger kingdom, but Sagondia was a military culture—every single child went through warfare and combat training no matter their economic status or eventual career goals. They grew up believing attacks could happen at any time and that it was their duty to preserve the land and their people. If it was true that the king planned to hit Sagondia first, then his father's goal was to eviscerate any and all hope within the less defense-oriented kingdoms. If Sagondia fell, then so could anyone.

Topp met the priest's eyes with steady ease. "I have no idea where she is, but trust me, you couldn't hold her if you found her. The woman's like an eel." And he meant that as a compliment.

The high priest's eyes darkened. "I suggest finding her if it's an audience you want." With that, he stalked out, robes flaring as the door slammed in anger.

Instantly, the air within the room began to pressurize until Rollie waved his arms and clapped his hands in front of Topp's face. "HEY. Don't you dare make thunder in here, you overgrown assmunch. Go outside if you want to do that."

The pressure vanished as Topp cracked a grin despite himself. "Did you just call me an *assmunch*?"

"I've called you worse," Rollie muttered. He eyed Topp suspiciously as if he might strike him with lightning for such a statement.

"You've been calling me names since we were kids. You told my girlfriend to break up with me repeatedly for years. Do you really think I'm going to lash out at you now?"

"Like I know what you're going to do. You almost just ruined our chances to assuage your masculine ego."

"My masculine ego?" He couldn't be serious. "That would have involved punching that twat in the face." *Which he hadn't.*

"Yes," Rollie shot back. "*Ohhh, they insulted my ex-girlfriend's honor. I must rage like an animal now.*"

"Are you done?"

"Are you done jeopardizing this mission?"

"Mission?" More amusement crept into Topp's voice.

"What else do you call this?" Rollie filled himself a glass of water. "I think we should bargain with them. Pretend we can get Elysia."

He disagreed. "They couldn't get us an audience with their

god even if they wanted to—look at this place. There's no god here. You'd be more likely to find the guy in Kava."

Rollie rested on a matching wicker chair and stared out the glass doors that led to the balcony. Dark green plants rustled in the breeze and a tiny lizard darted along the railing. "You might be right. What do you know about the original god—not the one they claim now?"

"He was a god of storms and beasts. Nature oriented. About as far from a god of wealth as you can get."

Rollickus raised his eyebrows and stared at Topp as if he was waiting.

"What?"

Rollie grunted in impatience. "Isn't it obvious?"

"I think you should operate under the assumption that what is obvious to you is generally *not obvious* to others."

Rollie's brow crinkled. "Interesting thought, but the goddess of pleasure stated that neither of us are her children, implying we belong to other houses. I think you could be one of the storm god's mortals."

Topp scoffed. "Should I run around calling out for my storm sky daddy? See if he answers?"

Rollie threw him a look and opened the glass patio doors wide to stand in the breeze. He kicked a dusty shoe at the shiny white walls. "Somewhere beneath all of this nonsense is the original temple, correct?"

He stepped past Rollie out onto the balcony. The smell of roasted meats and spices beckoned him to forget the temple and wander the streets in search of meat and fruit and sun. Maybe drink until his brain no longer knew how to rage or grieve, but only how to breathe and piss.

He leaned his hands against the balcony, forcing himself back to the conversation at hand. "That's what I was told. Not sure how much was demolished to build this monstrosity." He stared at a statue of what was presumably the god of the undead gods holding his own gilded cock. And people thought *he* was arrogant.

Rollie chewed his lip. "Just how destructive can your magic be?"

Topp's eyes slid to Rollie with a grin. "Are you asking me to desecrate a *temple*, Rollickus Timmons?"

Heat crept up Rollie's face, mixing with his sunburn, and he adjusted his glasses. "Turning in Elysia isn't an option, and I think it could work."

Topp had to agree. There wasn't a single bone in his body that believed the sleazy priests would be able to conjure a god even if they handed Elysia over tied up in ribbons and bows.

A smirk stretched across his face as he pushed off the balcony. He didn't care whether it worked or not. He was going to destroy this shithole. He pointed at Rollie. "Best advisor the Crown's ever had."

TOPP FINALLY HAD his sandwich of spiced roasted meats. Sauce dripped down his arm, and in between bites, he sipped on a cool rose mint tea. It was exactly what he had wanted.

At least it would have been, if he wasn't eating it with an arrow pointed at his chest. The man staring at him had a strange handheld contraption loaded with an arrow, and he had no doubt it would hurt like the underrealm if the man decided to shoot him. Rollie, oblivious, was arguing with the shopkeeper in the common tongue they had all learned as children of the Crown over the price of powders. Powders that Topp was afraid to ask about but would undoubtedly cause destruction when wielded by Timmons.

All in all, not the worst evening he'd had. He took another bite and smiled with his cheeks full of meat at the sweaty, portly man still holding him at arrowpoint. He swallowed.

"What's that called?" He gestured at the device currently dipping a little too low for his comfort.

The man just grunted.

Right. He glanced at Rollie, who was now fixing the shopkeeper with the famous Rollickus Timmons *you're dumber than shit* stare while the man babbled about price margins and something about illegal substances.

Rollie marched over, knocking the man's arrow device out of the way as he grabbed Topp and pulled him aside with his gaze hard on the shopkeeper. "How good are you at stealing?"

Topp looked at him. The man was dead serious. Wanted him to swipe the gods only knew what while the shopkeeper and grunting enforcer were close enough to smell their breath. How were smart people so dumb?

"Not *that* good."

Rollie heaved a sigh through his nose. "Sorry about this."

Topp's brow creased, but Rollie's pale hands were already launching him with unexpected strength straight into the enforcer. Their large frames tangled, arms grasping for balance and pulling down wooden shelving as they crashed. Spices and herbs poofed into a nose-tickling aromatic cloud, both men now sneezing as they rolled.

Rollickus was busy shoving goods into a cloth crossbody bag and yelling for Topp to get off his ass, but the enforcer had already wrapped a sweaty forearm around his neck, squeezing in hopes of cutting off his air. He was going to kill Rollie. Slamming his head backward, he broke the man's nose and sent his elbow at a sharp, downward angle, driving into the man's groin. There was a strange *pew* sound and rush of air, and then Topp let loose the roar of a wounded animal.

The bastard had fired that child-sized weapon straight into his ass from no more than a hair away. He shook off the enforcer and clambered to his feet, stomping on the weapon before ripping the arrow out of his ass and throwing it at the man's face.

Chest heaving and blood pouring out his ass, Topp glared at

Rollie standing over the shopkeeper, who now had a smattering of a dark purple powder smeared on his face. Rollie shrugged. "He'll be okay in an hour or two."

Topp made a restrained noise and practically flung Rollie outside. They hustled through the masses of people, darting in and out of perfume- and sweat-scented bodies, squinting in the light of the lowering sun. Several streets away, they ducked under a colorful awning in front of a fruit stand with their hands on their knees and breaths heavy.

"Your buttock is bleeding."

Unbelievable. "Yes, Rollie, my ass *is* bleeding because you threw me at a man *with a weapon and no warning*."

Rollie stood with his hands clasped behind his head as he tried to catch his breath. "I needed those powders."

"And I need to not die!"

Rollie let out a petulant sound. "*Sorry.*"

"I take back what I said about you being an advisor. You'd have me dead within weeks."

Rollie's head went side to side as he considered this before finally conceding. "That is possible. But that doesn't negate me being an excellent advisor. Case in point, we got the powders we needed, and your butt will be fine."

Topp wiped sweat from his stinging eyes. "Let's just get back to the temple before you get us killed."

CHAPTER 25

Elysia shivered as the wind picked up, the muddy scent of the river tangling in her nose. Aidan stood at her side, hands behind his back as he watched the incoming boats expectantly. The dead were arriving. They always were, but this was the first time she was participating.

A battered wooden boat sailed ahead of the other smaller boats. Its side was slapped with bright white and blue paint that read *Ferryman Tours, One Coin.* Standing tall in tan trousers and a light blue button-down with an anchor patterned silk scarf tied around his neck was a man with one foot propped against the edge of the hull, looking like he was sailing the high seas rather than the dark, oily rivers of the death realm.

The Ferryman's boat slid up beside the dock, and he stepped easily onto the rickety wooden slats, his pockets jingling with the weight of coins. Hands shoved into her coat, Elysia kept her gaze on him as he strode closer.

"Well, it's about time, isn't it?" Sea-green eyes swept over her face with interest, and he stuck out a soft dusky brown hand for her to shake. Elysia politely shook his hand, murmuring a hello even as her attention was pulled back to the countless plain wooden boats gently rocking against the river's current.

"Elysia, this is Sai. He acts as a guide for our newcomers."

"Someone has to introduce them to everyone! Gods know where they'd end up without me." At that, Sai's eyes narrowed onto a singular boat that was doing its damndest to turn around and paddle upstream. "You there! This was a non-refundable, one-way ticket, sir, please sit down and resume your spot. I'll be with you all shortly, and you can lose your shit then. Thank you!" he chirped before turning back to Aidan. "You asked for an easy one today?"

Aidan nodded, his face focused and somewhat tense. "Please."

Sai glanced at Elysia, then back to the boats. "I've got just the one. Don't you worry, you'll be a natural, I can feel it." He started to wind his way back to his boat when he stopped and threw her a blinding grin, his dark hair ruffling in the wind. "And if you ever want the real tour of your new home, you know who to find!"

Smiling, Elysia waved to him and allowed Aidan to guide her over to a bench on the riverbank. "Is he a reaper?"

Startled, Aidan took a moment to answer. "No, Sai is not a reaper. Both Sai and Grim were my right-hand men back when we were mortal. He's taken to this life better than any of us." Aidan shook his head, watching Sai offer a hand to an older gentleman struggling to step out of his boat onto the shore.

Soon enough, a plump woman with shoulder-length curly brown hair stumbled over to them, kicking up riverbank dirt with her eyes tired and blank.

"The jaunty one sent me over here," she mumbled.

Nodding, Aidan gestured to the space on the bench beside Elysia. "Please take a seat."

Agitation brought a little more life into her eyes. "Did I do something wrong already?"

"Not at all," Aidan soothed. "Sometimes the transition to this realm is more challenging for some mortals than others. We'd like to assist you if you're open to it."

She looked at Elysia warily. "Assist how?"

Nervous, Elysia cleared her throat. "I'd like to remove whatever is getting in the way of you being able to naturally process your life. Sometimes things get stuck—mortal life is hard, but here you can process and reset."

The woman was quiet. "You can try." The doubt was evident in her voice, but she didn't pull away or say no.

Remembering Aidan's instructions, Elysia directed her magic to search the newcomer. In her mind's eye, she found knots and snarls. Pain and responsibility that had never been the woman's in the first place, along with genuine fetid grief. Elysia carefully scanned every part of her before reaching in and removing the hardened clumps of energy.

One by one, stonelike objects of different sizes and weights fell into her lap as Elysia fought to stay within the flow of her concentration. The heaviness of loss, the debilitating squeeze of guilt, and other flashes of emotions all swam through her consciousness without settling. The emotions and sensations weren't hers, she was simply a surgeon, viewing and extracting from the woman's etheric body. She had no idea how long she worked, only that at some point increasingly familiar hands pulled her against a firm body, offering warmth and support as she worked. Dropping one final pebble onto her lap, golden light coursed through the woman's body, filling in the now empty spaces. Elysia came to and found the woman staring at her in shock.

"How–how did you do that?" The woman was fixed on the pile of blackened rocks on Elysia's lap.

Elysia held one up as the fog-soaked wind sent her hair flying and shrugged. "I've always been good at finding stuff."

Entranced with the rocks, Aidan stepped in for Elysia and walked the woman back over to where Sai was now waiting. Offering them a quick two-finger wave, he hooked his elbow through the woman's and escorted her away from the riverbank and into the city.

Walking back over, Aidan scooped all the rocks into a basket and pulled Elysia to her feet. "Final step."

He'd talked her through it all, but she still couldn't believe her magic was capable of *this*. She'd been fully expecting a whole lot of nothing to happen and then needing to awkwardly apologize to both the woman and Aidan for failing the realm. But it had been easy—taxing, but easy—to search for the hardened blocks of energy and draw them out.

Crouched down by the river's foamy edge with the basket of rocks between them, Elysia grabbed a handful and dropped them into the river. As the rocks sank, the water bubbled and foamed until the blackened stones glinted in shades of red, purple, and dazzling blue. Rubies, amethysts, and sapphires swept away in the river's current. She dropped a few more into the water, and this time, she kept her eyes on him, noticing how with each transmutation the quiet, but constant tension she associated with him softened a little more.

The last of the transmuted rocks drifted away, the river intuitively guiding them where they needed to go to support the Deathlands. Elysia sat back on the damp shore and wiped her hands off. "Promise me you won't attempt this anymore."

Caught off guard, Aidan tore his gaze away from the river to look at her.

She inspected her nails rather than look at him. "The screaming in your head. It was from trying to do this, right? Except you weren't able to properly remove the pain, so you've been carrying it. And based on what I heard, you kept trying anyway."

Aidan ran a hand over his face, his blue eyes bright and face tight with latent anxiety. "I was able to rip properly sometimes—it's not my natural magic, but I knew the theory and you weren't here. The rivers were willing to do the transmutation because the realm needed the power. The only reason we're in better shape than Kava is because I've been supplementing from the newcomers."

Elysia frowned. What she had heard and felt the day she first met him was indescribable. It was the type of pain that made people wish to stop existing. Her own brain had wanted to shut down after only moments of dipping into his.

Her voice became clipped. "You mean to say that you *knowingly* took on the pain of *how many people* even though you were well-aware it was beyond your skill set? Did it even turn into rocks or are you just *carrying it?*" She stared at the god beside her, who she was now sure might be just as stupid as your average tunnel rat.

Aidan exhaled through his nose and looked at her beseechingly, his dark hair breaking free from its carefully styled confines and falling against his skin. "What would you have done? It's my fault this is even happening. If anyone deserves to bear the brunt of the destruction, then it's me. Besides"—he smiled mirthlessly —"I'm a god. It takes an awful lot to kill us."

"You have to let me fix it." The same bossiness with which she directed her juvenile sister now rode her voice, her face fixed into a pissed-off mask that brooked no arguments.

And yet, Aidan stood, ignoring her offer. "Come on, you did well, and assuming you maintain your *platonic co-ruling* duties, then I'll never have to do it again." He stalked off, hunched against the wind. Elysia's eyes narrowed. She was damn-well familiar with wallowing in your own shit, and the stench of *I'm not worth it* was rolling off the god of the dead in undeniable waves.

She stood, fingering the tiny ruby she'd kept in her pocket as she watched him. One day he would let her help him, but she knew better than most that he'd have to be the one to decide he deserved it.

CHAPTER 26

THERE WAS a lightness in Aidan's step that she hadn't seen before. Focused and difficult to pull away from his work, Aidan was not what she would describe as easy-going, but watching the rocks transform into precious jewels had relaxed something in him.

She smiled as they walked through the spindly trees with their bony fingers scratching skyward. It was nice to see him like this. Soon they were back on the cobbled streets of the local village. Past all the brick houses and buildings, hills rolled and somewhere in the valley was the estate. Her feelings about Aidan remained conflicted, but it satisfied the gnawing anxiety eating at her to do something helpful for the Deathlands. Caught up in the moment, she hadn't asked for a better explanation, but now she puzzled over the mechanics of her magic.

The road curved, taking them into the business district filled with everything from candy shops with brightly lit glass windows to large red-brown brick warehouses with iron-paned windows. Elysia spotted a familiar man walking up to one of the warehouses across the way. Distracted from her questions, she nudged Aidan and tipped her head. "Isn't that Grim?"

Aidan's mouth opened, then shut. She looked at him with a

raised brow. "Is it a pleasure house or something? Even Kava has one, you know."

His eyes flitted back and forth, the debate inside his mind evident. "No, not a pleasure house."

Elysia pushed her hands deeper into her coat pockets. "You're being weird." Music started somewhere inside her then, giving her pause as she considered him carefully. *Oh, he has a secret.*

Aidan made a face at her, unaware of the magical scrutiny he was under, and pushed his hair back. "It's just work stuff that you don't need to worry about. You've done enough today." The music grew louder now, pulling her attention to the beautiful warehouse.

She drew back, slowing her steps. "Shouldn't I know about *work stuff*? As your deeply platonic future co-ruler?" Her words were a dare, giving him the chance to correct his mistake.

Aidan pointed at the street that would take them out of the city and onto the well-worn path back to the estate. "Funny, but as much as I enjoy your sudden interest in the workings of the realm, it's really not that exciting. Let's go home."

Elysia stopped and looked at Aidan bluntly. "I'll give you one and you just used it."

Glancing over his shoulder, confusion furrowed his face. "One?"

"One lie. Hope it was worth it."

And then she spun on her heel, darting across the street, quickening her pace as the warehouse loomed closer. A vibrant, tumultuous song filled with roaring excitement and pounding fists pulled at her feet. It was a song of both vengeance and dangerous, unlikely hope. The front door flew open, her feet barely touching down on the expansive wood plank stairs, her hand grazing over the iron handrail. Swaths of muted light shone in through the enormous iron-paned window onto the hardwood floors, and a ruckus of shouting and noise filled the warehouse. Huffing for air, she stopped at the top of the stairs with Aidan barely avoiding colliding into her back.

The back of the warehouse had a grid marked off on its white wall. Within each grid was a glimpse into the mortal realm—of some very familiar faces. Topp and Rollie stalking through the halls of the gaudiest temple Elysia had ever seen. Her sister yelling and waving a potion bottle in the face of a cowering man. Garrison stomping through the Relaclave castle. People she had never seen before filled even more grid spaces.

Grim spotted her, his posture straightening as he made a beeline through the mass of people all shouting and gesticulating at the grid. He looked between Elysia and Aidan warily. "We good here?"

Elysia looked at Aidan with death in her eyes. "*This* is how you know so much about me?"

Aidan appeared pained. Like he wished he could evaporate rather than deal with the small tightly wound package of fury in front of him. "This is not how I wanted to introduce you to this..."

Grim took one look at the two of them, and turned right back around, aiming for the group of reapers he had been minding. "I'll be over here if you need me."

"Traitor," Aidan muttered before glancing down at Elysia again, his face turning wary. "Please, will you allow me to explain?"

Plopping down onto the light-toned hardwood floor with her feet on the stairs and back to the grid, she gestured for him to get on with it. She'd already known the reapers were trailing her occasionally, but to have their lives thrown up on a wall for people to watch without permission was incredibly invasive. Anger writhed beneath her skin, convincing her there wasn't a single reason he could state that would make this acceptable, but she waited with her mouth clamped shut and fists tight.

Aidan sank down beside her, unbuttoning his winter coat and kicking one long leg out. "The more Grim trailed you the last few years, the more concerned we became about Garrison, but my *siblings*, if you can even call them that, can be difficult. We needed to find a way to show them the chaos that's on our doorstep if Garrison proceeds with his plans to exterminate magic. Because the gods *will* devolve into their basest forms. The fates assigned us roles because every time they didn't, the gods inevitably started fighting, destroying realms and mortals and whatever else got in their way. Instead of being stewards, they become tyrants."

He wove his fingers together, his scars turning silvery as they popped against his tightened skin. "They didn't listen when I explained that the death realm was on the verge of collapsing. They consider me the most responsible of the bunch and trusted I could handle it. They also assumed I was blowing it out of proportion—that my anxiety was getting the best of me." His mouth tightened.

"They didn't believe you or want to hear it," she summarized succinctly.

Fires blazed in his eyes as he met her gaze. "Exactly. It doesn't help that they're terrified of the fates. No one wants to lift a single finger that could be misconstrued as going against the fates' design."

She nodded as a slice of fear cut through her. Even the *gods* were afraid of the fates. "You told me the death realm was stable."

"It mainly is now—I didn't want to burden you when I was managing it."

Swiveling to face him better, she hardened her voice. "Honesty goes two ways, Aidan. You can't expect these things from me and not return them."

His jaw ground. "I am well-aware and working on it."

She questioned him again, realizing his independent streak might run as deep as hers. "The Deathlands are genuinely stable?"

He nodded. "I pushed myself too hard, but I knew what would happen if I didn't. The dead don't belong roaming the mortal plane, and none of my siblings seem to grasp the destruction they would wreak."

"And you think a wall of mortals bumbling around is going to convince them?"

Confidence deepened the blue of his eyes as his chest expanded. "Not just any mortals. Exciting mortals. Interesting mortals. Ones who could change the fate of the world and are worth betting on."

Elysia spun around on the wooden stair plank. People were still shouting and pointing at the grid. "It's a game? They're betting on us?"

"We're testing it. Everyone here right now is a Deathlands resident." Voice rough instead of his usual smooth, melodic sound, she could tell he was shoving his nerves down, trying to hide how anxious he was to hear what she thought.

That was how the bartender knew her.

Her gaze narrowed in suspicion. "What did you say you did when you were a mortal?"

His grin became wolflike, his usual self-assurance returning. "I ran the books for an organization much like Gage's family. I also handled all the gambling fronts," he admitted.

She ran a hand through her tangled hair. "Oh my gods, I was *right*. Why is this harder to take in than knowing you're a god?"

Aidan grunted a laugh, leaning back against the stairs and draping an arm in her direction. "Because one of which is far more real to you, and now you're wondering what kind of person I am."

"No, I'm not," she responded without hesitation. At his clear surprise, she continued with a shrug. "You have your stalking ways —you've seen me with Gage. Besides Beatriz, he's all I've got. He was a better brother-parent than I could have ever asked for. It's complicated, but so is everything in my life. It's harder to take in because it makes you human—the kind of human I happen to understand well."

Gaze heavy, he made a noise of consideration deep in his throat. Reaching over, he pushed aside her coat and gently tugged on her shirt until the Reyez branding was visible. His gaze tunneled onto the reddish-pink skin. "I have a mark just like this. Inside of my elbow." He looked up with a small smirk. "Hurt like a bitch at the time, but I loved my job, and I loved my life. I had nothing to lose back then."

He didn't say the rest of the words burning in his eyes.

Elysia diverted back to the grid. "When do you introduce it to your siblings?"

Aidan glanced casually over his shoulder. "We'll roll it out soon. Your friends are running around to temples right now, trying to stir the gods. The response has made me confident that this will do the trick. They might fear the fates, but they love competition and drama even more."

GRIM TENSED as Elysia stalked over, his reapers parting to allow her through and looking at her curiously. Nodding at them, she glanced at the grid and then back to Grim. "I have questions."

Folding his arms, he considered her. "You're taking this well."

Suspicion belied his statement, and Elysia couldn't blame him. She wasn't actually taking it well. Her brain was whirring through every possible private moment they could have seen over the past few years. Being forced to find cursed people who were then executed. Bending to her father's demands. Fawning and fluttering through the courts in delusional hope of wielding a crown. Moments she had thought were only between her and Topp.

Her gaze was cold by the time she answered the head of the reapers. "I want to know what I'm dealing with here. What has everyone seen?" She couldn't bring herself to ask Aidan, so now it was Grim's problem to tell her.

He looked disgruntled. "My reapers never stay present for intimate moments if that's what you're implying, and we do have a job to do reaping souls. We can't be following you everywhere all the time."

That should have soothed her, but it didn't. Intimacy wasn't just sex. A crowd of people seeing the best and worst of her without ever actually knowing her made her stomach turn. The worst moments of her life had been made out to be entertaining fodder.

Grim's stout, muscled body loosened as he examined her face. "We were desperate. We still are desperate. I'm sorry it came at the cost of your privacy, but if it means the rest of the gods come out to play, then I'd wager it's worth it."

Unsure of what she'd expected to hear from Aidan's right hand, she stormed from the warehouse before she could say or do something she would regret. She knew they'd been right to try anything they could to fix this mess, but for someone as guarded as herself, this was excruciating.

Halfway to her greenhouse, a jet-black bunny hopped onto the path with a wax-sealed envelope between its large front teeth. Dropping to her knees, she accepted the letter, and the bunny fled into the grassy hills. She ripped open the letter, hastily reading its contents.

Elysia Parker, former daughter of the Crown, mortal candidate for co-ruler of the Deathlands,

We greet you with the utmost interest and speak to you today in hopes of clearing confusion. While we did require you to take back your heart, we merely hoped to be of service as your first life splinters and turns to dust. Please remember the death voyage is the distance between you and claiming your crown. The threads of our fated tapestry are untied as we remain unconvinced. You would be wise to heed our advice as it comes. As such, we must give only the highest recommendation of visiting the temple of the god of the undead gods in the White Sands of Sagondia.

Even gods can't help but marvel at false religion falling.

Fates' Blessings

Cold damp spread over Elysia's knees as she stared off over the hills. She'd been watching Topp and Rollie while in the warehouse, catching glimpses of them in what looked like a hot, bustling street market. Rollie had stolen from a merchant. Topp had gotten shot in the ass.

It concerned her that the fates wanted her to stir up the gods, considering that was what Aidan and Grim sought as well. Call it intuition, or maybe just a lifetime of being hunted, but she had a terrible feeling about being sent to the White Sands. The note was a reminder to stay in line—if they wanted her to jump, she would jump. She couldn't say she cared for that.

Elysia stood, turning her face up into the brisk air, her anger fading into a sharp loneliness. The soot-stained purple evening sky was a balm, though. The dark fog drifted aimlessly, quieting the turmoil in her chest.

She'd once told Topp that she didn't believe redemption existed for people like them. She hadn't entirely changed her mind, but even if redemption remained out of reach, she was starting to believe they could do *some* good, and maybe that was better than none. She would go to the White Sands. Not for whatever end the fates desired, but to further her own aims—the aims of Aidan and Grim, and all her friends who fought to keep the mortal realm safe from Garrison and the fates' machinations.

She touched the ruby in her pocket.

If they wanted a show to wake the gods, then that was what she'd give them.

Chapter 27

Elysia was throwing trowels and rummaging through seed pouches to no avail. This was the *death realm,* was it not? So why had this man only gifted her *nice* plants? She needed snapping plants, poisonous plants, and ones that could be ground into fine powders meant for diabolical ends. Frustrated, she chucked another pouch filled with peony seeds across the greenhouse. No one ever pulled a god's head from their ass with *peonies.*

"Looking for something?" Dry humor coated Maya's words as she leaned against a workbench.

Elysia scowled at her, in no mood for jokes. "Obviously," she muttered.

Maya untied her cloak, dropping it onto a table, and smirked as she walked over. She tapped the crumpled letter from the fates, which was resting on a shelf near Elysia, with a black-smudged finger. "The fates are meddling again, then."

"According to them, they don't meddle at all."

Maya snorted, glancing over the note's contents. "I take it you haven't shown this to Aidan yet."

"No, I've been a little busy." She grunted as she lifted and released a heavy box of seeds onto the table. Sorting through them, she shoved at the box. "This is useless. I need something, something *explosive.*"

Maya rummaged through the seed pouches, humming as she did so. "I could help."

Elysia's mouth flattened. "And what do you want in return?"

"Come now, I'm supposed to mentor you. What did you think I'd be mentoring you in? All that mushy emotional magic you're doing with Aidan and the new arrivals?"

Elysia wasn't convinced. "What type of magic do you work with, anyway?"

Maya didn't answer, instead grabbing Elysia by the wrist. "All kinds. Come on, take a break. You've never visited my cottage, and I can tell you more about your magic. Did Aidan even *explain* what you're really doing?"

No, no, he hadn't.

Elysia threw her coat back on and followed Maya to her small stone cottage. The stark contrast to the reddish-brown brick buildings with iron accents everywhere else in the city piqued Elysia's curiosity. The cottage's chimney puffed happily, and the door was painted a dark burgundy with both dried flowers and nails hanging from its center. To the right of the cabin were several plots of tilled land that Elysia imagined Maya used for plants in warmer weather.

Stomping her boots on the porch, Maya unlocked the front door and Elysia followed her in, looking around and breathing in the smoky air. Maya immediately checked on several tinctures and paused at the stove to stir something that did not look remotely edible. Satisfied her work was progressing, she grabbed a bottle, popped off the cork and poured out two small glass goblets.

"Woodland berry wine. Tart, but good." She set one down in front of Elysia before taking her own seat.

Elysia sniffed the wine before sampling it, her face screwing up in shock at how sour it was.

Maya laughed, her gray eyes dancing. "Maybe it's an acquired taste." Standing up, she walked over to an apothecary cabinet and began to pull out drawers, talking to herself as she piled more and more ingredients into a jar.

Watching her gave Elysia a disturbing flashback to the old meela in Kava. Slamming the last drawer shut, Maya turned around and placed the jar between them before settling back into her chair. "Grim said the Kava boys want to light up a temple? These will do the job when mixed appropriately."

Elysia nodded, holding up the jar to peer at its contents. "Rollie is probably five steps ahead of me, but just in case."

Maya took a long pull of her wine, not even wincing as the sour alcohol went down. "Your goal is to destroy the temple or to garner the attention of the gods?"

Elysia fidgeted with the goblet before taking a breath. She'd been sitting on a thought all day, afraid to ask Aidan since he hadn't brought it up when it seemed like there had been an obvious opening. Finally looking at Maya, she kept her voice even, disinterested almost.

"When I extracted the pain from a newcomer today, I was able to hold it as raw energy, and the river transmuted it to support the realm." The rocks in her lap had been clods of hardened soot—giant hunks of raw magic waiting to be used.

A slow smile worked its way across Maya's face. While the woman normally wore floaty flower dresses and boots for mucking through the forest, there was something in her eyes that always reminded Elysia to mind herself, to pay attention when in Maya's presence.

"You want me to teach you how to use the raw power."

"Is that possible?"

"You'd be amazed at what I can teach you, Parker." Maya crossed her arms, considering the task before them. "That type of training will take more than the time you have before visiting the mortal realm."

Elysia deflated but nodded. "I figured. It's one thing to assist the dead in removing their burdens, but mortals are still living. I can't go around relieving them of their pain. I just figured there had to be another way to, I don't know, find excess energy, and use it." She frowned, maybe it was too crazy.

Maya placed her hand on top of Elysia's. "Allow me to be your guide. I will teach you what Aidan can't, and I promise, when you're ready, nothing will stop you."

Her mouth was moving, agreeing to Maya's offer before she could form a thought. "Teach me. Show me what I can do."

Even while under the laws of Kava and her father's thumb, she had trained, plotted, and ensured she never felt entirely powerless. But her trip to Bellia had left her afraid, all too aware of her current disadvantage. Luckily, she knew that even the most mediocre of natural talent could be trained into something greater with enough discipline and devotion.

Maya swept up the glasses and bottles. "Good, it's settled. I always wanted an apprentice." She grabbed a piece of paper and scrawled out instructions that she dropped into a small drawstring pouch along with a few handfuls of glass balls. "Follow those carefully. Aidan will murder me if you blow yourself up."

Elysia grabbed her loot, heading for the door. "Don't worry, I've made poisons before, it's practically the same thing, right?"

CHAPTER 28

Elysia strolled through the sculpture garden surrounding the god of the undead gods temple, enjoying the swish of her bright blue robes. It hadn't gone unnoticed that Maya had supplied her with appropriate garments in the exact color of Aidan's eyes. She wouldn't have pegged Maya as a romantic, which only made her wonder further about her motives.

Sewn into the endless folds and pleats of her strategically pinned robes were tiny sachets of explosives and one drawstring pouch of igniters. The igniters rolled quietly against each other. Each small glass ball was no bigger than the pad of her pinky finger. What mattered was that when she chucked them at the sachets, she would be in business.

Dressed like one of the acolytes, no one noticed as she marveled at the statues and sculptures while also lacing them with explosives. It was a pity she hadn't had time to learn how to utilize raw magic yet. She didn't know what she would be able to do, but she was imagining being able to light everything off at once in a grand finale of exploding golden statues.

Given that wasn't possible, she continued her work through the garden, relishing the warm sand squishing up against her sandal-clad feet and being able to see blue sky above her.

Assuming the boys hadn't gotten far, then she would find Rollie and Topp inside in a rather compromised position. She couldn't wait to scare the shit out of them.

Elysia stepped out of the sun into the cool air of the temple. It was every bit as gaudy as she had seen on the grid. Ostentatious and lacking in spirit, she was hard-pressed to understand how people still brought their money and pleas to this tomb of a temple. But then, she also understood the lure of a shiny promise and a little hope. Her mother had once said that religion was for scared, lonely people, and while she knew it was more complicated than that, she could see her mother's point. It was easy to prey on the downtrodden.

It was midafternoon—the time when everyone slipped off to their chambers to get out of the worst of the sun, to sip on cooling teas and juices and maybe even steal a nap. Not a single footstep echoed in the green-domed temple beside her own, but there were the hissed voices of two grown men squabbling far above her head.

Elysia's sensible sandals clacked against the white and black marble steps as she walked up past a blessing fountain onto the raised dais where the priest would speak from. She cupped a hand around her mouth, calling out with a drawl. "Hello, boys."

Someone's head thumped loudly. Cursing drifted down from above, making her smirk as she waited. Soon enough, Rollie was leaning dangerously over the scaffolding bars, his blonde hair poking into sight.

"Elysia?"

She'd never seen him look surprised before. She decided she liked it. Men like Rollie needed to be surprised occasionally if only to remind them that their calculations weren't always perfect.

Topp, on the other hand, looked hassled and one second away from lighting the temple on fire early. She assumed this was because of Rollie, not her. "Parker, what is it about you that you're always exactly where you shouldn't be? Get the fuck out of here," he barked.

Or maybe that face *was* about her. She smiled, thoroughly enjoying disrupting them. "You're hiding up there and planning to what? Drop a match and hope for the best during evening prayers? How are you even going to get out?"

Rollie crossed his arms. "They'll be distracted, and don't worry about how it's getting lit. I have it covered." Indignant, he didn't elaborate further.

She nodded, reaching over, and letting the blessing fountain water trickle over her fingers. "Sure, but not so distracted that they don't clock your faces." She gestured spectacularly. "Prince of Kava! Anti-religious zealot destroys the god of the undead gods temple in the White Sands!"

There was the sound of boots hitting metal, and then Topp's body came into sight as he lumbered down the construction scaffolding. Gracefully, he dropped to the floor beside her, slowly rising from bent knees to his full height. "We were going to wear masks."

She looked at him incredulously. "Topp, the first rule of being friends with Rollie is knowing when to point out when he's lost sight of practicalities! He was probably so enraptured with making his boom-boom powders that he doesn't give a shit whether they identify you or not. All he cares about is finding out if they work the way he imagined they will." Frustrated, she glared at him.

Rollie awkwardly descended until he was hanging from the scaffolding and refusing to let go. Elysia saw him and groaned. "For fuck's sake. Topp, help him down. He's stuck."

Topp reached up and gingerly placed one hand on either side of Rollie's waist.

"Let go already, I've got you."

Rollie looked down, paralyzed.

"Rollickus, it is a four-foot drop. Let go of the damn bar."

Elysia released a great sigh. Yeah, they would have escaped without a single problem. Exasperated, Topp gave a solid yank, ripping Rollie's hands from the bar, and set him on the ground.

Both men shuffled over to her, looking slightly embarrassed. "You're lucky I came. Gods know what would've happened if I hadn't." She chastised them while biting back a grin. This was better than yelling at Beatriz.

Topp glowered at her, knowing she was getting her rocks off. "Enough. How did you even find us?"

"That conversation will take far too long. What you need to know is that I am *all* caught up on your latest escapades and I have additions to your plan. How's your ass, by the way?" She held up a hand to the instant spluttering of both men. "I'll explain later, and yes, you still get to blow the place up."

Mollified, both Rollie and Topp shrugged.

Rubbing her hands together, she pulled them both in closer. "Listen up…"

By the end, there were no questions because both men were rendered speechless.

Rollie finally coughed awkwardly. "There's one minor thing that may clear up your concerns about our end of the plan. I made the bombs for efficiency but lighting them and destroying the temple won't be a problem. I'm a fire-worker."

Both Topp and Elysia stared at him.

"You didn't think to mention that? I asked you fifteen times how you planned to light these suckers," Topp groused. "I thought your brain was your magic."

Elysia smacked him on the arm. "You lived in a *tunnel*. What if you had set an uncontrolled fire?"

He shrugged. "Kava's dicey. But I usually can put them out."

Shaking her head, Elysia danced lightly on her feet.

"Never by halves," Topp muttered to himself.

Elysia repeated it back like a mantra for the night ahead.

It was just past dusk when the receiving line began. Evening prayers had ended, and the petitioners were in a long line streaking out of the temple and down the green-tiled path. The cool evening air scurried through the hopefuls, carrying sand and the faint lingering smells of early dinners. One by one and huddled in little groups, the line moved slowly.

Elysia wore a matching cobalt veil now. It wasn't uncommon for the women of the temple to cover their hair or even their faces. Once again, she appeared to be one of the many acolytes assisting with the evening petitions. Starting from the very end of the line, she lazily tossed Maya's glass igniters as she took slow, pious steps, her hands hidden in the folds of her robe and her gaze on the temple. She wasn't aiming for the sachets she had placed earlier. Those would come later.

As the igniters hit the hard ground, they sparked brightly and popped loud enough to startle those who were close. Many didn't go off until she had passed, and an unsuspecting patron stepped on the glass. She never once reacted. Acting as if nothing had occurred, she continued to glide and smile as she invoked the seeds of chaos into the crowd.

She wanted them uneasy. Spooked and wondering where the noise and sparks were coming from. Was it someone's errant magic? Had the god of the undead gods stirred? By the time she reached the temple entrance, people were looking over their shoulders and jostling each other as they tried to find the source of the strange sparks and pops.

Bowing her head, she entered the temple. The high priest would be starting soon, and she didn't want to miss it. Wooden benches had been brought into the main room of the temple. People squeezed in side by side and looked upon the priest on the dais as if he were a god himself. Dressed in pale gold robes, the gemstones that held the folds of his robe in place stood out magnificently, shining in the low dusk light. He stepped to the front of the dais, hands on the railing, and a hush fell over the crowd.

"It is good to gather, is it not?"

The crowd murmured their agreement.

"We gather today, as we do every week, to honor and beg the favor of the one true god, the god of the undead gods. And what better way to beg his golden light than to shower him with his own wealth? For as we know, the wealth belongs to him, does it not? And whatever we give is returned to us tenfold."

Elysia noticed the person sitting next to her clutching a single coin to give in offering. Her leather sandals looked ready to disintegrate, and her eyes gleamed with a desperate unshed tear. Jaw set, Elysia adjusted the pearl pin for her veil and waited.

The smallest of flames soared, striking and sputtering out against the priest's bare ankle. Giving an undignified yelp, the priest smacked at the burn with his opposite foot. Shaking it off, the priest opened his mouth to continue, but another fiery ember caught against his nape, scorching skin and leaving his hair smoking as it burned out. His hand hit against his neck, eyes wild as he searched the crowd.

"Who is doing this? Show yourself," he demanded, leaning over the railing.

But the crowd was silent, nervously looking amongst each other and the silent golden statues.

His voice bounced within the shining domed temple. "Which of you can command fire? Speak now." The priest loomed angrily from atop the dais, and the acolytes surged around the edges of the benches, hunting for the guilty party. Whispers ran through the people now, wary glances shooting left and right.

"Who besmirches this holy temple and its keeper?" The high priest was relentless, spittle coming off his pale lips.

Drops of fire fell through the air, singeing the circle of space all around him, and a nervous ripple went through the crowd. Benches creaked as people shifted uneasily, clothes rustling, and sandals shuffling against the floor. The acolytes' heavy pacing footsteps only added to the tension.

One brave voice sounded above the others. "What if it's the one true god?"

The tension in the air became thick and heady, people

twisting in their seats to stare at the high priest in suspicion. A fallen star in his pale gold robes, he tried to take back the room, afraid of the crowd turning against him.

"I am the mouthpiece, protector, and keeper of this mortal home for the god of the undead gods. He does not strike against me."

There was a great whoosh, and every oil painting in the room went up in flames, crackling and billowing colorful smoke.

"The true god has spoken!"

"This house is cursed!"

"Look!" shrieked a woman in the front row, pointing as she leapt to her feet.

Fire surrounded the dais, trapping the high priest but not touching him, the flames rising higher until his face could scarcely be seen.

People fled, and the acolytes did not stop them, most of them tripping after the crowd, hoping to escape. The flames held their circle, and over the din of stampeding feet and upturned benches boomed a deep voice.

"Today, this house will fall. Leave or perish."

The flames shot high and then extinguished. The high priest sprinted, shoving people out of his way left and right as he made for the doors. In minutes, the entire temple was empty.

Elysia slid out of the arched hallway entrance she'd been watching from and called to the rafters. "I do love an exciting first half! Are we ready to bring it home?"

Feet plunked against the out-of-sight scaffolding as the men lowered themselves down to the ground. Rollie grimaced as he dropped the last few feet, but successfully navigated that terror on his own this time.

Standing in front of the dais, all three veiled or masked and wearing the robes of the acolytes, they reconvened. Elysia was about to ask Rollie if he was ready, when the temple doors were thrown open and the priest along with a herd of acolytes stormed back in.

"I swear it's him and I'm going to prove it," the high priest was seething. Embarrassment had a special way of bringing out the worst in men, and Elysia could see in his eyes that he was determined to mete out the pain of his incompetence against them.

Elysia slipped in front of two of her oldest friends, giving them a passing squeeze. "Go," she ordered. Turning back to the oncoming rage of robed men, she slowly drew out a veil pin and dropped it to the ground.

A line of fire erupted before her feet, halting the priest and his acolytes in their tracks. The priest crashed to a stop, teetering dangerously over the flames and flinging out his arms to hold off those behind him. Elysia continued to unwind her veil and smiled.

Sachets and igniters in hand, she greeted them. "I heard you wanted to meet me. Here I am." She laughed darkly and slipped into a mocking curtsy. Dipping her head of dark brown waves in their direction, she lowered her voice. "He might live, but I still gutted the King of Kava. Did you really think you could hold me?"

"Your king will be the ruin of us all with his backward ways," the priest spat back, pushing against the line of fire.

Elysia nodded and rolled the igniters in her sweaty palm. "This is true, and for that I will give you a choice. First option, go back the way you came and get as far from this building as you can, and no harm will come to you or any of your people. Two, you give chase because you're a greedy, fraudulent fool, and I won't feel a shred of remorse over what comes next."

She spun, not waiting for an answer, smashing igniters into the angry line of fire, making it lash out viciously as she raced to a back exit of the temple. Hurling herself through the door, she chucked more igniters at the sachets she had placed earlier, explosions going off to her left and right, debris flying through the air. Elysia dared a glance back and swore. The priest and two men were gaining on her. She pumped her arms, begging her legs to move faster.

Now that she had given the cue, and the building was evacuated, Rollie and Topp would execute the mass demolition of the temple. Her only job was to escape with her life intact. Elysia sprinted down the sandy street, blue robes billowing as she tumbled in and out of people. There was a small bay not too far from the temple. Muscles burning, she pounded on in the direction of the water. The boys knew she could travel. She hadn't mentioned the need for a body of water to reach the death realms. If all else failed, she could escape to somewhere in the mortal lands.

Tearing around a corner, Elysia came to a staggering halt. There was a line of acolytes between her and the bay. *How did they get there?* She dared a glance back, her stomach sinking as her pursuers came into view. She couldn't use any of her explosives in this crowded of an area—not without injuring or killing civilians. *Change of plans.* She pictured the Bone Temple, the one place that would always be safe for her in the mortal realm.

And nothing happened.

Panicked, she tried again.

The head priest laughed as they closed in. "Problem leaving? Gerald here is a blocker. You're not going anywhere, you Kavian scum."

Gritty resolve replaced her fear. Her hand slipped between her robes, drawing out her dagger. She'd meant it when she said they couldn't hold her. That over-groomed, prissy priest had another thing coming if he thought he could fight her.

Surrounded, Elysia, met the high priest's red, enraged gaze. Dirt and sweat smeared his temples, and he lifted one trembling finger to stick at her face. "Seize her."

No less than ten acolytes fell upon her as the people milling about the market stared in confusion. Clenching her teeth, she ducked and sliced and fought. While they may have been trained in combat in their youth, they were now out of shape and used to the luxurious life of the temple. She slowly picked her way through them. The head priest watched as it came down to her and two final acolytes. She moved lightly on her feet, ready to end it, when one of the men threw out his hand in a fit of violent temper.

"*Enough* of this barbaric nonsense."

A blood-curdling scream released from her mouth. Collapsed in the dirt, the bones from her ankle to her knee hung strangely. Tears streaked down her face, but she clawed upright, still clutching her dagger, swiping at anyone who came near.

The bone-worker growled. "Cut me again, and I'll snap every last bone you've got."

Furious with pain, a filter of black haze overcame her vision. Elysia's magic roared, flooding and bursting through the dam of her body, hungry for the bone-breaking power torrenting out of the acolyte. In her mindless fury, there was no thought or choice. There was only self-protection and defense.

This wasn't the soft, beautiful magic that had occurred on the riverbank.

It was the long-buried instinct of a powerful but untrained woman lashing out. Elysia seized the man's power and ripped until it became hers. Unable to hold or form what she had stolen, she pointed the javelin of force back at its owner. The cracking and shattering of his bones became the song that drove her on. His shrieks layered with the bass of breaking bones until he became silent, his body overcome and no longer conscious.

Dagger still up high, her body wavered as her sight grew unfocused. Whatever she had just done was far beyond her magical capacity. Fingers unable to hold it, the dagger thudded to the sandy ground, and her body slumped as everything went dark.

Elysia came in and out of consciousness, her skin tearing and body thumping as she was dragged the many blocks back to the temple. *Maybe this is what the fates wanted.* Eyes bleary, she blinked them open to find the sky dark and the streets lit with both flaming torches and the occasional floating orbs. Even in the firelight, she could see how her ankle flopped limply while the burn of road rash stung the bottoms of her legs and arms.

Suddenly, the air changed. The delicious aromatic scent of herbal torches and food stands changed to the acrid blackened scent of an uncontrolled burn. Lifting her head, she saw the outline of the temple up in a blaze, black smoke billowing out into the night. Except the temple no longer looked like it once did. The golden statues were melted and blown to pieces. The iconic green dome had collapsed, and the once unnervingly white walls were charred and soon to be gone as the flames slowly, steadily consumed the entire structure.

Limbs heavy and shot through with unbearable pain, she still smiled. Topp and Rollie had pulled it off. She knew Rollie had been hopeful it would be enough to draw out the god of the original temple, but selfishly she prayed they were long gone and laughing as they safely sought the next temple. Elysia's head fell back again as her muscles gave out. She still had one trick left up her sleeve, and it was about time to use it. He had said it was only for emergencies.

Her bloodied hand lifted, but her body was jerked forcefully, cracking her head against the statue she'd been propped against. Head ringing, she blinked slowly.

The head priest kicked her shattered ankle. "One of you search her. Fucking bitch probably still has explosives on her."

If she hadn't been fighting the brink of unconsciousness, she would have sighed. Groping hands patted her down, snatching away the small number of igniters and sachets that remained on her person. She barely breathed as she waited for them to take it, but they didn't, so she lay there, compliant and clinging to alertness.

The head priest's knee dropped into the ash-covered sand. His dirty fingers grabbed her face, forcing her eyes to him. "We would have kept you as a guest before returning you to Garrison. But the warrant doesn't say you have to come back whole, does it?" The priest slapped her so hard her teeth clacked, but Elysia said nothing as she pulled in a ragged breath.

He stalked away just as the ground began to quake. Tremors swept through the sand, the particles moving erratically against her palms. But that was nothing compared to how the temple shook and swayed as it crumbled. Acolytes who had been futilely pouring water over the burning structure screamed, running haphazardly over the uneven ground, tripping and stumbling as the earth became determined to eat them whole. Down they went, hitting the earth, fingers and nails scraping against the hot, sandy ground as the growing chasm became slanted and they slid into its maw. Their cries grew fainter as they fell, swallowed up by the now temple-sized hole.

Doing her best to ignore the chaos, Elysia finally took hold of the old coin on a chain around her neck. Tarnished silver with a skull and dice on its face, it was warm between her fingers. Rubbing her thumb over its surface, she prayed the reaping prayer before struggling to her feet. Arms clutched around the remains of the statue, she leaned heavily against it, unable to put any weight on her right leg.

She pressed at her chest, coughing on the smoke as she squinted through the ash-heavy air. A remnant of power hung like static, prickling against her unnaturally. Her head swiveled, searching but finding nothing to account for the sudden carnage. Rollie and Topp may have set the temple aflame, but whatever had just happened was beyond their limited strength.

A loud crackling drew her gaze back to the cavernous hole. Dread coated her stomach as green spiky vines slithered out of the temple's grave. The thick, ropy vines covered every inch of the hole, overlapping and twining together as they sprawled and stretched out into what had been the sculpture garden. Snakelike, the vines roamed the grounds, finding collapsed and injured acolytes and dragging them without mercy into the hole. Their descent seemed to go on forever, their screams echoing in terror and pain.

Elysia pressed her back against the broken statue as if that would help if the vines decided she was next. Above, a storm erupted. The sable smoke-laden sky darkened further with heavy rain clouds and bolts of lightning that shot out in warning. Thick raindrops pelted down, plastering her hair against her head and stinging against her torn skin. Heartbeat tired but fast in her chest, fear took hold as the storm ravaged on, washing away the debris and ash of the fire.

Blackened water streamed past, over the fire-baked sand, flooding the impervious ground. Her body begged her to run, to do anything to get away from the ever-increasing electricity in the air as she stood now calf-deep in water, but she couldn't. Her ankle hung awkwardly, and she knew she couldn't make it more than a few hopping, hobbled steps.

She gripped the statue tighter. Grim had said he could be here in moments. And yet, there wasn't a reaper in sight. Once again, the fates' demand that she come here flashed in her mind. A sick taste filled the back of her throat. She'd walked right into this.

Her fear contorted into a silent buzzing as a hand the width of her body slapped against the cavern's edge, grasping the vines, and heaved. Hand over hand, the most enormous man she'd ever seen pulled himself out of the hole. A bear head hooded his face, and its thick brown pelt hung as a cloak over his naked chest as he stalked through the quieting storm. He stood in front of where the temple once was, his electric blue-green gaze hunting through the open land around him.

When his eyes landed on her, Elysia paled. She gingerly tested her ankle as if it wasn't smashed, never taking her eyes off the beast. Grim's coin heated against her rain-slicked chest as the bear-man crushed the distance between them. Standing no more than a foot from her, he reeked of the wild. The crack of fresh air, the hazy ozone of a storm, and the rich, warm scent of good soil all rolled off him. Up close, he had to have been seven feet tall. Barrel-chested, his muscles were thick and defined, his naturally light skin a deep leathery tan that made it clear he spent too much time in the sun. Channeling the defiance that had long kept her alive, she lifted her chin and met his strange blue-green gaze.

The rain relented to a gentle mist as he stared at her curiously, and when he spoke it boomed like thunder, making her flinch. "You stink of death."

Elysia blinked once, her knuckles whitening as she clung to the statue. "I am...connected to your brother." What was she? Did she have a title? *Death voyager extraordinaire.* Now would have been a really good fucking time to have a title.

His eyes swept over her, frowning at her broken bones. "I thought I heard rumblings of a death voyage. He should take better care of you, so fragile while still in this state. Very unlike him." He glanced back to where the temple had once stood. "Did you do this?"

She paused, unsure of how to answer that. "I assisted," she replied shortly.

"It was our doing," a familiar voice called out, and her shoulders sank in relief.

Topp somehow managed to make his burnt, smoky attire look purposeful and rugged while Rollie staggered closer with red eyes and angry skin, looking like he was two steps away from passing out as he hacked and coughed.

"Rollie, are you okay?" Elysia examined his drained face in concern. He stumbled to her in a daze.

"Too much magic, but I think I should be asking you that," he mumbled. "You were supposed to leave. Why didn't you travel?"

The bear-man interrupted them, bringing them all back to his question. "Son of mine, why did you wreck this empty place?"

"We hoped the destruction would act as a true offering and call to you."

The god's expression remained impassive but considering. "Why? I am not a god who seeks offerings. Feel a breeze. Plant a tree. Tend to an animal friend. This is what pleases me."

Rollie put one palm against Elysia's statue and cut in. "Because we seek to warn the gods."

A ground-shaking laugh carved a smile onto the giant's face. "You would warn *us*? Of what could you possibly warn the immortal, timeless gods you come from?"

Topp's voice went gravelly. "Of my father—he aims to eradicate magic from every land he can reach."

Blue-green eyes went back to Elysia now. "Aidan finally reached his counterpart despite your fates-crossed path, and here you stand on my ground, spent with misused magic that would have killed a lesser mortal. Tell me, lady of the dead, is this true? Does my brother fear this end as well?"

"He fears it so much that he struck a deal with me that if I succeed in my voyage and bring his talisman to him, then I am free to return to mortal lands as much as duty allows. He even stabilized the death realms at great cost to himself to prevent the dead from overtaking the earth."

"Unfortunate how the fates are handling this... My boy never deserved their wrath." His frown twisted into an odd smile. "But yes, I imagine the talisman will be key in the days to come if what you say is true."

Elysia took a great breath. "Grim and Aidan invented a new technology. It will allow the gods to see what is happening across the mortal realm in real-time. All the big players—Topp's father, my friends from Kava, perhaps even the gods. He'd like to set up a gambling game."

Both Topp and Rollie swiveled to stare at her, but she didn't say anything else, her eyes fixed on the reaction of the terrifying god weighing her words.

The silence thickened and Elysia grimaced. *Great.* They'd managed to get a god to show up and she'd blown it.

He finally gave a slow nod. "I am older than most. I stand as the only original fate-made god, lasting through their many purgings. Again and again, they have made new gods when it pleases them." The giant gave a weary sigh. "Nothing gives me greater pleasure than caring for the little mortals of storm and fauna, so while I remain cautious for fear of my godhood, I will hear what my favorite and youngest brother has to say."

Rollie pushed sweaty hair out of his face. "If the fates oversee the gods, and have the power to eliminate gods, then who could stand against them?"

The rain came down harder as the god looked off into the sky. "I hope Aidan is ready for the chaos he chases."

Putting a hand on the back of both Rollie and Topp's necks, he steered them in the direction of the gaping, vine-covered hole. Except now that Elysia looked again, a broad-leaved forest had sprung up all around them. Lush and green, the forest looked like it had stood in the White Sands for centuries rather than seconds. A red deer disappeared behind a tree, and Elysia shook her head. *This is too crazy.*

The god stopped, his bear pelt swinging as he turned back. "Tell Grim he's welcome and let your future husband know I'll be seeing him." With that, he carelessly threw down his hand. The earth cracked, icy water rushing and overflowing into a river that disappeared deep within the new forest past where she could see.

"Happy traveling." He winked and turned back to the boys, lifting them by their necks and jumping into the hole.

Elysia hopped on one foot to the water. She stared at the beautiful, fresh river, and tried to decide if a broken ankle or a pissed-off death god was worse. She took a breath and jumped.

CHAPTER 29

Elysia found it suspicious that she had made it through the
night with no one knocking on her door or barging in and
demanding to know everything. She laboriously changed into a
loose pair of cozy black pants and a soft oversized sweater. Maybe
they had already watched everything on the grid, but somehow,
she doubted this considering neither Grim nor any of his reapers
had responded to her call. Something had gone wrong, she just
didn't know what.

Her ankle was multicolored and bulbous, and the bruising
continued up her shin and calf, marking out the ugly map of her
pain. She poked at it with a wince. Seeing Maya was the first thing
on her agenda today. She'd arrived in a state of exhaustion so deep
that she hadn't even stripped off her river-drenched clothes before
collapsing into the armchair and passing out. Unfortunately,
bathing was still out of the question—it was a small miracle she'd
managed to change her clothing now, hopping around like a
strange one-legged bird.

Tediously, Elysia hobbled through the house, following the
sound of the daily breakfast din and clamor to the dining room.
The table was full with Aidan at the head when she entered.
Mouth tight and with bluish-purple under eyes, he snapped out

the paper he was reading a little too aggressively, tearing it down the middle. *Okay, then.*

Grim sat two chairs down sporting an obvious black eye while he ate a hearty bowl of porridge in pointed silence. His volt, the official name for Grim's flock of reapers, picked nervously at their food, afraid to converse with one another. Releasing the doorframe, she unceremoniously hopped into the room, making a beeline for the closest chair. One of the reapers quickly kicked out Elysia's seat, so she could grab onto the tall wooden post and slump down into the heavily embroidered seat.

She shot the woman a smile of relief. "Thanks."

Grim looked even more miserable as he took in her appearance while Aidan unconsciously bent the metal spoon in his hand.

"Seems like a rough morning?" She tentatively dropped the question.

Aidan's glare turned arctic. "You left a note. *Again.*"

Grim stared studiously at his porridge. He was obviously going to be no help. It made her wish Maya was here, both for her broken bones and a little support. Elysia paused, trying to think of an answer that would calm His Deadliness's rankled feathers. Somehow, she doubted explaining Beatriz's tried and true advice that it was easier to ask for forgiveness than permission would be well received or that the idea of *permission* was gross. She shifted her weight uselessly, the chair creaking beneath her as the pain distracted her. It was up to her knee now, her foot turning strangely cold.

"You asked for me to communicate... And a note *is* communication." Not her best work, but she was injured. Maybe he would take pity. There was a coffee carafe just out of her reach, and she was itching to grab it. She stretched, but none of the reapers helped her now, all of them either fixed on their breakfast or just flat out refusing to make eye contact. Bet they regretted coming in here today.

Aidan flicked his hand, and the carafe shoved forward roughly to where she could grab it. Her mouth quirked up. That was a neat trick.

"Thanks." Even as she poured out the coffee and added cream and sugar, she could feel the steady beat of Aidan's stare.

Once she'd taken a good long pull, she set the weighty mug down, and sighed. "I'm sorry, okay? You're so anxious all the time. I thought you would freak out and try to convince me not to go even though the fates are the ones who directed me to do it."

Aidan dropped the mangled spoon as his pale cheeks colored.

"I am appropriately anxious," he replied curtly, the angles of his face harshening as he looked away from her.

Her shoulders dropped. *Amazing.* She'd managed to make him feel bad for his singular neurosis when she was made of them. Taking another sip of coffee, she tried again, making her voice gentler.

"Really, Aidan, I'm sorry that I worried you. It looks like you were up all night." Her heart softened as she said it—when was the last time someone had worried after her? Gage did, but for some reason, coming from Aidan the sentiment was different.

His profile thawed, and he turned back to her, his blue eyes still intense. "A note may be communication, but you used it to avoid me because you knew I would fairly push back against the reckless haphazardness of your plan. The nearest body of water was over a mile from the temple, and you forgot you could travel to it! Did you think that made sense for an exit plan?"

"I thought I'd be able to go to the Bone Temple. How was I supposed to know they'd have someone who could block travel-ing?" Worked up, she leaned forward, putting a little too much weight onto her injury. Inadvertently, she let out a small pained sound, her hands reflexively reaching for her ankle.

Aidan's eyes flared wide as he shoved away from the table in concern. Straightening from his half-bent posture, his face went through a slew of emotions until there was only apology in his tone. "Maya conveniently disappeared last night, after...an unfor-tunate interaction of mine with Grim, and I don't know when she'll be returning." He hesitated. "But I would be happy to ease your pain if you'd like. These conversations can wait until you're healed."

She looked over at Grim's black eye, the reddish tones of the bruise making a half-moon on his brown skin.

"*Aidan,*" she chastised. "I asked him for help. If anything, you should thank him. It's not his fault that the enormous bear-wearing god did something to prevent him from helping."

Grim grunted, waving her off. "I let my best friend's," he paused, rolling his eyes, "*platonic co-ruler* almost get herself killed. At the very least, I should have been there for you, and I wasn't. I didn't account for Oren being a cantankerous, dramatic old bitch."

Aidan wasn't remorseful. "It was a punch. It was deserved. And we're nearly unbreakable immortals. He's fine. You, however, are not."

He sat back down with his face pinched, and it was all Elysia could do not to laugh. People thought she could be *prim,* but Aidan's tense rigidity when stressed was almost comical.

"I can wait for Maya to get back."

Aidan undid the top button of his shirt as if he needed the room to breathe, his voice turning blunt. "Don't be childish. You're clearly in pain, and will need assistance with a bath. There's sand and ash all over you, and you smell like a sweaty river."

"Way to not sugarcoat it," she muttered as she tenderly adjusted her leg, the mottled blackish-purple tones whitening then flushing with color as she moved. She flicked her eyes back up, her voice hardening in challenge. "And over my dead body am I allowing *you* to bathe me, so I guess you're just going to have to deal with my stench."

Grim rattled the table in his haste to stand. Cutting his hand through the air to the door like a traffic director, he growled at his reapers. "Time to go."

Relieved, the reapers mirrored his haste and practically flew out of their chairs, knocking against each other as they filed out of the dining room. Which left her alone with a wildly displeased god who looked like he would be more than glad to pick up the challenge she had laid down.

Room empty, Aidan's voice became painfully low and controlled. "Do you have any idea what it's like to be chained here, unable to do a godsdamn thing while the woman I've waited lifetimes for rushes headfirst into certain mortal death?"

Elysia stirred her coffee, avoiding his gaze. It had been shitty to leave a note instead of talking to him. It had also been shitty to include Grim and Maya in her plans, but not him.

Anxiety closed her throat, refusing to allow any words out. The space between the words in her head and them exiting her mouth was insurmountable. Her chest squeezed like an old rag being wrung out to dry as she tried to force them out. Her frustration mounted at her inability to extricate a simple apology, but the harder she tried, the further away the words slinked.

Aidan's sharp, observant gaze tracked her struggle, and with a sigh, he slumped into his chair. "This is hard for you."

Her frustration spiked even higher. He shouldn't have to always bend for her. She was grown, and yet when faced with emotional matters, she had no better skills than a child. Until now, she hadn't needed them. She knew how to hide her feelings, not express them, and she'd never had to learn to partner with anyone. She had been a one-woman show her entire life.

He poured himself a cup of coffee, adding cream, but not sugar.

"You never drink coffee," she said quietly.

"Tea didn't feel strong enough today."

"You were up all night."

"I was."

Guilt fell heavily, finally stirring the words on her tongue. "I knew going to Grim and Maya for help but not you was low, but I was afraid you'd say no, and then I'd have to blatantly go against you. Doing it this way... It was easier."

Aidan gave a barely there nod, his gaze hard, but said nothing.

Gods. He was going to make her say it. She pulled at the cloth napkin in her lap. "I'm sorry, okay? It was shitty."

He loosed a sigh. "And so was that apology."

Her head shot up. "I'm trying!"

His hands hit the table. "Then try *harder*."

"I don't know how! I've never apologized!" The words burst from her mouth in a sudden yell.

Aidan's lips curled in satisfaction as he rested his elbows on the table, perfectly calm in the face of her storm. "It's just a muscle, Thorn. I'm not particularly natural at it myself, but I've had practice. Now try again."

As pompous as he was being, she liked that idea. Anyone could learn to use a muscle. A weak muscle didn't make you horrible or bad—it simply created an imbalance, and that could be addressed. She took a sip of her coffee. "I think I have a lot of relational muscles I've never used."

An honest smile broke through his grumpy facade, and a flush of warmth ran through her at the sight of him tired, rumpled, and half-slumped over the dining table, but smiling at her.

She cleared her throat delicately. "I am *sorry* for not trusting you and making you worry."

"Thank you. Will you tell me about the instructions from the fates?"

Her ankle pulsed angrily, but she ignored it, only flinching a little. "They said the death voyage is the space between me and the crown, and that the *tapestry remains untied.* Basically, they don't trust me and sent me off to the temple to get killed."

Aidan made an annoyed sound in the back of his throat. "Manipulative little dictators. No two death voyages have been the same, but the one thing they have in common is the fates making sure the new queen will bend to their whims."

Elysia's brow quirked. He'd never been quite so direct in his feelings about the fates. "I knew getting to the water would be tough, but..." Her cheeks pinked as she trailed off. "After seeing the temple and the acolytes on the grid, I didn't think there was a chance in the realms they could keep up with me. They look like they just sit around staring at their own reflections and stealing people's money all day."

Aidan's shoulders shook. "So arrogant."

Elysia didn't bother to defend herself given how thoroughly she'd been humbled. "So, what exactly did you all see? I assumed I didn't have a tail since the reaper prayer failed."

His jaw worked, his gaze homing in on her swollen ankle and the smattering of road rash decorating her skin. "We had eyes on you in the temple up until you were dragged back and Oren arrived."

She cringed and looked away. She'd hoped he hadn't seen the bone-breaking and magic use. "I'm surprised you didn't make a reaper cart me away."

Aidan leaned back in his chair, folding his arms. "To be honest, I was shocked Grim offered you the option."

"Why? They're following us around anyway."

Aidan blew out a half laugh. "There are rules. Reapers are not meant to be seen or heard. And they're absolutely not allowed to interfere. To do so goes against the laws of the living and the dead. If the fates found out, they would have punished him severely for allowing his people to act on your behalf."

Elysia drew back, slightly shocked. "I've barely even spoken to him since being here. He shouldn't have offered that—why would he do that?"

Aidan looked at her with both frustration and something softer. "You matter, and you seem to keep forgetting that."

Sidestepping his comment, she mused on this new information. "That must have been why Oren said to tell Grim he was welcome."

Aidan nodded even as he bristled. "And how was Oren?"

Her eyes went big as she made a face. "He turned the temple into a sinkhole, sent vines out of it, which pulled *very alive* acolytes down into its abyss, and then climbed out wearing a bearskin cape with the head as a hood."

Aidan exhaled and stared at the ceiling. "I was an only child as a mortal, you know."

"I actually very much can believe that."

He shot her a look. "Oren likes to think he's less dramatic than the rest of our siblings, but really he just likes to be dramatic from his woodland isolation."

Elysia chewed on a muffin. "I could see that. I told him about the grid, and he said he's going to come by."

Aidan looked appalled. "You invited him *here?* To our *home?*"

"No, *he* said he was going to stop by." She set the muffin down as pain shot through her entire body. Gritting her teeth, her face betrayed nothing. She didn't need Aidan swooping in. She remembered how he had *eased* her pain last time.

Still aghast, he grunted, "Very well. We'll deal with that later. I imagine we'll have to put up with the rest of them then too."

"How else did you think it was going to work?" *Ohmygods, I'm going to pass out.*

Grimacing, he stood and stretched. "I was hoping to have the reapers set up viewing stations in all of their homes, and therefore, never have to see them."

He was serious. *Okay, then.*

Elysia attempted to get up only for Aidan to make a sharp sound of disapproval as he flashed to her side. His hands gently guided her to standing.

"You really do smell like a fish," he muttered.

She glared back over her shoulder. "I can do it myself."

He looked down at her from over her head, dark hair falling onto his forehead as his fingers pressed firmly against her ribs. Little zaps of awareness shortened her breath, but she ignored it and wriggled free of his hands only for her good leg to collapse when a wave of dizziness rocked her. One arm under her shoulders and one banded beneath her knees, Aidan cradled her against his chest.

"Yes, you're really doing it, aren't you?"

Tipping her head back, her eyes narrowed. "I made it from my bedroom to here, and I can do it again."

While it wasn't a look she was familiar with, she would have almost described the soft exasperation on his face as *fond*.

"Really, Aidan, I just got a little dizzy, but I can get back to my room and wait for Maya."

All traces of fondness disappeared, and his voice became a growl. "Maya is lucky I'm not allowed to throw her in my prison. Spineless witch disappeared right when she was needed." Aidan's anger washed over her, and Elysia silently allowed it, curious about how Maya fit into the death realm's court.

But that seemed to be all he was going to say, his long strides smooth and efficient as he carried her through the house back to her room. The door swung open magically, and Aidan shook his head at the sight of her many piles of clothes strewn about, stopping abruptly to stare at the small collection of pens placed in a glass goblet like a trophy on her fireplace mantle.

"You do realize I've been blaming Grim for my disappearing pens."

Elysia smiled innocently. "They're just pens. Was I not supposed to borrow them?"

His eyelid twitched as he continued staring at her stolen goods. "Just pens," he echoed, clearly wanting to snatch them all up and put them in their color-coded homes back in his office.

A shit-eating grin weaseled its way onto her face, and Aidan looked down at her, his blue eyes widening. "This is what you find funny? Torturing the anxious and organized?"

"Very much so."

His voice deepened as he kicked the bathroom door open. "I'd throw you in the tub like a puppy if it weren't for your damned ankle."

Elysia made to tell him exactly what she thought of being compared to a dirty puppy, but then he was sliding her slowly, carefully down his front, giving her time to settle onto her good foot while still gripping his upper arms for support.

Her response died as she drank in the tortured look on his face. His words were a dark rumble. "I was awake all night imagining every terrible thing that could have happened to you, knowing I was powerless to stop it. I sat outside your door for hours, listening to you breathe. Please let me take care of you."

Her brown eyes grew wider, her fingers digging into the strength of his arms.

"You have no idea what it does to me that you could be so easily broken, and I'm *stuck* here while you wage this battle for us. Because war is coming, and I'm chained to my throne." His lips were against her throat now, kissing softly, nipping as he came upon the juncture of her neck and shoulders.

Her eyes closed, chest moving of its own accord. She didn't want this, couldn't want this. She needed the lines to be stark. Him on one side and her on the other. He had done terrible things. His fingers inched beneath her sweater, warm and smooth against her skin, while his lips feathered lightly where he had nipped. Sensation flooded her, heating her from the inside out, and then he was tugging her sweater up and over her head, leaving her bare.

An appreciative thrum rolled through Aidan's chest as he pulled back to look at her. "Tell me yes, Thorn. I need to hear your yes."

Heartbeat in her throat and between her ears, she gave a shaky, wordless nod.

Ink-stained fingers gently gripped her face. "Say it."

"Ye-es." She felt like a fawn instead of the viper she had once been. "But no sex," she blurted, cheeks crimson as she looked away.

A delighted light came into Aidan's burning eyes as he turned her face back to look at him. "Define that."

Her brain stuttered. The number of times she'd imagined his hands all over her body, and now she couldn't even muster a single coherent thought.

Those same scarred and ink-stained hands slid from her shoulders, grazing her breasts as they moved down, down, down to push against her pants. His hands stopped there, her skin buzzing beneath his touch.

"How about this?" One hand moved back to her clavicle, his finger tracing lightly down her sternum, making her skin goosebump and nipples peak without even a touch. "I'm going to take off all your clothes, and put you in this bath, and rub every inch of your filthy body until it's clean. Yes or no, Thorn?"

She swallowed hard, nodding fast as his rough laugh tickled against her, making her squirm. "Out loud."

"Y-yes," she stammered.

"Good girl," he murmured, and she flushed instantly, heat pooling in her lower stomach.

Hands dipping inside the band of her pants, he held her gaze as he dragged the soft material over her hips, even more slowly down her thighs, and then with the utmost care removed them without ever touching her bruised calf or ankle. He knelt at her feet, still staring up at her, one hand running up and down her good leg as she held on tight to his shoulders. His gaze dipped to her broken bones.

"I told you I could ease your pain, and I can—" Aidan's shoulders tensed beneath her hands as he warred with himself. "I should have asked you first if you would like me to ease your pain, but I'm selfish, and I didn't because if I do, then your inhibitions will be lowered, and I won't be able to touch you."

Her voice was a rasp. "Bath. Then fix it."

"Thank fuck."

Her stomach dropped at his obvious relief. Depositing her onto the dressing chair, he turned the bath knobs, testing the water and adding scented salts until the wafting steam became a eucalyptus mint cloud.

Before her pulse could settle or self-consciousness could kick in, he was lifting her and placing her in the large claw-foot tub. He frowned at her swollen ankle, turned around, and went back into her room only to return with a small wooden footstool and several pillows.

Elysia lifted herself, trying to stop him. "Aidan, you're going to wreck those pillows."

Ignoring her, his brow creased in concentration as he placed the stool and pillows beneath her ankle. When he turned back, she swallowed at the sight of his attention narrowing to only her. His gaze dripped down her naked body from her head to her toes, a slight groan escaping him. The hot water slipped over her pebbled skin, both relaxing and torturous as her blood sang under the blaze of his fiery blue blown-out eyes.

Button by button, Aidan undid his white shirt before tossing it aside and fluidly pulling his undershirt off, mussing the dark strands of hair at the crown of his head. Her fingers clutched the sides of the tub, and a little grin toyed at the edges of his mouth as his hands went to the button on his trousers until he finally removed all his clothing in one motion.

There was no hope for her heartbeat now. It walloped into an embarrassingly loud and heavy beat as she drank him in. Wide, strong shoulders and a lean, defined chest tapered into a hard stomach she knew came from long, disciplined hours on the mat. Her gaze shuddered as it lowered, and she saw all of him. Gods, she wanted to touch him. It had been torture to spar with him and pretend not to notice every stupid line and cut of his body, not to let her hands explore as they rolled across the mats.

Cream candles flickered to life as the dark plum curtain fell in front of the window, blocking the natural light. Suddenly bathed in shadow and cozy light, the mood deepened and Aidan moved, coming to the back of the tub. He grasped the detachable shower-head. Kava may have started to utilize indoor plumbing, but the mix of magic and engineering in the death realm was *luxury*. Aidan dropped to one knee, adjusting the sprayer until it was the perfect temperature. His fingers tapped lightly against the line of her jaw. "Drop your head."

For once she was compliant, tilting her head back without

question, her long brown hair cascading into the tub in a mess of waves, river water, and dirt. The warm water soaked into her hair, running down her back and turning her locks weighted. With a gentle clink, Aidan set aside the sprayer and rubbed shampoo between his fingers, making the sweet almond orange scent burst into the air. Strong fingers massaged her skull, and her eyes automatically closed as her head fell back even further into his hands and she sank deeper into the water. Aidan let out a pleased hum, continuing his ministrations far longer than she knew was necessary. Too soon, he rinsed her hair and lathered the lengths in conditioner, twisting the strands up into a clip to set, and then his hands were on her skin, fingers dipping dangerously over her shoulders, sliding over the tops of her breasts as he rubbed away the tension in her neck and traps. Over and over, his fingers stroked, simultaneously relaxing her body and heightening the need that burned relentlessly below.

The pad of his finger barely grazed her nipple, but a sound still escaped her mouth, making her cheeks burn as her legs clamped together. There was a rumbling in his chest, and then Aidan's hands slid down her back and under her ass, sending her forward until he could step into the tub and sink into the water. Strong thighs wrapped around hers, and her body tensed as he settled behind her, the length of him hot and hard against her ass and back.

A warm, soapy washcloth stroked down her arm, his fingers massaging both forearm and hand until she relaxed against his firm chest, her head falling back to him. Carrying on, he meticulously washed every dirty part of her before finally rinsing her hair and pulling the plug on the tub. Her heart dropped, but she refused to turn around. *Was he done?* Sensing her tension, Aidan flicked on the sprayer, resuming his languorous rinsing and stroking of her skin as the used bathwater drained. She shivered against the cold air and made to stand, but Aidan's hands dropped the shower head and clasped her hips, pulling her solidly into him as he leaned so close his hair tickled her cheek.

"I promised to rub every inch of you, didn't I?"

Her breath went out in a rush as she nodded, and his fingers dimpled further into her hips.

"I thought you were done." She dared a glimpse over her shoulder to find his sapphire eyes still blazing in the candlelight.

His voice went low, raising all the little hairs on her skin and sending a fresh wave of heat between her legs. "You'll know when we're done, Thorn."

Tub emptied, he turned the hot tap back on, refilling it with fresh, clean water. "You were *filthy*, and the water was full of salt and soap. Couldn't have that touching what I'm about to," he murmured against her ear, making her chest rise and fall as she squirmed against him. He squeezed her ass lightly in response. "So impatient."

Her usual fire stoked to life, and she turned with a glare. "Hardly, this is just—it's nothing." Her chin lifted as she looked away, refusing to look at his beautiful face.

Aidan's hand brushed over her chest, teasing her nipple, while the other traced light, careless shapes on the warmth between her thighs. "Is this what you think platonic co-rulers do?"

He was using that voice again.

"If they want to," she gritted out, doing her best to ignore the tantalizing sensations of his gods-cursed hands.

"Mmm," the sound rumbled against her bare back. "So you're not impatient then, and this is strictly platonic?"

A single finger swept lower, dipping into her liquid heat, sliding right where she wanted him for the briefest of touches before his palm pressed firmly against her, and a soft mewl slipped out against her best efforts to contain it.

"Yes." Her hands gripped against his thighs now as she leaned back into him. "Very platonic. Has to be."

The sweet pressure of his palm paused, both hands gliding up her ribs to cup her breasts. His fingers expertly grazed and pinched until her chest was heaving and she was biting against the muscle of his arm, wishing he would give her what she wanted.

But then he stopped, leaving her writhing as his strokes became silky over her stomach.

"Tell me why it has to be." His voice was practically guttural, the sound reaching inside her and making her pant.

Ankle long forgotten, she made to turn, but she was immediately held in place with one arm banded around her waist and the other collaring the edge of her throat.

"Answer me." His mouth moved like fire down her neck, his other hand finally hovering over where she wanted it again.

Frustration built within her. "Why won't you touch me?" she rasped, unused to not being able to control a situation such as this.

He put the barest pressure on her throat, and she melted, her head fuzzing with pleasure. "I *am* touching you, Thorn. Now tell me why I can't love you while I fuck you. Tell me why I can't love you while you rule beside me. Tell me why the idea of my devotion makes you want to run."

Her eyes flew open, stomach clenching. "Because—" Her words cut off as she choked on them.

"Tell me," he demanded.

Worked to a frenzy, her emotions eluded her usual guard. "Because you're the one man I should never touch while somehow also being too good for me. What does it say if I allow this? You're the god who ruined my life." Her face burned now, but not for the same pleasant reasons as only moments ago.

She was smart. She was cunning and even brave. But she had also been selfish and the reason for so many horrible deaths. She had been born cursed and treated as such for over twenty years. A few weeks of Aidan's stable presence wasn't going to unearth and heal all the beliefs buried in her. She'd barely started to believe she deserved to be alive—something like love wasn't for her.

And worst of all, she *did* want him. She wanted to bathe in what he was pouring out. She was terrible enough to want the person who had caused destruction to sweep through her home.

Destruction that was about to steal the life of her sister and possibly reach its hands out through her whole world.

His arms wrapped around her, holding her body tight against him, voice rich and deep. "I've watched you for years, and I saw *nothing* that would change how I feel now. Hard lives make for hard decisions, and you never once made yours without bearing the cost. You carry every life lost somewhere within you as if it will pay penance, but there is no penance. There's only now, and *now* I see a woman doing her best to grow and change after a lifetime of being hunted and coerced without anyone showing her the way."

His fingers tightened and then slowly released as he loosened his hold on her. "I can only swear to spend the rest of my immortal life atoning for what I've done if you'll let me, but I understand why that isn't enough."

The promise crashed against her, bold and blunt and terribly unashamed in its honesty. Her hands gripped his thighs again before uselessly wiping at the lone tears leaking free.

"You can't possibly love someone just like that, Aidan. It's too fast, and you shouldn't make promises you can't keep."

The soothing, melodic tone she'd once been so enraptured with returned to his voice. "I will decide who I love and what promises I am capable of keeping. I only ask that you keep letting me in."

The hot water lapped up over her. "I think I have been," she whispered, afraid to say it aloud.

"And you've been doing it so well," he returned, moving her wet hair away from her shoulder with a kiss.

She hiccuped a laugh. "No, I haven't. I left you a note and could have died."

He buried his face in the crook of her neck, smothering a rough, pained laugh. "Not wise to remind me of your bad behavior right now." His teeth sank into her skin in reprimand, and the slow simmer of want and need surged within her all too easily.

Her breath hitched as he sent his hands down to the creases of her hips. "Tell me again."

She closed her eyes as his fingers squeezed her thighs, and she ground against him. "Tell you what?" Breathless, her voice floated.

"Tell me yes," he growled.

Her heart skipped now. "*Yes*. It doesn't have to mean something." The still breathless words were achingly hollow even to her own ears.

But Aidan accepted what she gave. "One day, it will only be yes," he murmured darkly against her skin.

CHAPTER 30

HER HEAD DROPPED BACK, her spine arching as his mouth latched onto her neck, his hands working her breasts until she panted before sliding down to tease her. His fingers circled and slid, always backing off right as she wanted—no, *needed*—more.

She placed her own hand over his, pressing his fingers against her and narrowing her eyes at him over her shoulder.

Aidan grasped her chin, bringing his mouth against hers, but not kissing her. "So. Impatient." His lips brushed over hers, sending tingles through her body. "Maybe you're not ready for this. Maybe we should wait."

A hot flush of needy irritation spread through her, and she found herself cursing her ankle since it stopped her from flipping around. If she could move, she'd have him *exactly* where she wanted him in moments. Instead, she was stuck with her leg elevated, waiting for this *infuriating* man to get the job done.

He smiled against her neck, wrapping her long, wet locks around his hand until he gripped close to her head, and then he pulled, so her head rested against his shoulder and pec, her brown eyes staring up into his blue. The water lazed over her chest, her rosy nipples peeking through, and Aidan once again stroked a thumb over her until she writhed uselessly in his hold.

"Unlike you, I have patience in spades, Thorn. Don't test me, or you'll hobble out of here with enough frustration to fight ten men, and we both know nothing you do will sate it."

In response, Elysia plunged her hand beneath the water, reaching for herself. "Oh, I'm sure this would do just fine."

Soot-stained wisps locked her wrists, forcing her hands to the side of the tub as she gasped, unable to move. Aidan tugged her hair, a wicked smirk gracing his face as he stared down at her. "We're clearly going to have to set some rules since you can't behave."

His large, scarred hand ran over her breast, tweaking her nipple, then continuing down until it reached between her legs and slapped gently. A thrum shot through her body. His mouth curved at how her face heated, and she pressed her lips together against a moan.

"When we're together..." His hand came out of the water and ran silkily down her face, over her lips and throat, to the softness of her stomach. He grabbed tightly onto the swell of her hips and ass. "This is mine."

Her chest heaved as she blinked up at him. Fuck her ankle, she was going to scream if he didn't take her now. Another smile twitched at his lips as if he knew what she was thinking.

"Do you agree, Thorn?"

He reached down, finally using the kind of pressure that sent stars into her vision.

Mindlessly, she pressed her hips up, still chasing the feeling he kept abruptly taking away. Two more smooth, perfect circles, and then his hand disappeared again, squeezing her hip, waiting for her answer.

"Fine," she bit out, looking away from the intense fire of his gaze.

The hand still tangled in her hair massaged into her skull. "That doesn't sound very enthusiastic."

He carefully undid his hand from her hair, and dislodged himself from the tub, sitting her up as he did so. She grabbed hold of the edges of the tub, turning slightly to stare at him aghast.

"Are you *kidding* me right now?"

He paused, still half-bent as he made to stand, and Elysia regretted her outburst when she realized she was now eye to eye with a very prominent part of his anatomy. Long, but not overly thick, she let her ankle slide into the tub so she could twist and take him by the base and slowly stroke him to the tip.

Aidan shuddered, his blue eyes flaring and soot-stained wisps of power leaking into the room. One by one, his power removed her fingers as he stared down at her, tortured and battling something she couldn't see.

"Fuck it."

She barely heard the growl, but the words slipped out. He lifted her out of the tub, water splashing everywhere as he stalked back into her room, and threw her down on the bed, his power snapping out to be a cloud beneath her ankle. She lay back, naked and sprawled as he stood at the end of the bed. His hands crept up her thighs too slowly for her liking.

She propped herself on one elbow, scowling at him. "I thought when I told you *yes*, you would do something about it."

Faster than her breath could escape, his warm, naked body lay partially over hers, his fingers suddenly filling her. She stretched into the sensation, a soft sound hissing in her throat. Dark hair fell onto his forehead as he held himself above her, easing his fingers in and out slow enough that it was excruciating. Writhing, she began to burn, clutching at his shoulders and arms.

"More," she demanded.

Aidan let out a low laugh, relaxed and unhurried at her side. "What was that, Thorn? You want me to go slower?" His pace lazed, slipping through her heat, and curling into her perfectly. Her hips lifted, seeking him, but his power shot out, holding her down.

"Is this mine?" he asked again, pausing and clearly enjoying the sight of her frustrated and wanting.

"Yes," she spat, her gaze narrowing to as much of a glare as she could manage.

Satisfied, he covered her with his body, pressing her into the mattress, and nipped at her throat with a growl. "Good."

He slid his fingers in, his palm grinding against her.

"That means *this*."

His hand left her, trailing lightly over sensitive skin.

"Is mine to pleasure."

His fingers slammed in again, finally allowing her hips to push up into him.

"As I see fit."

She panted. He could say whatever he wanted, so long as he didn't stop. She moved with him, his pacing becoming steady and building. He kept working her, but one hand grabbed her face, his lips an inch from her skin.

"I would wait a thousand years for you. But in here? I need you to let me have you. Let me worship and taste every part of you until your body knows the truth. I am safe. I will always wait for your yes, and even when you're a pain in my ass, your only cries will be from pleasure. Can you trust me with this?"

"Yes." Her brown eyes were likely wild, but for the first time her yes was emphatic without a single hesitation, and she watched the change come over him at the difference.

"Good girl," he murmured huskily. Lifting her, he brought them both upright, her arms wrapping and clinging around his neck so there was no space between them. One hand on her lower back, he fixed his burning cobalt gaze onto hers as he deepened his touch, increasing the pace until a hot flush spread across her chest.

"You flush so pretty when you're about to come for me." His low words sent her flying, lights and sensation tipping her over as she soared, collapsing against him in sweet relief. Limp against him, she pressed her lips to his skin.

Aidan laid her back on the pillows and crawled on top of her, the length of him even harder than before and brushing against her. She made to lazily pull him closer, but he stopped her, his power knocking her hands away with a slight growl.

"I'm not done."

In an instant, her good knee was bent, foot propped on his shoulder as he dove face-first between her legs. She fell back against the pillows, another orgasm building immediately as an embarrassingly low moan came out of her mouth. The sound of her pleasure didn't slow him now. Done playing, he worked harder, taking her small breast into his hand, pinching and flicking her nipple until she was gripping the bedding and shoving herself at his face. His soft laugh rumbled against her heat in a way that made her eyes roll back, and then his fingers slipped back inside her and she was gone. She broke with a ragged sound, coming so hard tears spilled from the edges of her eyes. Body shaking, she came undone as he continued to tease the very last drops of her pleasure out into existence.

Boneless, she melted into the bed as Aidan lay down beside her, brushing her wet hair away from her face.

"You're perfect," he said, his voice so serious and quiet that her heart swelled before she could hide from the words. She said nothing though, blushing as he settled in beside her, running soothing hands over her arms and relaxing her even further. "Would you like me to ease your ankle now?"

Turning to him, she laughed, finally noticing the persistent pain. "I haven't thought about it."

His smile was smug, and she shook her head.

"Drug me, Your Deadliness."

"As you wish," he murmured, his blue eyes still burning. The same intoxicating but sleepy feeling she remembered from when she first crashed through the realms to find the god who had promised her a deal swept through her from head to toe.

She smiled sleepily at him, and his chest moved with laughter.

"Rest," he ordered softly, and she did. She closed her eyes, more content and at ease than she'd ever been.

CHAPTER 31

ELYSIA PERCHED on the edge of a table they'd brought into Aidan's office, looking down at a map. Kava, along with two of the smaller southern kingdoms below it, had black flags pinned to them. Black meant Garrison had already overtaken the kingdom. Yellow, like the flag pinned to Sagondia, signified it was on the chopping block. Elysia knocked over the yellow flag in frustration.

It had been a month since the events in the White Sands. She'd been holed up in the death realm while her ankle healed, forced to watch the grid as her friends courted gods and built ever-expanding black markets for magical goods and weapons. Maya had set her bones and reduced the healing from what would have been at least three months to one, but still.

She was going out of her mind.

It didn't help that Aidan seemed to be keeping a solid distance from her. He was polite, he was attentive, but he was distant. She didn't want polite. She wanted him to grab her hair and talk in that godsdamn voice again. The aftermath of their bathroom escapade was that she had become painfully aware of every glance, every brief touch. And she loathed him for it. How the fuck was she supposed to get anything done like this?

She sighed loudly, and Aidan looked over at her from his desk, his pen poised in the air above a ledger. It was a purple pen. She was going to have to steal that, she didn't have a purple pen yet. Aidan noticed her gaze on his pen, and his eyes narrowed.

"Don't even think about it, you little thief."

Elysia threw him a completely untrustworthy smile. A chime rang throughout the house, and she straightened to attention. "What in the realms was that?"

Aidan stood with a frown. "The doorbell."

She jumped up, glad for the excuse to stop staring at the map. "I'll get it!"

His frown deepened. "The only people who ring doorbells are ones I don't care to see."

He strode out of his office, still gripping his purple pen protectively. Elysia laughed, he'd put it down eventually. *And she'd be there!* Trailing after him, she stopped in the living room, peering into the foyer. He had a point about unwanted visitors. Better to take stock of things from here. Crusher trotted up beside her, letting out a whine of annoyance as she stared into the foyer. Well, that wasn't promising, but she also hadn't turned into a massive man-eating creature, so maybe it was fine.

Aidan shrugged on his suit coat, buttoning the front, and cracking his neck like he already knew this was going to take something out of him. Then he flicked his wrist, the door swinging open to reveal the front walkway congested with people she assumed were his siblings. The garrulous chatter cut off as they all craned their necks to look at Aidan before flooding in the door with obnoxiously loud remarks about how they always forgot how *small* and *quaint* his home was. Elysia glanced around. *Small?* She still wasn't sure she'd seen all of the estate. It was like there were rooms for the rooms.

The woman she recognized from the grid as the goddess of pleasure spun around in a sleek, long leather trench coat. "Show us your magical wall then. Oren said your mortal mentioned there would be betting and games."

Oren lumbered in last, ducking his head to fit through the doorway. "Francesca, that's not how you greet someone." He clapped a hand on Aidan's shoulder, and Elysia bit back a grin as she watched Aidan grimace and shirk the touch. "Little brother, tell us of your troubles. Your mortal, whom you really should take better care of—you do remember how fragile they are, don't you? She said your realm is crumbling by the day. You never did take me up on my offer to teach you the art of realm stewardship, and now see where you are."

Elysia could practically hear Aidan's jaw grind from the living room. She grinned. Today was going much better already.

Francesca frowned, giving Aidan the once-over. "What is wrong with his lover? Have you not been able to woo the one fated for you? Is she turned off by all the...*dead*? Does she not know how we are made?"

Oren tutted. "She was helping my boy blow up an old temple of mine and got busted up by a bone-breaker. Looked like her foot was hanging on by its skin. Didn't look right at all."

She waved him off. "No, no, nothing so boring as bones. Where is she? I want to see her. I'll determine the cause of your bedroom problems, sweet brother. Nothing a little of my power won't fix."

A short angular woman with pin-straight brown hair, thick glasses, and chunky sensible shoes looked seriously between them all and interrupted. "I came here to see your invention. Can we get on with it, please? Oh, Loretta is going to make an entrance, so be prepared for that."

Aidan made a gesture down by his side that Elysia could only interpret as him silently telling her to get the fuck out of there while she still could, and though she appreciated that given the obvious headache his family was going to be...this was the most fun she'd had in weeks.

Elysia strolled into the foyer with a bright smile and years of Crown training in hand. "I can take you to the grid. It's a bit of a walk, but the weather really is warming up, and I think you'll be quite intrigued with what you see." Crusher cemented her butt to

Elysia's foot and glared at the gods, but none of them seemed to notice as they looked Elysia up down, judging and weighing her with zero effort to hide it.

Francesca pinched the bridge of her nose. "I am embarrassed to be your sister right now, Aidan. The woman is starved and practically enraged with neglect. *Look* at her sexual energy. She is young and ravenous, and you ignore her like an old maid." Her voice heated. "You should be flogged. Flogged and left to consider your actions for a few centuries. This is *not* how I taught you to please a woman. I would not love you either."

Elysia blinked, stunned and unsure of whether to laugh, cry, or run.

"*Franny.*" Aidan's voice chilled the room instantly. "I am well-aware of what I'm doing, and there will not be *any* further comments on the state of my future queen's sexual energy. Are we understood?" His final words could have cut glass.

She sniffed, the leather of her jacket squeaking as she readjusted herself. Ignoring Aidan, she wrapped an arm around Elysia's shoulders, pulling her into her side as she glared at him. "He always has been so delicate. You just come to me and we'll get you sorted." She walked toward the door, tugging Elysia along with a tight grip on her shoulder. "Now show us this grid before Ramona loses it."

Nothing like being called sexually ravenous and deprived in front of the man who had been acting like he hadn't pinned her down with his sooty little shadows and made her come harder than she ever had in her life. So much for acting unbothered. Francesca had just sold them both out in five seconds flat.

Elysia shook it off with a practiced smile. "Right this way." With a crew of gods on her heels, she guided them through the woods and into the village. Throwing open the entrance to the warehouse, she called back over her shoulder. "Now, once we're up these stairs, you'll be able to see the grid. Feel free to watch for a while, and then once you're ready, Aidan, Maya, and Grim can answer your questions." She was going to get the heck out of here before anyone else took a look at her *sexual energy*.

She lingered by the top of the stairs as they all traipsed in, oodling at the massive wall that held the grid. Eyes on the gods, she made to take a single step backward to begin her escape when she found her feet stuck to the floor.

"What the f—" she mumbled, ripping at her legs, trying to get her feet off the ground. Suddenly, he was there behind her, hands in his pockets, ducking his face down so his words tickled the back of her neck.

"Got that potion from Maya. You're not going *anywhere*, Thorn." He brushed his knuckles down the back of her neck and then he strode past her into the fray of his siblings, looking every bit like a god who had once run gambling rings.

Elysia tried to pick her foot up again to no avail. In the distance, Franny cooed at Aidan. "See? Was that so hard? She blooms for you, little brother, there is hope yet!"

"I am begging you to shut the fuck up, Franny." Aidan gestured to Grim and Maya, who begrudgingly wandered over from where they had been skulking and likely hoping not to be needed. Aidan cleared his throat, about to explain the magical mechanics of the grid, when an old woman with short white curly hair stomped up the stairs and shoved her purse at Elysia.

"Be a dear and hold this."

Elysia reflexively accepted the overly large carpet-style purse, looking over to the group in befuddlement.

Dressed in a smart skirt and lady-jacket, the older woman grouched as she approached the rest of the gods.

"Whatever happened to formal invitations? Sending a messenger?" She scowled at Aidan. "Poor form, young man, poor form."

Aidan stared over the slightly hunched woman's head out the window, his nostrils flaring briefly as he attempted but failed to look remorseful. "Loretta, this was an unplanned event, as I am sure you are well-aware. Had it been planned, you would have received an invitation."

She folded her arms and made a sharp noise. "You should have had us here months ago. I watch and I watch. I wait and I wait. And still you all sit on your immortal asses doing nothing. And *you* know the odds. I know what you've been fretting and spiraling over in those ledgers of yours."

Looking past Aidan, she glared at every single god in attendance for good measure. "Are we going to allow a *mortal king* to destroy the stability we have created? You do know he aims for our wellspring. Plans to cut off the very source of our imbuement, so that mortals will be born without their divine spark. We have jobs for a reason! If we can't do them, then the fates will end us and begin again as they have done before. Is that what you want? To be wiped from existence?" Reaching into her pocket, Loretta unwrapped a small hard candy and popped it into her mouth, sucking on it noisily while shooting everyone looks that made them duck their gazes, abashed and properly chastised.

Elysia vaguely remembered Aidan explaining how mortals received a drop of diluted magic, but she had no idea how the wellspring worked, or how someone like Garrison could impact it. Sickening dread filled her stomach as she watched the gods stay silent. They looked ill. Like they hadn't truly believed things could be that bad, but now that Loretta had spoken, they did.

"Oh, stop sulking," Loretta groused. "Show us your wall, Aidan."

Aidan rubbed his ink-stained fingers together, his face hardened in worry, but then he nodded. "Very well. As you can see, the grid gives us the possibility of watching the mortals who we have theorized as being key to the unfolding events. Interestingly, most of them fall into different houses, which led us to consider the possibility of gods championing mortals and giving points for behaviors that improve our overall odds of defeating Garrison. However, open betting could work as well where we place bets in live time on what we believe will occur. This would be messier, but possibly allow us to capitalize on the dramatics in a more effective manner, playing off our family's tendency to wish to outdo one another. We've been increasing our reaper team to handle the uptick in work as they are the ones following the mortals. Of course, we are open to suggestions at this point, as you all know the siblings much better than me."

Oren puffed out his chest. "My boy will trample you all. The fates already told the new lady of the dead that he's to go after Garrison. Basically, isn't even a contest at this rate."

Ramona adjusted her thick glasses dryly. "Your boy would be dead without mine." She paused. "That or mine might get him killed. And did you ever consider that he might die trying to kill his father? Aidan, what are the odds on Topp Blatz dying?"

Aidan cringed and muttered something Elysia couldn't hear that made Oren's face turn red. "How does she even know about my boy? Did she get to see the grid before us?"

Ramona stared at Oren like he was a bug. "Some of us actually do our jobs instead of getting drunk and making storms in the woods. Rollickus has been petitioning me for months. He wastes his brilliance on your axe-wielding forest brat." She leaned in closer, looking impressively menacing given her stature compared to Oren's. "And with odds like his, maybe your boy should stick to playing with the little animals and leave the real work to those of us with brains."

Elysia looked at the back of Aidan's head like she could burn holes through it. *Topp had bad odds?* Why hadn't he told her that? That was information she should have. Gods, she wouldn't have even told Topp about what the fates said if she had known that. She knew Aidan was tracking *the odds* in his ledgers, but she hadn't realized he meant *their* odds, as in who was going to live or die and the fate of the world. Her gaze narrowed on the anxious, number-spinning god. As soon as she could scrub her memory of being called sexually ravenous and force herself to look him in the eye again, they were going to have a chat.

Grim coughed loudly, breaking up the squabble. "Does anyone else have any questions or suggestions?"

AIDAN SAT SPRAWLED in one of the living room armchairs with the fire blazing. Face resting in his hand, his hair fell into his eyes as he stared tiredly into the flames. Elysia was curled up on the rug, wrapped in a blanket and clutching a cup of tea. Still peeved, she glanced at him. The man was drained, but she needed answers, and she wanted them *now*.

"Are you happy with the plan?"

Aidan nodded, eyes still stuck to the fire, his fingers now sinking into the skin above his jawline. "Loretta's help will be invaluable—she's an oracle, if you didn't realize. With her assistance, I can narrow down the most likely paths to success in a fraction of the time it would have taken me alone." He inhaled tiredly, shifting so he could look at her. "Once we have the most likely scenarios along with the odds, we can do a big reveal with *all* the gods, and the meddling will commence."

Elysia tucked her legs underneath her, allowing the blanket to pool around her lap. "What could possibly go wrong?" she murmured.

The corner of Aidan's mouth pulled up. "Only everything."

"What are Topp's odds?" The blunt, blurted question turned her stomach upside down. Aidan's breath deepened, his chest moving like there was a weight on it while his blue eyes cast over her and then pulled away.

Sitting up, he unbuttoned his jacket and leaned forward, clasping his hands together. "I'll have a better idea once Loretta and I get to work."

Her tongue pressed against the roof of her mouth as she stared at him. That was a shit answer, and he knew it. Her dark eyes bore into him. She could sit here all night if he wanted, but he *was* going to give her a real answer.

Sensing her mulishness, Aidan's hand dropped heavy on his thigh, his mouth pinched. "The most likely outcome right now is that he dies trying to kill his father. *But* defeating Garrison is still on the table, which tells me that either something needs to change, or even if Topp dies, it contributes to Garrison falling."

Elysia's eyes welled, and her nostrils flared as she swallowed. "You should have told me. I wouldn't have told him what the fates said. It was cruel to let me do that." She turned her face away from him, staring at the fire.

Aidan's voice became sharp. "The fates wanted you to tell him. I stood against the fates once, and I won't directly do so again. We have to be careful."

Anger overrode her guilt and fear. "You're *gods*. What could have possibly happened that you're all so afraid of the fates?"

Her condescension wasn't missed by Aidan, but he simply looked at his long, ink-stained fingers before coming to some internal decision.

"Ask me again another time." His voice was quiet but firm, and his blue eyes burned.

Her brows turned down. It wasn't his friend's life on the line. "I'm asking you *now*."

Aidan stood, brushing his hair back into place and tugging on the sleeves of his jacket. "No. I've respected your need for space. I've supported you the best I can given what you'll allow. And now I'm asking you to let this be. It's my story to tell, and tonight isn't the time, but I *will* tell you."

Elysia drew back as if he had slapped her. She stumbled awkwardly over her words. "Okay. I didn't realize—okay."

He nodded stiffly, color flushing the tops of his cheekbones. "I'll need to focus on my work with Loretta. You should continue training with Grim and Maya this week."

Elysia dipped her chin, still confused, but also embarrassed she had clearly overstepped a line she hadn't known existed.

Aidan stopped with his hand on the doorframe as he was leaving. "Odds are only odds, Elysia. Humans are too interesting to be beholden to calculations. Even magical calculations like mine that go beyond the math."

She twisted to see him looking at her with a sad, contemplative expression.

"I am the god of the dead. My magic is of death and renewal. My shadows are the soot of decomposing magic that will be reborn—raw magic as you know it. I am well-acquainted with the difference between the soul of a mortal with a well-lived life and one who never knew the satisfaction of purpose. I would be *cruel* to steal his volition and purpose from him. Death is not the worst thing that can happen to a man." He paused, his shadows gently brushing against her cheek. "The odds can and will change as the gods become involved."

Aidan walked away, leaving her with more questions than answers, and her magic rolled within her, seeking release to chase him down and give her what she wanted, but she held it. If Aidan could respect her sky-high walls, then she could back off... for now.

CHAPTER 32

"I THOUGHT you were going to *train* me." Elysia grumbled as she studied the organizational flowchart of the different types of reapers and their roles within the volt.

Grim gave her an unamused look. "You're going to need to know these things."

He was right, but it had been a month of this, meeting with Grim and being restricted to physical training and flow-charts. She had thought they were going to be working on mastering her magic, and instead, she was learning about how reapers could shoot acid to incapacitate anyone who stood in the way of their duties. Maya had said she wanted an apprentice and then continually disappeared whenever she was needed. Which meant Elysia's magical training had come to an abrupt and unfortunate halt given that neither Grim nor Aidan knew how to train someone with magic like hers. The extent of Aidan's knowledge had been what he taught her, and he had no idea how to proceed from there.

She eyed Grim and fought back a grimace. Death by unnatural stomach acid was not on her to-do list. Pushing away the paper, she raised her eyebrows hopefully. "Or you could show me your wings. That could be educational." She hadn't even known the reapers had wings.

Grim ran a hand over his short dark hair before shaking his head and tapping a finger on the paper. "Memorize this and I'll consider it."

An hour later they had moved onto the rules of reaping, and her innate curiosity had taken over. She'd scribbled page after page of notes, constantly interrupting Grim to ask questions and understand the function and limitations of his reapers. They were neck-deep in a discussion on which mortals were considered theirs to reap when Grim's office door flung open with a bang.

Maya stood in the doorway wearing a tiered lilac dress that floated around her body and made her gray eyes and freckles pop. She flounced into the room, the woven basket on her arm swinging. "Sorry I'm late, I knew this was going to be boring." She glanced around. "Gods, are you ever going to decorate in here?"

Elysia clamped her mouth shut. His office *was* extremely plain. It was like he had sucked out all the charm found in the rest of the house and then hung up two plaques for his reaping accomplishments as if that fixed things.

Grim's over-muscled shoulders hiked up as he scowled. "Foundational knowledge comes before practice." His fitted shirt bunched against his enormous biceps as he folded his arms.

Maya leaned against the wall and crossed her ankles delicately and smiled. "Well, it's my turn now. Come along, then." She nodded at Elysia and pushed off the wall expectantly.

"We aren't done yet. I haven't even taken her on a reaping," Grim growled.

Elysia perked up. "You were going to take me on a reaping?" She really wanted to see a reaping in action.

"Liar. You wouldn't have taken her on a reaping for weeks. I know how many lectures you have stored away in that terrifyingly dull brain of yours."

Grim heated. "You didn't get to go on a reaping because you were the worst student I've ever had."

Maya lifted one shoulder lightly. "I've met your reapers, so I find that hard to believe." She glanced at Elysia. "Dumber than rocks, some of them. Very strong, though. Great at lifting things and putting them down."

Elysia's hand went over her mouth as she pointedly looked away from Grim. Once she'd collected herself, she reached across the desk to touch Grim's arm. "Tomorrow, same time? I appreciate you teaching me. I learned a lot today, and I'd really like to go on a reaping."

Embarrassed, he flushed, clearing his throat and tidying the papers strewn across the desk. "Glad you found it helpful."

Maya made for the door. "He'll live on that compliment for weeks. Let's *go* already."

Grim pushed away from his desk, his chest puffing. "I'm monitoring."

Maya halted and slowly spun back around, a strange white light cracking through her eyes. Elysia barely held back her flinch, her gaze darting to Grim, who was now pressing his hands against the top of the desk and leaning over it as if daring her to cross him.

Her eyes flashed back to their usual gray, and Maya gave a tight smile. "I thought we'd moved past this."

His thick jaw tightened, but he didn't answer, and Maya's mouth thinned in response. "You want to waste your day watching me teach her what she should have been taught since infancy? Fine by me."

She stormed out of the office, her boots striking heavily as she disappeared down the hall. Elysia raised a brow as she looked at Grim, waiting for him to explain, but as a man of few words he remained true to form, simply rolling his shoulders and staring after Maya like he wished there could be more eliminating and less monitoring.

"You don't trust her," Elysia stated, trying to leave an opening for him to expand on.

His dark brown eyes cut to hers. "You shouldn't either. Aidan has his reasons for allowing her to be here, but I don't share them."

ELYSIA ENTERED a room in the estate she'd never seen before. With buttercream yellow walls, lace curtains on the windows, and floral upholstered furniture, it looked like a grandmother's dream.

Maya spun in a circle, her dress flitting out around her. "The boys have their offices, and I have *this*."

Elysia took a seat on a cracked warm brown wooden stool. "And what is *this*?"

Grim stationed himself near the door like some kind of silent, disapproving sentry. "It's where she tests her shit and her other unnatural practices."

Maya nodded and set her woven basket on a table. "I needed a magically reinforced space that could handle my inventions and *unnatural practices,* as Grim called them."

Elysia looked between them warily. "Which would be?"

Maya busied herself grabbing objects out of the basket. She placed an hourglass, gold-faded iron scissors, and what looked like one of Aidan's ledgers on the table. "We'll work with those later. First, you need to understand what you've even been doing all these years because, my gods, do you have it all wrong."

Elysia moved from the stool to the purple and gray rug, coming to a cross-legged position. She wound a strand of hair around her finger, thinking hard.

"How could my magic be anything other than finding secrets? Even here or somewhere like Bellia with full access, that's what happens." She gestured emphatically as she continued to process aloud. "I call on my magic, it homes in on what I'm seeking and yanks me around until I find it, or I can sort through the visual and emotional cues that flood in from whoever."

Maya gave Elysia her full attention. "You're not finding secrets. You're looking for power sources."

Elysia shook her head ,already disagreeing, but Maya cut her off. "As you've already learned from working with Aidan, there are different types of power you can transmute. When you were in Kava and magic was almost non-existent, you were most drawn to the few people who had magic you could have stolen to use for your own if you'd had the capacity."

"What about all the mundane secrets and information I collected in Kava? Or how I can purposely seek information now?"

Maya paused, giving her a soft crooked smile. "Our magic is in relationship with us. You're hypervigilant to emotions, mood, information because you needed to be, so your magic learned to use this as well. Growing up where you did, your magic would overtake you, latching on and dragging you around because you were finally giving yourself what you needed. I imagine the sensation of being controlled has lessened now, but you still trained yourself to be able to find weaker sources such as emotion or information, which is excellent. We can simply improve that skill instead of starting from scratch."

Elysia was dumbfounded. "But I never made or did anything once I found a source."

Maya shrugged. "It was Kava, and you had no idea to even try. You removed a stranger's pain, didn't you? I realize the realm did the transmutation once you dropped the solidified raw magic into the river, but you managed that with Aidan's awful teaching. It likely won't be that simple learning how to *do* something with the power you take, but if you'd grown up somewhere normal, someone would have explained all of this to you when you were a child and over years you would have mastered it. Some of magic is innate, some is always training and practice."

Elysia looked over at Grim. "Is this true?" Her mind was spinning, bouncing back through the years, wondering at every time she'd thought she'd been racing after secrets.

Grim sat on the floor with one knee bent and one leg out in front of him and nodded like this was obvious. "People used to call anyone with this power rippers. Usually, people have their proclivities and tend to rip from specific sources and transmute similarly. You developed an affinity for mental and emotional information, but given how drawn you were to plants in Kava, there's a strong chance nature may be a good source for you. Ripping other people's magic and power may prove difficult, but it's worth attempting for battle purposes."

Her eyes went wide as a very specific memory returned to her at his use of the word ripper. Her voice lowered. "Last time I was in the mortal realm, I—I used a man's power. When that man broke my ankle and was going to keep breaking my bones, and I don't even know what happened, but I took it and—" She paled, her stomach souring at what she'd done. "I broke *all* of his bones."

Grim's face remained clean of any judgment. "Common in child rippers. Instead of ripping and transmuting, you just returned it to the sender. You might not be able to do that unless in mortal danger—like I said, most rippers have specific sources they tend to draw from. Working with us will give you control, though." His eyes darkened. "And then you can break their bones on purpose if they try to harm you."

Still uncomfortable, she voiced another question. "What do you think I'll be able to do?"

Anxiety rushed through her. She just wanted to be able to protect herself again. She hated being the weakest one in a fight.

Maya's grin was vicious. "We'll dabble in the areas I think you're most likely to excel in."

"Such as?" she asked warily.

"Nature and death, obviously. We'll start with plants and work our way to necromancy."

Her stomach bottomed out now. "Necromancy," she repeated.

Grim grunted in dissent. "Not necromancy. Anything but

necromancy. You don't see Aidan running around abusing his chthonic powers or bringing corpses back to life. He keeps them here where they belong." Elysia was pretty sure he said something about a rule-breaking degenerate under his breath.

Maya's face flattened. "While your domain remains the harvesting and transport of souls, his is the entirety of death and the dead, and you would do well to remember it. He simply hides it—likely because of your hypocritical disdain. How do you think your reapers are made? There would be no reapers without Aidan calling them into new undead life. He's so ashamed, he doesn't even *look* at your reaper choices. He plunges his hands in the dirt, calls them, and *leaves*."

"That's not—"

But Maya was already breezing past Grim's protests. "Okay, first things first, you need to improve your ability to immediately find and rip magic from your surroundings. We'll start easy. I'm going to hide several highly magical objects, and your job is to find them."

Elysia nodded.

"Once you've collected them, we'll practice ripping."

She picked at a loose thread in the rug. "Do you think if I get better at this, I could find the talisman?" She'd tried every evening since coming to Aidan's realm, and every time she failed.

Grim looked at her intently. "You've been trying to subvert the death voyage?"

She turned to him. "Who's to say that isn't a part of my death voyage? I was told to find the talisman—we don't have time for the fates to decide I'm suddenly worthy of a grand reveal. Of course, I've tried. I've tried every day," she muttered.

Something shone in Maya's eyes at this. "You haven't felt anything when you try?"

She shook her head. "It's like slamming into a brick wall."

"They're blocking you then. Likely snipping any threads that would allow you to find it." Her face settled into harsh determination. "No matter. There are ways around that."

"This is the shit you both can't be doing. This is why you have a babysitter, Maya." He turned to Elysia. "And you, don't fuck directly with the fates. That's how we got in this godsdamn mess in the first place. If you want to push back, it has to be thoughtful and planned."

Elysia cocked her head. "We're in this mess because Aidan made a stupid deal with Garrison."

Grim's face tightened along with his posture, but he said nothing. His dark eyes fastened onto her though, telling her she didn't have the story quite right.

Elysia nodded to herself. It sounded like the conversation Aidan didn't want to have was becoming more and more pressing. He had explained his role in the Fall of Kava, taking the blame without hesitation or pause. She never sensed any deceit when he spoke about the deal with Garrison, but like most things, maybe it was more complicated than its appearance.

Then again, maybe that was wishful thinking. Because no matter how much she was attracted to him, she'd be lying if she said that his past wasn't an obstacle for her. A glaring obstacle. He was the reason her kingdom and people were dying. The reason her sister was sick. Fresh guilt constricted her. It was too easy to forget what he had done when she was near him. He'd done her a favor in withdrawing, and she needed to remember that.

Maya snapped her fingers to get Elysia's attention. The ledger, scissors, and hourglass disappeared, and her eyes sparkled with excitement. Handing Elysia a tiny brass bell, she instructed her. "Find all three objects and then ring the bell."

With that, she exited, leaving Elysia staring at Grim with her mouth half-open. *Okay...* Apparently, Maya was more of a sink or swim type of teacher. Unsurprising, really. She smiled tentatively at Grim. "Want to come along?"

Grim pressed up to standing, looking like he knew this was a bad idea. "I told Aidan she couldn't handle mentoring anyone."

Elysia took a seat on the stiff floral couch. Bad idea or not,

Maya was the only one who had even bothered to explain her magic to her.

"I'm going to look for the hourglass first." She paused, twisting to find him gripping the back of a deep-seated velour chair. "You've seen what can happen when I search for sources right? It's been better, but I don't want you to be surprised if I go into a trance."

He nodded seriously. "We may not know each other well yet, but we're going to be in each other's lives for a very, *very* long time. It's my job to have your back. You can trust me on that."

Tension left her at his words. Grim might not be the life of the party, but she could see why he was Aidan's right hand. She'd take his loyalty and common sense over frivolity any day. Rubbing her palms on her thighs, she answered the blunt, but strangely sweet reaper.

"That means a lot. Thank you."

She closed her eyes and envisioned the bronze hourglass and its white sand as she sent her magic out through the Deathlands. Seconds passed, and then there was a snag, her attention narrowing to a single spot. She tried to send herself into that pinprick of space, to see where it was, but as usual, there was a hook behind her navel, prompting her to her feet. She stood, hurrying out the door and through the halls of the house with Grim trailing closely behind her.

Grabbing a coat, she left the house, boots pointed at the woods. A haunting, mournful song played in her ear. In all the times she'd sought a secret or source, there had never been anything like the sighing, soulful cry reverberating inside her now. She stumbled on her feet, racing over the soggy Bonewoods floor. She didn't notice the gothic white fingers scraping upward, or the small branches snagging on her wool coat. Unlike in Kava, she wasn't ruled by the magic, but nonetheless, it bore down on her, demanding she listen and take note of what it told her.

They reached a small stone bridge that crossed over a stream to an enclave. Grim's large hand grabbed hold of the back of her coat, bringing her to a sudden stop on the bridge. His chest worked beneath the slim, flexible jacket all the reapers wore when on duty. Irrationally, she wanted to throw herself out of his grasp and sprint ahead. They were close, and the magic pulled as the music vibrated within her body now.

"What?" she snapped, her gaze already looking ahead over the bridge even as he held on.

Grim's grip didn't loosen as he forced her to look at him. "Eyes, focus."

She blew air out of her nose, sending her gaze to his. "Yes?" Her tone was still short, but she was listening.

"Up ahead, all you'll find is graves."

Annoyed, she shook him off. "Everyone's dead here. Why would there be graves?"

His expression faltered before hardening. "It's everyone who didn't pass the death voyage in time."

"In time?"

He stared off past her. "Some people run out of time. Or never earn the talisman. It's all the same in the end. If the fates don't decide to make you a goddess, you end up here."

Her brows rose as well as her temper as she connected what he was saying back to the item Maya had sent her here to find. Her voice went deathly low.

"Are you telling me that the hourglass SHOWS HOW LONG I HAVE TO LIVE?" Her yelling echoed out through the woods, causing a skittering of animals and birds as they fled.

Grim shifted into the ready stance of a seasoned general, his even tone telling her to calm the fuck down or he'd make her. "We didn't want you to feel even more pressure than you already do. You've been doing everything you can. It's impossible to know what will please the fates."

Pissed, she reached for the hilt of her dagger, but Grim held his hand over hers, stopping her. "You're right. We should have told you. It's been hard to know what's enough or too much. Maya was the only one who voted to tell you. I have a feeling this little treasure hunt of hers is going to illuminate a few things we'd decided weren't helpful for you to know."

Fingers gripping the handle, she didn't pull it from its sheath, but still she fumed. Having a clock on your life seemed like something that ought to be shared regardless of the anxiety it inspired. Spinning around, she marched off to find out just how much time she really had left.

The enclave wasn't beautiful like the rest of the realm. There weren't wild dead grasses waiting to turn green in the spring or spindly trees. It was just dirt. Dirt, tombstones, and a mausoleum. Gray marble, chipped and speckled with the mineral remnants of precipitation, it stood alone. Ducking inside, brass plaques marked two people whose time had run dry. She ran her chilled fingers over the fading plaques, but all they gave were their names. The bronze hourglass sat plainly on the dirty floor. Her heart turned cold as she stared at the trickling sand.

Less than a quarter of the sand remained. The priestesses had said some death voyages took years. She was not to be given years, it seemed. Her resolve hardened in a familiar manner. She'd survived a kingdom that wanted her dead since birth. Escaped that fate countless times. She wasn't giving up now.

Turning to Grim, she gestured around them. "Beyond the fact that we're almost out of time, is there anything else for me to know about the people who didn't survive their death voyages?"

Grim delivered the information like a cut. "The connection between them, their partners, and the Deathlands either never formed or wasn't strong enough. Your connection with the land and rivers seems well enough..."

Her mouth flattened. "If the fates wanted a love match, then maybe they shouldn't partner people with someone who set the end of the world in motion and is the reason why the other person had such a shitty, fucked up life."

Suddenly, the fact that she'd allowed Aidan to touch her made her sick. Her fear and anger blackened her thoughts until all she could think about was how she'd had to dodge execution her entire life and her sister was about to die. And it was *his* fault.

Grim's jaw worked, looking like he wanted to retort against her allegations, but instead he held out his hand for the hourglass. She shoved it a little too forcefully into his waiting palm and stalked out of the mausoleum while he situated the hourglass in the satchel he'd brought along.

"There's a third option."

She stared at him impatiently. "And?"

"You weren't supposed to make it here, were you?"

"Aidan said something like that once." She held his gaze, but Grim didn't break.

"It's a fine line with the fates. But at the end of the day, they want control. You've already broken their threads once, and Aidan has been on their shit list for a long time."

She absorbed this without response. Politics and manipulation were nothing new. She'd do what she needed to survive—just like every time before. Without bothering to sink to the dirt, or to find the zen she didn't want to feel, she plunged through her magical awareness like a knife through paper until she grabbed hold of the ledger. There wasn't a shred of doubt in her mind that Maya had stolen a specific ledger of Aidan's for her to crack open and read, and she was determined to see what he was hiding.

Back over the little stone bridge, she set off at a run through the woods until she exited the trees into a barren expanse. She didn't think it was the same place she'd fallen through to all those months ago, but she was quickly realizing how unfamiliar with the death realm she really was. Over the last few months, she'd retraced her steps from the house through the woods to the village, and that was basically it. She was regretting never asking for a map now.

Dropping a knee, she ran her fingers over the ground. She rubbed the tips of her fingers together, studying the familiar black-gray soot. She'd looked at this soot every day of her life in Kava, and now she stood in a desert of it. Decayed magic, raw power. Her own magic danced inside her as the soot fell from her fingers to the ground, whispering to her to take it, form it, *use it*. Forget ripping the newcomers' pain, she could eat here until ready to burst. *Wish I knew how.* She'd have to see if it could be used to further stabilize the realm. In the distance, she beheld the dunes and smooth mounds of either soil or raw magic that gave shape to the land. One of the Deadlands' rivers cut through the seemingly endless scape.

Getting up, she took off again, ignoring Grim's shouts for her to stop. Rather than the oil-slick colors of the river Aidan used for deals and protecting the realm, this river appeared molten. It glowed gold and orange with a steady simmer of bubbles bursting on its top.

She kept running, following the river as it disappeared into an enormous dune. Slowing down, she cautiously entered the cave. A heavy sensation weighed her down, her steps suddenly resistant and slow. The sluggish feeling dissipated as she forced herself further into the mouth of the cave.

Shaking out her limbs, she turned to Grim. "What *was* that?"

His voice was low. "Elysia, you shouldn't be here. Forget Maya's stupid game. You clearly have no problem finding objects. We should work on ripping and transmuting."

Plunging ahead, she wrinkled her nose at the disgusting smells drifting out from somewhere deeper in the cave. "Sounds like you don't want me to see what's in that ledger."

Grabbing her wrist, he pulled her up short. "I'll tell you what's in the ledger myself if you just turn around." Genuine fear roughened his words into a plea.

Undeterred, she kept moving. "What's in here?" She peered ahead but saw nothing except for the glow and steam coming off the molten river.

Voice urgent now, he overpowered her, pulling her away from the river and back in the direction of the cave's mouth. "There are realms within the realm. This is where the people and creatures you *never* want to meet are kept. Aidan is the only one who comes here and for good reason."

"As in the prison he mentioned?"

Relief poured through his features. "Yes, exactly."

"That means they're locked up."

Yanking her arm free, she took off again. If they were locked up, then there was nothing to worry about. She didn't trust any of them to tell her what was in that ledger anymore. She was going to get it herself.

Chapter 33

Natural light faded into gloomy dark as she hurled herself deeper into the cave. Eventually, an enormous wrought iron gate appeared, and two small familiar creatures paced in front of it. Crusher was nowhere to be found, but her siblings sat down staunchly at Elysia's approach, tilting their heads in question.

Crusher trailed her constantly when she was in the death realm. The little dog even slept in her room now, but these two remained Aidan's shadows. Tiny growled in the back of his throat, his tan fur bristling along his spine and little pointed teeth showing. Brutus didn't bother growling. He instead galloped over, headbutting her legs as if he could move her backward.

Hands on her hips, she pulled out her Georgia Parker voice, chastising them both. "Am I not to be Aidan's counterpart? Do I not have access to this place?"

Brutus paused, his enormous eyes suddenly uncertain, but Tiny snarled, making ungodly noises as he grew bigger. Thanks to Crusher, she wasn't caught off guard and recognized he hadn't grown to even a quarter of his full size. Her gaze narrowed.

"Your threats are empty. You wouldn't dare harm me." She skated around Brutus and walked right up to Tiny. "I'm going through this gate, and if you have a problem with it, then go get

Aidan and tell him if he had *communicated* better, I wouldn't be busting into his wretched prison."

Tiny gave one more low growl and disappeared, likely off to rat her out, but that was fine. She only needed a few minutes. The massive gate boasted thick iron bars with little space in between. Functional, it hadn't been made to be beautiful. She touched a brown splotch on one of the bars, her face twisting when she realized it was old, flaking blood, but then the bars hummed. Stopping, she experimentally wrapped both hands around the bars, and the humming grew louder. There was an ear-splitting creak as the gate lurched open.

She glanced back to where Grim was approaching. "Are you coming?"

There was a tearing sound, and then wings the same smooth brown as the rest of his skin emerged with lighter markings near the ridges of his bones. He stalked past Elysia into the prison.

"If I grab you, don't fight me." Tension radiated off the reaper. Wisely, she slipped through the gate, jumping when it locked shut with a clang, and didn't argue.

"Understood," she murmured.

The river reappeared and she stared at it in consternation. Hadn't the river ended?

Grim flicked his gaze from her to the boiling river. "All the rivers are sentient. They can move and appear as they will. That's how Aidan called the river to the throne room the day you made your deal. They listen to him occasionally."

She gave the river a little wider berth. "You're saying the river could decide to *boil* us?"

Grim gave her a look that finally sent the smallest sliver of guilt shooting through her. "It's a *prison* for the worst people ever to grace the godsdamn realms. Mortals, gods, and everything in between."

Squinting, she quickened her pace as they came to a split in the path.

"This way." She turned to the right. The ominous minor

chords echoing in her mind did nothing to ease the tension in her body as they hurried through the dark with strange moans and scraping sounds traveling out of the dark.

"It's just a little further," she said only to stop abruptly, Grim slamming into her back.

Maya had chosen the first cell, which could have been a kindness...if it hadn't been a cell in a magical prison for demons that looked like *that*. She took a tentative step closer to the cell, and Grim swore as he realized what was happening.

"Listen, Aidan would rather read you every single page of that ledger aloud than have you take another step."

That was probably true. She stood at the rusted bars now, staring at the humanoid creature huddled in the back. Gray skin and yellowed eyes, she'd never seen anything like it. Its limbs were longer than a human's with hands and feet more like that of a rabbit's. Between the limbs, feet, and protruding curve of its spine, she imagined it could lope and jump in a manner that would be enough to give her nightmares.

Yellow eyes glommed onto her frame, and she stilled. It was practically skin and bones. Maybe it was weak. Maybe she could just grab the ledger and walk out.

"Elysia, I'm counting to three, and then I'm fucking taking you out of here like a toddler over my back. He'll kill us both if anything happens to you. And by us, I mean me."

"Okay, okay," she relented.

He was right. Whatever that creature was, she didn't feel like getting eaten by it today. If nothing else, at least she had likely made Aidan piss himself when Tiny delivered the news of where she was right now. She wrapped her fingers around the bars, peering in closer to look at the ledger. She wanted to know exactly which of his ledgers Maya had stuck in there.

"Number fifty-five," she muttered, but her words turned into a yelp as the bars hummed and disappeared. Suddenly leaning on nothing, she crashed through the open air into the cell.

Frantically, she scrambled upright, shoving backward, but the formerly motionless creature had pinned her in one silent bound, its long curved black nails scoring into her throat and yellow eyes trailing over her.

Off to the side, there was sizzling as Grim shook the bars and cursed. The demon held her gaze, leaving her frozen and terrified as its rancid breath billowed out over her face. Inside her mind, she screamed at herself to grab her dagger, but her arms wouldn't move. Nothing would move. *I'm paralyzed*. Fear claimed her, her gaze still stuck on yellow eyes. She was going to die here.

All at once everything went dark as a soot-drenched sky.

There was a sharp slice down her throat as the creature was ripped away, her head lolling now that nothing held it in place. A terrible wet sound squelched too close to her ear, bones crunching as it slammed into the cell. Unable to move, she watched the demon slide down the wall, motionless as its blood splattered out around it.

White button-down speckled in gore, Aidan didn't waste a second glance at the disposed-of creature. He shoved his hands beneath her body, stopping only to reopen the cell and the enormous barred iron gate. Still paralyzed, she stared at his bloodied face. His normally bright blue eyes burned darkly, and his pale face was chiseled into an unreadable mask.

Once outside of the cave, Aidan stopped his heavy, purposeful walk, and traveled them both into the infirmary. Her body buzzed uncomfortably, pins and needles poking her as sensation returned. Setting her on a clean table, Aidan held her upright.

"Can you sit?" Voice gruff and angry, his eyes blazed as he waited for her to answer.

She forced a nod. *Fuck*. He was incredibly pissed this time. Walking over to a sink, Aidan rolled his sleeves even higher and roughly scrubbed his skin clean. He returned, carrying small white cotton pads and a liquid solution. Aidan soaked a cotton pad before meticulously cleaning the gouges the creature had left behind. Thumb on the base of her neck, the rest of his fingers held her firmly, guiding her movements as he searched for any other wounds. Silently, she allowed him to hover, her heart rate slowing to normal as he examined her. Relenting, he pulled back, squeezing her shoulders as he stared into her brown eyes, emotions flitting through his.

Drawing away, he backed into the table opposite the one she sat on, leaning against it with his hands pressed to its edge. Wordlessly, he shook his head, looking off and away from her.

"Aidan," she tried, but he waved a hand, his brow creased and mouth drawn.

Unbuttoning his bloodied shirt, he removed it, casting it aside on the table before folding his arms. The blood had soaked through to his undershirt, but he didn't seem to notice.

"What happened with the fates?" She blurted out the words anxiously, but she didn't wait for him to answer. "You're right, okay? We do need to tell each other what's going on, and I don't blame you for not telling me everything immediately. Or at least, I get that you didn't at first, but I think we're past the point where that's going to work. You need to tell me everything. The fates, the ledgers, all of it."

Aidan nodded, but he didn't look pleased about it. "Are you well enough to go out?"

Perplexed, her voice lifted in question. "Yes?" The paralysis had quickly worn off, leaving her fine though shaken up.

His shoulders turned inward as he put his hands in his pockets. "Then clean up and meet me at the front door."

ELYSIA HAD NEVER BATHED SO FAST in her life. Scrubbed clean with wet, wavy hair, she beat him to the foyer. She'd thrown on the first thing she could find, and now the longer she stood there waiting, the more concerned she became that the dress had been the wrong choice over the functional trousers and sweaters she'd been wearing lately. Burgundy silk crisscrossed and draped her upper body, flowing out into fluttering sleeves and gentling around her legs. It was the kind of dress she would have worn dancing in Kava—not that she'd ever gone, though she'd wanted to. She'd always been envious of the people spilling out of Shakes, the dance hall Remy and Daphne had talked about countless times. Topp had said he'd rather stab himself than get caught there.

Mind made up, she twisted to run off to her room and change, and plowed straight into a hard chest. No longer covered in a demon's blood, Aidan's scarred hands wrapped her shoulders, steadying her. Usually, he looked caught between being the death realm's most attractive accountant and the guy you didn't want to show up and collect.

Tonight, he looked like the god of the dead.

He'd traded his usual attire for all black. Black shirt, black vest, black jacket and trousers. Hair damp and slicked back, his blue eyes were full of swirling fire ready to consume anything in his path.

Given she was directly in said path, she swallowed, stepping delicately out of his grasp. Smoothing her hands over the silk, she avoided his eyes. "Sorry, was just going to go change."

He spun her back around, grabbing their wool coats and tossing her hers. "Why would you do that?"

Before she could say anything else, they were out the door and his hand was on her lower back, guiding her in the direction of the village.

"Where are we going?"

"Remember when you crashed into my throne room—were literally dying, and then promptly went out and got wasted?"

Her gaze slid to his. "Yes." She made the word as caustic as possible, but his mouth curved anyway.

"I thought you might like to go again with someone who actually knows what the potions do."

For a brief moment, she was excited at the prospect of having a drink and being out like a normal person, and then she remembered he was probably ready to murder her. Anxiety slowed her steps, and she glanced back at the diminishing figure of the house, considering making a run for it. She exhaled a chilly cloud—she didn't really want to run, she wanted answers. He might be angry, but she was too.

"Can I pick yours? Your drink, that is."

His steps faltered. "I had one in mind, but I'll let you be the judge."

Quickening her step, she grabbed his hand, forcing him to keep up as she weaved around people on the street. The long walk was going to kill her. She just wanted to get there and get on with it already. The streetlamps flickered, casting a familiar glow. Hand in hand with the god of the dead, she drank in the warm orange-tinted light and how the soot looked so natural here rather than a curse of decay like it did in Kava.

A sudden knowing hit her like a brick. "Did your realm always look like this? The streetlamps? The cobbled streets? Your home?"

Half-turned toward her, Aidan looked uncharacteristically sheepish as if he'd been caught. A wisp of hair blew into his eyes, but for once he left it there. Setting his anger aside, he shrugged as if it wasn't a big deal. "You're giving up so much. It was the least I could do to make it feel more like home here."

Her jaw almost hit the ground.

"I couldn't do anything about the soot, as you call it, because it's natural here, which I'm sure you hate, but adding some lamps, a little iron, and cobblestone streets? That I could do."

Shocked, she gripped the nearest black lamppost. "Your realm is barely stable, and you used your power to make it feel more like home to me?"

He took a step closer, facing her completely. "You forget I was mortal, and I too once woke up here and hated everything I saw. I didn't want that for you. I wanted your experience to be different, better than mine."

"But your house—it was already like this when I visited you for the deal."

His face was wry. "I'm the plotting kind of stalker—I saw how you loved the dark beauty of Relaclave, and I refused to give up hope that you would make it here somehow."

Reflexively, her hand gripped his tighter, her heart mimicking the motion as his fingers responded in kind. Dazed, she allowed him to guide them all the way to the bar. The estate with its mix of oil lamps, electricity, and lush rugs and rich paintings. The dark red-brown brick buildings with black accents and iron touches. There were even a few curving cream buildings like the ones in old Relaclave in his village. He'd recognized the heart of what she loved in her city and brought it to life here as much as he could.

The lounge was quiet when they entered with only a few people seated at the bar and at the small round dark wooden tables. Settling in at a table away from the others, Elysia perused the drink menu.

"Which one were you thinking?"

She looked up to find Aidan already sliding onto his stool with two flutes in hand. The liquid glimmered a rosy gold, and juicy red seeds floated down to rest on the bottom. "It's called the Ultimatum."

She raised a brow, pulling hers in closer and giving it a sniff. It smelled like pomegranate and citrus. "Quite the name."

The flame of the candle on the table highlighted the hollows of his face as he gave a mirthless smile. "Couples like to use it when they think the other has been lying or cheating."

Elysia sat up straighter. "Because it...?"

"Forces you to tell the truth."

Her gaze moved from the effervescent drinks to the god suggesting they use drugs to fix their relationship. Inevitably, her mind slipped back to her earlier thoughts. Hand in hand, it was terribly easy to forget who he was and what he had done when he was revealing he'd altered his entire realm to put her at ease.

She studied him openly. Rough, but purposeful, she wouldn't call him impulsive. And yet, that was the story he wanted her to believe. That as a young god, he'd impulsively made a deal with a grief-stricken king.

She downed her drink in one go, wrinkling her nose as the bubbles hit. Serious as the grave, Aidan followed suit, setting his delicate flute down and folding his hands.

"First question goes to you."

She didn't hesitate. "Why didn't you tell me about the fates' involvement with the deal between you and Garrison?"

His mouth pressed tight as he huffed a silent laugh. "You had to start with that." Fingers tapping on the table, he considered his answer. "Because regardless, I am at fault."

The words were barely out of his mouth when he gasped, doubling over and clutching at his stomach.

Oh. "Liar, liar," she sang sweetly under her breath, watching him with a dark expression.

Tugging on the lapels of his suit, Aidan straightened, looking slightly sweaty and green. His words were half-growl now. "I didn't tell you because I didn't want you to hear the full story and take pity. I meant what I said, I was young and angry. The fates were right to punish me for what I did. I only wish it hadn't been through you."

"Explain." She was doing her best to keep her magic leashed, but even without it, Aidan's anxiety was palpable. Fingers drumming, his chest barely moved, but still he nodded, his spine going straighter and chin lifting. She couldn't help but recognize the posture. This was a god who thought he was about to take a hit and was bracing for impact.

"The fates chose me to replace the last god of the dead because he'd grown dissatisfied with his lot. He wanted to be able to leave the Deathlands freely, he grew envious of the other gods and their lighter, easier lives. He stopped tending to the new arrivals, stopped managing the prison. The realm was in shambles, so he was removed."

A chill ran over her skin. "Removed?"

"Yes. The fates expect a certain amount of difficulties from the gods, but there are lines they expect not to be crossed. As you know, they eliminate the gods who don't meet their requirements. My selection for this role meant cutting my mortal life short, which I did not take kindly to." Bitterness sank into his words.

"They killed you?" Horror washed over her.

"Me, Grim, and Sai. They wanted a fresh start for the realm."

"What happened?"

His brow twitched. "They showed up one night at the club I managed the gambling from, talking about my new fate and how I was the perfect candidate to become the god of the dead. I thought they were high or insane. I told them no, that I'd never give up my life. They pulled out their tapestry, grabbed a string, and snipped. When I woke up, I was here, alone in a pile of dirt, and everything was different." He paused. "I realize many mortals would be elated. Chosen by the *fates* to become a *god*."

"You loved your life." She remembered him saying this now, the meaning suddenly different.

"I did," he replied softly. "I had no respect or love for the gods. I followed the customs of a follower of death, but only in rote action, never heart. I had built my life brick by brick—no one ends up at the top of a crime empire without getting their hands dirty. More than thirty years of blood and sweat over in an instant. I wanted my life back. I was furious over the loss of control. Being trapped here and destined to tend to the dead. I understood why my predecessor had revolted. They had chosen me for my unfailing discipline and sense of duty, never considering I wouldn't feel I owed them it."

Elysia went quiet. "What did you do?"

Aidan smiled humorlessly. "I also got drunk shortly after arriving here. Except I had managed to steal something from the fates." He made a motion with his fingers, the silvery scars shining in the low light. "Their precious scissors. The scissors are how they change fate. Cut threads, create gods, end them. All with nothing more than some thread and a pair of old scissors."

She steeled herself, already knowing where this was heading. "You didn't want to be a god."

He tipped his head. "They found me bleeding out, but they'd just replaced one god and weren't about to do it again. They'd always planned for me to be a replacement, but the timeline had moved up, and instead of acknowledging how that had affected things, they punished me."

She was almost afraid to ask. "How do you punish a god?"

"Same as anyone, by changing their fate." Regret filled his eyes, and he gripped the table. "It's still all my fault, Elysia, everything they set in motion was because I tried to avoid my duty."

Her fingertips reached to him tentatively, grasping his arm and knowing he wouldn't hear her if she tried to point out the fallacy in his thoughts. "What do you mean?"

"My punishment was to rule my realm alone. That I could never leave the Deathlands or find my counterpart. That I would bear the weight of a crumbling realm by myself, unable to fix it. That I would be cursed to watch my counterpart live a harrowing life, but neither of us would be able to reach the other. The singular blessing of this role is that the fates always bring the god of the dead their match. Yes, there's the death voyage, but in exchange for rarely being able to leave or live like the other gods, they bring you love. It's a quiet life of duty, but it's meant to be shared and cherished with another."

She nodded. "Where does Garrison come in?"

Aidan's body tensed, and his chin tilted away, giving her only his profile. "The fates delivered Garrison to me while I was still in a spiral. I tended to the Deathlands the best I could with my limited power, but receiving the fated words of their punishment and watching our threads change had only made me angrier. Instead of falling in line, I stewed and obsessed over the possibilities, running the odds over and over, but it always came up the same. My fate had irrevocably changed. And then in walked this king, demanding a deal and spouting nonsense about magic being evil and wanting to rid his kingdom of its plague. He cried and talked about his wife dying, how he had loved her. And because I'd run the odds and knew there was no hope, I decided to take one last strike at the fates, hoping to anger them enough to put me out of my misery. I went against the natural fabric of the realms and made the deal. I imagined it would be an annoying mess for them to clean up in the morning. When in reality, they had simply allowed me to make my own bed. Your kingdom decayed and so did mine. You lived every day of your life in fear of death, and eventually, I was forced to watch. Not only did I have to watch, but I got to feel you flash in, then out of my realm like a shooting star when you'd sleep, but I couldn't hold you here, and your magic couldn't sustain you either. Everything they'd promised came true because of me—is still coming true because of me."

Elysia released his arm, exhaling as the story filled in. "Sometimes you sound so human."

The more Aidan drew back the curtain on his inner world, and how he'd gotten to where he was, the more difficult it was to sustain her anger. He had undoubtedly fucked up. And she also couldn't entirely blame him for his anger or messy actions. He'd lost his life and wanted to escape a fate he hadn't chosen.

Aidan's gaze drew hers back. "I mean it when I say the fault is mine. I was in my early thirties when I died, and unlike so many mortals, I loved my life. I know being a crime lord and bookie might not sound like a dream to many, but I hadn't grown up with much, and my gift for odds had brought me into a life I wouldn't have traded for anything. I worked hard and work was all I did. The crew was my family, and I was fine with that. It took time for me to see the beauty in my new life, and I naively thought the consequences of moving against the fates wouldn't be permanent. But again, the fault is still mine."

Now that Aidan was talking, she didn't want him to stop. "How long had you been a god when Garrison came?"

"A little over a century. The longest any god of the dead had ever gone without their counterpart entering the death voyage, so I assumed they'd made good on their curse."

"And you didn't have your talisman."

Aidan paused, blinking rapidly. "Any luck with that by any chance?"

She made a face. "That's how today started. Well, it started with a hand-drawn flowchart of the volt, but then Maya showed up and explained more about ripping and trans-mutation."

Clucking his tongue, he nodded. "I'd forgotten that's what people used to call it."

Elysia tried to scrabble together the theory she'd been stuck on all afternoon. Embarrassment made the words heavy on her tongue. "Are you a power source for me?"

Both of Aidan's brows flew up. "How did you jump there?"

"Because I somehow traveled here while living in Kava, and I can't think of another explanation."

Putting an elbow on the table, he put his chin in his hand, his eyes zoning out before pulling out a small version of his usual ledgers from his jacket.

His pen flew faster than Elysia could track. "You keep a minia-ture version in your suit?"

Ink smeared, but he wasn't done, pages flipping as he wrote. Eventually, he stopped, reviewed his impossible handwriting, and let out a discontented sound. "I hadn't taken into account you being a ripper. I'd assumed it was the fates fucking with me—allowing you to appear, but then disappear before I could even reach you, but it seems you're onto something."

Grabbing the small notebook, she slid it in front of herself. Despite being barely legible, Aidan had scrawled out at least twenty different scenarios in less than two minutes, detailing their odds with thorough explanations. She pushed the notebook away like it was poison.

"You're a psychic math nerd?"

Aidan's face flattened, but there wasn't any actual bite to his voice. "I'll take that, thank you." He tucked the ledger back into his jacket.

"Seriously, that's what you're doing all the time? Writing out endless possibilities and spitting out their likelihood? That sounds more like a curse than a gift. Wouldn't the numbers constantly change?"

Exhaustion bled into the faint lines on his handsome face. "It was a lot easier when it was just races and sporting events."

Elysia snorted. "So, what's in ledger *fifty-five*? I almost died trying to get it. I think I deserve to know."

Aidan glowered. "I'd argue that's exactly why you don't deserve to know, but lucky for you I'll throw up if I lie."

"Lucky, lucky me."

"Brat," he muttered before continuing. "Ledger fifty-five is all of my notes on how the world might end." He instantly clutched his stomach.

"Is it? Cause you're sweating."

Grimacing, he tried again. "It might as well be. Right now, in every single scenario I can come up with, Garrison wins, you don't complete the death voyage, and people die. A lot of people, including the people you care about."

Sweat rolled down his face, and Elysia tapped her fingers on the long empty glass. "What aren't you saying? What could possibly be worse than what you're saying? Because I'm pretty sure that not completing my death voyage is the soft version of *you die, Elysia.*"

Aidan looked at war with himself. "I'm sorry, I can't. We're toeing the line of death interference, and I *cannot* give them another reason to make this worse."

Elysia leaned away, resting her head on the wall behind her. "You're turning green."

He closed his eyes. "Mortals can't know about impending deaths. I shouldn't have even mentioned the possibility of yours."

"You sound like Grim."

"He does know the reaping rules better than me."

"What happens if you don't tell me?"

His blue eyes blinked open. "The intestinal pains will increase until the drink wears off."

"Fun night for you then." Elysia stood up, slipped on her coat, and helped him off his stool. "Come on then, let's get you home."

Arm draped over her shoulder; Aidan looked down at her as they awkwardly shuffled out of the lounge back into the night. "Do I even get a single question?"

The wind blew her unkempt waves around her face. "Maybe," she responded cautiously.

"With all I've done, is there any hope for us?"

She didn't have an answer for that. It looked like they'd both be writhing in pain tonight.

CHAPTER 34

Elysia sat on a roof beside Grim, twirling a dagger and trying to enjoy the sun on her face. Her stomach growled loudly, and Grim shot her a look. Like she could help that they'd been sitting here for hours. No one could see him, but they would be able to see and hear her if she were to slip into view or make too much noise. She sheathed her dagger with a grumble. The local butcher still hadn't keeled over, and she was getting impatient and hungry.

"There he goes," Grim murmured, dropping onto the dusty street with the slightest flare of his wings. Elysia remained on the roof. She'd been given firm instructions to *not* move. He'd said this countless times in the last five hours along with several scarily calm reminders that he'd throw her in the boiling river himself if she pulled anything.

Aidan had been well-aware that the prison fiasco was thanks to Maya's *mentoring* and Elysia's choice to push for answers. That didn't stop him from threatening to put the soul of Grim's mother in the prison. She'd decided to leave them to their couple's fight when Grim grunted about how at least Aidan had gotten over himself and told her the truth.

Grim's wings flared again, and Elysia squinted. The bastard

did that on purpose. He'd agreed to take her on a reaping because it was *educational* but was refusing to fly with her because *assholes who try to get us killed don't get flights*. Grim dropped to his knees beside the corpse and held his hand over the man's forehead until a blindingly bright prismatic ball of energy bounced lightly before his palm. Elysia audibly gasped. He'd warned her, but to *see it*.

Grim cupped the soul reverently in his hands. Gently he lowered the shining ball, holding it near the bone strung along a cord on his neck until it vanished. He stood, bent his knees, and jumped into the air. Two strong pumps of his wings and he was soaring.

Touching down beside her, Grim chuckled at her obvious delight. "You're so easy to please. You're like a little kid with this stuff."

She held out her arms in faux offense. "Are you kidding me? That was a *soul*. You just sucked a soul into a bone shard and flew up here on *wings*. You know I never saw any magic until recently. I'm not going to pretend it isn't cool when it is."

Still smiling, he held the bone shard away from his chest. "Bones and souls. The best and the worst magic come from these."

Elysia opened her mouth to ask a question when three people appeared on the roof, startling and surrounding her. A hand gripped each of her arms, the third person clamping down on her shoulders, and then they were gone. The last thing she saw was the burning rage and fear in Grim's eyes.

In a blink, she was sitting at a long rectangular table with a lone lightbulb hanging overhead. Dim orange light sheared out in a conical shape over the whole table, the illumination barely enough to make out the faces of the people who had stolen her. Darkness blanketed them outside of the dim light, leaving Elysia digging her feet down to reassure herself there was, indeed, floor beneath her. Discomfort roiled in her gut. Wherever they were, she didn't like it.

Across from her at the table were the three people who had

forcibly removed her from the roof. Front and center sat a person in flowing linens with waist-length white-blonde hair and bone-structure so sharp their bones seemed to protrude, pushing against their fair skin. Large and feminine, the person to the right was decked out in lush turquoise velvet and silks that shone against their brown skin. Around their neck were piles of jewels, and every finger boasted a precious metal. To the left sat a person who reminded Elysia of a painting she had seen of the people who lived in Arctan, a never-ending tundra. Straight black hair hung in a no-nonsense collar-length cut, and an overly starched black suit formed rigidly to their body. While the people in front of her presented as feminine, there was a distinct otherness that left Elysia positive they were beyond such a distinction.

Elysia folded her hands. "The fates, I presume."

The person in velvet patted the locs they'd twisted into a high bun. "You remember us, how sweet. I'm Monica, that's Skiel, and Adla."

Liquid black-brown eyes slid over from the left side of the table. "Monica."

Skiel, the blonde, exhaled as if this interaction played out ten times a day. "We wanted to speak with you."

Elysia's magic coiled tightly inside her, wary of even brushing against them. While the gods walked with power, they had once been mortal. She didn't think the fates had ever been mortal. Silent anxiety overtook her, her posture growing more rigid the longer she sat in the dark nowhere with them, but much like she had endless times with her father, she appeared poised and ready.

"I gathered that."

Skiel smiled, but their ice-blue eyes held zero warmth. "You've done well on your voyage."

The suit, Adla, looked Elysia over carefully. "I had my doubts, but getting to the Deathlands was quite the feat. We underestimated the power of the original fate we had woven and how its remnants lingered in you. We learned much from your lesson, and we thank you for this. Now tell us, how do you feel about the king of the dead?"

She refrained from shifting in her seat. No matter how it was phrased, it wasn't a compliment. They hadn't planned for her to make it to the Deathlands. She had somehow bypassed Aidan's punishment, and now they were adjusting accordingly.

Elysia's grip on her magic was strangling, but she was at a loss. She wasn't foolish enough to attempt to read the fates. Gods only knew what would happen if she did, which left her in the terrible position of having to resort to honesty. She measured her words. "Aidan's choices are why I lived every day in fear of execution. He's why the mortal world is now in fear of losing its magic and livelihood."

"But what do you think of *him*?" Adla pushed.

Elysia met her gaze. "He's a good ruler now that he's accepted it."

All three of them smiled now, and Elysia tensed.

Monica rested her soft fingers on Elysia's comfortingly. "But you can't imagine forever with a man like him. A man who brought about the decay ravaging your world."

Adla tilted her head, gaze focused and unblinking on Elysia's reaction.

Elysia hardened herself against the sinking in her stomach. "It's been a point of contention for me," she admitted, tone flawlessly even and cool.

Tossing their hands into the air, Skiel brought endless shimmering strings into existence over the table. They motioned again, and the strings rushed together into a massive tapestry. "We'd like to offer you a proposition. It was always fated for you to take the throne."

"But you shouldn't have to rule beside a man of such little ethics," Adla chimed in seamlessly.

"You shouldn't have to loathe yourself for what would inevitably happen," Monica added with a knowing, lascivious raise of their brow.

Skiel swept their hands back down, and the tapestry disappeared. "Time changes all things. Aidan has provided an opportunity for us to release old customs and begin again. We are threading you in as the sole goddess of the dead."

Face neutral, Elysia leaned back in her chair. Beneath her skin, her heart thundered. "What's the catch?"

All three fates dropped their smiles, but it was Monica who spoke. "Eliminate him. We'll give you what you need."

Time froze, yet seconds passed. Clearing her throat, Elysia asked quietly. "What about Kava? Garrison?"

Adla readjusted the sleeve of their tailored black jacket. "Handled. Garrison will be removed. We can even allow the young Blatz to do it as was intended. The magic will slowly return with Garrison's death as the deal will be broken. Better for it to return naturally than to flood the little mortals."

Skiel fixed her with a hard look. "We don't tolerate our gods shirking their duties or divine roles. Aidan will be removed one way or another. The question is, what do you want, Elysia Parker? How do *you* want to spend eternity?"

She showed nothing, forcing her breath to rise and fall even as her thoughts and emotions warred. Manipulation or not, even the gods feared the fates. Cool and clinical, she reviewed every point against Aidan. With every point, her body remembered his touch, his steadfast care and attention. But self-preservation's only job was to keep her alive, and she'd spent a lifetime fostering that instinct. She had been fooling herself to think she could have it all. She'd decided to be a *better person*. A person she could be proud of, who looked beyond simply surviving, but what did that mean? A hollow knowing settled like a rock in her chest. *Good people* made sacrifices. They didn't choose a man over the world. His love, touch, friendship—she shouldn't have let them even graze her skin. It was a fitting punishment. She'd had a taste of hope, love, and what a life worth having could look like, and now she had to give it up. She could do the right thing though, save her kingdom, and the realms. *They'd said they would remove him either way.*

Elysia considered the fates, and with a sense of foregone resignation slipped back into an older version of herself. One who had made hard decisions in the name of staying alive. Her words were cold.

"I'll do it."

CHAPTER 35

ELYSIA HURRIED along the cobblestone streets. She was a void, a vacuum, and she needed to see the one person who would always tell her to save herself. She needed to see a Parker.

Sooty muck kicked up with every step, hitting the back of her trousers. Early spring was such a disgusting time of year. The snow, the rain, the soot—nothing escaped the decay. Eyes fixed on the poison green door of the House, she walked even faster, shoulder checking strangers and not giving a damn that she was wanted dead or alive by the Crown.

Pounding on the door, she stepped back half a step, impatient and ready to bust her way in. An unfamiliar face opened the door, and Elysia shoved inside.

"Where's Beatriz?" She'd decided it wasn't safe to travel immediately to her sister. Not with her sister's new ventures.

The woman who'd answered the door pulled her plush robe closer. "She's with the Doorman. They left about an hour ago."

"And where did they go?" Elysia bit off the words like the woman was stupid.

"Why in the realms should I tell you?"

The sharp end of Elysia's dagger went to the woman's throat. "Because I have this. Now where are they?"

"You're her sister, aren't you? The one with the massive bounty?"

"And you're the one who'll be dead if you don't answer my question."

Blood dribbled down the blade, and the woman flinched.

"They're at the Nightshade Market. Down in the tunnels."

Elysia was gone in an instant, traveling away.

Plodding down the time-worn steps, she wrinkled her nose immediately. Still smelled like rat shit. Hustling through the tunnels, she let the scraps of her magic loose. A slinky tune drew her in, and she shook her head. Fucking Beatriz. Holding a gods-damn underground market, *literally underground*. Not only underground, but beneath the fucking castle. She hated how much she loved it.

Skidding around a corner, she came to a stop, her mind going blank in disbelief. Sensual and mysterious, the market glowed with lanterns. Delicious scents drifted in the air, and small wooden booths lined one side of the tunnel while market goers glided past, sampling and examining the goods. Everyone wore veils or masks with dark cloaks hiding their bodies.

In the distance, a silver head bobbed above the others, her long thin fingers pointing and directing newcomers into the Nightshade Market's throng. Tempted as she was to take a look at the booths herself, she kept her gaze on her sister as she went against the crowd's current.

She tapped two fingers on her sister's shoulder, grinning darkly when Beatriz let out an unholy shriek at the sight of her.

"I needed a sisterly chat."

Nails digging into her arm, Beatriz dragged her away from the market into the familiar dark of the tunnels.

"What are you doing here?" she spat through tight lips. "You can't be here. We've talked about this."

Alone, Elysia leaned against the crumbly wall of the tunnel. "If you had to choose between your life or Lily's, what would it be?" She played with her dagger as she stared unflinchingly at her older sister. "Love or survival?"

Beatriz drew back. "What's this about?"

"Just answer the question, for fuck's sake."

Beatriz looked at her in bewilderment, running silver-ringed fingers through her matching hair. Uncharacteristic vulnerability washed over the harsh lines of her face as she looked up out of gray eyes. "I'd choose Lily. She's a better person a thousand times over than me, and I wouldn't want to be without her."

Elysia slammed the dagger back into its sheath, her mouth pursed.

"That wasn't the answer you wanted."

She shook her head, staring at the top of the tunnel. "I don't know what I wanted." She gave Beatriz a tight, unconvincing semblance of a smile. "Sorry I bothered you." Stalking off, she had no idea where to go, only that she couldn't go to the death realm. Not yet.

"Wait, you annoying shit," Beatriz called out to her back, jogging to catch up. "Why are you wearing this face again?"

Elysia scoffed, pushing away Triz's reaching fingers. "What kind of stupid comment is that?"

"You look like you used to after meeting with Father."

A terrible burning ache filled Elysia's eyes as she looked away. "The market is incredible. You should be proud of yourself." She paused. "And I don't care if Lily is better than you. I'd pick you."

Concern crossed Beatriz's face, but then the yelling began.

Side by side, Beatriz and Elysia raced back to the market, but the calm, sensual evening market was gone. Smoke wafted through the air, but every booth, lantern, and person was nowhere to be seen.

Beatriz went pale. "We need to get out of here."

Elysia grabbed her hand, turning them around, already breaking into a run. "Don't worry, I know how to get out."

Soon she was nearly dragging Beatriz. "It's not much further. We'll exit into the main square. I used to do it all the time."

Staggering to a halt, Beatriz put one hand on the tunnel wall, dark specks dotting her lips. Chest heaving, she closed her eyes. "Just need a moment."

"The guards are coming. We can't stop yet. Come on, you can make it." Fear tightened Elysia's lungs. She couldn't leave her sister, but she could already hear the guards clanking and stomping in the distance.

Beatriz nodded, and relief coursed through Elysia as she grabbed her sister's hand again and took off. Two more tunnels and they were slipping out into an old shut-down eatery and then into the square. Laughter tumbled freely out of both their mouths, and Elysia grinned, mirroring the wide curve lighting up Beatriz's face.

She squeezed her sister's hand. "We made it."

"That's her!" a male voice shouted from behind her back.

Twisting to look, she never saw it coming.

But Beatriz did. Beatriz, who tackled her to the ground without a second thought. Elysia groaned, rolling over only to see a cracked, wooden hilt protruding from Beatriz's chest. An unskilled, lucky shot straight through her ribs to the heart.

"No, no." Tears were already spilling as her hands frantically pulled her sister closer. Ripping her own dagger from its sheath, she returned fire at the man who approached. He wasn't even a guard. Merely a hungry commoner who had seen the notorious Parker girl emerge and wanted his chance at the prize. Her dagger stuck out of his eye socket, his body hitting the ground hard.

Elysia clutched her sister's too-thin body closer. "Beatriz, you can't. You're all I have."

A strange, murky mix of blood and soot spilled out of the cavity in Beatriz's chest, but her fingers weakly grasped at Elysia, her gray eyes straining to focus. "I pick you too."

Sobs wracked her as the sharp, ever-present light in her big sister's eyes went out. Someone let out a blood-curdling scream and through blurry vision, the familiar shape of the Doorman hurdled closer. Her sister's body was torn from her arms as the

Doorman poured herself out over it, rocking and murmuring agonizing pleas.

Makeup smeared, she pierced Elysia with a look she would never forget. "You were supposed to stay away. We *told* you to stay away." The Doorman stroked Beatriz's smooth, silver hair, whispering something in her native language that sounded like a blessing or prayer.

Endless silent guilt claimed its home in Elysia as she slowly backed away. It was another death in the square, and for the first time in years, she was unable to tear her eyes from the sight. A crow flew past, its wing knocking into her face, and then she was running, throwing herself into the ether, traveling to the only other person she could think of to see because now, more than ever, she couldn't go home.

CHAPTER 36

A PLAIN, unremarkable off-white building stood in front of Elysia. It might have been the most boring building she'd ever seen, functional and bereft of any character. Topp Blatz's broad back had just disappeared through the temple's faded and scratched black door.

Hurrying, she slipped in behind him, trailing Topp down several flights of stairs and into what looked like barracks. Topp strolled down the long hallway, dim orb lights brightening with a quiet buzz as he passed them. Built into the walls were beds, stacked atop each other from floor to ceiling. Each bed had a singular small white pillow and a black medium-weight blanket on the mattress. Whatever temple this was, it gave her the creeps.

The prince stopped in front of a bed that looked exactly like all the others and picked up a small red gift box. Untying the golden bow, he opened the flaps, and pulled out a cute chocolate confection. On edge, Elysia's magic shot out, blaring an alarm.

Sprinting as fast as she could, she was screaming. "Don't eat that!"

Jolting, Topp spun around right as she smacked the chocolate down to the ground where it splatted against the dull white floor.

"Elysia?" The prince looked between her and the now inedible confection, his eyebrows going up as he took in the sight of her. She knew her eyes were probably red and puffy, but a glance down informed her that her clothes and hands were covered in soot-riddled blood. *Right.*

She bent down, tentatively poking at the viscous red filling of the chocolate and sniffed it. "That's poison."

"You're sure?" He frowned at the scuffed floor like he was still thinking about eating it.

"Positive. Smells like branson weed. I wanted to use it for Scarzan, but there was no way to cover the odor." She stuck out her finger, and Topp ducked his head, nose wrinkling as soon as he got close.

"Gods, that's awful."

"Maybe you shouldn't eat surprise chocolates when you're a wanted prince and staying somewhere that looks like they have a protocol for murder." Her tone fell flat, leaving the joke lifeless despite her attempt.

She kept touching her chest. But there wasn't a cracked wooden handle protruding from her. There was only a gaping hole, slowly solidifying into something she didn't think would ever leave so long as she lived. Still, her mouth moved, and her face creased into expressions that might as well have been painted on. A horrible pressure increased behind her eyes.

Topp once again looked cautiously at her presentation, his demeanor shifting into one she'd seen him use with skittish and aggressive animals.

"How'd you know to be here?"

She shrugged. "I didn't. Guess I'm one and one tonight."

He frowned, not understanding her comment. "The goddess here is weirdly protective of Rollie. Can't stand me though. Woman acts like I pissed in her wine."

Comprehension dawned as she looked around again, the minimalist building now making sense. "This is the temple of Ration and Reason?"

He nodded.

"Oren didn't fill you in?"

Topp's jaw twitched. "Was dragged to his woods for a bit, but I've been ignoring his summons."

"You should let him help you. You and Rollie had the right idea, but Aidan's got it covered now. His gambling game will rope them all in."

He looked at her in pure confusion before a flash of something crossed his face. "That bitch of a goddess said something to Rollie about Ration and Reason needing to have a strong start."

Elysia backtracked, knowing she was tired and struggling to make sense. "Aidan is tracking all of the most likely outcomes with his magic, and basically we're all probably going to die, but he's hoping if the gods watch us all stumbling to our doom, they'll start to interfere and change the odds."

Topp kicked at the smushed chocolate. "She just tried to kill me. How is that helping?"

She stared at the mess. "Yeah, they're weirdly fixated on helping the mortals that belong to their houses. Could be a problem."

"You mean to say the goddess of Ration and Reason is trying to off me because she wants Rollie to what? Be the star of this strange bullshit game?"

Elysia stepped back, leaning against one of the smudgy white walls, too tired to care if she left it even worse and smeared with blood.

"Something like that. The gods need to remember they'll be eliminated by the fates if they can't do their jobs...and they can't do their jobs if there's no magic." She rubbed her eyes. "Gods, the fates are just going to wipe everything and start over, aren't they? They could, you know. Erase every mortal and god and start over. They're that powerful."

Sighing, he sat down on the bed and gestured at her appearance. "If you weren't here to save me, then why are you here?"

What *was* she doing here? Staring down at her waterlogged

boots, she shook her head. "I don't know." Her voice was quiet, worn.

"You're covered in blood."

"It's not mine." *But it should have been.*

Topp had lost a sister, but it wasn't that. It wasn't even that he used to be the person she would show up to in the middle of the night, asking his body for the comfort that the man was unable to provide. It was simpler than that. She'd wanted someone who didn't just know her but knew Beatriz and their life. Someone she didn't have to explain everything to.

"I wanted to talk to Beatriz. I *needed* to talk to her." Her voice broke, as if she were begging him to believe her. Her eyes ached, but they remained dry as she stared off, away from him.

Topp was silent, his bright green eyes already bracing for what was to come.

"The Nightshade Market got raided. Maybe that was my fault too, I don't know. But I got her out. Took the tunnels to a shut-down spot, but when we exited into the square, someone saw me. I didn't have my face covered." Her head thudded against the wall. She should have had her face covered.

"Where's Beatriz, Lys?"

Eyes finally glistening, her throat burned as she choked out the words. "She's d-dead. A man threw a dagger at me, and she tackled me. It should have been me." A muffled sob escaped her as she clapped a hand over her mouth, shoulders shaking, and slid down to a crouch.

The bed creaked as Topp stood, dropping to the floor beside her, so he could reach one large, warm arm around her. Pulling her into his side, he rested his chin on her head.

She wasn't sure how long they stayed like that. Long enough that his shirt became stained with salty tears and her eyes were raw. Wrapping her fingers into his, she whispered, "I never should have gone there. I wanted her to make me feel better about what I have to do. It was selfish and reckless. You should have seen Lily."

His palm was familiar against hers as his thumb brushed against her skin. "What do you have to do?"

"Fix things before it's too late."

He leaned back so he could see her face, his gaze scanning over her. "Why do I feel like you're about to do something stupid? Like stab a nearly immortal king at a ball stupid?"

Her face was blank, her emotions draining out of her until she was empty and blunt. "Stabbing your father wasn't in the plan. He went off script. Imagine if the fucker had just died..." She winced, realizing who she was talking to, but the prince just nodded darkly in agreement.

"Should I be worried?"

"Probably," she admitted.

His groan was heavy in his chest. "I know better than to think you'll tell me, but I wish you would."

She stretched out one leg, knocking her boot against his. "Where are you going now that you don't need to keep enticing the gods?"

Topp considered this, waving his hand to keep the orb lights from dimming. "If what you're saying is true, then maybe it's time to focus on my own plans." Elysia tensed, and he frowned. "What?"

She bit down on her lip, unsure of what she could tell him, but she'd had enough death. She knew there would likely be more before all of this was done, but after today, she didn't care what rules it broke to tell him.

"You need to be careful. Whatever you've been thinking, I would scrap it and come up with a different plan."

Absorbing this information, his eyes shone in calculation. "Slow down and regroup."

She nodded. "Garrison isn't mortal anymore. I know he's working up to sailing for Sagondia, and it feels like time is running out, but you're going to need more than a half-cocked plan run on emotion." She faced him fully, her gaze taking in his familiar spread of freckles and electric presence. "You need to let other people help you. Maybe even the gods."

"Ouch." He clapped his hands against his chest like he'd been struck. "Is that what you thought I was going to do? Run in screaming and try to stab the bastard in broad daylight like someone else we know did?"

She slumped back tiredly. "Maybe."

"I'll be thoughtful, alright? Maybe I'll go to Oren, but I hate to leave Rollie here with that emotionless bitch. Gods know what they'll do together."

"He loves her, doesn't he?"

"Thinks she's brilliant."

Elysia laughed hollowly, but Topp was looking at her again a little too knowingly.

"Why aren't you in the Deathlands doing this with him?"

She twisted her fingers together but said nothing.

Topp sighed, running his fingers through his wood-brown hair. He opened and shut his mouth more than once as he tried to find the words. "Lys, don't make the same mistake we did. If you went to Beatriz, that means you feel bad about whatever it is you think you need to do. He's not really in a place to judge you, just tell him whatever it is."

Elysia slid him a look. "It's annoying when you pay attention."

"Everyone always thinks I'm all brawn and no brains, but I can work a thing or two out." He grinned and she scoffed.

"No one thinks that. You're just rash and don't get all the facts before reacting."

He spread his large hands. "Sometimes it's better to act than to wait. Will you talk to him?"

He nudged her, refusing to drop his point. "Can't."

"Bullshit. Just like we couldn't?"

Glaring, she sent an elbow into his side. "You could have killed me! You *did* leave me to die."

"Water under the bridge."

"Yeah, the water I almost fucking drowned in that night."

He cringed. "Still, you should talk to him."

"Maybe." Brow scrunching, she looked at him. "The little raccoon? Is she okay?"

Topp gifted her a genuine smile, his eyes warming. "Lina? She's been living with Kava's Shadow."

Elysia gaped. "*What?*"

He nodded like he couldn't believe it himself. "I jokingly asked her where she'd like to stay since I was going to be gone, and she took me to his front door. I'm not sure who was more shocked, me or him. I think she liked all the food he had."

"She always seemed too smart for a raccoon," she mused. "Larkspur's been with Jessa. I miss the pompous little shit."

They both went silent. He may have been the worst boyfriend to ever exist, but she was starting to think that Topp Blatz might make an okay friend.

Chapter 37

Elysia stood on the shores of the river as the Ferryman guided the boats in. She'd been in the Deathlands for over a month, and every day she came here. Winter had broken, and yet it still misted and rained, cold and miserable against her skin. But it didn't matter, she barely noticed the precipitation slide down her face as she waited for the new arrivals and offered to ease their entrance into their new life. From sunup to sundown, she worked until exhaustion overcame her, and only then would she finally stagger back to the estate, disappointed and ready to collapse. No Beatriz and no indication of any progress learning to rip and transmute despite Maya finally coaching her.

After she'd left Topp, she'd traveled to Bellia, back to the Bone Temple where she'd been welcomed as promised by the priestesses. She'd needed somewhere to rinse her sister's death from her surface, somewhere to sit in her grief until it hardened enough that she could disappear into strategy and manipulation. Emotionless, she'd sat in the dark amongst the bones, staring at the skeleton throne.

She'd seen Grim and Aidan in passing since returning, but after weeks of unsuccessful attempts to approach her, they'd backed off and surveyed her from a distance. Maya was the only person she spoke to, and she only allowed that because Maya was content to speak strictly of practice. There wasn't any time to waste lazing around or avoiding how abysmal she was turning out to be at progressing past her current skill level. She'd master her magic even if it killed her.

Most days she would see the faint outline of Aidan down the riverbank as she relieved newcomers of their burdens and fed the death realm the raw power. Other days there would be the strong, powerful flap of Grim soaring overhead. Silently, they watched, waiting for her to come to them. Food and drinks were delivered as she worked, but she had no appetite and barely any thirst. Crusher napped near her feet, periodically opening an eye and then closing it again until it was time to go home.

Today, the Ferryman gave a sharp whistle with his fingers, announcing his arrival, and sent the first resident over to the bench where Elysia always sat. She gave the woman a frayed smile. She wasn't her sister, and neither was the next person, or the one after that. But she would come here and work until it was her sister who walked up with her silver hair swinging, overconfident even in death.

It was late, the sun already set on the soot-tinged evening, when he finally dared to wait for her to be done for the day. His posture was familiar to her now. Hands behind his back, long wool coat gently waving in the wind, and face drawn. It was getting harder to look at his face, knowing what she did. Day to day, the scales tipped from left to right.

Topp's advice hung like a stone around her neck as she peered silently up at Aidan, cataloging every beautiful line of his face. The slow-burning fire in his eyes, the chilled flush against his high pale cheeks, even the ever-moving smudges of ink that traveled from his hands to elsewhere when he lost track of himself in his work. She stopped on the wet riverbank beside him, waiting for him to say or do something. He was the one who'd sought her out after all, but Aidan didn't speak. He simply crooked his elbow, offering her his arm.

She took it hesitantly, wary gaze on his, but again, he said nothing, allowing the strength of his presence to wash over her and ground her. Leisurely, he guided them back, except instead of turning to the estate, he veered onto a path that cut deeper into the woods. Her feet came to a stop. She was tired and wanted nothing more than to sit under a hot stream of water before sinking into her bed.

Aidan pressed a hand to her lower back, his voice dropping into the soothing, melodic sound she usually loved. "It will only take a minute. I'll travel you home if you don't like it."

A rasping breath sounded in her chest, but she nodded, eyes half-glazed as she slipped back into the numb state she'd been coming in and out of. Silent once again, they walked on, and Elysia realized where he was taking them. The only thing in this direction was her greenhouse.

Glancing at him, she couldn't even muster up the energy to push back aloud, but she had zero interest in flowers or visiting her greenhouse right now. Her brain conjured the image of her pressed flowers in the transom glass where Beatriz met clients. *She named her market after my favorite flower.* Opening the greenhouse's iron-wrapped door, Aidan gestured for her to walk inside. The warmth swallowed her as she lifted her tangled hair off her neck and unbuttoned the top of her coat.

The first workbench was piled with new seed pouches. Aidan walked over to them, holding up the first pouch. "I sourced some new seeds for you from one of my siblings."

Tired, she leaned against a table, exhaustion pulling her face down. He'd dragged her out here for new seeds?

"They're all native to Kava, but now likely extinct unless magic returning revives them one day. I thought you might like to plant them in your sister's honor. You can plant them inside the house for all I care, rip out the hardwood and create a wildflower field. Just please, when you're ready, talk to me." Worry creased his face, his hands gripping the seeds a little too tightly as he waited for her to respond.

Elysia's eyes grew wet and her skin hot beneath her coat. She pressed her mouth shut as her eyelids pinched against the sting of brimming tears. Clenching her hands, she fought the unbearable emotion building in her chest. She didn't want him to see this. She didn't want him to be so kind or thoughtful when every night she went back to her bed and forced herself to envision how she would complete the fates' bidding.

Eyes shut, she didn't see him come closer, but the amber and bergamot scent of him hitched her breath as she pulled it in, her lungs shuddering against unreleased sobs. His fingers cradled both sides of her face, sliding into her hair. She opened her eyes to find a grief that mirrored her own.

"I'm so sorry, Thorn, I am so fucking sorry."

Just like that, the dam broke, and she was sobbing, face buried in his chest, his scarred hands gripping her so tight it was like he thought she might disappear. Over and over, he smoothed one hand down her back as he murmured gentle nothings to her. When at last her tears had run dry, she panted against him, barely able to breathe. Without a word, he scooped her up, traveling straight into her bedroom.

Setting her on her feet, he methodically stripped her down, disappearing for only a split second to steal one of his own large undershirts to tug on over her head. Drowning in soft cotton and the scent of him, her body slowed as Aidan pulled back the bedding and patted the mattress for her to climb in.

With her safe in her own bed, he sat at the edge of it, fingers brushing back her hair. "Do you want any tea? A sleeping tonic?"

She shook her head, her swollen eyes glued to his face. The bed dipped as he made to stand, and before she could think better of it, her hand snaked out, taking hold of his wrist. "Stay."

It was the first word she'd spoken to him since Beatriz had died, and in her heart, she knew it was more. Because she wasn't simply asking him to stay tonight—she wanted him to stay for good. She'd envisioned every potential path. Tried to find the Elysia who had turned in innocent Kavians and put her own life above all else. Again and again, she lay down in this bed, forcing herself to imagine plunging the fates' scissors into the heart that had revived her own, but every time she failed. The scissors held high but never stealing down and snipping him away.

She had no desire to be the goddess of the dead on her own. She wanted him squirreled away in his office, fussing over details she never would have thought of, organizing the arrival schedule of all the new souls, and doing everything in his power to ease the transition for his people from mortal to embodied soul, and beyond. Aidan was an excellent ruler who had made a terrible mistake that the fates had fanned into uncontrollable flames. But he had worked himself to the bone trying to restore both his land and the mortal realm. In the face of a terrible future, a future that promised him nothing but misery and death, he got up every day and fought for a new ending while knowing the odds were against him.

Much like him, Elysia didn't believe in accepting the fate handed to you. She'd escaped death and fallen through realms to find him—to find a different fate. Slipping her hand into his, she spoke quietly, drawing on the thin connection between her and the Deathlands. The same connection that had allowed her to open the prison gates and partner with the rivers to transmute raw magic.

"You made a deal with me, sending me to seek your talisman and free your power. You made an oath and wager, promising me freedom if I succeed. But this is my oath to you—I have never loved freely or easily. I've hidden and failed to find the words you deserve. But if you give me time, then I will learn. I will learn to love and protect with the same ferocity that I learned to survive. I will be your queen."

Voice catching on gravel, he questioned her. "Do you know what you're doing? Tell me before I accept your oath and damn the consequences."

All she knew was that there was no future in which she ruled over the Deathlands without Aidan by her side, and even if it meant the world catapulted past redemption, there hadn't ever been a chance she could harm him to save them all. There would be more than enough time to sort the idea of *them* so long as they both managed to stay alive.

Her gaze never left his. "Stay," she said again. "Stay for always and I will too. I can make no promises beyond that." *I evaded fate once and I will do it again.* A burning anger entered her words, furious that the fates had tried to rob them of this, and at her rage there was pride in his face.

"Yes, Thorn, I accept your oath," he murmured, a softness shining through the harsh hollows of his face. Dark hair trickled onto his forehead, and his lips pressed to her temple.

Golden strands dashed out into the air, glimmering against the barely there light of the oil lamp. The strands danced over their hands and forearms, and Aidan inhaled sharply at the sight, the cobalt flames in his eyes shooting high. The sparkling strands of gold wrapped and plunged into their skin, binding them irrevocably. Her fates-created death voyage would continue as her time dwindled to naught, but the connection between them and the death realm itself had already told the truth.

The god of the dead twisted, his gold-branded hand grasping her chin. His gaze burned brighter in the dark, his low voice sweeping through her. "Your trust won't be wasted, Thorn. I promise we'll find a way."

Chapter 38

ELYSIA STUDIED HER AUDIENCE. Maya lounged in her usual overstuffed chair, her legs flopped over the sides. Grim, unfamiliar with the idea of comfort, had carried in a stiff wooden chair from the dining room and sat at attention like he was ready for orders. One leg crossed over the other, Aidan relaxed on the couch, patiently waiting for her to begin as he pushed his dark blue sweater sleeves up.

Ever since her oath, he had been walking around with his sleeves at his elbows, silently showing off the golden strands that had sunk into his forearm, hand, and fingers. Without saying a word, he was loudly making sure everyone knew what she was to him now.

The light caught on the shimmering strands, and Elysia's attention stumbled as a rush of both attraction and fear overwhelmed her. She'd made her decision and now everything she had to lose was smirking at her from across the room.

Unaware of her thoughts, Aidan grinned and stretched his arms in front of him, making both the floral torch and the golden strands from her oath obvious. Maya clomped her feet onto the rug, looking disgusted. "Funny how she still seems to be dancing around you like you have a disease."

Elysia's glare turned icy. "Deal with your shit, Maya. I'm moving at a pace that works for me, and I won't apologize for it."

A dimple appeared on Maya's freckled face as if both surprised and pleased at Elysia's backbone. "Well, good for you. I've been meaning to catch you—my offer still stands about teaching you necromancy. I know we've stalled with moving past ripping into transmutation, but I really am the best at all things necro. We could have your sister here in no time. Can't say what state she'd be in, but there are always options."

Aidan didn't even look angry, just annoyed. "One, you almost got her killed, so your mentoring permissions are permanently revoked. Two, you know you're not allowed to practice necromancy anymore. And *three*, Elysia is not your conduit just because you're banned."

Frowning, Elysia glanced at Maya. "Why can't you practice necromancy anymore?"

Slumping into her chair, she pouted. "Because people are prejudiced against *unsavory* types of magic!"

Aidan drilled his fingers against the back of the couch. "Maya."

Sighing, she relented. "And because I reanimated a corpse and sent it to murder my father—that's how I died as a mortal. Then after I died, I realized I could travel realms, so I tried again." Her smile was bone-chilling. "That time I pulled a spirit all the way from the death realm and shoved it into a corpse. That was a mistake. Much easier to simply animate a corpse and steer it. The fates didn't like my murder beyond the veil attempt, but they did realize my *potential*, so I was let off with a light punishment. As king of the dead and master of necromancy, Aidan is my babysitter. One day I'll get my full powers back from the fates, but until then I'm studying everything else."

Elysia couldn't manage to school her face as she blinked. "That explains a lot," she said slowly before abruptly turning to face Grim and Aidan. "The fates are why I called a meeting. I need to know how much I can tell you. Do they see everything? Know everything?"

Grim sat up even straighter, if that was possible. He'd been on edge ever since she'd returned even though she'd assured him that he couldn't have done anything. A fates kidnapping was a hard thing to stop. "Their magic works in broad strokes. For most people, the threads that are sewn never change. In a situation like this, they'll be watching for changes in our individual tapestries, but it's difficult for them to notice minor changes—just because you have a thought, the threads don't change. Concrete action can be a problem."

She chewed on this, sliding up her sleeve to stare at the golden strands winding around her light skin. Holding up her arm, she said quietly, "Then we have a problem."

Aidan's voice became bland. "Maya, go to my office. Grab ledger seventy-eight, please."

Maya looked at Aidan like he had grown another head. "Do I look like your maid?"

He leveled her with a cold stare. "I wasn't asking."

Glaring, Maya disappeared, traveling out of the room.

Aidan gestured for Elysia to continue.

Relief filled her that Maya was gone. She'd asked Aidan to divert her before coming in here, and he'd agreed easily enough, always happy to irritate the witch of the woods. But now she had to admit the truth. The fates had asked her to kill him, and in her grief and panic, she'd considered it. Her stomach tightened while the gold glinted reassuringly on her wrist.

"We have to find a way to trick the fates into believing I've accepted their offer to rule the Deathlands and kill Aidan. Maya has the scissors somewhere in the Deathlands. I can feel them, but I haven't found them yet."

Aidan and Grim's gazes met only for Aidan to hold out his hand expectantly. Lifting off the chair, Grim dug in his black tactical pants. Sitting down, he slapped a pewter pocket watch into Aidan's waiting palm.

Aidan clicked the top and the face sprung open. He smiled in satisfaction, clicking it shut and tucking it into his own pocket. "All these years, and you still think you can win a bet against me." He shook his head, but his mouth was smiling.

"Are you serious right now?" She told them she'd been asked to assassinate one of them, and this was their response. She'd been expecting surprise, shock, anger even.

It was Grim's turn to smirk, his tone low and easy. "That watch has gone back and forth between us since we were mortals. We made a bet on what the fates wanted from you. We were already well-aware of Maya's...lack of trustworthiness."

"You do understand how his magic works, right?" she asked.

Grim interlaced his fingers, relaxing a little. "I'm his reminder of the three percent."

"The three percent." She glanced over at Aidan in question.

Grim nodded. "Three percent error margin."

Hope drained out of her, leaving her a husk. "I thought it was more variable than that!" Elysia fought to keep the hysterics out of her voice. She'd made the wrong decision. She should have agreed to off him. The scissors couldn't be that hard to find.

"You made it here, didn't you?" Aidan murmured.

"First time he'd been wrong in a *long* time. That's how I got the watch back." Grim looked like he was two seconds away from clapping her on the back.

She threw Grim a weird look but kept talking. "The fates promised me they'd handle Garrison. That they'd restore Kava." Despair drenched the tiny flame of courage she'd walked in here with as she realized how stupid and emotional her decision had been.

Aidan's gaze remained steadfast on her, unfazed by the torrent of fear and doubt driving her response. "That's quite the deal you're turning down. Goddesshood. A whole realm. Your kingdom restored."

Her hands fisted as she stared at the luxurious hand-woven

rug beneath her feet and muttered. "Maybe I shouldn't. The smarter choice would be to do what they asked."

"To kill me," he prompted helpfully.

"Yes, to kill you," she spat back, her brown eyes flashing murderously.

"You're welcome to try. Keep them guessing till the end."

Elysia pinched the bridge of her nose, the heat of the fireplace suddenly suffocating. This meeting was not going how she wanted it to. She'd come in here ready to discuss her plan, and now, she doubted any length of planning would matter in the end.

Elysia glared at him again. She didn't *want* to kill Aidan. She *wanted* to be locked in a room with him for a few solid hours without any interruptions.

Steadying herself, she slowed. She needed to trust her decision. In the past she had pushed past her natural revulsion of ending someone's life, her tips and leads bringing innocent people to their deaths. She didn't want to do that anymore. Surviving wasn't living, and unfortunately, she knew that now. She was grateful to still stand here, but she'd changed—half in love and tumbling closer, the thought of throwing Aidan at the feet of the fates made her ill.

His burning blue eyes didn't flinch as she worked through her tumultuous confusion. She swallowed hard—what if she was wrong? What if protecting herself and ridding the world of Garrison in one fell swoop was the right choice?

No, love might have been a liability and affliction, but Beatriz, the most selfish person she'd ever met, the very woman who had imparted those words of wisdom, had said she'd choose Lily. Elysia's chest loosened as she reaffirmed her choice.

"There is one other option. We kill the fates."

Silence overtook the room. The only sounds were the sharp crackle of wood burning in the fireplace and shallow breaths.

Grim and Aidan spoke simultaneously.

"No."

"Yes."

Elysia leaned back on one hand from where she sat on the rug in front of the fire, waiting for them to get it all out of their systems.

Turning to Aidan, Grim lifted a shoulder. "You know we considered it in the past. We said if things ever got dire enough that it was on the table."

Aidan's body was stiff, his answer unyielding. "That was before."

Grim argued in his unruffled way. "She knows what's at stake. We don't have time for the gods to interfere anymore. The hourglass is close to running out."

"No, we stay the course. We're releasing the grid to all the gods soon. They'll get involved, and it will change the available paths." Aidan's jaw was so tight, Elysia thought his teeth might grind through.

Thick chest puffing, Grim pushed back. "Tell her. Then she can decide with all the facts in hand. It's her life."

Soot-stained shadows shot out from the outline of Aidan's body, and the blue fire in his eyes blazed unnaturally, but he said nothing. Standing, he began to pace until Elysia grew impatient and snagged his trouser pocket, stopping him from burning holes in the floor.

"It can't be worse than me contemplating murdering you."

Exhaling harshly, he stared down at her. "Killing the fates is a possibility."

Surprise lightened her. "Then what's the problem?"

"Your odds, specifically, are not good if we were to go in that direction. You need to understand, mortals *cannot* kill gods, much less fates. If anyone says otherwise, they're lying. If we were to move in this direction, it would take time and planning. This isn't a one-woman job."

Elysia deflated, letting go of him and sinking back to the rug. It didn't take her long to shrug. "There are no good odds—I say it stays on the table. Besides, they said they'd kill me if I didn't kill you."

Aidan's gaze was heavy on her. "Involving the gods is a longer path, but safer. Every time I consider killing the fates, the odds don't make sense. I can't even be sure of what I'm calculating. It's like my magic can't conceive of a world where the fates are not dictating what is or isn't. There have been many gods. There have only ever been these three fates."

While it was likely the opposite of his intention, an ever so tiny flicker of possibility came back to life within her at his words. It was an incredibly long shot, but if it worked...

"Killing them can wait, but the fates are hiding the talisman from me to stop my apotheosis." Decision made, she continued. "Which brings us back to where we started, I need to retrieve the talisman. My tapestry won't change—I've been after the talisman the whole time."

Aidan's gaze darkened, easily surmising there was something she wasn't saying. He ducked his brow to hers in acquiescence before quietly exiting the room.

His office door latched in the distance, and her shoulders dropped. No doubt he'd be in there all night now, filling ledger after ledger with possibilities and odds. As a mortal, his magic had made him successful, impossible to beat. Now, it seemed to be a curse. He lived in possibilities, never able to stay long in what was, and it was akin to unending distress.

Maya reappeared in the living room, ledgerless and irritated. "I couldn't find that number."

Elysia grabbed a bottle of red wine off the black tray resting on the couch cushion. She poured out a glass and handed it to Maya.

"Don't worry about it. He's pissed because we're running out of time."

Grim's brow creased for the barest of seconds before smoothing. Nodding to Elysia, he stood and brushed a hand over her shoulder. "Need to check in with the reapers."

She smiled at him. He could wonder all he wanted. She'd told them what she could. They would have to trust her now.

Grim stalked out, and Elysia poured her own glass.

It was better this way.

She took a sip of the bittersweet wine. "So, you tried to murder Garrison with a corpse?"

Astonishment flashed across Maya's face before she recovered herself and took a seat on the dark brown leather armchair. Pulling a throw blanket off the arm and onto her lap, she toyed with the fringe of tassels. "You've known then."

Elysia nodded without emotion, continuing to study the woman across from her. "I didn't immediately. You looked familiar, obviously. Your father's eyes. Your brother's freckles."

"What gave it away?"

She shrugged. "I read you."

Maya's mouth twisted. "And you never said anything."

It wasn't an accusation, but there was an edge to Maya's tone that made Elysia smile. She didn't like being found out. It made her nervous that Elysia had rummaged around, searching for her secrets.

"Neither did you." She set her wineglass down. "Help me and I'll help you."

Still miffed, Maya hedged. "What are you thinking?"

"We both know you have the scissors. You put them in front of me for a reason that day. Do you work for them?"

Maya's face went blank. "No, the only person I work for is myself."

"Hmm, well, either you stole them from the fates, or they gave them to you. Which is it?"

Her magic curled around Maya, and the woman bristled. "That won't work on me. I've been shielding you for weeks."

Elysia took a sip. "I know. You're going to give me the scissors."

Maya scoffed. "And why would I hand you a pair of gods-ending scissors?"

"Because I think you stole them. I think that you stole them and wanted to see if you, as a demigod, could wield them. But you can't, you're not strong enough. Are they still in your possession?"

"No," she bit off, eyes flickering with white. "They would have noticed if I kept them for long."

"Right. I need you to steal them again."

"*Why* would I do that for you?" Her face wore a sneer.

Elysia calmly put aside her wine. "Because if you don't, I'll tell Aidan that you stole the scissors hoping to murder him. You're an easy read, Maya. There are two things you want. The death realm, and your brother. So, here's what's going to happen. You're going to get me the scissors, and not only will I keep this from Aidan, but I'll convince him to give you a pass to the mortal realm for a day. He can't restore your ability to travel realms, but he can manage a pass like he did for me. You can see your brother."

It was a few moments before she said anything. She looked older when she answered. Older and angrier than her whimsical dresses and antics ever showed. "I raised him, and they want to use him to end Garrison. They don't care that he'll die, but I do."

Elysia nodded. "I don't want him to die either. Do we have a deal?"

Chapter 39

Rollie was still shrieking when Lucy dropped him at Elysia's feet in the musty cellar.

Elysia smiled down at Rollie, who hurriedly brushed himself off and stood up, ready to blast her verbally.

"Hello, Rollickus, grab a chair. Lucy still needs to retrieve some of the others."

He stuck a finger in her face. "You can't just *do* that to people. I was about to have dinner!"

Topp's low chuckle had Rollie turning. "Really? Because I thought that was the only way you and Lucy traveled. Grabbing unsuspecting people and yanking them around."

Scowling, Rollie sat in an empty chair and crossed his arms, uncomfortable at the sight of Topp.

"Glad to see you haven't gotten yourself killed yet," he muttered, looking around the old cellar as if trying to place where they were. Cold concrete, cobwebs, and old wooden chairs that one of the Reyezes had lent them were the only furnishings. Oil lamps bolstered the bleak light coming in from the singular tiny window, but it was still a shadowy gloom in the damp cellar.

Topp smiled viciously, a shred of his old mask in place. "Oh, you know I'm not so easy to be rid of. Oren's been so helpful ever since your bitch of a god tried to kill me."

"*Goddess*," Rollie corrected. "And I didn't know she was going to do that."

Ignoring them, Elysia turned her attention to the cluster of women to her left, not expecting the sudden sharp pain in her chest that almost keeled her over. Inhaling as the pain returned to its usual dull throb, she straightened. It would be a long time before she got used to seeing Jessa or the Doorman without Beatriz. She still half expected her older sister to barge in and take up all the air in the room with her foul mouth and secretly big heart.

There was nothing to do about that, though.

She took a step closer, and the Doorman threw a hateful look her way, as if Elysia needed the reminder that she was why her sister was gone. Jessa grimaced and clamped a hand down on the Doorman's shoulder like she was afraid the woman might spring up and attack. A fucked-up part of Elysia almost wished Jessa would let her. She shoved the masochism out of her brain. This was delicate, and she couldn't afford to be distracted.

Lucy popped back into the room, delivering both Remy and a blindfolded and tied up Daphne. Remy was dressed to kill, like always, in a fitted sleek skirt and brass-buttoned military-esque jacket. She forced a tight smile, and dragged Daphne up the creaky cellar stairs.

Remy trotted back down the stairs, this time with Emmellin Reyez at her side. They both took a seat and motioned for Elysia to begin. Crusher, Elysia's often present shadow, grunted and plopped down next to her worn-in black boots. She tossed the sweet but terrifying creature a treat from out of her pleated charcoal trouser pocket.

Clearing her throat, Elysia allowed her gaze to run over the roomful of familiar faces. It hadn't been easy to round up everyone, but she wasn't going to pull this off alone.

"You all know that I agreed to find Aidan's talisman and was initiated into the fates' death voyage. While some voyages take years, the clock on mine is almost up. I need to retrieve the talisman, and I need your help to do it."

Several voices broke out at once, causing Emmellin to soundly rap the blade of her dagger against the wooden chair beside her. "Oy! Everyone shut the fuck up. She's talking."

Elysia tipped her head in thanks at Emmellin's unconventional support. She'd gone to the Reyezes first, running part of her plan past Sylvia and Gage. They'd offered one of their many safe houses, allowing her to take advantage of the anonymity of Lucy traveling everyone directly in and out.

She continued now that everyone had quieted down. "The fates kidnapped me and offered me a deal. If I kill Aidan and usurp the Deathlands throne, then in return, they will handle Garrison and restore Kava. Alternatively, I don't kill Aidan and they kill me. To be clear, they never had any intention of allowing me to step foot in the death realm, much less complete the death voyage, so their word is thin."

Jessa let out a low whistle. "Still, you said no? He's why we're in this predicament in the first place."

Elysia nodded, and the knots in her stomach twisted. This is where she knew she might lose them. She couldn't expect anyone else to see past Aidan's mistakes. Not when they'd lived exactly as she had—afraid of dying and watching people they loved fall prey to the soot and execution.

"While you're right, it was more complicated than that. To become a god, you must die and be remade. The fates offered Aidan his role years before it was intended to be his, and he declined. They killed him and his friends and carried on with their plan. Aidan stole a fated object, one of the only ways gods can die, and tried to complete suicide. He had been killed and brought back as a god without his consent, and he rebelled."

"Damn," Emmellin remarked. "They don't tell these stories in the temple."

Elysia nodded. "As punishment for trying to end his life and escape his divine role, the fates altered his fate and mine. All of ours, really. They promised him he'd never be able to reach his counterpart, never fully claim his power or throne. After a century, he believed them. He made the deal with Garrison to spite them, hoping to provoke them into ending him, not realizing what would happen when so many natural laws were broken." She grew quiet, afraid of their response. "Again, you're right. In some ways, it is very much his fault. At the same time, he was manipulated and violated by the fates the same as us. I can promise you that he's worked tirelessly to undo what he set in motion and will continue to do so now."

The prince broke the tension with terrible, off-time humor. "Bet I'm looking pretty good right now, aren't I?" He stretched, his arms folding behind his head and a lazy grin sliding across his face.

"I don't know. Given that my standards were at *can't leave me for dead*, I'd say he's doing okay." Grateful he'd eased the room, she threw him a small half smile, and he winked.

"Killing Aidan is the cleaner option." Rollie's clear blue eyes held hers. "I'm surprised you're considering other plans."

Swallowing, she nodded. She'd known someone would point this out, but it was still uncomfortable to address aloud to a roomful of people she cared about.

"Yes," she said softly. "It is the easier option, and it may even be the better option. Garrison gone. The kingdoms restored, but I can't do it."

"Why?" The Doorman's voice was the crack of a whip.

Elysia met her anger solemnly. "Because I think I might be able to love him. In the short amount of time, I've known Aidan —I've changed. For the first time, I can picture a life worth having, and it's because of him. He made a foolish, short-sighted mistake, but I've made so many more, and he's never once judged me. He's only ever offered to stand by me, support me, tried to love me." She lifted her arm with the golden strands shimmering against her skin. "You don't have to help me. No one could blame you, but I already made my choice, and it's him."

The Doorman's dark eyes misted over, and she quickly averted her gaze, before looking back with her eyes brighter and voice rough. "What did Beatriz say when you went to her?"

Elysia held her own tears at bay at the mention of her sister. "I asked her if she would choose love or survival, and she said she would choose you. That you were a better person than her, and she wouldn't want to live without you."

Face dropping into her hands, the Doorman's quiet sobs filled the silence in the room. Jessa put a hand on the Doorman's silk-clad back. "Not that we're agreeing to help but...tell us how this would go."

Emmellin gave her an encouraging nod, and Elysia gestured at the stairs. "You might have seen Remy escort Daphne upstairs."

Jessa snickered at this. "Fucking Garrison is gross, but what exactly are you going to do with her? Shame her for being a horrible person?"

Topp made a noise of discomfort, and Elysia almost laughed. "I considered finding a random mortal who can summon others, but I decided to try to sway Daphne first. If I know Daphne, then as ambitious as she can be, she's not fucking him for the fun of it. If I'm wrong, then we'll find someone else and handle her."

"There's the cold bitch we all know and love." Rollie commented, his scrutiny on her unwavering, still waiting for her to deliver them a plan.

The Doorman interrupted, her eyes puffy but her makeup somehow still perfect. "Since when can Daphne Reynolds summon people?"

"Since she started going to other kingdoms in Garrison's entourage. Aidan's reapers reported it to me, and I decided it was worth seeing if we could use her." She turned to Rollie. "Daphne is going to summon the fates, and I'm going to retrieve the talisman."

SHE'D HELD up her end of the deal. Maya had traveled to the safe house at the appointed time, and Elysia had the painful pleasure of reconnecting the siblings postdeath.

Holding back the dingy window curtain, Elysia ignored the ache in her chest as Topp and his older sister walked away from the safe house. Given Kava's godless beliefs, it was rare that the current generations passed from their realm to Aidan's. Instead, their souls skipped the pleasant respite of the death realm, and went straight into the beyond. The god of the dead had explained this as gently as he could to her. That Grim knew every soul meant for their rivers, and Beatriz was not on the list. Forced to acknowledge that Beatriz was never going to step off one of those shitty old boats, she'd stopped working from sunup to sundown after that.

Gaze on Topp's strong wide back, she remembered the festering grief inside him—how years after losing Maya, it hadn't relented but only darkened. Looking out the window at Maya's soft brown hair blowing back in the wind, Elysia swore she'd end the bitch if she hurt Topp after he'd lost so much of himself to the grief of her death. She knew how bad Maya wanted vengeance and that Topp wasn't far off in that desire. It had been a risk to connect them. He threw his head back, roaring at something Maya had said.

A hand on Elysia's arm drew her attention, and she dropped the curtain.

"Are you ready?" Emmellin asked.

She nodded, following her into one of the dilapidated safe house's bedrooms. Blindfolded and huddled in the corner of the plain mattress lying on the floor, Daphne was terrified. The others who had hidden out of sight from Maya's arrival were already pressed against the wall, waiting for Elysia. She lifted the opaque blindfold from Daphne's face.

"Hello, Daphne." Elysia spoke calmly. "Apologies for the rough travels, but we needed to talk."

Her old friend gaped, shaking like a leaf. "You don't understand."

"What don't I understand?" Elysia's hand settled on the handle of the dagger at her waist. She almost felt bad about it, but she needed her to talk, and it seemed fear was a heady motivator for Daphne Reynolds.

Blonde hair unkempt and pale eyes frantic, Daphne pleaded. "You were gone, and he started issuing all those bounties. He placed one on *Topp,* his own son. And then he went to my parents, saying he needed a new heir because of Topp, and I didn't have a *choice.*"

Someone made a sound of disgust from the back wall, but Elysia ignored it, understanding all too well what Daphne was saying. Nonetheless, she pressed her. "But you always wanted a crown. We all saw how you looked at Topp. Heard your little comments about him. I just never thought you were fucked-up enough to go after his father instead."

Daphne flinched, drawing back even further into the corner as she quivered. "Who wasn't jealous of you? But I'm just trying to stay alive, and if that means being with an old man, then I will close my eyes and do it. You don't get to judge me." She hissed, suddenly coming off the wall only to fall back when she realized what she was doing.

Elysia smiled and ran her blade along the edge of her finger until the point pressed into the tip. "I have an offer for you. If you take it, you'll be bound by magic and blood because not everyone believes or trusts you."

Suspicion entered her gaze. "What's the deal?"

"We need you to summon a few people for us, but the deal will prevent you from speaking of it to anyone."

"And what do I get? I'm next to Garrison all the godsdamned time. Do you think I can just leave and do a summoning without it being noticed?"

If the situation had been different, Elysia would have laughed.

She liked this version of Daphne. Less frill, more teeth. "You get to keep your head."

Her old friend went ghost-white.

"And...your disappearance could be arranged."

Daphne froze, hope entering her eyes.

"Or you could agree to help and stay where you are. It may turn out that we need someone there."

"Need someone where I am," Daphne repeated back dryly as she licked her lips.

"Yes, in his bed. In the court. We may have eyes and ears, but they can't be everywhere, and Garrison is about to lay siege to every kingdom he can."

Daphne looked down at her bound hands, shaking her head, and adjusting her awkward position on the mattress. "You have no idea what he has in store."

Fear sluiced through Elysia, but she ignored Daphne's baiting. "So, what will it be?"

"How would you get me out?"

Elysia shrugged. "It's not foolproof, but we have people who can keep an eye on you. Could have a traveler grab you and take you out of Kava. There are people you could stay with where no one would ever find you."

"How reassuring," Daphne muttered, suddenly scanning the people in the back of the room. "Remy?" Her brow wrinkled and her voice softened to a more familiar sound.

Remy walked over the stained carpet to stand beside Elysia. Her mouth was a hard, flat line as she stared at their tied-up friend. "I'm the one who demanded you be bound by blood and magic."

Daphne was speechless, but Remy wasn't done. "I have made *endless* excuses for you over the years. I thought you would grow out of it—the utter lack of self-awareness, the blind climbing for better position, never giving a shit how anyone in our kingdom is affected by what's going on within our protected castle walls. I don't know that I've ever seen you do a single thing for another human out of the goodness of your own heart. Let me be clear, I will handle you myself if you screw this up and Elysia dies."

A mixture of shock and shame held Daphne in place. She rested against the wall in defeat, but still her voice was scathing. "Not all of us are smart enough to be philanthropic, local business-saving mavens, Remy Peraldine. I might not have given a shit about the people outside the castle walls, but that was because I knew I was one bad day away from being one of them." She flicked her eerie gaze to Elysia. "You're not so different from me. That's why you're the one offering me a chance."

Elysia shook her head. "No, we're very different, but someone helped me climb out of a hole, so I'm throwing you a rope. Do you want it or not?"

Daphne refused eye contact, staring at the water-marked thin plaster wall. "I'll do the summoning. If I disappear, he'll kill my parents. The only reason yours aren't dead is because your father had all his apprentices executed for being cursed. There's no one to replace him yet."

This news should have stunned her, but it didn't. She'd waited and waited for Beatriz to casually mention their parents had been killed for her betrayal of the Crown, but as the months went by and they remained alive and at the castle, she knew Jack Parker had done what he did best, and pulled every string he could to keep his position. She tapped her nails on the handle of her dagger.

"You're sure?"

Daphne ignored Elysia's question to glower coldly at Remy. "You think you're better than me, but you're not. Just be thankful you're not the one warming his bed." She turned her face away from them all again.

Elysia sighed. This wasn't the outcome she'd been hoping for. "If you change your mind, get word to Jessa at the Salty Rim."

Daphne's shoulders curved, but she didn't face them. "The steamships leave soon for Sagondia. You should do it then. He won't know I'm gone."

Grim's reapers had already gathered the intel, but Elysia thanked her, knowing Daphne was struggling to make sense of how to keep herself safe. It wasn't so long ago someone had called her selfish and given her a chance. She glanced at Remy, who was still staring at Daphne like she wanted to slap her. They'd always been closer, and she knew Remy hated nothing more than not being able to help someone who needed it.

Gaze on Daphne, Elysia spoke. "Everyone out." Quiet but commanding, everyone filed out except Emmellin, who hung in the doorway.

"You sure you don't need a hand?" Her already split red knuckles held onto the peeling door frame.

"I'm good," Elysia answered with a low laugh, giving her dagger a pointed wave.

"Fine, fine." Emmellin swaggered off with her blonde hair rippling, leaving them alone.

Elysia turned back to Daphne. "Before we get to the deal. I have another request."

"What else could you possibly want?"

Elysia shut the door. Five minutes later, she drew blood from them both and sprinkled Deathlands dirt into the wounds, whispering the words she'd been taught. Daphne Reynolds would see her part through or the magic of the Deathlands would take her.

Chapter 40

For the first time since her death voyage began, Elysia traveled back to the Deathlands without being sopping wet. Rollie had handed her a squishy waterskin of lake water and wished her luck. She stared at the now empty water pouch, deeply irritated that she hadn't thought of trying something like this months ago.

She washed the day off, hoping it would relax her enough to get some rest, but the hot water and steam did nothing to slow the constant battering of worry holding her mind hostage. After drying herself with a fluffy towel, she slipped into a butter-soft maroon nightgown, knowing sleep wasn't going to happen.

Resting on her bed, she examined her bare arms. Both were marked by the death realm now. Her left golden and glimmering, declaring her promise to stand beside Aidan, and the right dark and beautiful with Deathlands flora spilling out of Aidan's helm, a reminder of her promise to find the talisman in exchange for Aidan's help. She studied the flora that sprawled out of the helm onto her skin. If Beatriz was gone, she wasn't sure there was any point in going home even if they did manage to survive this.

She refocused on the golden strands. It had been days since she'd called on her faint connection to the Deathlands and spoken her oath to Aidan into existence. She stared at the strands curiously. They glowed warmly at her attention, and then to her surprise, her consciousness shot along invisible strands that carried out her door and down the halls to the man she hadn't brought herself to go see yet. Through the strands, his fixation and tension crashed over her, the scratching of his pen echoing loudly in her ear. Her chest grew tight as the incessant, unyielding *need* to find another solution bore down on her.

The scratching paused. There was a soft flicker of inquisitive interest, and then he returned to his work with even more vigor than before, as if the touch of her presence had renewed whatever lagged within him.

Elysia withdrew and slid her feet into slippers.

She stood in front of his office door, fussing with the smooth ties of her black robe. He probably didn't want to be interrupted. It was late and he was practically possessed by his work.

A soot-stained shadow darted out through the door's keyhole, twisting the knob so that the door fell open. Invitation clear, she entered his office and leaned against the wall silently. The orange-tinted light of an oil lamp cast over Aidan's desk, giving her a glimpse of his relentless concentration. Brow furrowed, stress lines apparent even in the dim light, he had a stack of ledgers beside him that looked ready to tip and an uneaten plate of long-cold chicken and potatoes shoved off to the side. A fire carried on in the black stone fireplace, and Elysia drifted over to it, standing with her back to the flames. She'd come here with every intention of interrupting him, forcing him to rest or at the very least take a break, but she waited, soothed by the sight of him at his desk, fighting against every odd with only a pen and a ledger. She hadn't known that things like steadfastness and responsibility could even be attractive until she'd met him.

It was a fact that he was obsessed. He was obsessed with the infinitesimal chance of them and the life they could have. Yes, he wanted to right his wrongs and save their realms, but he didn't burn for them. His cobalt gaze caught hers, the flames brightening as if he could hear her thoughts.

He burned for *her*. And yet, she doubted it again and again.

Her feet drifted closer again until she was gently lifting the pen from his ink-smudged hand. Aidan paused, allowing her to take the pen, both hands flattening on the open ledger.

"Give me the pen back, Elysia."

She clutched it to her chest like it was gold and grabbed the replacements he kept within arm's reach, tossing them to the winds. The pens clattered against both the hardwood and rug-covered floor, and the fire in his eyes turned to a slow, simmering burn as he pushed his chair back, angling it so he could spread his legs wider. Grabbing the knot of her robe, he swiftly jerked her, so she stumbled between his knees. His hands slid back around her waist, holding her to him. Pulse flying, she kept the fountain pen clutched to her chest.

A muted sound of surprise escaped her when he tipped forward, his forehead crashing against the softness of her stomach. Warm breath against the fabric of her nightgown, the hard sound of his voice sent a rush of blood through her body.

"Either give me my pen back and leave, or I'm going to spread you across this desk and work this out on you."

"I don't believe you," she murmured, clipping the prized fountain pen onto the plunging neckline of her nightgown. If he wanted it, he could take it, but he didn't move as she brushed her hands over him. Rhythmically, she repeated the motion, sweeping her hands over his back and shoulders, pleased at how his tension dissipated under her touch.

Aidan groaned, slumping even heavier against her before he finally lifted his head, his sapphire eyes now aglow with the dare of her quiet challenge.

"And why is that?" He forced himself upright, plucking at the ties of her robe.

"Because I've realized you're obsessed," she said simply,

allowing Aidan to relieve her of her robe, his scarred hands smoothly pushing it off her shoulders to fall to the ground.

His sharp grin glinted in the lamplight as he leaned back, his gaze roving over her as she stood between his legs. "Obsessed, am I?"

Elysia brushed back his dark hair. "Yes."

"And what exactly am I obsessed with?"

Her smile was small. "When I first met you, I wondered what it would be like to feel the weight of your intensity on *me*." She laughed, and Aidan's eyes flared brighter.

His hands grasped her soft skin, running up over the backs of her thighs, pushing her nightgown up to rest his hands just below the curve of her ass. His gaze remained on her, his rich voice as serious as the grave.

"I'm *obsessed* with finding a way to keep you. I'm *obsessed* with having you until immortality runs dry and we both finally cease to exist. Tell me how that equates to letting you walk out this door instead of throwing you down on my desk."

Forcing herself to speak, she unstuck her tongue and slipped her hands over his half-buttoned shirt, the firm muscle flexing beneath her touch.

"Sometimes I believe that. Sometimes I think I could have been anyone—any random girl, selected by the fates we now work against."

It was a careful probing comment. A fear that lingered, ready to taint the fragile, newborn alliance between them. Harshly beautiful, she gazed down at Aidan's sleep-deprived face and how he lounged confidently beneath her. Her fear didn't know how to believe him. It pushed her both to run away and to wait here in his purgatory, not knowing if he would rip her heart out or pull her into his current so they could finally drown in the tension she had tried and failed to ignore.

Her throat worked as she waited, the thorny stems of anxiety in her stomach piercing up through her chest and heart. His mouth parted to answer, and she stayed there in the tender discomfort of his hold because, for the first time, an almost painful longing rose in her. She *wanted* it to be real. She *wanted* to lose herself in the possibility that spurred him on to fill ledger after ledger in the middle of the night.

A new, different kind of fear sprung up as soon as she acknowledged this desire. That if he managed to convince her of his love, of his loyalty, that she would do terrible, unspeakable things to protect the seedling of what grew between them.

A thick band of soot clamped over her mouth just as she made to speak again, and Aidan's thumb caressed her thigh. "I find myself unsure of how to prove to you just how untrue that statement is."

Disappointment coursed through her, her body curving as she fought against his hands to take a step back, but his voice swept out again as dark and soothing as the soot-stained mist of Relaclave.

"I could tell you how the first time I saw you I thought you were beautiful and sweet, making art in such an ugly world. Or how the second time I saw you, it was relief in my bones as you sat on the roof of your home, quietly crying after you sent a poor boy to the gallows because I knew you would understand the complexity of a life intimate with death. Or how I grew to admire your tenacity and cleverness and how you loved your sister no matter how many times she showed up empty-handed asking for more. And then you changed, and I loved how you grew angry and violent as you found the undying rage that tore the wool from your eyes."

Elysia tried to speak against the band of soot, but it gently tightened.

"I'm not done," he growled, the sound rekindling the slow smolder of heat inside her. He began again, holding her gaze steady. "Then you showed up *here*, in my world, against all odds, and asked your fates-destined partner to make you a deal, so you could save the kingdom you have every right to want to raze from history, still wanting to return to a man who had betrayed you, and I agreed, knowing damn well I didn't deserve you either, not after everything I'd done."

Vulnerability shone in the fires of his eyes, and his grip shifted, lifting and settling her on the cool wood of his desk as he stood. Two more soot bands solidified around her wrists, keeping her arms in place. Mouth covered and hands bound, her heart threatened to burst in her chest. He studied her, watching the rise and fall of her pebbled skin, how her pulse battered in her throat, and a flush crept up her chest.

"Are you uncomfortable?" He knocked her knees out, standing between her legs now, one hand on her inner thigh and the other making a slow ascent up over her nightgown-covered stomach to brush over her breast. "Do you want me to stop?"

Drunk, she shook her head, dark hair tumbling over her shoulders.

He smiled. "Good. Because the last thing you need to know is the day you crashed into my throne room and almost died in my arms, I made an oath. I took the Deathlands dirt, your blood and mine, and I promised that if you didn't survive the death voyage neither did I. I called upon the realm and the rivers and prayed for the Deathlands to protect and receive you as their queen before it was your time. Caught between life and death, your soul responded, answering my oath and agreeing. I no longer cared if I deserved you, only that you would have me, and if you would then I would do everything in my broken power to assist and protect you on your path, wherever that may lead. I have watched every version of you—the conniving survivor to the cautious but learning woman—and I want them all."

His hand moved over to where her heart labored beneath his touch. "Do you believe me yet?"

Her gag disappeared, and the words spilled out before she could stop them. "You stupid, stupid man."

He smiled against the darkness. "I knew what I was doing."

Fury darkened her words. "You *knew* the odds. You knew, and you bound yourself to me, and it's—it's irresponsible!"

His grin was blinding, but his voice became gruff as he clutched her face. "You wouldn't have survived. I know these lands, and they wouldn't have given up their right to a mortal death for anything less than the promise of two souls for one, and not any souls, but their king and queen. It was an easy choice."

Looking him in the eye, she spoke. "Till death?"

Soot-stained shadows drenched the room. "Thorn, I've told you, I *am* death."

CHAPTER 41

Elysia's hand went to his belt, but she stopped, her fingers curled around the buckle. "Anything else I need to know?"

Aidan leaned over her, planting his hands on the desk, and invading her space until she was gripping his belt and pulling back away from him. Her abs quivered, but she stayed there, face tilted up, waiting, and drowned in his scent.

He smiled at the sight of her clinging and hovering beneath him, a breath away from falling onto the desk.

"Sure," he said casually. "The talisman is yours."

She blinked in surprise, losing her coy composure as she let go, catching herself sharply on her elbows.

"What do you mean, it's mine?"

Aidan drew back, placing his hands above her knees. The firm pressure of his palms inching up her thighs was an exquisite torture. His hands stopped on her hips, her nightgown bunched up and simple black undergarments exposed. Thumb twitching over the seam of her panties, his brow creased. No longer paying attention to their conversation, he stepped back, his fiery gaze once again roving over her. One maroon strap had fallen down, exposing the soft swell of her breast, the rest of her nightgown shoved up around her hips, her body propped up on his desk on display.

"Better than I ever could have imagined," he murmured.

"Aidan," she chastised, "how is the talisman mine?"

He shook his head as if to clear his thoughts and fixed his heated attention on her face. "I confess my love, my obsession, and you sink your teeth in for another secret?"

One corner of his mouth curved up as his movements turned predatory, his trousers brushing against her bare skin as he came close enough to press his large palm over her clavicle and throat, adding force until she narrowed her eyes and allowed him to lower her completely to the desk.

Still holding her down, he extricated the pen from her nightgown, and ripped the cap off with his teeth to reveal the curved metal nib. Focused, he held her still, and began to write on the smooth skin of her stomach.

Has he lost his mind? She attempted to sit up, but soot-stained shadows shot out, holding her for him, freeing his hand to slip under her nightgown against her ribs as he wrote.

"Aidan, what in the realms are you doing?" Heart tender from his professions and panties damp from his touch, her irritation knew no bounds.

His smirk grew wider the longer he scratched away at her skin. Intent on his work, he spat the pen cap to the side so he could talk. "I told you what I was going to do."

His earlier words played back in her mind. *Either give me my pen back and leave, or I'm going to spread you across this desk and work this out on you.*

"You are *not* running odds on my skin right now." Her voice became dangerous, but she still couldn't move.

"I am," he returned, voice matter of fact.

Peering down as much as the shadows allowed, she saw her stomach was an illegible mess of scrawling black ink, and he was moving dangerously close to her panty line.

"Aidan."

"Thorn."

His fingers hooked under the black cotton fabric, and his brow furrowed in concentration as he slid her panties down just enough to write another line. The side of his hand smeared the wet ink across her skin, extending words and numbers past their form. A pillow of soot slid beneath her head as he continued his work. Lazily, her hooded gaze followed his every movement, her breath inhaling as he incrementally slid down her panties again.

She squirmed, the soot shadows tightening, then relaxing when she held still. Wet heat dampened the space between her legs, and the pen briefly stopped, his fingers gripping against her as his nostrils flared before he returned to his work. His blue eyes never wavered from her skin, the pen nib scratching and teasing with its cool sensation on her warm body. He paused, stretching the fabric over the flare of her hips as he lowered them just enough for another line.

Hovering the pen over her skin, he looked up at her, blue fires blazing and dark hair out of place. Desire dripped through her, her mind going blissfully empty of every single thought as his mouth and hot breath grew close to her core. Sleeves rolled and shirt half undone, his forearms flexed, showing off both his golden strands and asphodel torch as the metal nib glided over her most private skin.

"The odds are steadily improving." His low voice vibrated over her, and she squirmed.

His mouth twitched, a soft laugh falling from his lips. Thumb brushing over her ribs, he grazed the bottom of her breast, making her squirm even harder, fighting against the dark bands that held her as he wrote.

Already breathless, she murmured into the dark. "And what odds are those?"

The pen stopped.

"You naked on my desk letting me fuck you until every doubt of how I feel is forever gone from your mind and body."

She choked, her gaze locking with his. "You could try." She

hadn't meant the words to be a taunt, but by the dark grin on Aidan's face that was exactly how they'd been received.

The words had barely left her mouth when her nightgown and panties were gone. Aidan once again paused, the moonlight illuminating his skin. Down to fitted shorts, he admired her, his hand stroking over himself.

He nodded slowly, his voice deep. "I've never been much for *trying*."

Restraints gone, she lifted one bare shoulder in invitation, and he chuckled before stalking between her dangling legs. Abruptly lifting her upright, he slid her ass to the edge of the desk.

"Last chance." Both hands held her head now, his thumbs framing her jaw.

Distracted, she gripped the wooden desk, swaying into him and kissing his chest. "For what?"

"To keep your distance. You can walk out and go back to your silent wanting."

The tips of her breasts scraped lightly against his bare chest, her hands moving to his back, exploring as she pressed up against him. "As if I'm the only one who's been silently wanting."

He lifted her chin, claiming her gaze, his voice turning smoky like his power. "I've bound you to me through death and realm. You spoke your promise to stand by me, and it gleams on our skin. But do you want to be *mine*?"

Her tongue refused to move as she stared up at him.

"I'm not a half-in sort of person, Thorn. I need to hear you say it."

She nodded with her face in his hands. In the past, she would have found a way to twist what happened between them until she could write it off as only sex, or to flit anxiously between emotion and the physical, never allowing it to come together all at once. It was unsurprising he needed to hear her say it.

"Tell me what you want," he coaxed. The dark music of his voice drew out shivers of need, making her want to pull him tighter against her.

Her gaze nervously fled from his. "I want—"

"Eyes on me," he corrected gently, and a heady heat washed over her again.

"I want to be yours," she whispered.

A flash of a blinding, satisfied smile rewarded her, and then he moved.

Hands lost in her hair, the god of the dead kissed her mouth for the first time, his lips worshipful against hers. Her body rocked back under the weight of his touch. Relief, desire, and want all threaded together, overwhelming her as he groaned with his mouth still pressed to hers, his breath ghosting over her.

"Finally," he exhaled. The word was only half out—likely escaped without permission—when his blue eyes brightened, the flames shuddered in the dark of the room and his mouth stole hers again.

His kiss changed then, deepening as he held her to him, lifting her until she rose to her knees on the hard wood of the desk. Bergamot and the warm scent of his skin lulled her as her head dropped back, his kisses exploring her jaw to her neck, fingers tangling in her hair before he retraced his steps to her face where he drank deeply from her mouth.

Aidan continued to taste her. Plunging into her mouth, tongue sweeping hers as she clutched him, needy in her want for more. The taste of him had her spinning, her body bending and seeking his without thought. Molten beneath his touch, she was ready when his strong fingers finally slid through her heat. Over and over, he teased her with smooth, gentle strokes that left her desperate for more. Still on her knees, her mouth parted on a heavy breath and a flush spread across her chest. Elysia clamped down on his shoulders and writhed against his fingers, chasing what she wanted. Pausing, he cupped her firmly, and she moaned at the pressure.

He kissed below her poplar-leaf-marked ear, his voice a rumble against her. "Patience. I've waited so long."

Her blood sang at the yearning ache in his words and how

they flooded her with a sense of power. One arm behind her knees, he lifted her again and wordlessly sent every last item on his desk flying on a sharp crack of soot-stained shadow, leaving the desk empty but for her. The oil lamp crashed against the rug, flames spluttering as they died out, and his precious ledgers lay useless and stained from dirty oil.

Sprawled out on his desk, naked with her hair fanned out around her, her pulse thumped in her throat as he finally dropped the last of his clothing to the floor. She swallowed, her mouth going dry as he stood over her.

Moonlight cast in through the window, catching every lean, sculpted line and scar of the death god before her.

"You're beautiful," she whispered.

"That mouth," he answered, propping himself over her on one forearm and stroking her face before turning her lips to his. "Who knew it could be so sweet?" He spoke between deep, plunging kisses, tasting every inch of her again. Hand trailing lightly up her thighs, his fingers returned to his slow, relentless task, bringing her to tiny gasps, while she wished he'd take her further.

"Please," she said between quickening breaths.

His hand stopped again, moving to grip her hips, squeezing them as he brought his mouth to her stomach and groaned, kissing her soft skin. He laved kisses and nips over her until he reached her breasts and paused.

"I've never heard you so polite. I think I like it."

And then he took her peaked nipple in his mouth, sucking until her back arched and she was grasping at his flesh, one hand tugging his hair.

Pulling her down the desk, he settled his weight over her, his length slipping through her slick heat as he moved his hips. The hard, warm length of him set a fire in her, her hands trying and failing to pull him closer. A soft rumble sounded in Aidan's chest as he watched her writhe beneath him. He rolled his hips into her again, making her release a throaty sigh as a ripple of pleasure sated her for the briefest of moments.

Looking down, she bit her lip as Aidan took himself in hand, his crown teasing her entrance. Lifting her hips, she offered herself, but he withdrew only for a pathetic sound to escape her. She squirmed impatiently, and he appeared over her, his hand sweeping up over her throat.

"Hush," he chided, his fingers now brushing her lips. She bit down, narrowing her eyes, tired of his teasing. He shook his head, a little grin playing on his lips.

And then the god of the dead dropped to his knees, kissing her feet that dangled off his desk. His kisses crawled up over her skin until his mouth replaced where he had just taunted her with his cock, his warm breath teasing over sensitive skin. Hand on her stomach, his mouth sank onto her, sucking and licking until her cries were wordless, and she was a sopping mess.

Satisfied, he stood and held her gaze as he wiped his mouth, and notched himself at her entrance. He waited, gently moving his head through her wetness as she panted, but he still didn't move. The slow, torturous sensation continued until she broke, her eyes latching onto his burning blue ones.

"Please," she said again, the sound half breath and barely formed.

"Your words are honey," he murmured, one hand trailing over her breast, eliciting a shiver as his fingers grazed her nipple. Cock held against her, he canted her hips and sunk into her, controlling the motion even as he closed his eyes in strain, and a broken groan fell from his lips.

Breath by breath, he stretched her with his fullness. Leaning down, he bottomed out within her, capturing her mouth as she inhaled sharply, her eyes rolling back and a flush of heat sending her spinning.

He nipped her jaw. "See what happens when you say please?" He rocked against her gently, the subtle movement flooding her with pleasure as he allowed her to adjust to his size. She once again tried to encourage his movements, her body becoming increasingly desperate after being brought to the edge again and again with no fall, but he denied her, kissing her throat.

"Do you trust me?" His words vibrated against her skin, and she nodded. He hummed, softly running his hands over her waist. "Then relax. I promise you I won't leave you wanting."

The frantic energy within her melted back into a sweet, endless pool of anticipation. Her focus narrowed to every last tantalizing sensation, from the drift of his fingertips to the aching heat between her legs.

Pliant, she was a puddle of lust on his desk wearing nothing more than the small smile on her lips as she gazed up at him.

"Good girl, just like that." He looked down at her with such pleased adoration it made her whole body boneless. She sank even deeper into her bliss at his praise, no longer worried, but simply lost in the heady space he had led her into. Aidan's hands stroked her sides before firming his grip on her hips and adjusting his stance.

Holding her hips, he finally lengthened his thrusts, pausing at her entrance before sliding even more slowly back home to her. The slow drag of him against her walls had her breaths deepening and cheeks turning rosy as she allowed the sensations to pull her further under.

He had chased every thought from her mind, and all she knew was the rhythm of the god above her stoking her higher and higher. From her dark cloud, she bit down, the taste of his skin satisfying something in her even as she wanted more.

His thrusts turned languorous. Slow and luxurious, his cock moved in and out of her like he was savoring it. A deep, burning heat began to build, and this time she couldn't control it. Liquid light poured through her, and every touch brought her closer to the beautiful death she sought. In her haze, she asked for more, her nose drawing up his neck and pulling in the drug of his scent.

"You asked so nicely," his low voice slipped out, caressing her. "But I don't think you're ready."

Aidan straightened from his half-bent position, bringing her upright against him only to take his time, watching himself disappear into her over and over. Lips against his chest, she kissed up his sternum, barely coherent and hanging off the edge he'd held her to.

"Fuck," he groaned, forehead crashing down onto hers. "You're perfect."

Bringing his hand down between them, he pressed firmly against her, making small circles as he continued to pump in and out of her. A low moan from deep in her belly sounded, a harbinger of the pleasure about to consume her.

"Yes, *that*," Aidan praised her, suddenly gripping the back of her neck and slamming her back onto the desk, leaning over her again and thrusting deeper and harder than before. The same almost guttural sound left her mouth, her legs wrapped up above his hips, digging in as he brought her closer. Eyes closed, the liquid light turned scorching and she lost herself to its waves. Sweat broke out across her skin, and his name fell like a plea from her lips into his mouth.

Hand in her hair, he tugged until her hazy eyes blinked open to meet his, her mouth half-open on a cry.

"I'm right here," he growled. "Now *let go*."

He thrust into her again, and her head threw back against the desk as she completely broke. The sweet endless bliss shocked through her in shimmering waves and convulsions against his skin. Through it all, she clung to him as he spoke softly against her hair.

"Just like that," he whispered as she floated on, still shaking with tears rolling down her face. She couldn't have stopped them if she tried, the tears continuing even as mindless pleasure still cascaded through her.

She pressed her face into his shoulder. "I'm sorry," she hiccupped. "I don't know why I'm crying."

Her stomach convulsed again, and she groaned as more heat swept through her, pressing her hips closer to him. Understanding, Aidan slid his hand beneath her low back, fingers spread across her ass as he pulled her onto him as close as physically possible. Arms tight around him, she exhaled in relief at his closeness. He held her there until she drew back, easing herself off him, and settling onto the desk propped up on her elbows so she could see him.

The look on his face brought a blush to her face, and she tried to look away. He was looking at her with such gentle but fierce devotion it made her heart stutter.

"Stop." She flicked her fingers against his skin, leaving them there so she could finally run her hand over his beautiful chest and stomach like she'd wanted to all night.

He smiled down at her less than subtle attempt at feeling him up before grabbing her fingers and kissing them. "That was new for you then?"

She paused. "Crying?"

He nodded.

If her cheeks had warmed before, now they burned. He was never going to have sex with her again. She was so embarrassing.

He kissed her palm now, noting her distress. "I'm honored."

She froze, her brow quirking. "You're honored that I acted like a teenage virgin?"

A rough laugh escaped him, his abs flexing over the top of her. "How do you feel right now?"

She stretched, her whole body languid. "Spent, but new. Like you cleared everything out and I can breathe again. Like I want to do it some more," she purred, pulling him down to her so she could kiss his mouth. "Mmm." She couldn't help the little noise, he tasted so good she nipped his lip.

Another laugh rumbled through him. "I've created a monster."

She nodded. "You'll have to deal with the consequences."

Shaking his head, he traced his fingers over her skin. "I don't need or want to know what kind of sex you've had before. That's your business, but I want you to know that it's normal for certain kinds of sex to elicit that type of response, and I'm *honored* because it means you gave yourself over to me. You trusted me with all of you, and I know how difficult that is for you."

Her throat suddenly had a lump, but she nodded, and he sat up, scooping her onto his lap. "Hold on." In a flash, they were on his bed, and Aidan was drawing the covers back, gesturing for her to crawl in.

Once they were under the covers, her hand slid across the sheets, trailing over the length of him. Wrapping her fingers around him, she smoothed her hand up, then back down in one smooth stroke, and Aidan closed his eyes, groaning as he put his own hand over hers, stopping her.

Confusion cramped her stomach. "But you didn't...? Do you not want...?"

His bright blue eyes flashed open, practically glowing in the dark as he moved over the top of her faster than her eyes could track. Hot and ready, he pressed against her. "Does that *feel* like I don't want you?"

He ground down against her already sensitive front and laughed darkly as he rolled off her. "Go to bed, Thorn." Grabbing her, he pulled her into his side, her face on his chest.

Sitting up, she dug her elbow into his ribs and glared, knowing damn well he could probably see her with his stupid immortal vision. "I don't understand."

He sighed. "I can't."

"You can't have sex? Hate to break it to you, but I think that ship has sailed."

Aidan bent one elbow, putting his head on his hand, sounding patient now. "I can't risk fully finishing inside you while you're mortal."

She paused, anxiety rising inside her. "Do regular contraceptive herbs not work?"

Face to face in the dark, the high points of his defined cheekbones colored. The mighty death god was finally *almost* embarrassed. He tucked a piece of hair behind her ear. "They work."

"Then what's the problem?"

"The problem is that I'm not willing to risk harming you."

"Aidan, you're going to have to spell it out."

Rolling onto his back, he slid one arm behind his head as he stared up at the ceiling. "I might have run some numbers, some scenarios."

"About you...finishing inside me?"

"Yes," he snapped without any bite. "I don't want to alter your mortal makeup in any possible manner. It was dangerous enough that the realm accepted you the day I made the oath to keep you alive, but I'm concerned that any serious amount of my essence within you could interfere with your transformation."

"And *why* would it interfere?"

"I don't know! It was just a thought, so I ran the numbers, and it *is* a significant possibility, and we don't need any more things that could go wrong."

Elysia bit her tongue, studying his clenched fingers and the forearm covering his eyes. She wrapped her pointer and thumb around his wrist, delicately lifting his arm as she draped herself across his chest. Stubborn light shone out of the low fire in his eyes. Dropping his arm away from his face, she folded her hands and rested her chin, continuing to gaze quietly at him.

His shoulders dropped. "You think I'm ridiculous."

Her brow scrunched, but her voice was gentle. "No, I think your brain wouldn't know what to do if it wasn't worrying. The odds for all of this are terrible, and you can't control that no matter what, and that's hard. Your brain is stuck. It can't find a solution, and it doesn't know how to rest, so it makes more problems to worry about."

He huffed lightly, shooting her a look. "I'm not risking you."

She rolled into the crook of his arm, staring up at the ceiling like him. "There *are* other options."

"I've waited this long. I can wait a short while longer."

"Okay."

"Okay?" The word was suspicious.

She lifted a shoulder. "Sounds like I need to give you more actual things to worry about. I could tell you about how today went if you'd like. Might help."

Even though she couldn't see him, she could feel his silent grin as he shook his head.

"You know I'm never going to be able to sleep unless you tell me now, right?"

She glanced up, tilting her head back. "You're a very strange man."

He pinched her ass and she squeaked.

Voice barely a whisper, she rolled back on top of him, nose to nose. "I have an idea. Will you run the odds?"

Hands cupping where her thighs met her ass, the god of the dead kissed her so intensely she lost her breath and saw stars.

"Tell me what you need," he rumbled, and she smiled. Maybe letting people in on her plans wasn't the worst thing in the world.

Chapter 42

Elysia paced in the empty warehouse. Her black boots struck hard against the concrete floor of the wide-open building as she walked back and forth. Jessa's gaze trailed her as she leaned against the wall with her arms crossed.

"You're making me nervous, stop."

She came to a halt, spinning to scowl at Jessa. "Remember when we were so convinced I could make a deal with Aidan, and it could fix things?"

Jessa lifted a shoulder. "I was never that enthusiastic, but sure."

"This feels like that." She hadn't looked at the fated hourglass today, but intuitively she knew the sand was almost at its end.

"Like it's going to go sideways?"

She twisted her fingers together. "Something's wrong."

Pushing off the wall, Jessa grabbed her by the shoulders. "Of course, something is off. This plan is insane, but it's the best we've got, so get your fucking head on straight, and pull it together."

Elysia nodded rapidly, bouncing on her toes. "I think Aidan's rubbing off on me."

Jessa's eyebrows drew together in question, and Elysia pulled out of her grasp. "He worries. About everything. All the time. He's anxious," she clarified.

"Right, well, cut it out because you need to nail this."

She closed her eyes, slowing her breaths until the ragged expansion and deflation of her lungs consumed her nerves. "Focusing."

Jessa's voice reverberated weirdly in the empty building. "She summons them. You find out where the talisman is and nab it before you're dead. Easy."

Elysia's gaze darted away from Jessa just as a banging on the door echoed loudly. Jessa grabbed her shoulder again.

"That *is* the plan, right?" Menace graveled her voice, and somehow it soothed Elysia to hear it.

She smiled sweetly, wishing her sister were there. "Definitely the plan."

Jessa dropped her arm and cursed, but Elysia was already flinging open the heavy door of the Reyez warehouse. The whole crew filed past her looking grim as she gripped the metal door tight enough that her knuckles turned white. It appeared she wasn't the only one who was a barrel of raging nerves.

"Everybody ready?" She stuck her hands into her pockets to hide how they shook. Even if this did work, there was a strong chance she wouldn't be walking out of here, but they didn't know that, and she couldn't let them. She fisted her hands, forcing the shaking to stop.

Topp stood tall above the others, shifting his weight from foot to foot as he cleared his throat. "Can I talk to you?"

Lucy and Jessa grumbled at his interruption, clearly wanting to just get on with it. They were on a tight schedule.

He held his hands up placatingly. "Just take a minute. I swear."

Elysia nodded, following him outside the warehouse to where it sleeted steadily. Spring in Bellia was a sloppy, dangerous time where rain froze into wet sleet that iced over all the roads at night before melting into dirty gunk. It was disgusting. Hunching into herself, she squinted up at him.

"What is it?"

Topp rubbed the back of his neck, his face creasing. "I can't help."

Sleet smacked her in the face as her mouth slid open, her honest surprise plummeting like familiar betrayal through her chest. Voice dangerously low, she strung him up with her gaze. "We are two minutes away from trapping the godsdamn *fates*, the most ancient of beings, and you want to cut out *now*?"

Sleet flattened his hair, making odd pieces stick out as he ran his fingers through it. He sighed tiredly. "Lys, you don't need me."

She stopped, shock coursing through her. "You don't know that. My magic isn't battle ready yet. I've been trying, but I'm just not there." She was rambling, unsettled by this last-minute change in the plan, with old feelings of Topp letting her down surging and dictating her response.

He looked at her with icy flecks dripping off his nose, his green eyes dimmer than usual and begging her to see reason. "You have a woman in there who could blow up this entire building."

"But she sucks at limiting it to people!" Elysia exploded back, her barely restrained anxiety now rampaging. It was one thing for her to die, but she needed to know everyone else would make it out, and he was threatening that.

She walked a fine line, drawing the fates here to retrieve the talisman without tipping them off about any of her other plans. She'd come up with idea after idea, making Aidan run the odds. She'd taken stupid, concrete action in a hundred different directions all to ensure the threads never solidified into what she truly hoped to do. Even Aidan didn't know her exact plan. It was the single idea she *hadn't* run the odds on. And now *Topp fucking Blatz* thought he was going to ruin it all?

His hand covered his mouth for a moment, then gestured to her belt. "Oren has a lead on killing demigods that isn't the scissors. I need to follow it."

She stared down at the wet, rocky ground, only now realizing he was dressed in heavy boots and had an overstuffed rucksack on his back with a canteen hanging off it. "Are you taking Rollie too?"

Guilt shone out of his eyes.

Ire stirred in the bottom of her stomach as her brain put it all together. "You can't have Lucy. Not today. She's the only one who can group travel."

He tilted his head in acknowledgment and adjusted the strap of his rucksack. "We've got it covered."

With a hand on her dagger, she spat out the question she knew would put their friendship in the grave. "Fuck Oren's lead. You're helping her, aren't you?"

Topp looked uneasy, his mouth fumbling for an answer he didn't have. Because he wasn't supposed to know about the scissors. No one knew about the scissors strapped to her belt except her and the woman who had stolen them.

Venom dripped from her voice as she pressed her dagger to his stomach much like she had his father only so many months before. "You're lucky I don't gut you right here, Blatz."

She spun on her heel, gravel spitting out from her boot, but stopped with her hand on the chilled metal of the door handle. Looking over her shoulder, Topp had turned away from her. Shoulders curved and back flexed with his fists clenched, he warred with himself.

But she wasn't wasting another breath on Topp Blatz.

Shaking her head, she marched back into the warehouse, leaving him behind for good.

She shook off the sleet from her all-black attire and stormed over to Rollickus, grabbing him by his shirt collar. Disgust thickened her voice as she held him in her grip. "Anything you want to say?"

Rollie jerked away, attempting to smooth out his shirt. He frowned at the ruined material before giving up. Adjusting his glasses, he studied her and glanced at the closed warehouse door. "So, he is up to something then."

Face devoid of any warmth, her jaw ground. "I have a job to do. Go follow him if you want, but don't be surprised when he leaves you for dead."

Rollie's sharp eyes became calculating. Buttoning his jacket up, he spoke. "Do you really think I would ever trust a Crown squinch?" He almost reached for her but dropped his hand when she stepped back. Rare uncertainty flashed across his face. "You're sure you've got this handled?"

Her mouth flattened. "Just get out."

* * *

RESPONSIBILITY FELL HEAVILY ON HER. Down by two people—two people with physical magic—they were far less protected than before. Worse than that, she'd been played *again* by the same man, but the cards were already in motion, and it was too late to stop the game now. She threw up one hand with an irritated breath.

"It's better this way. Everything else remains as it was."

Jessa rubbed her palms against each other and nodded in agreement. "Never liked working with that asshole. Should've planked him when I had the chance."

The Doorman, cunning as ever, scanned Elysia for signs of an impending breakdown. "He has his uses. Are you going to tell us what happened?"

Face tight, Elysia shook her head and brushed her thumb over the hilt of her dagger. Forget planking him, she should've stabbed him. Turning her stare to Daphne, she practically growled when she asked, "Are we ready?"

Pale and trembling, Daphne did not look ready for what was to come, but she nodded weakly, and that was the best they were going to get from her. Elysia glanced at her watch impatiently.

Just then, a reaper with a flight-ruffled braid and torn uniform appeared in the warehouse.

Bloodied with satisfaction in her eyes, she addressed Elysia. "The Grim requests I inform you the reaper mission is complete. The fates are in the mortal realm, and he is engaging them. Work fast." She disappeared.

Her plans had changed, but she couldn't dwell on that. She'd gotten one beautiful night with a man she knew she could love, and right now he was probably losing his mind as the odds tanked and her death grew unavoidable. Good thing he was stuck in the death realm.

Elysia ran her fingers over her belt, checking off each item—water pouch, dagger, one already used potion, and finally the gods-ending scissors. Chest tight, she looked every single woman in the eyes before she spoke.

"Tonight, we change fate. Don't doubt, don't hesitate, or we're dead."

The Doorman lifted her voice. "For Beatriz." Normally enchanting, tonight she was the lethal edge of steel.

"For Beatriz." Their voices echoed out in the warehouse, pinging back to them smaller and tinnier than they'd left.

Grabbing a heavy box, Elysia held it out. In silence, hands reached into the box, pulling out the gas masks she'd asked Rollie to devise. At least he'd come through with that. Her jaw ticked as everyone slid the masks on. Black masks molded to look like skulls hid their faces and protected them from what was to come. Elysia slipped on her leather gloves, quickly tucking in the icy blonde hair flowing out from beneath Daphne's mask.

Taking a seat on the floor, Daphne's eyes closed.

The summoning had begun.

Elysia quickly handed out potions from the bottom of the box. A brutal invention from the Nightshade Market, the whole crew began smashing the glass vials all over the concrete floor. Thick-soled boots crunched on broken glass as the noxious white vapors clouded into the air.

Cursing, the fates shuddered into existence, furious they'd been summoned. A smirk formed behind her mask. Grim had been right. Their protections didn't extend past their own realm. *Arrogant pieces of shit.*

She flew through the air, tackling Skiel to the glass-covered concrete floor. Bones crunched to her left as Jessa's fist smashed against Adla's face. Still wrestling Skiel, she couldn't spare a glance to anyone else. They didn't need to conquer them, they just needed to distract the fates long enough for the poison to over-whelm their systems. Elysia grunted as she took a knee to the groin, but her grip remained tight on the much taller fate as they rolled. Arm snapping out, she grabbed Skiel's neck and squeezed, knowing that if she lost the upper hand for even a second, she would be dead.

Anger in their eyes, Skiel's movements jerked as they lost their strength, but Elysia didn't dare move until the fate was completely in the poison's grip. Panting, she dropped her hold and took in the mess around her. Jessa's hands were bloody, but she stood over Adla victorious and alive. Tiny Lucy had paired off with the Doorman to wrangle Monica. The Doorman was clutching her nose, blood seeping out from her fingers.

The fates had been unsuspecting and unprepared, but more than that, their unique powers were restricted to fate magic. Their power lies in the tapestry they wove, not in physical prowess or battle. While they were ancient and feared, it was for the broad-scale destruction they wrought, ruining an entire life with the tug or snip of a thread. Throw them in a bar fight, and the Kavian women had them by the throat. *Too bad they can't die.*

Skiel's head rolled to the side, eyes blank and mouth ajar. Elysia had tested the potion three times on Aidan but had still been afraid it wouldn't be enough to hold them down given how old the magic and blood that ran through their veins was.

"Chain them, now," Elysia ordered on winded breath as if the rest of the crew didn't know exactly what came next.

Grunting, they lugged the fates' motionless bodies over to the prepped spots. Elysia's nails tapped against the empty potion bottle on her belt. Maya's famous glue. It didn't matter how powerful you were—that shit worked.

Elysia leaned back on her heels, taking in the sight of the slumped fates stuck to the concrete floor. Lucy and Jessa crouched, pulling the fates' arms behind sturdy warehouse support poles, and chaining their wrists and ankles.

Knowing what came next, her emotions slid down and away, leaving her functional but cold. Cold was easier than scared. Because she *was* scared of what came next—but she'd met death and knew what awaited her. No matter what, she was going home today. She just wasn't sure how she was arriving. Her foot tapped, eyes narrowing on the chains, wondering if they'd hold.

Her foot tapped again. Time for them to wake.

"Thirty seconds, everyone."

Daphne continued to work, her body swaying as she lost the strength to stay upright. She sank onto her side, exhausted, but not done yet. Jessa glanced back at Daphne, confused that she was still summoning, but the bartender stayed where she was, returning her gaze to the fates.

Elysia rested in front of the fates when their eyes opened. Down on one knee with her dagger prodding at Adla's cheek, she forced them to meet her gaze.

"Tell me where the talisman is." Despite the quiet chill in her voice, her demand still made Adla smirk.

The blade scraped a thin line of blood as Adla looked off to her siblings and laughed.

Skiel shook their head, their long blonde braid swaying. "She thinks she can harm *us*. We are endless, child. No matter what you do today, we will go on tomorrow and every day after that. We do not fear pain or our end."

"Is that so?" The flat part of her blade quieted Skiel's lips.

They spat their words around steel. "You could have become a *goddess*. Now you're just another woman who gave it all up for a *man*." Skiel's stare bore down on her, condescension snarling out.

Elysia stared at them, disgusted. "All your fucking bullshit. It never ends." Without another word, she dove into all three fates' psyches at once, searching for not a secret, but something more. It was her talisman they hid, and she would find it in their abyss.

She'd loved chasing secrets. The thrill and danger of the trail, the satisfaction of stealing and escape. But now she knew what it was she truly sought: *power*.

Power that would take her from fragile mortal to nearly untouchable god. The high of it swam through her like ecstasy, the promise twisting her reason. She spun through the thick molasses of their psyches, discovering what it was to be ancient beyond measure. The hopes and fears that had crumbled to dust with their humanity. How they saw puppets instead of souls and games instead of lives. How the gods were weighed down with the threat of death while the fates did as they pleased, threading wars and famine and loss beside joy and triumph.

Someone put their cold leather hands on her skin, the touch so distant it barely registered. There was a prick on her arm, warmth trickling down and pooling at the edge of her glove. The strange sensation drew her long enough to refocus her scattered, immaterial self. She'd been warned that to swim through the fates' psyches would be akin to warping through time—ill-recommended and likely to leave her broken or lost forever, unable to find her way back out. She was everywhere and nowhere at once, powerful, and bereft.

Tunneling through their waters, she left the shallow puddle of the fates' inner machinations and began to hunt for the object that was hers to claim. Time extended dangerously, but she couldn't leave until she found it. The shell of her body sagged, but that didn't matter. She had no body now. And this would all be for naught without the talisman. The sharp pricking dug in again, and a bell rang somewhere outside of her. A signal for her to come back to herself.

She wasn't ready. She couldn't leave.

Consciousness shot like an arrow through them all until the

arrowhead pinged off something heavy and iron. Invisible hands groping, she tried to pick it up, lost to the fact that it wasn't real, but merely the memory of what she sought. Again, she put her hands on it, prying with all her strength as the bell grew louder and louder while a hot, sticky substance streamed down her arm.

She needed it. It was hers, and it needed to come with her.

The whisper of a soothing, dark melody touched her spirit, and her left arm burned. Familiar, she listened, relaxing into its enchantment, and loosening her grip on the object in her hands. Dark and powerful, she wanted this even more than the power she'd been searching for in the abyss, so she followed it. Out of the thick, endless well of fate, and back into the present now.

Gulping for air like she'd truly been underwater, she re-emerged.

The Doorman held Elysia's bloodied dagger, her face pale and dark eyes relieved. Jessa exhaled, chucking the bell she had been ringing like it could wake the dead to the floor and grabbing at the back of her head with her elbows wide. Glancing down at her blood-soaked arm, Elysia barely registered the pain. Blood streamed over the golden strands on her arm. The strands burned wildly, glinting and shimmering as if alive. She had been in their minds for hours.

Shaking off the fog, she strode to the fates before she could lose her nerve.

It was time.

Ignoring the vitriol spewing out of the fates' mouths, Elysia tore the old golden-bronze scissors from her belt. She'd been to enough executions that she knew better than to talk or hesitate. Bracing herself for what was to come, she lifted the scissors like a dagger, ignoring how they hummed in warning against her mortal touch, put one hand on Skiel's shoulder, and plunged.

Chapter 43

The scissors bounced off Skiel's chest, the gods-ending magic reverberating back up Elysia's arm with shocking speed. Doubling over in pain, she grunted as the scissors clattered out of her hand.

The voice she'd been waiting for finally emerged from the cacophony like a peal of traitorous bells. "You knew it wouldn't work, but still you tried."

At least she'd expected this Blatz to double-cross them. Funny thing about lying to a ripper who had grown up feeding on emotion and information—it was possible—but it wasn't easy.

Jessa's arms swooped under her shoulders, dragging Elysia upright against her chest even as her bones became brittle and skin hot to touch. Maya strolled into view with a light pink gas mask strapped to her face. Walking over to the fates, she administered the antidote to her glue potion and muttered an incantation over the locked chains.

Staggering out of Jessa's hold, Elysia fell to the hard concrete, snatching the scissors and crawling over to an unconscious, face-down Daphne. Fire roared through her body, and she stopped, panting as her vision blotted out with black. Girding herself, she clung to consciousness with everything she had.

The power it took to kill a god was destroying her. A punishment for daring to wield an immortal weapon. She knew she couldn't kill them, but if she was going to wield scissors that would cause her death, then she had wanted the satisfaction of stabbing them first. They might not be able to die, but they could still bleed, chained up and forced to watch what she did next.

Out of the corner of her eye, most of her crew disappeared into thin air. Her relief burned away as the pain scorching her body battled on. Rolling Daphne over onto her side, she grabbed the thick tapestry out of her hands.

She knelt and held the tapestry in the air, waving it like a flag. Her fingers cramped painfully on the golden-bronze handles of the scissors, delirium carrying her on.

"I might not have the strength to kill a god, but I can rip fate." Voice thin and fading, it still reached the fates' ears, and she smiled as their faces changed. She wanted them to see her shred the nightmare they had painstakingly crafted over the millennia.

Channeling every last drop of her strength and magic, Elysia ran the scissors through the fates' tapestry as she ripped and ripped and ripped. The scissors tore fate in two, the tapestry fluttering to the floor in pieces as the threads turned black, disintegrating as they fell. Body bowing, she ripped like she never had before, drawing it all in and stealing the power they had wasted in their twisted manipulations. Her body sprung back as she collapsed, but Jessa was there, hoisting her to her feet as the power of the fates coursed through her like violent electricity.

Her mortal bones weren't made for this just like she wasn't made to wield the scissors, but she had done both, knowing full well how it might end.

Because now the slates were clean.

She'd ripped fate and wiped the odds, leaving destiny open.

Open for a mortal prince to kill a demigod king.

Open for a mortal girl to rule death.

Endless paths blinked into existence, waiting for them to rise up and rewrite their endings.

Bloodcurdling, pain-filled screams shook the warehouse as Jessa dragged her to the door. Adla keeled over on their knees with a bone needle in hand. Monica lunged for the shriveled tapestry, holding one half in the air with a gasp. Skiel simply stared, unmoving as if they couldn't believe it had happened at all.

Maya was ashen, slowly backing away before sprinting past them out the door.

"We have to get out of here." Elysia's voice was nothing more than a reedy rasp.

Nervous, Jessa's catlike eyes settled on her. "Do you trust me?"

"No," Elysia grunted, pointing at Daphne still on the floor.

Her heart beat strangely now, the off rhythm fast and pounding in her ears. There was no way she could travel herself, much less another person.

Fearful gaze stuck to the writhing fates, Jessa's words were almost silent. "Me neither."

Grabbing Daphne, Jessa awkwardly hauled them both out of the warehouse. She dropped Elysia once they were out, carrying Daphne off and dumping her beneath a tree. Elysia tripped over her own feet, slipping on sleet and ice as she tried to follow them. She didn't have much time, her body was giving out, but she didn't want to leave them here.

Hurrying back, Jessa slung Elysia over her shoulder and brought her to rest beside Daphne. Ducking to a crouch, she slapped Elysia's cheek, forcing her away from the edge of blackness. "They can't die, right? A mortal can't kill them?"

Elysia blinked slowly, her friend's words like mush. She shook her head. "Can't die."

Jessa nodded resolutely, her nostrils flaring as she put her hands on her knees and pressed back to standing. Stalking closer to the warehouse, her hands became fists and her whole body tensed. A foreign, ear-shattering hollow bang rocked the atmosphere, deafening Elysia as it passed. Brick became ash as the warehouse exploded into nothing but flame.

Dazed, she watched the flames grow. This was nothing like what Jessa had done in the Endless Forest. There was a crater where there had once been a massive building.

Jessa stalked back over, her cheek bleeding from shrapnel, and looked down at Elysia warily as if expecting her to recoil or cringe.

"That...was incredible." Rust and metal filled her mouth, her vision fading before the internal fire finally consumed her whole.

CHAPTER 44

ELYSIA WOKE in a cottage with the smell of sea in the air. Unlike in Kava, the briny scent rustling in through the cracked window didn't smell of rot. It was clean and fresh with a meager sun shining through the blue sky and clouds.

Her golden strand-marked arm had tight white bandages wrapped around her elbow, and overnight her joints had become stiff and arthritic, detesting even her slow, careful movements. Propping herself upright, she took in the room with a sinking gut —lace curtains and delicate half-drunk teacup on the wooden stool beside a rocking chair with a knitted blanket tossed over its arm.

Throwing back the covers, she stumbled to her feet, swaying as a bout of dizziness overtook her. She needed to leave. Hurriedly, she searched for her water pouch and dagger, or anything that could be used as a weapon.

The door creaked open, and Maya stood there in a pale-yellow dressing gown, holding a fresh cup of steaming tea. "Do you really think I'd leave anything sharp out around you?"

Mouth tightening, Elysia forced her aching body to straighten as she turned around. "Where are Daphne and Jessa?"

She sipped her tea. "They're fine. Dropped them back off in

Relaclave now that I can travel freely again. Thanks for that," she smiled, but it lacked any warmth, her gray eyes unreadable.

Elysia put a hand on the tree stump serving as a nightstand. "You can travel freely again."

"Indeed, all fates-woven restraints and rules are gone." She dipped her chin at the bed. "You might want to sit down before you pass out."

Begrudgingly, Elysia shuffled to the bed, never taking her eyes off Maya. "If you can go anywhere, why are you here? Why aren't you off murdering your father like you've always dreamed of? Do us all a favor," she mumbled.

"You're a bargaining chip." She took a tiny corked vial out of the pocket of her dressing gown and tossed it at Elysia. "And don't worry, Garrison will die, but I'm dreaming bigger than that these days."

Elysia fumbled the potion, her fingers not working properly. Grabbing it off the bed, she held it with no intention of ever drinking anything from the backstabbing bitch in front of her. "It doesn't matter if you healed me. Aidan and Grim won't forgive you."

Maya slid one finger around the rim of her teacup consideringly. "Who says I healed you?"

Elysia shot her a dry look and wiggled her stiff fingers. "I'm not dead, and I'm in your wretched seaside hovel."

The former Blatz princess set her teacup down and folded herself into the rocking chair. "You might remember I offered to teach you necromancy."

Dread poured through her empty stomach.

Maya watched her reaction carefully. "You're not reanimated if that's your concern. You're simply in-between."

"In-between," she repeated, her face falling as she looked around the cottage room with new fearful eyes.

"Yes, you were hovering when I came back for you, and I simply helped you along. Guided you into the other. No one will find you here. Your body is safely in stasis. You would die quickly if awoken."

Elysia gripped the blankets, her voice hardening. "What do you *want*?"

Maya looked out the window as the sky muddled into gray and rain drizzled down. "What do I want..." she repeated before glancing back at Elysia. "You know, I'm not sure anyone's ever asked me that. I was the eldest unwanted Blatz daughter, never even considered for the crown despite clearly being the better fit. Instead, I raised Topp for the role he never wanted, and I should have had. Still, it wasn't until I learned what my father had done to my mother that I tried to kill him."

In another life, Elysia could have empathized. Families were complicated and their world misogynistic. She knew what it was to be angry and want vengeance, but that didn't mean she was willing to be held hostage in a strange limbo. Her magic nudged her though, heeding her to keep quiet and allow Maya to unburden herself. Elysia held her tongue.

"As a necromancer, death went differently for me than others. I had no need for coins or guides to a new realm. I traveled between them all initially, watching, waiting, learning new skills. I couldn't stand how Garrison was ruining Kava, so I tried to rid the world of him again. At the time, I wasn't fully corporeal, which made my task of using a death realm spirit and driving a human corpse more challenging... Not only did I fail, but I also incited a new level of radicalism within Garrison that I couldn't have imagined. As you know, the fates stepped in."

She said nothing and Maya continued.

"They assigned me to monitor Aidan while Aidan believed himself to be babysitting me. They birthed me anew—a demigod —and promised me that if I reported to them, followed their instructions, and learned how to rule the realm, that it would be mine." Her gaze cut sharply to Elysia. "You were never supposed to even arrive."

Resignation and anger burned away Elysia's restraint. "Again, I am asking you what you *want*."

Maya looked up in surprise. "Isn't it obvious?"

She bit her tongue once more, holding back the scathing reply she wanted to fire at the batshit bitch. "Tell me."

"I want the talisman, of course. The death voyage is a joke. A way for the fates to flex their power and ensure you're obedient before they make you a god. The little priestesses love to wax poetic over it with their painted walls of stories, but all that really matters is the talisman, and you're going to tell me where it is."

Elysia scooted back on the bed, resting her head against the wall. "Couldn't tell you if I wanted to. Maybe you should have trained me better. Besides, what would you have done if I *died* using the scissors you gave me?" She shot a sharp, vindictive smirk at her captor.

A flash of anger whitened Maya's eyes. "Either I eliminated a threat to my throne, or I gained the knowledge I sought. Now let's try this without lying because I know how good you are at finding power sources. You managed to travel the realms to get to Aidan while in the godsforsaken cesspit of Relacave. Tell me where the talisman is, or you will never leave here."

She smiled now. "You think the talisman will give you what you want?"

Maya's hands gripped the wooden arms of the rocking chair. "Aidan doesn't deserve the Deathlands. They handed him a throne, a kingdom, and he *spat* on it because he wanted to carry on being a *thug*. I would care for the dead properly. Give them so much more than he ever has. He never even allows them to *visit* the mortal realm."

Elysia's chest quivered with a silent laugh. A worrying, brilliant thug—just her type. It wasn't her fault she'd been raised by a Reyez. Stretching her aching shoulders, she threw Maya an unimpressed glance. "You're not the only one the fates tried to play—they offered me the crown and realm in return for Aidan's life.

The difference between you and me is that I was smart enough to know it was shit, so I destroyed their work and stole their magic."

"Yes, fate-ripper, you will be known for what you have done, but you forget your mortality."

"Well-aware actually," Elysia drawled even as a terrible knowing deepened the ache in her bones.

Maya smiled like she knew she had her caught. "You wielded a weapon not made for mortal hands and drank the magic of ancients. You're lucky I want answers from you, or you'd already be dead."

"If that's how I go out, then so be it. I played my part well."

Maya stood to leave. "Tell me where the talisman is and I'll return you, mind and body intact, to the mortal realm."

Elysia scoffed. "Not even you're good enough to make a promise like that."

"Perhaps not, but I'm the best chance you've got."

A broken laugh escaped her, her head cracking against the wall as she held Maya's confident gaze. "Don't you understand? The only thing I can do now to help the people I love is to refuse you, and how fucking *easy* it is to do. I'll stay right here, and you'll never find the talisman. Good luck taking over the Deathlands as a demigod. The restraints are *gone*. Aidan has his full power with or without me."

Silent rage stormed across Maya's face. "If you won't make a deal, then we both know *he* will."

The door slammed and Elysia stared unseeingly ahead. He wouldn't, but still her stomach churned. He couldn't—Grim would stop him. Their lives were tied, he couldn't promise Maya his life without forfeiting hers, and for that relief calmed her heart even though her guilt was strong. She'd known there was a chance she'd die—that it would take Aidan with her, but Grim would have filled the gap. Destiny was open now, and as morbid and terrible as it was, she knew it was worth it.

Aidan didn't even know where the talisman was, so what kind

of deal could they possibly strike? She pulled the blankets around herself, certain of only one thing.

She needed to get back to her body, no matter the cost.

Chapter 45

Topp Blatz hated himself more than usual today. He should have been proud of himself. It wasn't an easy feat to trick Elysia Parker, but he'd been counting on their tenuous past to kick up enough emotion that she missed the truth. Still, it stung she'd so easily believed him.

The venom and hurt in her voice had been real, reminding him of how deeply he had fucked up while they were together. The image of her face and ribs smashed, breath rattling as she damn near died at the House still haunted him. It was a miracle she'd tolerated his presence at all since then, but she'd done more than tolerate him. On some level, she'd forgiven him. That much had been clear when she showed up at the temple of Ration and Reason, destroyed and looking for a friend.

He'd blown that to smithereens now. She'd told them the plan was to retrieve the talisman location. Per the usual, she'd failed to mention a few key details like the part where she planned to use the fated scissors to tear up their tapestry. He'd only known about the scissors because Maya had warned him that Elysia might show up with them and that he shouldn't touch them if she did. He'd ducked out for two reasons: Maya was going to double-cross her, and he wanted to be able to swoop in when she did.

Obviously, nothing had gone to plan.

Rollickus fidgeted next to him anxiously, trying to peer around Topp's massive shoulders and failing.

"Stay back, will you?" Topp growled. He wasn't in the mood. He needed Rollie for what was to come, and he liked to think Rollie benefitted from him, but once again he found the road to patricide to be a lonely, assfuck of a thing.

"Is she gone?" It was Lucy squeaking away now. The money he would pay to be able to travel himself, so he never had to watch her drool over Timmons again.

"No, she isn't fucking gone. For the millionth time, I will *tell* you when we can enter."

Clothes soggy and boots filled with water, none of them were having a good time, but it was a waiting game now. The ramshackle cottage in Briar's Cove of Lyden, the island kingdom near Kava, looked like it was one bad storm away from caving in, and he was tempted to help it along. Truth be told, the shit weather might have been partially his fault.

Wiping water off his brow, he glanced at Rollie. "You're sure they'll be able to help?"

Rollie yanked at his wet clothes, making a face. "Not at all. I've told you that, but what else are we going to do?"

Topp nodded, going back to his watch. There she was, the demigod, once dead, but now very much alive princess of Kava, holding his ex-girlfriend hostage. Gods, was he the only remotely sane person in his entire family? Aggravated, he pushed his questions away.

She'd seen the monster their father was becoming and tried to stop him only to end up murdered herself. And fuck, maybe Elysia's pale-ass death god didn't deserve to run the death realm, but from what Oren had told him... Aidan was the most responsible among them. Painfully aware of his duty and role. They all knew about his rough start and none of them blamed him. The other gods had received warning and consented to their godhood.

Aidan and his friends had been murdered and reborn after saying *no*.

Maya was straining a pot of tea now. He'd loved his sister. Mourned her every single day of her absence and relied on her memory to carry him through his worst days. But the woman humming and stirring sugar into a teacup wasn't the same person he'd known.

She didn't just want the death realm. She wanted to unleash the dead and force the fates to bend to her, weaving new stories that suited her aims. She had a prison full of creatures she could control and had no qualms about doing so. Their father wanted to kill magic and conquer kingdoms, but his sister wanted to bend the line between mortality and death. The vision she had painted him had chilled him to his core—she spoke of Aidan as rigid in his role, but Topp couldn't think of anything more terrifying than the death realm spilling over into the mortal realm. Look what had happened to Kava from a simple deal gone wrong. Decay. Illness. Death. He had no interest in the laws of magic as it applied to the mortal physical plane, but it didn't take a genius to understand it would not end well.

Ten minutes later a door slammed, and Lucy perked up. "She's gone."

"You're sure?" They couldn't risk her seeing them.

"I managed to ride her coattails all the way here. Are you seriously questioning whether I can tell if she traveled?"

Topp started walking to the cottage, his heart suddenly thumping harder. He'd made a promise that night in the House, and in spite of his failures along the way, he intended to keep it now. *Love or hate. He would do what he had to, to keep them both alive.*

Leaving Kava had granted him something beautiful. Yes, Rollie drove him insane, and had almost gotten him killed multiple times, but the last few months had given him distance, perspective even. He wasn't any less angry. He still barely controlled his temper and wanted to leave everything for the woods. Unlike Elysia's poignant speech at the safe house, he didn't see a love or future for himself. But the fact that she had found that? It made him wonder if maybe, there was simply something *better* for him than this. And to find whatever that was, he needed to keep his head and stop cutting through his relationships like they were deadweight. He glanced at Rollie beside him and resolved to build alliances rather than competition if they made it through this and the death god's gambling game took off. *Easier said than done.*

Jogging ahead, he tried the front door only to find it locked. Frustration bit through him, but he directed it, gathering the wind like it was his to command. Grunting, he released the gale, forcing it at the front door. The metal hinges flew off and the weather-worn door shattered inward.

Steps behind him and huffing, Rollie finally reached the cottage porch. "Gods, you're dramatic."

"Worked, didn't it?" Topp stepped over the debris, his ears alert for any sudden sounds, but there was nothing. Stalking through the cottage, he walked straight to the only closed door. His hand hesitated on the knob for only a second, and then the door was open, and his heart cracked.

Still in the all-black clothes she'd worn in the warehouse, Elysia was on the bed. Her skin rippled and shimmered unnaturally, and her eyes were no longer a sensual, liquid brown, but iridescent with light.

"Rollie," he managed to choke, but Rollie was already shoving past him, checking her vitals with an efficiency that surprised him.

"We need to move her. Lucy, let's go," Rollie barked. Lucy broke into motion, grabbing Topp's hand as she passed before slipping her other hand into Rollie's.

They landed in a heap on a cold white dusty platform. Topp stood, scooping Elysia into his arms, not so much as glimpsing the extraordinary sights around them before walking inside the temple. Shifting Elysia's weight, he took hold of a skeletal hand and pulled once, twice, thrice.

The clanging resounded, echoing throughout the eerie chamber, and he waited with Rollie and Lucy shivering behind him. Finally, the floor opened, and two women emerged in plain black robes.

Topp didn't wait for the priestesses to greet him. "You need to tell your god that Isamaya Blatz is coming and not to take her deal." He clutched Elysia tighter, pain leaking into his voice. "I promised she wouldn't die—not because of me. You have to save her."

TWO WOMEN HOVERED over Elysia's supine form. They'd laid her out on a long stone table, and with her dark hair splayed out around her the scene looked far too much like a funeral rite. Skin shimmering and eyes iridescent, he knew she wasn't dead, but it was still unsettling.

Fear and uncertainty sharpened into a much more comfortable foul temper. "Can't you do *something*?"

They shouldn't have come here, but he hadn't known where else to go. It wasn't like they could travel her to the death realm.

The woman with tight, twisting braids and sculpted muscles turned to him. "She cut through the tapestry of life?"

He didn't care for her disturbed expression or questioning tone. Both were unnatural on her and told him well-enough how fucked they were.

"Yes, she wielded the scissors even though she's not a god and ripped their magic." Impatience rode his voice. He'd explained this ten times by now.

Nia, the woman's name was Nia. She heaved an exhale and spoke to her partner. "Gather everyone. I can't imagine what will come of destroying the tapestry of life, but it may mean that some of Aidan's restrictions are gone. We will call on him."

The shorter priestess, who had initially been chatty until he'd bit her head off, nodded and raced down the hall.

"You're going to call on him?" His skepticism was obvious, but it was Rollie who talked him down in his own irritating, but factual way.

"What else are they going to do? Between the scissors and fate magic, and whatever your godsdamn sister did this isn't exactly a normal situation for a healer." Rollie's brow lines deepened as he stared at Elysia's body. "I told her not to trust you fucking Crown squinches. Sister included."

Topp glared at him. "We didn't know that was going to happen."

"Still blame you."

Nia draped a thick blanket over Elysia. "Come. You can watch if you'd like, so long as you don't interfere."

Curiosity brightened Rollie's eyes, and Topp swallowed what he'd been about to say. He really was trying to be less of an asshole—he knew the priestess was doing everything she could, but it wasn't good enough. All he knew was that it would be his fault if she died. More than once, he'd almost changed his mind and warned her about Maya playing every angle she could, but Rollie had convinced him not to—he'd said that he was positive Elysia knew more than she was letting on. That whatever she was up to was delicate and she was too smart to be unaware of his sister's obvious machinations.

So, he'd agreed, and now she was dying.

The woman had spent her entire life avoiding his father's execution squad only to almost die twice now from his shitty choices and his sister's grandeur plans for vengeance and control. He glanced up above them to the muffled sounds of feet stomping. Maybe he should just let his bloodline die out with him. His gaze flicked back to her. And maybe she should never come within five feet of a Blatz again.

Rollie paused in the archway. "Are you coming? I want to see this."

Nodding, he selfishly allowed his hand to dust over her hip as he passed. When this was over, he wasn't ruling Kava. He didn't care who bore the crown next, but it damn well wasn't going to be him.

Upstairs, the entire temple's worth of acolytes stood in a layered circle. Layer by layer, they began to chant until the resonance of their voices pitched through him in waves. In the center of the circle, Nia painted a skull and dice on the temple floor with her hands. Another priestess lit incense and wafted smoke until the air was saturated. Nia poured dark liquid over her painting and arranged food and gifts as the litany continued. The chanting increased until Nia held up her hand and at once their voices cut off.

"We call now on the god of the dead. King of the Deathlands, god that we serve, hear our petition and remember us." Nia lit the paper she held in her hand and placed it on a plate to burn. Curling and blackening, the petition went up in seconds leaving only ashes behind. Wiping her fingers through the dust, she sprinkled it out over the floor, murmuring. "May your strength and wisdom prevail."

The temple became uncomfortably quiet. Topp's shoulders tensed as Rollie's hot breath misted on his neck. There were too many people in here, incense was tickling his fucking nose, and *why* wasn't anything happening? He moved from foot to foot in agitation. Did these people even know what they were doing?

A man landed in the center of the skull, his smooth dark brown wings flaring wide. Ducking his head, he spoke softly yet his deep voice carried through the silent chamber. "Clear the temple. He's coming."

Instantly, as if they had drilled for this, the temple doors opened and everyone exited, fleeing down the temple steps. Hand on Nia's wrist, the winged man's eyes landed on Topp and Rollie. "Not you two." He stood there, alert, and watchful, waiting until every last acolyte had poured out of the temple, and then he disappeared.

Rollie whispered from behind him. "Maybe I should call for Lucy. I don't think we should be—"

A soot-like haze cloaked the room so darkly he could not see. The pulse in his throat quickened, and his hand shot out to grab at Rollie. He was right, they needed to get out of here. The blinding shadows cleared just enough to make out the outline of a tall, imposing figure.

"Where is my *wife*?" The voice that licked out matched the haze. Dark and dangerous, this was a god he had a feeling would have no qualms with burning him alive.

Dropping Rollie's wrist, Topp adjusted his stance, bracing for the worst, but the god of the dead was already striding past him, calling out over his suited shoulder. "You're lucky she cares for you." And then he was gone, down the stairs into the true heart of the temple where Elysia waited.

Taking a breath, Topp and Rollie looked at each other and followed him into the dark.

CHAPTER 46

THE GOD of the dead's cold fury was now painful. Face stricken, his bright blue eyes appeared to be made of flames as he stared down at Elysia. Unafraid, his hand slipped beneath her neck, thumb moving delicately over her skin as he stared at her shimmering form.

Turning to Nia, his intonation pitched low, and the walls trembled. "I'm going to find her now." The priestess swayed but held upright, and Topp unconsciously stepped back realizing why all the acolytes had been sent out.

The god of the dead was not in control.

Entwining their fingers, golden strands Topp hadn't noticed on her skin lined up with Aidan's, and the god of the dead lowered his face to her ear, whispering something only for her. Standing upright, his eyes burned even brighter until every semblance of mortality melted, and the sootlike shadows rushed from his being to cloak the room in darkness save only for the flame of his eyes.

Both Topp and Rollie collapsed to the shuddering floor, but the shadows didn't physically hurt them as they crawled over their skin. He didn't know how much time passed, only that the shadows left him with goosebumps and plunged him into the unavoidable icy waters of life and death, forcing him to examine much.

The darkness cleared and with it his mind. The god of the dead appeared calmer now, his body deceptively relaxed. Yet Topp's instincts tightened—whatever Aidan had found, he was even closer to the edge than before.

"I must retrieve something. Please wait with her," the god of the dead requested with lethal politeness and then he was gone. All the air flooded back into the room, and Rollie collapsed again, his head smacking against his forearms as he groaned.

"I take back everything I ever said about wanting to work with the gods. That son of a bitch should stay wherever it is he came from," he finished with a shiver.

Topp nodded silently, situating himself so he was seated with his back against the wall, but he could still survey the room. Nia stood at Elysia's head like a sentry, waiting for her god to return. He tipped his head toward Rollie with his eyes still on her. "What do you think he's getting?"

Rollie shook his head. "Didn't seem confident, did he?"

He shrugged. Hard to say. His foot twitched back and forth as they waited, the minutes turning into an hour and then longer.

There was an ear-splitting crack and Aidan was back, holding a heavy iron crown. Setting it gently on the table, he spoke to no one in particular. "If you'd like to stay alive, don't touch that. I must retrieve *her* now."

Once again, the blue flames shot high in his eyes and his pale, hollowed face grew bright against the darkness swallowing the room, except this time the golden strands on both his and her hands became a beacon. The light from the strands danced in the darkness and despite his inability to see through the shadows, Topp registered the strain emanating from Aidan.

Something melodic and enchanting played around them as the god of the dead ceaselessly whispered into the dark. Topp cocked his ear, wishing to hear what was being said, but all he could catch were murmurs of what sounded like adoration and enticement. Aidan's voice changed, suddenly stern, as a prismatic ball of light appeared, dancing around his head. The ball of light stopped, quivering in front of the god of the dead's face.

Tilting his head, Aidan's voice became droll. "*Thorn*, now isn't the time. Focus, sweetheart." His ghostly hands cupped the orb as if it were everything, guiding it over Elysia's chest. The blinding orb dropped into her without hesitation, plunging through skin and bone. She had shimmered before, but now she glowed.

Topp leaned forward. Was she waking?

A scream tore from Elysia's parted lips and slammed him back against the wall with its force, but Aidan didn't hesitate. Swiftly he took the crown and nestled it against her hair, holding it to her. Her scream became guttural and then silent, her mouth still gaping and eyes iridescent, and for the first time, Aidan's face stuttered in worry, his knuckles whitening as he gripped the crown to her dark locks like it could save her.

Slowly, the shimmer over her skin dissipated, her eyes returning to their familiar liquid brown, but she didn't stir except for the slight hesitant rise and fall of her chest.

Aidan closed his eyes as he made to cradle her unmoving body. Lifting her against him, he rocked, clutching her tightly. Topp wasn't sure if it was pain or the letdown of relief that made the god of the dead's shoulders shake as held her, but he knew in that moment if Elysia didn't live they would have a far larger problem on their hands than his sister, father, and the fates combined. Gods help them all if she didn't survive.

Eyes glassy, Aidan shifted his hold on Elysia, so she was draped in his arms with her head on his chest. Voice thick, he spoke. "Thank you all for your part today. I need to return my wife to the Deathlands so the apotheosis may complete."

Soot washed the room, and when it cleared, the god of the dead was gone.

CHAPTER 47

ELYSIA STOOD ALONE in the throne room. Her bare feet were quiet on the burgundy runner that led to the naked thrones. Placing her talisman on what was now her seat, she stepped back. Her long silk dress swirled gently against her ankles. Foreign power nestled inside her, some hers, some unbelonging and burdensome.

Slipping her hands into her pockets, she studied the iron crown. Aidan had cleaned it for her. The dark grayish silver now shone brightly and the small skulls adorning its base stared back at her with blank, empty eyes. It was fitting. Much like the thrones, her crown was not a thing of beauty, but a reminder of the role and responsibility that was now hers. Her gaze drifted to Aidan's helm. She had yet to see him wear it, but the design covered all his face apart from his eyes and lips. She imagined the burn of his eyes would be a sight when he wore that iron monstrosity.

She'd been prepared to wait out her days in the strange in-between Maya had dragged her soul into. What she hadn't been prepared for was the god of the dead bursting into her limbo with all the fury of death in his wake, demanding she tell him where the talisman was while also petrified she hadn't been able to secure its location. She was still proud of him for trusting her. Allowing

397

her to walk into that warehouse and execute her plan without knowing all of it, only that there was more she couldn't say. She hadn't asked him the odds, but she knew they hadn't been good. None of the odds had been good before, but now everything was a blank slate. The fates no longer held all the cards and while it would likely be a bloody, terrible end—both mortals and gods once again stood a chance.

Her fingers traced the sharp geometric edges of her crown. If she hadn't known its location, she would already be mad. Her mind and mortal body broken from ripping ancient power she wasn't designed to hold. The apotheosis had healed the physical injuries of ripping their power and wielding the scissors—after all, she was a god now, but she still wasn't a fate, and their power sat inside her, threatening her with the descent of madness.

It was inevitable.

She hadn't even mastered the basics of transmutation. She could search and she could rip, but thus far, she still relied on the death realm's rivers to transmute even the most basic of human emotions. Fat lot of good that would do her.

Bending her fingers, she examined her nails. Soil still lined a few of them, which wasn't surprising given Aidan had half-buried her amongst her own wildflower plantings. Her memory of her soul being returned to her physical form was thankfully blurred, but she did remember ever-present citrus and bergamot, and the sweet relief of Deathlands dirt surrounding her and easing her death and transition into godhood.

Three full days in the dirt with the rivers cutting through the land to wash over her feet and hands, and then she'd woken. No longer shimmering or with iridescent eyes, she'd sat up with soil in her hands and flowers in her hair as the goddess of the death realm.

She smiled faintly, still unsure how to process all that had occurred over the last few days.

One of the throne room doors creaked open.

"Wife?"

She glared at the god of the dead, the man who had done the unthinkable only days before and saved her from an excruciating end. "You have to stop calling me that."

"Why would I do that?"

"Because it's not true!" She huffed, walking closer to the door.

His brow creased and he held up his arm, exposing his golden strand covered wrist and forearm in rebuttal. "I'm starting to be concerned about your comprehension skills."

Exasperated, she stared up at him with her hands on her hips. Unbeknownst to her, her oath and the resulting binding on their skin was the equivalent to marriage amongst the gods, and Aidan had decided to proceed as if such was true. It was *not* true. "I agreed to nothing."

Now he stared down at her, smirking. "Whatever you say, wife. Are you ready to meet with Grim?"

A sharp pain shot through her temple, and she flinched, but hurried to smile. "Yes, all ready."

Aidan's mouth flattened, his hand running over her hair, tugging lightly until she met his eyes. "You promised."

Flitting out from beneath his touch, she sashayed under his shoulder and to the living room where they were meeting Grim. "I'm aware." But she didn't say it. How the little bolts of fated power were like lightning in her brain, or how her thoughts sometimes twisted strangely.

Elysia curled up in one of the big leather chairs. Last time they'd had a meeting, Maya had sat in this chair. Gods knew where the woman was now or what she was up to. The reapers hadn't seen hide nor tail of her.

Grim stalked into the living room. He looked to Aidan in question, but Aidan simply kicked back, stretching his legs out as he lifted his hands as if whatever the question was it was up to Grim.

Grim rubbed his neck, his jaw tight before walking directly in front of Elysia and dropping to one knee. His brown eyes were intent on hers. "I did something."

Startled, she stared at him in open confusion. Why was he kneeling? "Okay?"

"Something I should have asked your permission for."

Elysia made a face. "You've been running the realm with Aidan for years. You don't need my permission for things."

He dipped his head in acknowledgement, but gently pushed back against what she'd said. "You're correct, but this time, I should have asked."

Grim's out of character behavior was making her nervous. "What did you do?" she finally asked.

His face was soft now, his round brown eyes guilty. "I thought you might need...a friend. Motivation even, and I overstepped."

"Grim, *what* are you talking about?"

"You should go back to the throne room."

Standing, she threw Aidan an exasperated look, but he shook his head, following on her heels. Shoving the throne room door back open, a strangled cry escaped her.

Wings as wide as she was tall, Beatriz Parker stood on the dais. She pointed at the helm. "Does he wear that when you f—?"

Elysia plowed into her sister, arms tight around her middle, tears flowing. "I don't understand. I waited. I waited every day at the arrivals, and you never came. Aidan said you weren't ours."

Grim's cheeks deepened in color. "I didn't want you to be upset if it didn't work out, so I didn't tell him, and like Maya said, he never looks at who I choose for the volt even when he calls them into undead life. I reaped her myself and brought her straight to the village to offer her the job. If she declined, I would have made sure you at least got to see her before her soul chose its path."

Elysia was still clinging to her sister. Gripping her reaper uniform, Elysia's lungs took their first full breath since Beatriz's death. "You're going to *work* for him?"

A familiar glint overtook Beatriz's eyes. "You could say we came to an arrangement."

That sounded like trouble, but Elysia didn't care.

Kava continued to decay with Garrison laying waste to the mortal world. The fates slumbered somewhere, healing and readying to seek their vengeance. And Maya wouldn't stay down for long.

Arms around her sister, she beamed at Aidan and Grim even as a soft, slithering voice wound around her neck and into her ear. *You could keep it just like this. Write the ending you deserve.*

Elysia's teeth ground together even as her smile grew wider, a zing of pain shooting through her as she forced the voice from her mind. She was strong enough to stave off the madness. Aidan's gaze caught hers and her heart tripped as Crusher raced in to see what was happening.

For the first time in her entire life, she had something to lose beyond life itself—love and a strange, budding family of gods, mortals, reapers, and creatures.

She would be damned before she lost it all.

Acknowledgments

As I'm writing this, it's been exactly one year since Undead Gods was released into the world. I won't lie—it's been a bit of a crazy year. Jarring dips between excitement and doubt, flopping down on the floor and then popping up again. But one thing has remained constant long before publishing Undead Gods, and that's my love for story and words. That love is an easy and familiar thing to return to when the noise (or silence) gets too loud. The writing and creating itself is where I feel most myself, and I hope I always feel this lucky to craft stories and worlds for people to fall into. There is something incredibly satisfying about being the one who creates the magic—the elusive feeling of slipping away into some otherworld—that I myself long to find every time I pick up a book.

To my little family—I love you so much. Al, you are my favorite and always will be. I may have even written one of my favorite quirks of yours into this book. You're my best friend and the one I always want to see. Devi-dog, you are my tiny soul dog, and I love you forever. Thank you for being my friend, companion, and snuggle buddy. Dobs, you are the sweetest angel-baby cat in the world. I'm so glad you're still here with us.

To my beta readers [Amanda, Alexis, Julie, Layne, Amy, Lauren, & Laura!] You are all the most fantabulous and you truly helped make this story the best it could be—thank you so much for all your time, effort, and feedback! (But also for all the laughs and reactions. LOL)

To my wonderful street team, thank you a million for every

repost, comment, and share about Undead Gods. I appreciate you all so much! If anyone would like to join in on the street team shenanigans—the application is open! You can find it through my instagram.

To my editing team—I'm so lucky to have such great people in my corner. You all truly make the editing process as smooth as it can be, and I'm so grateful for your expertise. Britt, thank you for your story instincts and love for Undead Gods! Emily, I'm sorry I love dangling modifiers so much (loool), but thank you for always catching them and every other silly little error. Julia, I'm so glad to have met you—your sharp eye for detail and humor is so appreciated!

Finally, thank you so much to every single reader of both Undead Gods and Undead Oaths. It really can't be overstated the difference it makes when you choose to yap and shout about a book you love. Again, thank you so much for every single review, conversation, and post on socials telling other people about the Undead Gods trilogy. I consider myself a cute little indie potato in the book world, so please know, it does make a significant difference when you share about a book. If you loved Undead Oaths, then I would be incredibly grateful if you took the time to share that love with other people.

If you'd like to come along on this wild ride and stay in touch then you can sign up for my newsletter below!

All my love—I'll see you in the next one!

Caitlyn

About the Author

Caitlyn grew up on faeries, folklore, and late-night reads. Her dream is to write fantasy stories that will keep you turning the page long after everyone else is asleep. She lives with her partner, tripawed floof of a dog, and the world's friendliest tuxedo cat. If you can't find her, then she's probably escaped to the forest, but will provide updates from @caitlynbattellebooks on social media. You can sign up for her newsletter below.

Content Advisory

Death.
Graphic language.
Violence and gore.
Open door sex scenes.
Discussion of past torture.
Illness and death of a family member.
Addiction (drugs and alcohol references).
Reference to past emotional and physical abuse.
Discussion of past suicidal ideation and a past attempt.